The Resurrection Maker

GLENN COOPER

Lascaux Media

Cover Art by Davide Nadalin. Design by Asha Hossain.

ISBN 10: 0692266712
ISBN 13: 9780692266717

No one knows what existed before zero time.

Perhaps it will never be known; perhaps it is inconceivable, existing beyond the ability of the human mind to comprehend the abstraction—because prior to a singular moment some 14 billion years ago, our universe simply did not exist. There was no time, no space, no matter, no gravity, no energy.

Yet, at the precise instant of zero time, everything presently in the universe was condensed into a single point, a unified force of unfathomable infinite density and heat.

At the instant of zero time, the hottest possible moment, matter and energy erupted from the single point.

The Big Bang.

Within a trillionth of a trillionth of a trillionth of a ten millionth of a second of the Big Bang, space and time were created along with all the matter and energy in the universe. The temperature was 100 million trillion degrees.

In a hundred thousandths of a second the universe had cooled to a trillion degrees and the most basic forces in nature had come into existence: gravity, the strong force that holds the nuclei of atoms together, the weak and electromagnetic forces.

Within one second after the Big Bang, ordinary matter formed into fundamental subatomic particles including quarks, electrons, photons, and neutrinos. Protons and neutrons followed; and it is perhaps during this second that a mysterious second kind of matter was also created: dark matter, a material so elusive that although physicists know with absolute certainty it exists, they have no firm idea what it may be.

Dark matter became the dominant building block of the universe. This pervasive relic of the Big Bang, invisible and nonluminous, exerted gravity much like ordinary matter. It permeated the universe. Everywhere ordinary matter existed, so too did dark matter. When galaxies formed, for every particle of ordinary matter there were six particles of invisible dark matter.

Over the first billion years, trillions upon trillions of stars were formed and so too were hundreds of billions of supermassive black holes, one at the center of every galaxy.

And here is where the story begins.

Some 800 million years after the Big Bang, at the center of our Milky Way galaxy, a huge dying star went supernova, producing a massive cloud of antimatter and radiation.

Antimatter collided with the nebula's existing hydrogen and helium just as a supermassive black hole started to form. The coupling of matter and antimatter created the greatest explosion the Galaxy would ever experience, violently pulverizing dust and gas within the surrounding reaches of space.

As the Galaxy cooled, pulverized bits of ordinary matter and dark matter fused. Virtually all the fused lumps were sucked into the black hole but a precious few glanced off its gravitational boundary.

Thus began the 13 billion–year journey within the vast Milky Way of one stray lump, an exceedingly rare hybrid of dark and ordinary matter.

A billion years ago, when the earth was 3.5 billion years old, that lump of matter entered the planet's atmosphere and fell as a fiery meteorite onto a region that, in the course of millennia, would become Egypt.

The fire stone lay buried for eons as the earth became a living, breathing planet sprouting an abundance of life.

With the passage of time and the erosion of the desert floor, the lump would work its way to the surface and would be found in a.d. 31 by an alchemist, Nehor, son of Jebedee, who had an eye for rare minerals. He marveled at the wondrous properties of the melon-sized rock. He would soon cleave the fire stone, and use his skills to fashion it into a chalice—and he would devote himself to studying how to harness its strange power.

In two years' time, Nehor's chalice would be placed into the hands of an itinerant preacher named Jesus of Nazareth as he sat among his disciples in Jerusalem at the Passover supper before his execution.

And Jesus would die on the cross and he would be resurrected. And some would come to say that the chalice played a role in that divine act.

Soon after the resurrection, the chalice was lost.

Generations of seekers would feverishly pursue the Holy Grail, sensing its power as more than symbolic and believing that it might hold the greatest answers to the greatest questions.

And to this day, the quest for the Holy Grail continues unabated.

1

JERUSALEM, A.D. 33

A sandstorm swept the land, whisking the dry earth like a giant broom. An hour after it had passed, the air was still noxious and tinged with yellow.

Judas, son of Simon Iscariot, removed the scarf from his face and coughed a few times to clear his lungs. His eyes and throat stung from the grit. A sip of cool water would have gone down well but he had left his goatskin in his room; here, in the alleyway behind the stables, there was no one to provide a cupful.

The sun was directly overhead. He squinted at it through outstretched fingers. The storm had rendered the orb the color of blush roses. He dropped his hand and began to pace the alley. After a while, he sat on the ground and slipped off his chafing sandals to wipe the sand from his feet. He became so absorbed in the task that the man's voice startled him.

"I am sorry to be late. The storm delayed me." The man spoke Aramaic with a guttural Egyptian accent.

Judas rose and asked him, "Do you have any water?"

Nehor was taller than Judas, perhaps ten years older, with a longer beard and straighter shoulder-length hair laced with gray. He had two straps across his chest, one attached to a cloth bag, the other to a skin. He unshouldered the skin and gave it to Judas, who removed the plug and gulped a mouthful.

"No one knows you came here," Nehor said; though meant as a question, it came off as statement.

"I told no one."

"Good."

"I wouldn't want them to know I had anything to do with you."

"Then why did you come?" Nehor asked, reclaiming the skin.

They both knew the answer. Nehor was strong, Judas was weak. Often in the past when Nehor had commanded, Judas had obeyed.

"Your man said it was urgent," Judas said. "A matter of life and death."

"Indeed. Life and death."

"Whose life? And whose death?"

"To both questions I have the same answer: Jesus."

Judas's face contorted into a scornful twist. "You were cast out. He refuses to have you involved with his affairs any longer."

"That does not mean I have stopped loving him."

Judas shook his head. "Please. Your actions were abhorrent. To do what you did showed contempt for his teachings—hatefulness."

Nehor shrugged. "Only I can know what is in my heart."

"So … you wish to talk to me about his life and his death. Tell me, do you want to kill him or save him?"

"Both."

Judas dismissed the older man with a wave of his hand, turning to leave.

"Do not be a fool," Nehor said. "Everyone knows the Temple elders are baying for his blood. They have petitioned Pontius Pilate to have him arrested. As we speak, the Praetorians are looking for him. You know what they will do when they find him. The Romans are short on mercy."

Judas stopped to consider. "I will tell him to flee. He could go back to Galilee."

"He won't flee."

"You are right," Judas said sadly. "He will not."

"He wants to be martyred."

Judas wiped a tear. "I do not want him to leave us. None of us do."

"That is why you must listen to me! I have a way to let him fulfill the destiny he has chosen—*and* for his followers to keep him forever."

Judas had never been comfortable looking into Nehor's dark magnetic eyes, lest they suck his soul from his body; but at this moment he could not resist.

"What way?"

"When will you see him again?"

"Tonight. We are to break bread with him at the Passover meal."

"Where?"

Judas, as if commanded by Nehor's eyes, pointed toward Mount Zion where the wealthy men of Jerusalem lived. "At a large house. A follower's house. On the hill."

Nehor reached into his cloth bag and produced a bowl the size of a pair of women's hands, cupped together. It was the color of night, perfectly smooth and polished. He cradled it in one palm.

Judas inched closer, unable to take his eyes off the object. It wasn't the bowl that was so remarkable but the thin halo surrounding it: an opalescent haze that obscured everything behind it. He was mesmerized.

"What is it?"

"A bowl; a chalice."

"No ordinary bowl."

Nehor nodded. "If you love Jesus you must have him drink from it at the supper tonight—but *only* him. Later, wherever Jesus goes, you must go. The soldiers will come to arrest him. Make sure they know who he is."

"A betrayal?" Judas exclaimed. His gaze remained fixed on the bowl.

"No, a gift. The greatest gift you could bestow upon him. Have no doubt, Judas, if it is not you who delivers him to his fate, it will be another. Better it should happen at the hands of one who cherishes him."

"The others will know I have betrayed him. What shall I say for myself?"

Nehor removed a small leather pouch from his belt and secured it to Judas's belt.

"Tell them you did it for silver. Now take the bowl."

Nehor placed it into Judas's trembling hands. It felt warm, the temperature of a forehead burning with fever.

"What will happen to him?" Judas asked.

"Something glorious," Nehor said. "Something that will change the world."

2

ENGLAND, THE PRESENT

It was unseasonably warm for early March. During the short walk from the car park to the office, Arthur Malory sniffed at the rich organic smells emanating from the moist soil and turned his face to the sun long enough to set his skin tingling. For the first time since the dead of winter he had left his heavy coat home on a peg and taken only a thin sports jacket. Free of extra layers and woolen hat and gloves, he felt as liberated as the crocuses breaking through the earth. He happily swung his briefcase at his side. It was a damned good way to start the week.

Harp Industries, Limited had its administrative and marketing functions centralized in Basingstoke. Harp's only fabrications plant in the UK was north in Durham. Otherwise the company had scattered manufacturing to the four winds, following the trail of cheap labor, much of it now in Asia. Arthur relished traveling to the plants, meeting with the engineers and floor workers, eating their food, soaking up their culture, making side trips to historical sites. He argued to his superiors that he couldn't market Harp products properly if he wasn't immersed in all aspects of the product development cycle. But the age of Skype and video conferencing was upon him and to his dismay his wings had been progressively clipped.

In the lobby, the receptionist, a plain woman with a big smile, greeted him with a particularly beaming one.

"Morning, handsome."

"I know I am, but unless you had a bad row this weekend you're married, luv."

"It's not me sayin' it," she said, waving a stack of company newsletters, "it's this here."

"Oh, Christ, give me one. I never should have agreed to it."

On his way to his office he had to endure good-natured taunts from his colleagues, which he deflected with "I'll get you for this" or "Your time'll come, mate," but when he closed his door he was positive his cheeks were brightly flushed. He sat down and started to read the front page, which sported a photo of him sitting on the corner of his desk staring at the camera with sincere blue eyes.

MONDAY PROFILE: ARTHUR MALORY—A MARKETING MANAGER WHO'S A REAL TREASURE

by Susan Brent

When you ask his co-workers to describe Marketing Manager Arthur Malory you are likely to hear words like dedicated, brilliant, handsome, considerate and respectful. Everyone around HQ at Basingstoke knows he's an organizational treasure but how many know he's a real treasure hunter!

Arthur joined Harp Industries eight years ago straight out of university where he earned a BSc in chemistry from University of Bristol. What's a chemist doing at a physics company?

An article he wrote for the student newspaper on the challenges of communicating complex science to a lay audience caught the eye of Martin Ash, Marketing Director at Harp. "I could tell that this young man had a knack for communication and distilling key messages from a complex brew of information. He didn't know it himself at the time but Arthur was a born marketer. He thought one of his mates was playing a prank on him when I rang him but, as they say, the rest is history."

Arthur has risen through the ranks and is now in charge of the marketing efforts for industrial uses of our neodymium magnets. But how many employees know that in his spare time Arthur is a real-life treasure hunter? Armed with his trusty metal detector, Arthur prefers to spend his weekends tramping the countryside in search of buried goodies rather than pubbing or clubbing. And it's not just to keep fit now he's no longer playing rugby. He's got a trove of old coins including some from the Roman era, Victorian jewelry, even a valuable old pocket watch to show for it.

To what does he attribute his fascination with the past? "I'm not completely sure it's true but the family lore and a bit of genealogy has it that we Malorys are descendants of Sir Thomas Malory, the 15th *century author of* Le Morte D'Arthur. *Hence my given name, which has been imposed on many of my predecessors! When I was a boy I was mad about everything to do with King Arthur and I suppose that's where I picked up my interest in history."*

When asked whether that interest persists to this day he assured me that it did, and when further asked if he ever set his treasure-hunting sights on the Arthurian legend he said that was indeed the case.

"I'd love to find Camelot. I'd love to find Excalibur and most of all I'd love to find the Holy Grail."

Does he know where to look for the Grail?

"I have some ideas," he answered, laughing. "But if I told you I'd have to kill you. Honestly, if I ever get a whole month off to travel I think I'd make some good progress."

There was a knock on Arthur's door and he tossed the newsletter down.

"Come."

It was Susan Brent from HR.

"Like it?"

"Actually, it's quite embarrassing."

She issued a loaded grin. She was single. He was single. But because she was in charge of the company's sexual harassment policies she had, mercifully from his perspective, left him alone beyond the mildest of hints.

"Don't be embarrassed. Everyone says it's brilliant," she gushed. "Besides, maybe you'll meet some like-minded people in the organization. We have two thousand employees. You never know where a connection might arise."

By late morning Arthur had grown weary of fielding e-mails and phone calls from far-flung Harp colleagues ribbing him about the article; so he almost ignored his ringing desk phone when, from the corner of his eye, he recognized the caller ID. It was Andrew Holmes.

"Hello, Andrew," Arthur answered cheerfully, putting the call on hands-free. "This is a surprise. How've you been keeping yourself?"

Holmes was one of the more popular professors at Oxford, his lecture course *Introduction to Medieval Britain* a perennial must-take for first-years. Among his myriad draws was an *uber*-eccentricity marked by a quasi-Edwardian way of dressing and a ridiculously plumy oration. His high elocution wasn't reserved for lectures. Arthur got a full measure of plump, rounded words through the speaker.

"Hallo, Arthur! So glad to catch you. I become rather gloomy when I have to leave one of those awful voice messages."

"At your service."

"Marvelous, marvelous. Listen, Arthur, you know I have an egalitarian bent when it comes to keeping the Loons up to date on interesting tidbits but I rather thought I should inform you initially about a recent discovery."

This was a first. Though he and Holmes were close, Arthur had never knowingly received information before other members of their group, the Grail Loons, as Andrew dubbed them. A group of up to ten, depending on the night, convened several times a year at Holmes' favorite pub in Oxford to trade often wild theories about the Holy Grail and drink, but mostly drink. If this was, as some of them joked, a modern Round Table, then Holmes was King Arthur, not the oldest but the wisest and certainly the one with the deepest academic footprint. No one in the field would dispute that he was the preeminent Arthurian scholar in Britain.

Arthur had been brought into the fold some eight years earlier by a mutual acquaintance, Tony Ferro. Tony and Arthur had met at Bristol. At the time Tony was a graduate student in history teaching a section in a course that Arthur had taken to diversify his undergraduate science curriculum. As soon as Tony found out that Arthur was a likely descendant of Thomas Malory he became interested in the younger man and they had become fast friends. Tony was now teaching Medieval History at University College London and had recently added a course: *King Arthur—Myth or Reality*, which Arthur hoped to audit one day.

Holmes always had been highly selective of whom he allowed into his Grail inner circle. He had zero tolerance for New Agers, crystal gazers or religious zealots. Each of his Loons had to bring something concrete to the table so most were serious scholars in one field or another, although if they did not possess the requisite admittedly intangible "spirit" Holmes blackballed them. Arthur had made it over the goal line during their introductory pint. His answer to Holmes' first question had sealed the deal.

"Why am I interested in the Grail quest?" Arthur had repeated, giving himself a moment to collect his thoughts. "Well look, I think this modern world of ours has diverted our attention from lofty goals. We're barraged with the notion that we can achieve instant gratification for many of our needs. Hungry? There's fast food. Need information about something? Google it. Lonely? Online dating. Sad? There're drugs for that. But there's no instant gratification for a spiritual quest, is there? That takes work and commitment. Maybe by the end of one's days you've achieved a measure of spiritual fulfillment, maybe not. I see the Grail quest as a real embodiment of that spiritual quest. It's an ancient pursuit but I don't see why it shouldn't also be a modern and relevant one. Besides, what if it's more than metaphorical? What if the Grail really exists? How cool would it be to hold that beauty in one's hands?"

Now Arthur picked up the handset and took Holmes off speaker. "I'm all ears, Andrew. What is it you've found?"

"Well, I rather feel as if I've been struck by a cart-full of horseshoes. No one has a right to be so lucky. Or perhaps it's skill, I wonder?"

"Is this something to do with the letter you told the group about two months ago—from Montserrat?"

"Well, no. There are more details about the letter which I'll publish presently but that's not why I've called. It's a second find, much more important, seismic, really, as documents go. It concerns you, old boy."

"Me?"

"Yes, one Arthur Malory, resident of Wokingham, England, Marketing Whiz by day, Grail-hunter by night. It arose from some shoe-leather work I'm rather proud of. It had a low probability of paying off, which is why I'm especially pleased that it did—and in a spectacular way."

"God, Andrew, would you please spit it out?"

After a lovely Holmesian pause, Arthur heard, "How'd you like to find the Grail, my son? I mean really find it?"

Arthur found himself smiling. "You know I would."

"Good. Because if I'm right, the Grail has your name written all over it. I think it can *actually* be found but I'm going to need your help."

"Anything, Andrew. You know I'm always game. Busy, but game."

"Yes, I'm reasonably swamped myself. Besides being immersed in the salutary things which have happened, I've got a heavy teaching load and I've got to deal with a nitwit who broke into our departmental offices and ransacked several rooms, including mine. I don't think anything is missing but there's still an inventory to complete. Fortunately I keep my important papers at home. Arthur, between the two of us perhaps we'll be able to crack this glorious walnut. Can you come over Thursday night? It's Anne's birthday and we want you to have dinner with us. We've got reservations at her favorite place. I'll tell you everything then."

"Of course. I'll be there."

"Just one thing before I let you go back to your work enticing people to purchase things they may or may not require. You wouldn't have an extra rib, would you?"

Arthur scrunched his face in surprise at the question. "Actually, Andrew, I do. How in God's name would you know that?"

3

When the doorbell chimed Andrew Holmes grabbed his zippered portfolio and bounded down the stairs. He tossed the case onto the sofa but his aim was poor and it overshot, slipping behind the furniture. He swore but left it and answered the bell instead. He'd get it later after dinner—or rather, he'd have Arthur retrieve it, as he was younger and more limber. He hadn't decided if he would tell Arthur about the new letters before showing him or simply have Arthur read them unprepped. Either way, it was going to be epic.

Arthur was at the door smiling broadly and clutching a wrapped present for Anne.

"Ah, right on time," Holmes said. "I can't tell you how much I've been looking forward to this. Help yourself to a drink while I fetch my keys and try to get Anne out the door."

Soon Holmes was in a lather trying to find the car keys. He mumbled that he was certain they were in the house because he'd driven home from college only two hours earlier.

"I'm far too young to be this senile!" he bellowed loud enough to make Arthur wince.

"Are you looking for your keys?" his wife called out from upstairs.

"Yes, I bloody well am."

"Near the kettle. That's where you put them down."

Anne appeared wearing a nice green dress, perfect for a spring evening. She came into the kitchen as Holmes was pocketing the keys and merrily waved at Arthur but he could tell straight off she didn't look well. She was unsteady on her feet and more reliant on her cane than he'd seen before; and it appeared she'd since lost weight.

"I don't know why I put them there," Holmes said absently.

"If you leave them in the front hall whenever you get home, think how much more time you'd have to do other things: added up, it would probably equal a whole extra day of life."

"Very amusing."

"I'm sorry to involve you …" Anne started to apologize.

"Not at all," Arthur replied, handing her a wrapped present. "Happy Birthday."

"You needn't have done that," she said, putting the present down on the kitchen table. "I'd give you a hug but I've got some sort of a bug."

"A bug?" Holmes asked. "Can't a microbiologist be more specific?"

"All right." She sighed. "An enterovirus."

Holmes grunted. "You sure it's not Eloise?"

She was on medical leave from her job at a university research lab for a flare of her multiple sclerosis that had left her weak in one leg and a little dizzy. She was the kind of optimist who couldn't bring herself to call it MS. So she gave her disease a cheerful name.

"No, it's not Eloise," she said.

Holmes nodded and inspected her present. "Looks like a book."

"A book it is," Arthur said. It was a photographic volume on English gardens, a subject that interested Anne. "You can open it now if you like or save it for later."

"Later," she said, "after dinner. I enjoy the anticipation."

Holmes dangled the keys as a signal to make way to the car. "You're going to have to wait too, Arthur. I'll show you my discovery after dinner when we return. Anticipation."

Holmes focused again on Anne, peering at her over his narrow glasses with an air of concern. "Your color is strikingly similar to your dress. Are you sure you want to go out?"

"It's my birthday. I'm not going to miss out. It's hard work pinning you down to a dinner date."

They left at dusk and night was coming fast. Five minutes after they were gone a man emerged from the driver's side of a car parked down the road. Griggs walked to the side of their house and opened the gate to the back garden as casually as someone returning home from work. He was tall and broad with cropped hair. His leather jacket fit tightly against a flat belly. He had a coarse face—a brawler's face—but handsome enough to attract the kind of women who appealed to him.

There was no burglar alarm; he knew from a previous reconnoiter. The back garden provided a shield against intrusion from neighbors. He took a rock from a flower bed and lightly tapped it against a back door pane until it shattered with a musical tinkle. He reached in with a gloved hand to turn the lock.

The wandering beam of a flashlight would be more suspicious to passersby than a lighted room, so he switched lights on and off as needed. The downstairs rooms were uninteresting—a formal sitting room, dining room, kitchen, and TV lounge. It took a few minutes to vandalize them. He did so in a desultory manner, tipping over lamps, emptying drawers, quietly breaking a few pieces of china. Then he climbed the stairs and immediately found what he was looking for.

Arthur sat in the backseat of Holmes' car and felt as though he were watching two characters in a play act out a semicomic scene involving two fuddy-duddies in a domestic dispute.

"Must you take these corners so sharply?" Anne complained. "It doesn't do my stomach any good, you know."

"They should straighten out the road."

"Yes, of course they should. What a thing to say."

The GPS mounted on his dash announced a turning.

Anne pointed at the device. "We've only lived here twenty years and been to the restaurant several dozen times. How is it possible you need this box to get us there?"

"You didn't marry me for my sense of direction," Holmes objected. "But I do miss those bygone days when you'd sit with your folding map and berate me like a screeching bird."

"I daresay I was a better navigator than this Tom."

"I believe his proper name is TomTom."

Anne suddenly clutched her belly and moaned faintly.

"I don't think this is going to happen, is it?" Holmes said. "I'm sorry but I think I should have TomTom return us home."

Holmes had a generous study that had been constructed by knocking down the wall between two bedrooms. As it was front-facing and well above the height of the hedges, Griggs pulled the curtains before switching on a lamp. He checked his watch. With yards of shelving, filing cabinets galore, and books and papers everywhere, the job had the potential to be a needle-in-the-haystack affair.

He went for the desk first and unplugged a laptop computer from its charger. A quick rummage through drawers instantly yielded one of his targets: a folder marked in Holmes' calligraphic script *Montserrat Abbey—The 3 Amigos*. The folder contained handwritten notes, a typed manuscript marked *draft*, and several photographs. Griggs pursed his lips and said to himself, "One down, one to go."

Griggs was having no luck completing his task. He emptied the desk drawers onto the floor as a burglar might have done. For effect he also pocketed an envelope stuffed with euros and other international currencies from Holmes' trips abroad. He wasn't sure if his second target was inside a folder or notebook or just loose papers, but whatever its form, it was not in or on the desk. He started on the filing cabinets, hoping that Holmes and company would have a long, leisurely dinner.

He heard a car door closing and before he could part the curtains, a key in the front door. He did not panic; it wasn't in his nature—but he swore under his breath at a plan gone bad. *Time to go to Plan B.* With Griggs there was always a contingency. He mentally activated it as the door was opening.

Arthur was last in. He heard Anne exclaim, "Oh my God! We've been burgled!" The three of them stared at the disarray.

"Let's leave," Arthur said quietly. "They may still be inside. I'll ring the police from the car."

Before they could leave, Griggs appeared at the top of the stairs, smoothly drawing a gun from his waistband, a Bersa .40, a deadly little Argentinean piece that was his preferred carry weapon. He descended slowly, pointing the gun at Anne for maximal psychological effect.

"All of you. Move to the sitting room. Now."

Arthur was immediately struck that this man was no burglar. He was too cool, too confident. Burglars didn't swagger.

They were scared. Shielded behind Anne and Andrew, Arthur thought he could cleanly make it out the door but that might have drawn fire. So he did as he was told and retreated to the adjoining room with the others, the intruder following.

Holmes was breathing heavily, the threat of violence plunging him into apparent turmoil. "My wife is unwell. She has to sit down."

"Then sit," Griggs commanded.

"Take what you want," Anne said, "then please leave."

Griggs ignored her and aimed the gun at Arthur. "You're Arthur Malory."

The pronouncement made Arthur's knees buckle. "How did you know that?"

"I know a lot about you." He used his gun casually as a pointer and let it drift toward Holmes. "You too."

"Who are you?" Arthur asked.

"That's not important."

Holmes noticed that in his free hand the man was clutching his computer and *Amigos* folder. "Whatever do you want with those?"

Griggs ignored the question. "I need one more thing. If you give it to me, I'll leave quietly. If you don't, things won't go well."

"What? What is it?" Holmes asked sharply.

"I want everything you have concerning Malory and the Grail. Documents, notes, all of it, all the material you recently found."

Holmes sprouted a look of utter incredulity but said nothing.

Arthur heard him perfectly well but wanted him to repeat it. "What did you say?"

"We listened to your phone call. Don't bother to deny it."

"We?" Holmes asked. "Who the hell is *we*?"

"Interested parties."

The notion was incongruous. Scholars were interested in the Grail. Readers. Laymen. Not people with guns who tapped phones and broke into houses.

"Who are these parties?" Arthur asked. "And why are they interested in the Grail—and me?"

"Don't waste my time. Where's the new material?"

"It isn't here," Holmes said.

"You're lying." He pointed the gun at Arthur. "He showed it to you already, didn't he?"

Arthur stared at him angrily and refused to answer.

"Don't give it to him, Andrew!" Anne said. "We've seen his face. If you give it to him he'll hurt us."

Holmes looked at her hopelessly and sadly. "I expect we're buggered either way."

Griggs shook his head ominously. "I'm not going to give you more time. Be a good bloke and hand it over."

"Please, just go," Holmes said wearily. "We won't call the authorities. It's not that important. It's just an old relic, bound for a museum if it's ever found. It's not worth hurting us."

"You're wrong. It *is* that important," Griggs said. He put the computer and folder down on an end table and plucked a throw pillow from the sofa. "Last chance. Will you tell me?"

Holmes was defiant. "No! Go away!"

Griggs put the pillow against the barrel of the gun and immediately fired a muffled shot. For a moment no one moved. Then Arthur saw Anne looking profoundly puzzled as the bodice of her dress turned from green to red.

Holmes lurched to her side and at that instant Arthur acted more from instinct than premeditated intent. He'd been a good rugby player in his day and went low for the larger man, aiming to tie up his arms at his waist before he could get off another shot, then sweep him off his feet and body-slam him to the floor.

It didn't go as planned.

Before he made contact he heard a blast, saw a muzzle flash and felt a searing pain in his side. But he kept charging and drove the man against the wall, knocking down a painting. He ignored the pain and tried to get the intruder to the floor but the man seemed to be glued to the wall and nothing he could do would tip him.

He knew it was only a matter of seconds before the gun was pressed against him and fired so he suddenly pulled away enough to get his hands up against the man's face, desperately groping for his eyes with his thumbs.

When Griggs brought the butt of the pistol crashing down on the dome of Arthur's head, the jolting pain short-circuited his nervous system. His arms went limp and his vision stopped working, replaced by something flashing and bright, as if he'd been made to stare into the sun with eyes wide open.

The blow didn't seem to hurt at all. There was hardly time for it to register as the blazing sun suddenly set and Arthur fell into blackness.

4

Something was wrong, very wrong.

The light was flat, artificial, muted, and the sounds were mechanical—all whooshing and beeping.

Arthur's head hurt and so did his left side. His throat was tight and sore. He blinked and the ceiling came into focus. *Off-white acoustic tiles.* He moved his fingertips and felt coarse linen.

He was in a bed, on his back.

He tried to sit up and discovered his arms were tethered to rails and in a few moments a woman filled his view, a young nurse with a friendly face.

"Mister Malory. You're awake. Let me fetch the doctor."

A doctor. Why? What had happened?

The nurse returned, undid his restraints and elevated the bed. She offered him juice from a straw. His mouth was desperately dry and he sipped aggressively. His chest felt tight and he had a spasm of coughing.

"Take it slowly."

"Where am I?"

"You're in the John Radcliffe Hospital. This is the Neurosurgery Intensive Care Unit."

"How long have I been here?"

"Three days."

"What happened to me?"

"Let's have your surgeon, Mister Singh, answer that. He's on his way."

The doctor was a diminutive man in blue scrubs, unsmiling, clearly hurried. Before Arthur could open his mouth he saw a penlight in the doctor's hand and felt stinging bright light in his eyes. After a brisk neurological exam checking the strength of limbs and sensation, the neurosurgeon was ready to talk.

"You had a skull fracture and a small subdural hematoma, which I evacuated. We'll leave the bandages on until tomorrow or the next day. You sustained an injury, a fracture to one of your ribs."

"My side hurts like hell."

"Did you know you have an extra pair of ribs?"

"Yes."

"Well, the one on the left probably saved your life. The bullet glanced off it. Otherwise it might have struck your spleen, in which case you would have bled to death."

"A bullet?"

"You don't remember what happened?"

"No."

"Post-trauma amnesia is common. Your memory of the events may or may not return. There's no way of predicting."

"Tell me what happened."

"I'd rather leave that to the police. They're champing at the bit to interview you. I'll hold them off as long as I can. You also had smoke inhalation, which required breathing assistance and sedation until early this morning. But at this point you seem to be doing quite well. We should be able to send you to the wards later today."

Arthur spent the next few hours grinding away, trying to remember what happened. He recalled driving to see Andrew Holmes, arriving, giving Anne her present, heading off to the restaurant and returning prematurely. At that point he confronted a black curtain that stubbornly would not part to reveal anything more.

His nurse readied him for transfer and told him that various friends had tried to visit the past few nights but had been turned away. She was having trouble recalling their names.

"Was one of them Andrew Holmes?"

The nurse looked down and answered, "No, not him. Some other men. One of them had a beard."

"Tony Ferro?"

"Yes, I think that was his name. A woman was with him, tall and striking."

"Sandy Marina?"

"Yes, I'm sure of it. They'll be coming again tonight they said."

The moment his bed was rolled onto the lift to take him to his ward he had a spontaneous memory flash. The nurse seemed to notice the surprise on his face and asked if he was all right. He nodded. But a snippet had formed in his mind.

Anne had opened the door to their house. They had stepped inside. The sitting room was in disarray. They'd been burgled.

But what happened next?

The black curtain closed again.

That afternoon he was settled into a room with an elderly roommate who seemed to do nothing but sleep and fill a urine bag. The television didn't work. There were no books or magazines. He asked a ward nurse if his mobile phone and wallet were anywhere to be found but was told he had no personal belongings when he was brought into the ICU. He requested telephone service and waited for it to activate. Left to his own devices, he tried without success to further part the black curtain.

A respiratory therapist came in to give him a breathing treatment to loosen the mucus in his irritated lungs. While breathing vigorously into a tube, trying to lift a row of floating balls to the tops of their columns, Arthur was struck by a series of flashes.

A large man at the top of the stairs.

A gun.

Questions about the Grail.

Agitated, Arthur waved off the therapist and frantically tried to push the limits of his memory. What became of Holmes and Anne? How had he been injured?

And then over dinner, while slurping Jell-O, the rest of it came as if a dam had burst in a spontaneous flood of disturbing images.

A gunshot. Anne bleeding. Bull-rushing the intruder. Another gunshot. Pain in the side, a frenzied and primal fight for survival, terrible pain in the head.

That was all. Maybe there would be more but he thought not. He sensed the recollection was complete. He still didn't know if Anne had survived her wound. He didn't know what had happened to Holmes but the way the ICU nurse had avoided eye contact at mention of Holmes' name disturbed him.

The answers came soon enough.

Tony Ferro and Sandy Marina arrived during visiting hours, both of them a study in concern and sadness. Arthur hadn't seen them since the last time the Grail Loons had met in Oxford at the Bear Inn. Sandy was a professor of religious studies at Cambridge, a stately, vivacious redhead in her forties with a wicked wit and a cackling laugh to match. Tony was a bear of a man with a heavy full beard, his gut bulging over his omnipresent sweater vest. Though not yet fifty, premature graying made him seem older. Both he and Sandy awkwardly approached Arthur's bed, seemingly unsure of what to do or what to say.

Arthur had them draw the partition between him and his roommate and told them to pull up chairs. He could tell from their faces and Sandy's tears that Holmes was gone. He held out his hand and Sandy took it.

"We were told you might not remember anything," she said.

"I didn't but I do now. It all came back. But nobody's told me what happened to Anne and Andrew. Please."

Sandy and Tony exchanged difficult glances before Tony nodded and cleared his choked throat.

"Whoever did this set the house on fire. They think it was petrol taken from Andrew's shed. A neighbor saw the flames and managed to get the front door open. He found you near the hall and managed to pull you out. He couldn't reach them. The fire brigade found their bodies after they knocked down the fire. The newspapers are saying that they were both shot and were probably dead before the fire consumed the house. They're gone, Arthur, they're both gone."

The three cried softly for several minutes until Arthur started painfully coughing and Sandy insisted they leave until he settled down. In a minute he called them back from the corridor and asked whether the intruder had been caught.

"No," Sandy said. "We've been told the police have no suspects. They're looking for one or more burglars."

"Burglars?" Arthur exclaimed. "It wasn't burglars."

"What then?" Tony asked.

"There was one man. He wasn't a house burglar. He was after the Grail."

"Whatever do you mean?" Sandy asked with a startled look of fresh concern.

"He broke in while we were out to dinner. We came back early because Anne was unwell. We surprised him and he pulled a gun on us. He had Holmes' laptop and one of his research folders from his study. He said he wanted the documents Holmes had recently discovered."

"What documents?" Tony asked.

"Holmes rang me a few days ago and told me he'd made a new discovery, something really significant—something that involved me, believe it or not. He told me that he thought the Grail could actually be found and that he needed my help."

"How did this man know about this?" Sandy asked.

"He said that *interested parties*—that was the way he put it—interested parties had tapped our phone call."

"Who the hell would be interested in the Grail in that way?" Tony asked. "It's a bloody historical artifact that may not even exist! It's been sport for us, a wonderful exercise in academia, perhaps a grand metaphorical quest."

"If it did exist and were found," Sandy interjected, "it *would* have substantial monetary value."

Tony nodded. "But still—to kill for it when it hasn't even remotely been found? It doesn't make sense to me."

"I'm only telling you what the man said."

"Did Holmes show you what he'd found?" Sandy asked.

Arthur shook his head. "He was going to tell me after dinner. He never got a chance."

"Everything was burned," Sandy said. "Everything. His wonderful library, all his papers. We may never know what he discovered. A small tragedy heaped upon a far greater tragedy."

There was a rap against the open door and two men in suits entered.

"Sorry to interrupt," one of them said, "I'm Detective Inspector Hobbs of the Thames Valley Police and this is Detective Sergeant Melton. We'd like a word with Mister Malory if we could."

Sandy bent over to kiss Arthur and Tony patted his shoulder.

"You get better," Tony said. "We'll see you as soon as you're able at the Bear to continue our chat."

When they were gone, DI Hobbs and DS Melton stood over Arthur's bed.

Hobbs, the older man with the demeanor of an undertaker, said, "We know you've had an ordeal, Mister Malory, and we understand you've only been off the respirator since last night. In light of your head injury we don't expect you'll have a clear memory of what happened but we want to see if you recall anything, anything at all."

Melton, young and eager, added, "This is the start of a dialogue, Mister Malory. As time goes on, victims tend to remember more and more and we'll want to know every future recollection because—"

Arthur stopped him midsentence. "I remember everything."

"You do?" Hobbs said.

"I don't know why—perhaps it's unusual, but it took me only a few hours for it all to come back."

Melton took out a pad and pen. "That's excellent, Mister Malory. Why don't you start at the beginning and tell us everything you recall about the events of the evening in question."

Arthur methodically told his story, interrupted only by periodic coughing fits that forced him to press against his side to control the pain. As he talked, he absorbed the facial expressions of the detectives and wasn't at all surprised in the end when they barraged him with questions marinated in skepticism.

"So this fellow in the house," Hobbs asked, "this Caucasian man … you're saying he wasn't a run-of-the-mill burglar?"

"Hardly."

"Despite the fact that your wallet, mobile phone and wristwatch were stolen, despite the fact that when you came in the place had been ransacked, despite the fact we haven't found Mrs. Holmes' purse or Professor Holmes' wallet or watch."

"Yes, despite all that," Arthur said.

"This Grail you've talked about," Melton asked, "this would be the same as in *Monty Python and the Holy Grail*?"

"Are you mocking me?" Arthur's mood further darkened.

"No, hardly," Melton replied unconvincingly. "It's just that I'm not all that familiar with the Grail and those kind of things."

"The Grail has been an object of fascination for two thousand years, widely written about by scholars, playwrights, and novelists. I've been studying it myself for quite some time—as an interested layman—and that's how I met Andrew Holmes."

"Do you know if the Grail is even real?" Melton asked.

"No, of course not."

"I see," the young man said, smirking.

"You say this man claimed to have tapped a recent phone call with Professor Holmes?" Hobbs asked.

"He said that interested parties were responsible."

"And who might these interested parties be?"

"I've no idea. He wouldn't say."

"People who would commit serious offenses—including murder—in pursuit of an object that may not even be real? Does that make sense to you, Mister Malory?"

Arthur shook his head. "No. But it's what he said and more importantly it's what he did."

"Head injuries are a funny thing, Mister Malory," Hobbs said gravely. "In my considerable experience people's memories are often dramatically altered by this kind of trauma. And you had it even worse what with being shot and sustaining smoke inhalation. You're probably on pain medications too, right now, aren't you?"

Arthur nodded, unhappy with the direction this was taking.

"I've talked to specialists about the subject," Hobbs continued. "The mind plays tricks. You went to see Professor Holmes about some Grail business of his. That's what was on your mind. It's understandable that you're remembering things through that prism, isn't it?"

"I remember what happened," Arthur said emphatically before succumbing to a paroxysm of coughing.

"Well, we'll send the nurse in," Hobbs said. "And we'll have a police artist visit you tomorrow morning to make a sketch of the perpetrator. I'll leave my card on the table if you wish to change your statement. And we'll return in a day or two to see if your memory of that night changes, all right then, Mister Malory?"

5

Arthur woke to the pleasant chirping of birds outside his bedroom window and groggily went downstairs to turn on his coffeemaker. While the brew was dripping he stepped out the back door to see how nature was getting on.

As his fractured skull, cracked rib, and irritated lungs mended, Arthur had been able to gradually up his activity level. He had always been fit—jogging, cycling, tramping the countryside with his metal detector—and recent inactivity had hardly led to decrepitude. With his doctor's blessing, he was now doing some gardening and light jogging, still favoring his sore ribcage.

Arthur's house was a cozy, three down, three up affair situated on a fairly busy street in Wokingham. The road noise had never bothered him because it came into play only when he needed to rise on weekdays; but staying at home for a month had set him thinking about a quieter place.

It was his first house and suited him in a Goldilocks way: not too large, not too small. He used the smallest bedroom as an office and furnished the downstairs with legacy furniture. His parents were gone, both in their sixties, his father, Arthur Sr., from heart disease, his mother from cancer. Now with his parents dead and no sibs to share memories he liked the familiarity of having the same sitting and dining room pieces he'd grown up with. He filled the bookcases with the volumes his father had collected: history, geology, archaeology, and travel books as well as a nice collection of Arthurian material that he supplemented from time to time with his own purchases.

Periodically he shared his house with a girlfriend but only to a point. He had never been engaged, never opted for full cohabitation, and as his friends pointed out, he was chronically tepid on the commitment side. His last girlfriend was even blunter on breakup day.

"You're a bloody narcissist, Arthur, did you know that?" she'd ranted.

"Is it narcissistic to be passionate about my work and my hobbies?" he'd replied.

"Yes! When it trumps what I want at every turn!"

"I'm sorry I didn't fancy taking a Caribbean cruise. Not my scene, I'm afraid."

"The only thing that matters is *your* scene. I'm sorry, but digging for treasure in a muddy field and listening to all your boring King Arthur friends—those aren't *my* scenes."

Arthur had stared at her coldly and had responded, to his later regret, "Perhaps it would have been different if I were in love with you."

And with that her parting words had been deservedly unpleasant.

From the garden Arthur heard his doorbell ringing. He wiped his shoes and went back through the house snatching the cricket bat by the door and using his newly installed peephole before putting the bat down and opening up. It was DI Hobbs, very much his dour self.

"Do you have a minute for me, Mister Malory?"

"Come in. Coffee? I've got a pot on."

"Thank you, no."

They passed into Arthur's sitting room. Hobbs kept his raincoat on and looked around.

"Nice place you've got," Hobbs said.

"Thank you."

The detective inspector noticed a rose-colored kerosene lamp on the sideboard and picked it up.

"This is nice. Antique?"

"No, it's modern, actually. Handy for the odd power failure. How can I help you?"

Hobbs put the piece back down. "We've been investigating a series of burglaries in and around Oxford and I wanted to show you some photos of potential suspects to see if one of them might be your attacker."

Arthur put his coffee mug down, shaking his head. "I don't know how many times I have to tell you. This wasn't a burglary."

"I appreciate that and we've taken note of your official statements. However, we have to operate on facts. Forensically, we are now convinced that Professor Holmes' house was subjected to a burglary. There have been other break-ins at the university. We are operating under the theory that the perpetrator may have been responsible for the earlier burglary at his university office and gained knowledge of his home address at that time."

"Look, I—" Arthur began but Hobbs cut him off.

"And furthermore, an antiques dealer in Reading received some suspicious silver items and called the police. They clearly belonged to Professor Holmes. We identified the man who tried to sell them, a drug addict who was in a treatment facility the night of the murders. He obtained the goods from a lowlife who got them from another lowlife. That daisy chain of scum has led us nowhere useful at this time but reinforces our view that this was, at its roots, a burglary."

"You continue to ignore the Grail," Arthur said. He didn't sound frustrated, just weary.

"Candidly, I find the notion that this heinous crime is related to some kind of pursuit of the Holy Grail, well, fanciful. It's not what you may wish to hear but it is the truth. Now will you please review these photos of burglary suspects? They include photos of the aforementioned drug addicts."

Arthur sighed and scanned the photographs. It came as no surprise that none was his man.

"It must be clear to you that not one of these bears the slightest resemblance to the police sketch," Arthur said.

"I understand. We did print the sketch in the newspapers, as you know, and have received no credible leads as a result."

"You're basically saying you completely doubt my account of the night?"

"I'm only continuing to say that you took a nasty blow to your head."

"Did you at least look for evidence that someone tapped my phones or Andrew Holmes'?"

"We did, actually. There was nothing."

"Fine, all right," Arthur said testily. "If you'll excuse me I've got things to do."

Hobbs made for the door but paused to take note of the cricket bat.

"Do you still think you're being watched, Mister Malory?"

"Why bother telling you what I think?"

"Very well, then. You've got my card if you wish to speak with me."

After a day of gardening Arthur decided to take advantage of some residual energy. He donned his running gear and headed out into the cool darkness. There were few passing cars on his road but he stuck to the sidewalks anyway out of an abundance of caution. His favorite place for an easy jog these days was the recreation ground near Langborough Road, a short distance away.

His side throbbed with every strike of his left heel but he tried to tune out the discomfort and concentrate on the simple sweetness of the night air.

As he turned onto Fairview Road, he was vaguely aware of a car approaching from his rear so he clung to the sidewalk. He had to cross Fairview to get to the grounds, an easy task even during the day as it was a quiet little road. Ahead no cars were coming and the car from the rear no longer seemed to be about. But as he reached the middle of the road, he heard the roar of a motor and saw a flood of headlights.

A large car was coming fast and wasn't braking.

Arthur glanced over his shoulder. All he could see were headlights like the bright eyes of a nocturnal predator.

He did the only thing he could. He pushed off with his right foot and launched himself across the road. He heard himself yelling.

The car missed him by no more than inches.

He did a barrel roll onto his right side and landed on the grass on the verge of the recreation ground.

The car hurtled forward without slowing, made a left onto Gipsy Lane and disappeared, the sound of its motor fading.

The pain from his cracked rib took his breath away. He rolled onto his back, grimacing at the stars.

A woman came running out of Number 7. "Are you all right?" she called out.

"I think so."

"I heard you shout," she said, clutching a robe to her chest. "What happened?"

Arthur painfully pushed himself to a seated position. "It was a car. He almost hit me."

"There are too many bloody stupid yobs about," she said. "Did you get his number plate?"

"No."

"Shall I call the police? Do you need an ambulance?"

"No, I'm all right." He stood up, pressing against the sharp pain in his side with the flat of his hand. "I just live on Crescent Road. I'll be fine. Are there any security cameras on this street?"

"There ought to be with all the children who use the ground but the council's priorities are mucked up. Are you sure you're all right? I can easily ring the police."

"No. It would be a waste of time, I'm afraid. But thank you, you've been very kind."

The woman went back inside and Arthur began to walk home, eyes darting around, ears straining to hear any approaching car.

He imagined what the driver looked like and in his mind's eye it was the large man with the coarse face and cropped hair: the man who'd been haunting his dreams.

Walking into the Bear Inn was like walking into a wake. Tony Ferro spotted Arthur right away and by the time Arthur had pressed through to the crowded bar there was a pint waiting for him.

The Bear had been Holmes' favorite not because it had the best beer in town but because it was the oldest pub in Oxford, which meant something to an historian. Besides, it was close to his College, Corpus Christi. Invariably, when the Grail Loons got together this was the venue and this night was no different—except for the painfully glaring fact that Holmes was no longer among them.

Someone had placed a photo of Holmes on the bar. It perfectly captured his quirky charm: chin thrust out, full head of bushy hair, silk bow tie, five-button suit jacket, and an ivory-handled walking stick that he had used quite a lot lately to make his wife feel less self-conscious of her cane. Somehow this stick was one of the few items to survive the fire. A neighbor—perhaps the same hero who had pulled Arthur from the fire—had found it on the sidewalk amid blackened rubble, cast there by firefighters clearing out the collapsing front rooms. Now it lay on a table in one of the pub alcoves, a forlorn object if ever there was.

Arthur tried and failed to suppress a sob at the sight of Holmes' photo. Holmes had always liked Arthur to sit across from him at the pub so he could engage him easily. At one of the Loon meetings he had famously spouted, "With four pints in me and a good squint, looking at Arthur's like looking at Sir Thomas Malory, the old rogue, in the flesh!" Another time he had said, "If I ever finish the book I'm writing about Sir Thomas, I'm going to have you write a foreword."

"What would I say?" Arthur had asked.

"I don't know." Holmes had chuckled. "Why not something about why a fascination with King Arthur appears to be an inherited trait."

Tony spearheaded their push through to the alcove staked out by the Grail Loons. Aaron Cosgrove stood and gave Arthur a bear hug, making him flinch from rib pain. He was an Australian, a linguist teaching at Reading with a penchant for bad jokes. "Shove over, Sandy," he told Sandy Marina. "Make way for Arthurus Rex."

Sandy moved beer mats and glasses to accommodate one more on the bench, gave Arthur a pat on his leg and said, "It's good to see you looking hale and hearty."

Arthur couldn't stop staring at Holmes' cane, the small ruby eyes of the whimsical dragon head dull with soot.

Sandy noticed his gaze and touched its shaft. "We asked the publican if he'd keep it here for us."

There was no need for further explanation. That one simple sentence said it all. They would continue to meet as a group and Holmes would continue in their hearts.

"To Andrew and Anne," Tony said, lifting his mug.

"To Andrew and Anne," the rest chimed in.

Arthur drank half of his pint in one go, feeling positively numb that Holmes, this force of nature, was no more. The strong beer was medicinal.

There were gentle questions about Arthur's health and state of mind. Most knew nothing more than the official account—that the three interrupted a burglary and that mayhem ensued. Arthur responded mostly with grim, monosyllabic responses and told everyone he was returning to work soon. As far as he was concerned, this evening was about Andrew and Anne.

Tony wiped at a tear before it disappeared into his moustache. His signature sweater vest bulged over his gut and in honor of the departed he wore the Corpus Christi tie Holmes had given him, a Cambridge man, as a joke one Christmas. Holmes had told him, "I'm giving you this tie to irritate you, Tony, since I know your love for Oxford has no bounds. I expect you to keep it tucked away and produce it only on the event that I should ever require a funeral."

Aaron noticed the tie, pointed at the pub walls lined with cases of old college cravats and asked whether this specimen ought to go under glass too.

"No, I rather think I'll keep it," Tony said.

There were hushed words about the horror of it all, the tragic loss of two great people, and then Dennis Lange, an old Arthurian author, ruefully exclaimed, "All his books and papers! It's devastating."

Someone said, "I don't give a toss about the bloody books. It's Holmes I want back."

"Dennis is right to lament the books," Arthur said. "It would have been Andrew's thought as well. People die but books have a way of living on."

Dennis finished his pint and gave Arthur a thin-lipped smile for his support.

"So, we may never know what Andrew was going to conclude about the Grail and Montserrat," Aaron began, taking up the subject of the last Loons get-together. "I presume his manuscript is lost to the ashes or a melted hard drive."

"Maybe the Grail doesn't wish to be found," Sandy suggested.

"All of us are so bloody busy," Aaron went on, "but one day one of us needs to go to Montserrat and find Holmes' letter again. See if there's any fire behind the smoke." He realized what he'd said the moment it escaped his mouth, blubbered an apology and offered to buy the next round.

As Sandy rose to help Aaron with the drinks, she said to every one of them, "We all sit about our little round table and drink and talk ad nauseum. What we need is a knight to get on his horse and really and truly pursue the Grail—a modern Galahad."

As she said this, Arthur was keenly aware that she was looking straight at him.

Tony excused himself and Arthur followed him to the loo. When Tony finished up at the urinal Arthur coaxed him through the rear exit for a private chat.

"Tony, you realize I don't want to broadcast the details of that night to the entire group."

"I understand. Sandy and I have told no one."

"I've been doing a lot of thinking."

"I'm sure you have."

"The police don't believe anything I've told them. They think it's all the product of a scrambled brain. To them it was a garden-variety home break-in."

Tony huffed. "Outrageous."

"None of it makes any more sense today than the day it happened. I can't fathom a reason anyone would go to these lengths to find the Grail."

"Unless they were rather convinced—more than any of us—that it really exists."

Arthur nodded. "And unless they believe it's extraordinarily important. Tony, I think someone's trying to kill me."

Tony looked distressed. "Are you sure? Have you seen anyone?"

"At first it was just a sixth sense, really, of being watched when I'm driving, in the supermarket car park, that sort of thing. But a few nights ago someone tried to run me down while I was out jogging."

"Did you notify the police?"

"There wasn't any point. I didn't get the license plate, there were no witnesses and there weren't any cameras in the area. They already think I'm a nutter."

"What are you going to do?"

"That's what I've been thinking about. I'm a loose end. Why shouldn't the killer come back to clean up his mess? I'm the only witness to a double murder."

"Surely the police understand that."

"That much they do understand but they're absolutely convinced it was a burglary gone wrong and that I've got the Holy Grail on my addled brain. They'll provide protection if and when I receive an identifiable threat; but some drugged-out burglar—even one who committed murder, so they say—isn't likely to go after a witness. Look, Tony, if I thought the man that night was just a burglar I'd accept it and move on. But there's more to it. This was about the Grail. The Grail almost killed me. Now I think it may be the only thing that can save me."

"Whatever do you mean?"

"Holmes made some kind of breakthrough. This man was looking for it. At one point he asked me if Holmes had already told me what it was. For all they know, Holmes did tell me—and the gunman said *we*, I remember thinking at the time: he isn't acting alone. Anyway, I figured maybe that would give me a bit of a protective cushion. Until I almost got run down. He'll try again and eventually he'll get me. I know he will."

"Christ, Arthur."

"It's a long shot, but I really believe the only way I can be safe is to try and find the Grail, and if I do, loudly and publicly announce its discovery. These 'interested parties' the intruder talked about—the way I see it, it's the only way of neutering them. I've got to find the Grail and I've got to find and expose the killer. Otherwise the Loons are going to be drinking at my memorial too."

"We don't even know if it exists!"

"Someone thinks it does."

"How can I help?"

"I'm only a layman, Tony. I may need a real academic to chip in along the way. But we'll need to be careful. I don't want to get you involved."

"Of course. I'll do whatever I can."

"Do you know if Holmes kept an appointments diary?"

"I've no idea. You can check with his departmental secretary. Her name is Madeleine—*Maddie* he called her. I'll send you her number."

"Thank you."

"For God's sake be careful, Arthur. I don't want to lose another friend."

The History Faculty at Oxford was on George Street, set back from the road in a distinctive gabled building that, in the nineteenth century, had been the City of Oxford High School for Boys, the school T. E. Lawrence of Lawrence of Arabia fame had attended.

Arthur had visited Holmes there in the past but had never met Maddie. The moon-faced woman in an oversized jumper received him in her cubbyhole office and offered him a cup of tea from her personal electric kettle. Speaking of Holmes made her eyes go damp and Arthur quickly learned that he had been her favorite professor.

"And how are *you* doing, Mister Malory?" she asked. "The professor spoke so highly of you."

"Very much on the mend, thanks. I'll be returning to work on Monday."

"I'm sure that will help you take your mind off of ..."

She faltered and he helped her out. "I'm sure it will."

Arthur got to the point. He told her that Holmes had planned to tell him about a recent discovery concerning the Grail. Did she have any idea what it might have been?

"I'm afraid not," she said. "We mostly discussed departmental business, not academic affairs. Occasionally I'd type a manuscript for him but none lately."

"Did he keep a diary of his meetings or travel?"

"He had a small personal diary which he always kept with him. He arranged all his own travel and appointments. I generally don't get into that with the faculty. I do know that the police inquired about a diary a few weeks ago and searched his office without results, so I presume he had it on his person or in his house."

"He kept no other records of his schedule?"

She sipped her tea. "He has a calendar desk blotter and there are the occasional scribbles on it, I believe."

"May I see it?"

"I'm not really allowed," she said. "Our chairman has yet to make a determination on what's to become of his office."

Arthur smiled at her as warmly as he could and her objections melted away.

"Come along. I suppose it can't hurt anyone. The police say they're done with it."

His office was tidy and organized with calligraphic labels on folders and binders. The desk blotter was sparsely used with only a handful of notations. The one that first caught Arthur's eye was painful, from the day of his death: *Anne's b-day/dinner cum Arthur*

He scanned previous weeks. There were mostly references to faculty meetings or student appointments. Only one entry was of interest, a tantalizing note on 12 March: *Out of office. GQ!*

"Do you know where he went on this day?" Arthur asked Maddie, pointing at the box.

"I've no idea."

"Can you think of any way to find out?"

She shook her head. "Only Mrs. Holmes, and we can't ask her, can we?"

"If he had taken the train somewhere or perhaps a flight, would he have made those arrangements himself?"

"Not a chance. He was clueless about those things. I would have done it for him. But I didn't."

"So he would have driven."

"Presumably."

"Do you know who GQ might be?"

"I'm afraid not. I don't know of any faculty members or colleagues of his with a surname starting with *Q*."

Arthur sighed and gave her another request, so plaintively that she nodded. She granted him ten minutes and closed the door on her way out, leaving him alone inside. He immediately set to work going through desk drawers and filing cabinets, aided by Holmes' precise labels; but by the time Maddie returned, having allotted him extra time, he had found nothing about the Montserrat letter and more importantly, nothing on the matter Holmes had intended to broach with him.

After a circuit around the ancient courtyard at Corpus Christi College to clear his head, Arthur returned to the car park. As he was about to climb into his Land Rover, he once again had the prickly sensation that eyes were on him. Turning and scanning the surrounding area, he settled behind the wheel and uneasily headed back to Wokingham.

Arthur's return to Harp Industries was more difficult than anticipated. It felt like he'd been away far longer. People who didn't know

him well gave him furtive, uncomfortable glances; closer friends and colleagues lavished attention. By the time he reached his office he had tired of answering all the same questions.

His administrative assistant, Pam, was breezier about his return. She'd been in close contact for a fortnight and had begun feeding him some work items and meeting agendas.

"Coffee?" she asked.

"Yes, please," he said, "but funnily enough, I've started taking sugar. Must have been the bump to my head."

"Sugar it is. Martin's on his way. He wanted me to let him know the minute you arrived."

Martin Ash was soon at Arthur's door flashing a big smile and holding a couple of envelopes. He was in his early sixties, a consummate executive, capable of swinging from avuncular to headmasterish. Today he was full of warmth and empathy.

"We are so very glad to have you back with us, Arthur," he said, helping himself to a chair.

"I appreciate your coming by the hospital. I understand I was having a scan that day."

"We were worried as hell. I've brought you a card welcoming you back signed by every member of the magnets division."

Arthur looked it over then put it down.

"I'm ready to get back into things, Martin. I realize it's budget season so I know I've got to really get stuck into it to make the deadline."

"Look, we don't want you to overdo it. You went through some serious business. I've had Stu Gelfand pick up the slack while you've been out. I think he's started working with your managers on getting their numbers in shape."

Stu Gelfand headed the smaller magnets consumer division. Arthur headed the industrial side of the business. There was a clear rivalry between them for Ash's job when he retired, and Arthur wasn't best pleased to have Stu nosing around his department.

"I'll have to get Stu a fruit basket," Arthur said.

"One other thing. I received a DHL from Dr. Harp with a letter he wanted me to deliver personally. Here it is."

"I didn't think he knew who I was."

"Everyone knows who you are now."

Arthur used his finger as a letter opener and scanned the handwritten note.

"I can't believe it," he said.

"What does he say?" Ash asked.

"It seems he's invited me to his house."

6

Arthur's boxy Land Rover swayed in the crosswinds driving north on the A12 toward Suffolk. He'd gotten away well before the worst of the Friday traffic to arrive in time for his dinner invitation. The countryside was rain-soaked, the fields beyond the hedgerows ripe for planting. He drove with his window open a crack to allow earthy smells to permeate the vehicle.

He'd never met Jeremy Harp in person; he'd been in the audience a few times in the days when Harp would waltz into Basingstoke for one of his pep talks. He knew about him mostly from what he'd read on the company website: that Harp had received his degree in applied physics from Manchester and had gone on to do some of the key early work in neodymium magnets. Were it not for him, so the narrative goes, the world might not have disc drives, MRI machines, servo motors, and cordless tools. Harp had been a serious scientist earlier in his career but now that his company had matured, he had backed off from operations to pursue other activities, such as collecting art.

The portable nav system alerted Arthur to his turnoff. Binford was east of Bildeston. It was a tiny village with a handful of thatched pastel cottages, one pub, and a post office with general store. *Entering Binford, leaving Binford*, Arthur thought as he passed it by. Binford Hall was located off a very narrow stretch of B road. Had another car approached, he would have been obliged to pull off onto the shoulder.

The entrance to the property was modest, to say the least, a ratty gravel drive marked by a small wooden sign with a privacy warning. Apparently, the superrich didn't like to advertise.

Around a sharp bend in the drive a gatehouse came into view. There was a high iron gate and a sturdy boundary fence with electrocution hazard signs affixed. When Arthur pulled up to it a blue-blazered young man with short sandy hair emerged from the house carrying a clipboard.

"Hello Mister Malory," the man said crisply. He removed his sunglasses and peered into the car. He seemed to soak up the Land Rover's contents and when he was done with the inspection he put his glasses back on and said, "I'll announce you."

The gravel lane on the other side of the gate was twisty and thickly sown with impossibly white stones. When the drive straightened Arthur mumbled, "Bloody hell …" at the sight.

The house was magnificent, a masterpiece of ruddy brickwork, turrets, and gables laid out in an E-shape amidst an expansive parkland. He would soon find out it was early Tudor, circa 1490, though continuously embellished and improved upon over the centuries. Arthur guessed it had forty rooms, an estimate too low by twenty. As he approached he slowed the car the way one slowed a boat when entering a no-wake zone lest he dislodge any precious stones from the drive.

Arthur parked in the front courtyard. When he got out he wondered if he'd be able to find a bell on the massive oak doors but one of them swung open and out came an animated short man waving an arm in enthusiastic greeting.

"Hello there!" Harp called out. "Welcome to Binford Hall. How was your drive, Arthur?"

As they exchanged the requisite pleasantries, Arthur registered first impressions of his host. Harp had a florid complexion and a red, drinker's nose, which on closer inspection was really a knobbly rash. When Arthur returned home he would do an online search and decide it was rosacea, a stubborn condition that even a billionaire couldn't defeat. In fact, during the weekend he wouldn't see Harp drink all that much. The same could not be said for Mrs. Harp, who always seemed to have a glass of something at hand.

Harp had a white fringe of longish hair and glistening, intelligent eyes. His protruding belly might have made anyone else appear chubby but his clothes were so impeccably tailored and pressed that he merely looked prosperous. Arthur imagined that each and every garment peeled from his small frame was sent to the cleaners immediately, and even the man's pristine buttery loafers, subjected as they were to the horrors of a gravel drive, instantly would be sent for resoling.

Harp beckoned him. "Come inside. Leave your bag. I'll have it taken to your room. Have a quick freshen-up then I'll show you around while there's still light. Marvelous to have you here. Absolutely marvelous. You'll meet my wife later."

The entrance hall was cavernous and paneled, soaring two stories, dwarfing visitors. A gracefully swooping staircase led to a bannistered gallery. The walls were lined with portraits and landscapes in heavy ornate frames, and on the stairs Arthur swore he made out Rembrandt's signature on an amber-toned portrait of an apple-cheeked peasant.

Harp must have been tracking his eyes. "Yes, indeed. It's a Rembrandt. You might be confused by the way it's spelled: *Rembrant*, without the *d*. That's the way he signed his name prior to sixteen thirty-three. Bought it with a de Gelder and a Hals at the same auction a decade ago. Should have bought more when I had the chance. Dutch Masters always seem to be in a bull market."

Arthur resisted the urge to ask what it was worth though he was reasonably certain Harp would have been more than pleased to tell him.

At the top of the stairs, Harp pointed down a long hallway and said, "Fifth door on your right, the open one. That's yours. When you're ready come back down, give us a shout and we'll have our tour. Is that all right?"

"More than all right," Arthur said, bewildered by the grandness of it all.

His room was large, well-appointed, and en suite with a large claw-footed bath and a separate steam shower. There was even a flat-screen TV mounted at bath level.

A porter brought his bag and returned a short while later with a cart of beverages: bottled water, sherry, premium liquors. He considered having a nip but he wanted to be perfectly clear-headed for the chairman so he grabbed his coat and headed downstairs for the walkabout.

Though his legs were short, Harp beat out a fast pace in his Wellington boots, compelling Arthur to lean into his stride to keep up. He took him on a meandering tour of the property barking out facts about previous owners of Binford Hall, pointing out architectural, landscape, and horticultural features, glibly spewing the Latinate names of plantings. According to Harp, none of his predecessors at Binford had been much good at anything other than inheriting money. Not a luminary among the lot in arts, sciences, politics, or commerce—until him, of course, which seemed to be the subtext of the discourse. He'd bought the house in the early nineties from a bankrupt ne'er-do-well who could trace his lineage there back to the sixteenth century. Apparently, the fellow took his proceeds and decamped for Spain where he promptly killed himself in a road accident.

"He left Binford in a complete and utter mess but it had potential. I could see that from my first visit. How much do you think it took to make this place right?" Harp asked.

"Millions, I should think," Arthur answered.

"Times ten!" Harp crowed, puffing out his chest. "Spared no expense. Right now I'd rate it as one of the finest country estates in England. And it's not just the house and gardens. We've got almost four hundred acres of prime Suffolk farmland out that way beyond the stables. Had to introduce all the new methods to make the enterprise profitable. You know, I still haven't gotten my Nobel Prize in physics—though rumors do swirl about this year's slate. If by some travesty I never get it in physics, I should damn well get one in agriculture. My farm manager goes around giving seminars on how we turned it around. We are, without doubt, the highest tech farm in the country."

The light was fading but Arthur made out an expanse of tawny hues in the distance.

"That's where you'll be doing your prospecting tomorrow," Harp noted. "The weather's supposed to be fine."

"I'm looking forward to it," Arthur said.

"We dress for dinner."

That's what Harp told Arthur as he deposited him back at his room. If the notion of dressing for dinner would be satisfied by a sport coat and striped tie then Arthur would be fine.

The dining room was extraordinary: a high Tudor hall with a musician's gallery, heraldic banners, and an elaborately coffered ceiling. The long table, perfectly centered in the cavernous room, was set at one end for three with Harp at the short side.

Harp was dressed in a dark suit with a silky lavender tie, his wife in an elegant dress. Mrs. Harp started the evening with the pinched look of someone forced into hospitality but she brightened at the sight of Arthur and delivered compliments on his blue eyes and thick hair to Harp's apparent irritation.

"I read, of course, of your tragic happenstance and communicated with Martin Ash about it," Harp began when the starter was cleared by the server. "I would have reached out earlier but I wanted to make sure you'd convalesced. Are you all right now?"

"Close to a hundred percent," Arthur said. "I'm back to work and feeling quite fit, thanks."

"I'm sorry you had to go through something like that. The state of this country! Brazen burglaries are out of control."

Arthur nodded. There was no reason to correct Harp's impression.

"You know, I find our company newsletter very informative," Harp said, changing the subject. "How else would I have discovered that someone as interesting as you worked for me?"

"I'm really not all that interesting," Arthur demurred.

"This is a modesty-free zone!" Harp insisted. "You have a first in chemistry from Bristol, you're a bloody good marketing chap according to Martin Ash, you're a descendant of the man who put King Arthur on the map, a student of history, and something of an explorer. That spells Renaissance man, Arthur, and I like Renaissance men. It takes one to know one."

"Thank you, sir."

"Don't give me that 'sir' nonsense. It's Jeremy to you. So you're a Grail aficionado, is that right?"

"I am. The subject fascinates me." He caught himself. The Grail had fascinated him before the murders. Was it still fascinating, or had it mutated into something darker, more ominous?

"I'm a bit of a Grail hobbyist myself," Harp said, reaching for his wine glass.

"Is that right?" Arthur said. "Why the interest?"

"All work and no play … Even when I was doing physics day in and day out I had outside interests. That particular one probably sprang from reading your ancestor's *Le Morte D'Arthur* as a schoolboy. The Arthurian quest is very alluring, isn't it? It's a metaphor for all sorts of pursuits in life. I've periodically dabbled in the subject matter though I daresay I probably don't hold a candle to your knowledge."

"I don't know about that, but I agree with your views on the appeal of the subject," Arthur said, "though there are those who might say the quest is more than metaphorical."

"Are you among them?" Harp asked, helping himself from a platter of meat cradled by the server.

In light of the murders, Arthur dodged the question. "As you may know, the Catholic Church has obliquely endorsed the chalice kept at the Valencia Cathedral as the true Grail, so it might be argued that a real, physical artifact has already been found."

Harp laughed. "But you don't believe that, do you? I can tell by your face."

"It's certainly an interesting object. I mean the Valencia Chalice dates to the first century and it is unquestionably from a piece of

Middle Eastern agate; but none of the serious Grail people believe it's the genuine article. I could certainly go on." He looked at Mrs. Harp and thought better of it. "It might be a little tedious for your wife."

"Nonsense!" Harp exclaimed. "Much more amusing than talking about the weather or neodymium magnets! You agree, don't you, Lillian?"

Mrs. Harp poured more wine for herself and delivered a thin smile.

"You made a provocative statement in that article," Harp continued. "You said you had some ideas where the Grail might be located."

"I suppose I did say that."

"Tell me more."

"Well, it's not my personal research. I belong to an informal group of Grail hunters, most of them academic types who meet periodically to share ideas." Arthur stopped talking to wipe an unwanted tear that suddenly had formed at the corner of an eye.

"Are you all right?" Harp asked.

"I'm sorry," Arthur said quickly. "It's just that the founder of the group and his wife were the people who were killed."

"Good heavens. Terrible, terrible," Harp clucked, and his wife parroted him.

"Andrew Holmes was a history don at Cambridge. He had recently made some notable progress."

"Yes?" Harp looked at Arthur keenly, resting his utensils on his plate.

"I really shouldn't say much about it because he hadn't published his findings. I don't think he would have wanted anyone speaking about it prematurely."

"You can trust me, Arthur," Harp said. "Now that you've piqued my curiosity, I'll be like a dog with a bone. Anyway, who would I talk to about it? You have my vow of silence as a gentleman and your boss."

Arthur glanced at Mrs. Harp, who piped up and said, "You don't have to worry about me. I'm hardly paying attention."

"Go on," Harp insisted.

Arthur wasn't keen to say more but he felt like he had no choice. "I'm not sure anyone's going to know the full extent of what he found because the house fire destroyed all his papers. But here's what I was told. As you know, the Grail quest entered into the public consciousness via the Arthurian legend and subsequent literature. Thomas Malory may have definitively put the topic on the map in the fifteenth century with *Le Morte* but everyone knows that he relied on antecedent works."

Harp chimed in almost mechanically. "Chrétien de Troyes' *Perceval, le Conte du Graal*; Robert de Boron's *La Grant Estoire dou Graal*; and Wolfram von Eschenbach's *Parzival*."

Surprised, Arthur said, "You seem to be more than a dabbler."

"No—really not, I assure you. I'm blessed or perhaps cursed with a photographic memory. When something makes it inside my brain it never seems to leave."

"Don't I know it," his wife said without a touch of humor.

"Well, you've cited the troika of relevant twelfth-century texts, two French, one German," Arthur said. "And of course there were other versions produced over the centuries prior to Malory's definitive work; but the really interesting question is why did the original three manuscripts pop up within one or two decades of one another? Was it coincidence? Did the first one out, Chrétien de Troyes', spark some quick copycats? Is there another explanation?"

"Copycats?" Harp repeated.

"Well ... perhaps that's not the best word, as each work presents a unique version of Grail events."

"And you're about to propose an alternate explanation, aren't you?"

"Perhaps. So, as I'm sure you know, in addition to the Valencia Cathedral, there are a host of other possible sanctuaries for the Grail."

"Besides the theory set forth in *The Da Vinci Code*," Harp said teasingly.

"Oh please," Arthur laughed. "My interest has always been in a physical Grail, not a metaphorical one. So besides Valencia, the most commonly cited ones are Rosslyn Chapel in Scotland, Glastonbury Tor in Somerset, Oak Island in Nova Scotia, the monastery of Montserrat in Catalonia, and most recently, the basilica Of San Isidro in León, Spain. Montserrat has, perhaps, had particular appeal since the monks there have long championed the notion that Montserrat is the

'Munsalvaesche' that von Eschenbach cites as the Grail castle in *Parzival.* Even though Montserrat has been picked over exhaustively by Grail hunters, Andrew Holmes always favored the location for a variety of historical reasons.

"Several months ago the monks at Montserrat gave Andrew unusually broad access to the medieval library there. In a folio that probably hadn't been touched for nine hundred years he found a letter written in 1175 to the abbot of Montserrat thanking him for his hospitality during a pilgrimage. It was signed by three men: Chrétien de Troyes, Robert de Boron, and Wolfram von Eschenbach."

Harp swallowed. "All three at the same time and the same place? Amazing. Was the letter more than a thank you? Was there any mention of the Grail?"

"I don't know. Holmes hadn't shared its contents with the group. He was playing his cards close to the vest. I think he expected to make a splash when he was ready to present his paper. But we could tell from his body language that he was more firmly than ever in the Montserrat camp."

"Did he have a copy of the letter?"

"The monks let him photograph it, I believe. But it's gone in the fire. I'd like to retrace his footsteps one day and try to find the letter again. Maybe if Martin Ash gives me a long holiday."

"And this Holmes chap; that's all he told you about his recent research?"

"Actually, he *had* made a new discovery that greatly excited him. He was going to share it with me the night he was killed. I'm afraid he took it to the grave."

"A pity," Harp said. "Perhaps it will be rediscovered one day. It seems to me …"

"Jeremy," his wife implored, "save some of this for tomorrow, won't you?"

Harp nodded. "She's right, of course. Let's have some pudding and talk about something that interests everyone. Arthur and I can speak more about this at tea tomorrow. What time do you want to start your prospecting?"

"As early as possible. Four hundred acres is a lot of ground to cover."

"What are you hoping to find?" Mrs. Harp asked.

"Anything more interesting than a rusty tin of baked beans would be nice," Arthur said. "Not far from here at Hoxne, in 1992, a hobbyist with a metal detector found a hoard of some fifteen thousand gold, silver and bronze Roman coins in a field. The British Museum paid out roughly two million pounds for it. Something like that would be particularly welcome."

"Wish I could join you," Harp said. "I've got a bloody agricultural meeting to attend. The man from the gatehouse, Hengst; he'll be about if you need anything. Let's see to some brandy, shall we?"

"Of course."

Harp looked up at the empty musicians gallery as if listening to the interlacing melodies of an unseen string quartet. "We'll drink to the memory of your friends."

Arthur swept his Garrett metal detector over the clodded, pebbly earth. It was sunny and crisp, cool enough that when he had begun his hunt at 8 A.M., his breath had been visible. His boots sank into a wet soil rich and full of promise—of a bountiful fall harvest of winter wheat; of treasure.

Although the best find of the morning had been an old horseshoe, Arthur was contented. This was his first outing in the countryside since being hospitalized and to feel the wind on his face and listen to birdsong felt wonderful. Like a golfer who didn't much care about his score but relished the time outdoors, he happily tramped about the fields east to west then west to east, mindful not to scan the same ground twice.

Through his headphones he heard the muffled sound of an engine. He looked up to see an ATV approaching from the direction of the house. It stopped about one hundred yards away. Arthur recognized the guard from the gatehouse, lifting binoculars to his face; then shrugged off the snooping. He reckoned the fellow was grateful for having something to do on a dozy Saturday.

At noon he stuck his trowel into the earth to mark his place and ambled back to the car for the packed sandwich lunch Harp's kitchen staff had provided.

As the afternoon progressed, Arthur's arm and shoulder began to take the achy brunt of back-and-forth sweeping. The sun was getting low. His minder had come and gone but returned again, watching afar from his idling ATV. Arthur had increasingly hiked the detector's iron discrimination settings to cut down on the number of junk targets and it had been over an hour since the last decent tone through his headphones.

He was in a faraway place, thinking about small things like the flock of ducks streaking overhead when a beep brought him back to the soil. It was a pleasant, crisp midtone, fairly faint. His screen showed a reading of 64, a good number, one that included precious metals. The depth reading was about a meter. He swept the detector head a bit further on and got a clear double tone, also at a reading of 64. Two objects.

He swept another arc just to the north of the double tone and suddenly there was a symphony, beeps galore.

He'd never before heard the earth calling to him like this.

Suppressing an urge to fall to his knees and begin knifing the dirt with his trowel, he carefully mapped out the boundaries of the tones. When he was done he planted his trowel in the middle of the area, left his metal detector behind, and fast-walked to the Land Rover for his spade.

He began taking down the topsoil, periodically checking the signals with his detector until he had carved out the boundaries of a roughly two- by three-yard zone. His side began to ache but he wasn't going to let pain slow him down.

Each of his neat spadesful of earth was the size of a book. He had volunteered on archaeological digs and knew how carefully and methodically professionals liked to work. When he had produced a mound of slices he passed his metal detector over it and verified the absence of metal. He climbed into the shallow hole he'd made and scanned it with the detector head. The symphony was louder.

The hole was getting deeper and the mound of discarded earth higher. Arthur had decided to take everything down to the same level rather than pot-hole it. He didn't want to be embarrassed by poor technique on the chance that a real archaeologist had to be called in. He took the trench down almost a yard and when he scanned the fresh surface the beeping in his ears was so loud he had to dial back the volume.

Troweling from here on, he thought.

He began scraping thin cuts of earth away, scooping the debris with his hands and inspecting each handful before tossing it onto the pile. Every so often the trowel caught on something hard but each time the obstruction was a piece of flint.

His trowel caught again but this time a stone didn't pop out of the ground. He probed the obstruction with his hand to see if it was a larger rock that needed digging out but it didn't feel like a flint nodule. It wasn't as smooth as an exposed flint surface or as rough as a chalky matrix—and as he ran his finger over it hard, he saw a glint of unmistakable color.

Gold!

He used a ballpoint pen as a scraper lest he scratch the surface of the object with the tip of his trowel. When the pen wouldn't complete the trick he used his fingernails. Before long a flattened piece of gold the dimensions of his hand lay exposed to the pale afternoon light. He spit on it and smoothed away the adherent soil to get a look at its intricate tooling and held his breath at what he saw: an engraved menagerie of stylized animal-like figures emerging from the golden finish.

It looked like the cheekpiece of a helmet, Anglo-Saxon perhaps.

He eagerly scraped at the earth adjacent to the cheekpiece and another object was revealed. After a minute, Arthur had exposed a braided bracelet, chunky, golden, beautifully crafted.

Judging by the cacophony coming through the headphones, he guessed there would be more. Lots more.

He looked to the ATV in the distance and waved his arms to summon the guard.

When Jeremy Harp finally arrived he made his security man jump into the excavation first and help him down. Three crowded the space, so the guard climbed out to give them more room. Arthur crouched alongside Harp and showed him the cheekpiece and bracelet.

"Extraordinary!" Harp exclaimed, touching the cool golden surface of the cheekpiece with a chubby forefinger.

Then Arthur took him over to the far end of the oval where, while waiting for Harp to arrive, he had uncovered another extraordinary piece, a gold pectoral cross with a central garnet, twisted up rather like a pretzel.

"How old are they?" Harp asked.

"Seventh century, eighth century, somewhere around there, I'd guess. I'm no expert but I reckon it's Anglo-Saxon. Probably buried for safekeeping in leather or cloth bags, which have long decomposed."

"Is this it? Is there more?"

"Definitely. All the way to the edges. There could be dozens, maybe hundreds of pieces."

"Well get digging then while there's still light. Let's see what I've got."

Arthur noted the first sign of trouble—*what I've got.* He chose his words carefully. "Actually, Jeremy, we really shouldn't do any more digging. We need to call in the professionals."

Arthur saw how the small man stiffened. Despite his plea to be called by his first name, it seemed that *Dr. Harp* would have been a better choice. And Harp didn't seem best pleased to have his instructions challenged.

"Professionals? Whomever do you mean?" he said gruffly.

"Suffolk will have an Archaeological Service. All the councils do. They'll send a team out to make an assessment. For something like this I wouldn't be surprised if they'd come out tomorrow morning. I can see if they've got a weekend number."

Harp had the guard help him out of the pit and he peered down imperiously from the edge. "This is my land and I'll do whatever I please on my land. I don't want strangers on my property."

Arthur felt his face burn.

"Look—Dr. Harp—I'm afraid there are certain procedures to follow even on private land. As someone who does this kind of prospecting, I'm reasonably up to date on these things. The Treasure Act of 1996 mandates that all possible discoveries of ancient and valuable artifacts—whether on public *or* private lands—be reported to the local coroner for a determination whether it does indeed meet the definition of treasure. And best practice is to call the archaeologists first."

"And the definition of treasure is?"

"Artifacts more than three hundred years old and containing at least ten percent gold or silver. I'm quite sure we're going to meet the definition."

"And what if I tell you not to call the archaeologists or the coroner?"

Arthur took a deep breath. "I'm obligated to make the call, sir."

Harp looked volcanic. "And should the coroner and his minions make an investigation, what happens when they are done?"

"The hoard would be excavated and catalogued by the county Archaeological Service and its value assessed by the Treasure Valuation Committee in London."

"How much might it be worth?"

"Quite a bit I should think. I hesitate to speculate but as I mentioned last night, some hoards have been valued at millions."

"And this value would accrue to me?"

Arthur decided to hold his ground. "Well, actually to us, sir. As the finder who did the treasure-hunting with the permission of the landowner, I'd be entitled to half."

Harp began to walk away in a furious state but he turned long enough to say, "You do whatever you feel you must, Malory. My wife and I have another commitment tonight. We'll have food sent to your room. It would be most convenient if you departed first thing in the morning."

The next two weeks streaked by like a tornado, which had left Arthur decidedly de-roofed. The maelstrom had begun, as most large things do, with a small thing—a one-minute conversation with a newspaper man.

A team from the Suffolk Archaeology unit had, as he had predicted, arrived early on the Sunday morning before he'd cleared out. Hengst tried to shoo the archaeologists away but the threat of police involvement greased open the gate. Hengst watched from a distance as the team members did preliminary investigations, excitedly pointing out each new find to Arthur. Harp was nowhere to be seen that morning.

The buried pieces were indeed Anglo-Saxon, a combination of militaria and jewelry. Peter Saunders, the head of Suffolk Archaeology, a lanky, erudite fellow, guessed from the density of objects at several hundred pieces when all was said and done. He was correct. The dig lasted four days, and each evening Saunders kindly sent Arthur an e-mail attaching photos of cleaned-up artifacts. The final count was 663 gold objects: sword pommels, hilt plates, scabbard loops, buckles, helmet pieces, fittings, strips, studs, buttons, brooches, crosses, and rings. Some of the pieces, the brooches especially, were achingly beautiful renderings of birds, snakes, and lizards. From the clustering of artifacts, Saunders surmised that some

East Angle lord, or perhaps someone who had sacked him, had buried two bags of loot in an eighth-century forest with the unrealized intention of returning for it.

Arthur knew, of course, a hefty value would be placed upon the hoard but the preliminary assessment of four million pounds staggered him. The Suffolk County Council made attempts to keep things quiet until a suitable time could be found for a press conference but the leak couldn't be stopped. Almost instantly, Arthur found himself fielding a call from one Laurence Cole from the *Daily Mail*, who knew essentially all there was to know and wanted to confirm it. The man sounded breathless, as if rushing to a deadline.

"So, Mister Malory, how do you feel about making the discovery of a lifetime?"

"I mean it's quite unbelievable, really. I've been prospecting for years with rather little to show for it. I couldn't be more pleased."

"Would I be mistaken to take you for the same Arthur Malory who was tied up in that nasty business in Oxfordshire back in March?"

"I'm afraid that was me."

"You're having quite the eventful time of it, aren't you?"

"Unfortunately, yes."

"Well, sounds like you're on the mend. So you work for Jeremy Harp."

"Yes. I'm in marketing at Harp Industries."

"Yeah, I got ahold of the company newsletter which features you. Says you're a descendant of the bloke who wrote *Le Morte D'Arthur*."

"That's the family lore. I've done some genealogy work but nothing really definitive."

"So a guy who's a descendant of the man who made King Arthur famous finds a treasure hoard that could've come from King Arthur's days."

"Well … I think most believe that King Arthur lived a few centuries earlier than the Binford hoard."

"Close enough, though, don't you think? It's the story that counts and this is a good 'un. So, the archaeologist, this Saunders chap. He tells me the British Museum's keen to buy this off of you. Were you aware that your cut could be worth two million quid? Does that put a spring in your step?"

Arthur remembered exactly how he had felt at that moment. He'd said his piece and never once regretted the sentiment. He just wished he hadn't stepped in so large a cow pie.

"There's no way I'd accept a penny. This kind of treasure belongs to the country. It's our collective heritage. I may be entitled to money by law but I will certainly donate my share to the British Museum."

In the pause that had followed, Arthur heard the journalist furiously typing on his keyboard. "What would you say if I told you that when I informed Doctor Harp about the British Museum's cash offer he replied, and I quote, 'The more the merrier, I'm sure I'll put it to good use on my estate'?"

At that moment Arthur had caught a glimpse of a thorny future but he refused to backpedal. He thought long enough for a diplomatic response to come to him. "I think one has to do what one is comfortable with under the circumstances."

"But you're not a billionaire like Harp, are you?"

"Of course not!"

"Not wealthy at all, are you?"

"Hardly."

"And yet, you're giving your country a gift worth a couple of million."

"Look, is there anything else I can help you with?"

"No, Mister Malory. I think we're good. You have a nice day. I expect it'll be the last sane one you have in a while."

Cole's newspaper story begat other stories that begat TV and radio pieces that begat a torrent of blogs and postings and tweets until Arthur and his brave recovery from a brutal attack, his treasure and his altruism, became a self-perpetuating set of memes that eclipsed all others up and down the British Isles.

For his part, Jeremy Harp, when informed by the press of Arthur's intention to donate his share, quickly changed his mind and announced that he too would make a donation. But the damage was done. A billionaire belatedly donating millions wasn't news.

At first, Arthur had been merely shy about the attention; but as the phenomenon built up steam his sheepishness turned to embarrassment and finally irritation when it became more and more difficult for him to perform everyday activities. There were incessant phone calls to his home and office and somehow his mobile number and e-mail address became known too.

To his amazement, he now had become the target of paparazzi, shadowing his every mundane movement, trying to land photos of the handsome young man. That Arthur's house was on a busy road worked to his advantage. No parking allowed police to move the paparazzi along but they congregated on side streets, prowling the sidewalk outside his home wielding telephoto lenses and calling to him to poke his head out the door.

An unpleasant thought plagued him as well: wouldn't the presence of a mob make it easier for a man with a gun to mingle and get close?

Stu Gelfand appeared at the threshold of Arthur's office, interrupting the spreadsheet work he was doing on his departmental budget.

Stu looked at the cluttered desk. "Looks like you're waist-deep in alligators. All right, then?"

Arthur bridled as always at Gelfand's smarminess. "I'm doing fine, Stu, and more to the point so are my projections. Next year should be outstanding."

"I'm sure it will be. Well, if there's anything I can do to help, just give us a shout. My presentation's in the can so I've got buckets of free time."

"You're too kind."

Gelfand grinned. "The least I can do for a real-life British hero."

Jeremy Harp was well into a bottle of Armagnac. Binford Hall was large enough that he and his wife usually saw each other by appointment. But they surprised each other by their accidental collision in the kitchen when he wandered in for leftovers and she for a cup of herbal tea before retiring.

She watched him peel the plastic wrap from the lamb joint. "Do you want me to get Marie over to heat that up? She's probably still awake."

"I'm a bloody physicist, Lillian. I can operate a microwave oven."

She watched in disdain as he fumbled unsuccessfully with the timer clock and elbowed him aside to set it for him.

"You're a drunken physicist, I think."

He sat down hard on a chair and mumbled. "Now you know what it's like living with you, darling."

She clammed up at that and when the microwave beeped she loudly slid his hot plate of meat in front of him. Before departing to her bedroom with her mug she said, "I realize you've endured a period of rare rebuke, Jeremy, but it's beneath contempt to take it out on me."

Here he was, a man who preferred to keep out of the public eye, enduring withering attacks at the hand of cartoonists, bloggers, and chat show hosts as the most haughty, out-of-touch man in Britain, the embodiment of all that was rotten about the wealthy elite. He had no idea that his offhand comment to a reporter would turn him into a caricature—and no doubt it wouldn't have happened without Arthur Malory's ridiculously altruistic stance. He had hoped rather naïvely that reversing his position on the treasure would repair his image, yet that had hardly happened.

He carved into the meat, stewing in resentments. Drink only fueled his anger, aimed at all those who had belittled him throughout his life. Although richer than most rich men in the corridors of power, his was new money, earned in the grubby world of modern commerce. He wasn't one of them. He was a northerner. His father had been a surveyor, his grandfather a pipe fitter.

As a small lad with more brains than brawn, he'd been accustomed to taunts and beatings. But hard work and inventiveness had elevated him out of poverty to the ranks of the ultra rich. With his kind of wealth he had bought his way into most of the right clubs but he never truly belonged. He had come to hate those smug bastards with their correct schools, correct accents, and sniggering inside jokes.

And now, his head swimming in Armagnac, he conflated all those smug bastards with one new one—Arthur Malory.

A mouth full of lamb didn't stop him from lifting his head and speaking to the emptiness of the kitchen.

"I own you, Malory," he said, spraying bits of meat onto the table. "And when I own something I can bloody well do whatever I want with it. You have no idea who you're dealing with, do you?"

Arthur was on his computer working through a Singapore supply-chain problem when Pam knocked.

"Martin would like to see you."

"Topic?"

"He didn't say."

If he wanted to chat about something Ash usually grabbed him as they passed in the hall or cornered him after a meeting. Their important sit-downs were always prescheduled affairs, so Arthur ran through scenarios on his way to Ash's office. Maybe there was a problem with his budget, or perhaps Martin had gotten some client feedback he wanted to pass along.

Ash was normally gregarious so Arthur could tell by the assiduous avoidance of eye contact that trouble was afoot.

"What's up, Martin?" he asked, settling into the subordinate spot—the love seat. Before Ash could answer there was a light tap and Susan Brent came in.

"I'm sorry to be late," she said, taking a chair, also avoiding Arthur's gaze.

Arthur scowled. "An unscheduled meeting involving my boss and HR. This can't be good."

Ash heaved his chest dramatically, a gesture that came off as practiced. "I'll just say it. There's been a reorganization. It affects you."

Arthur steeled himself. "All right ..."

"The board wants to streamline things, achieve some rationalization, trim costs, et cetera. Next year could be challenging."

"My forecast says otherwise, Martin. You signed off on my numbers."

Ash had the appearance of a patient awaiting his turn for hemorrhoid surgery. "It's not necessarily as challenging for your department. It's a companywide issue. In any event, the decision's been taken to merge your department with Stu Gelfand's. Stu's come out on top."

The flush of anger scorched Arthur's neck. "Stu's group is half the size in revenue and half the size in headcount! And I've been here longer. That's absurd, Martin!"

"I hear you, Arthur. I assure you I argued against it but the decision was taken at higher levels."

"Who else is being let go?"

Ash turned away and looked through his window. "For the moment, only you."

"You know what this is about, Martin," Arthur seethed. "I understand you may not wish to acknowledge it but this is blatant retribution for what became a public contretemps with Dr. Harp over the treasure. I never had any intention of embarrassing him and I took pains to avoid media attention. I made a decision dictated by my conscience. He did what he thought was best for himself and I have no problem with that. But this is wrong, Martin. It's wrong."

Susan stepped into Ash's silence. She seemed uncomfortable, laboring to sound professional. "Whenever companies endeavor to control expenditures there are human costs but I can assure you that this decision had nothing to do with anything but financial and strategic objectives."

"Susan's right, Arthur," Ash said. "I don't have any evidence this is coming from Dr. Harp. He's always been a supporter of yours. Did you know how you got hired here in the first place?"

"You saw something I wrote at university."

"Dr. Harp was the one who saw it and passed it to me. He said he could spot talent and he was right."

Leaning forward, Arthur said, "I wasn't aware of that but it doesn't change anything. This is blatant retribution for making him look bad."

Susan started in with more boiler-plate babble and Arthur stopped her.

"For God's sake don't patronize me with that kind of nonsense. Look, Martin, I've always respected you. I'm sorry you've lost your mettle. This is an open and shut case of unfair dismissal and I shall be taking it to an employment tribunal."

Susan placed an envelope before him and with a pasted-on smile said, "I'm sure you're disappointed, Arthur, and I'm sure you're angry. That's perfectly understandable. The company wishes to address your termination amicably and avoid any legal actions which would only serve to distract both parties from productively moving forward."

"Spit it out, Susan," Arthur snapped. "And spare me the HR-speak. What are you offering me?"

The terms emerged fluidly. A lump sum equal to eighteen months of salary and bonus with appropriate pension contributions and the maintenance of his company car lease for six months—plus a good reference. In return, Arthur's agreement not to take any legal action against Harp or publicly disparage the company.

Arthur shook his head, laughing. It was rich. No one at Harp got that kind of severance package. They wanted him gone and they wanted him quietly forgotten. After endless tribunal hearings he'd be lucky to get half. He picked up the envelope.

"You'll accept?" Susan pressed.

"I'll take it but the both of you should be ashamed of yourselves. When is this effective?"

"Immediately," Susan said. She looked like she wanted this over as quickly as possible. "You'll find security waiting in your office to supervise the removal of your personal effects."

"Great. Why don't you take a photo of me packing up for the newsletter?" At the door he said, "Good-bye, Martin. Sorry it had to end like this."

Ash looked at the carpet and mumbled, "I'm sorry too, Arthur. I really am."

Arthur went into his garden to soak up the sun carrying a mug of tea and a pad of paper. He had woken, newly unemployed, with Sandy Marina's exhortation playing in his head: *What we need is a knight to get on his horse and really and truly pursue the Grail—a modern Galahad.*

He now had the time to get on with it. The carnival sideshow of the treasure was behind him. His departmental budget wasn't a concern anymore. His personal finances were cushioned by a severance. And his nerves were fraying waiting for the man with a gun to reappear.

The Grail was going to get his full attention.

He made two notations on his pad: *12 March* and *Montserrat.*

He had to find out where Holmes had gone on the twelfth. He'd already had a word with the Loons to see if Holmes had mentioned anything to any one of them about his destination that day—a library, museum, an archive—and had come up empty. It occurred to him that Holmes might have said something to an Oxford faculty member or one of the fellows at Corpus Christi. There was a list of names to compile. Then there were Anne's friends. Who knows, maybe she even accompanied him that day and told one of them about it.

Then there was Montserrat. It was a lower priority but it would be easy enough to send a letter to the abbot of Montserrat informing him of Holmes' untimely death and requesting permission to reexamine the twelfth-century letter in their archive.

He began making calls. Holmes' secretary agreed to e-mail him contact numbers from Oxford. The director of Anne's microbiology lab at the medical school helpfully put him through to Anne's best friend at work, and after a heart-wrenching chat, which shed no light on 12 March, he obtained a list of Anne's other friends who may or may not have heard something.

After a couple of hours of further unproductive calls, he decamped from the garden, rinsed out his mug, and went upstairs to change into running gear for some exercise to clear his head.

Few cars were on the road to foul the spring air. A quick glance up and down his street convinced him the paparazzi had subsided for the time being.

He started jogging, periodically looking over his shoulder for the odd photographer or someone more sinister. Along the way, mothers pushing prams checked out his bare legs and gave him sly smiles. In twenty minutes he had gone a good way down the London Road on his way toward a giant circuit around the town, the steady exertion settling him into a contemplative state.

He breathed rhythmically, smoothly rolling from heel to toe, trying to ignore the bother of his sore ribcage. Arthur's thinking drifted to Holmes. It was still impossible to believe that the eccentric dear man was gone.

Once again he found himself painfully reliving that night. Arriving at their home, giving Anne her present, hearing he'd have to wait until after dinner to learn about Holmes' big discovery, driving to the restaurant, turning around abruptly and heading back, the intruder, the mayhem. The night played in a loop, repeating itself with every mile he ran. And on the third replay, legging down Murdoch Road with the circuit almost done, his mind stuck on the car ride to the restaurant and Anne's snide remarks about the Holmes' GPS.

The GPS!

Holmes couldn't find his way around his own patch without sat-nav. If he drove somewhere on the twelfth, the address was bound to be on the TomTom.

He sprinted the last half mile and when he got back home he kicked off his trainers and gulped a glass of tap water.

Breathing hard, Arthur rang up Holmes' secretary and asked if she knew what had happened to the professor's car.

"I was wondering about that myself," she said. "No one's called down here asking about it. A week after the fire I went there with one of the girls from the department, you know, just to have a remembrance and drop off a bouquet, and we saw the prof's car at the curb, a bit battered. We wondered whether the fire service dragged it out of the drive that night."

"Did he keep a spare set of keys at the office?"

"He did. He was forgetful, not about his work but about things like keys, so I made sure he had extras about."

"Do you think I could pick them up? I may have left something important inside the car that night."

Arthur never wanted to return to Holmes' house but it wasn't nearly as traumatic as imagined. It had been leveled as a safety caution and all the detritus carted away. It was harder to assign emotions to a blackened lot and a garden rutted by heavy machinery.

The car was indeed out front, askew to the curb with its passenger side bashed in courtesy of the fire department. Arthur looked around for neighbors and seeing none, unlocked the driver's side door.

The TomTom was suction-cupped in place and it powered up with the ignition key. The list of saved locations was long, presumably in chronological order, but there was no way of knowing which, if any, had been visited on 12 March. He pulled out a pocket notebook and began writing down the full list of Holmes' destinations from the device's memory.

Back at his house Arthur settled onto his sofa with his laptop. The addresses were mostly in Oxfordshire and London with a smattering of others in Cumbria, Warwickshire, Scotland, Wales, and Devon. He found a website for reverse-address lookups and got to work.

Straight off he had to chuckle. Some of the destinations were places that Holmes had frequented for decades, including his own office and his favorite pubs. Anne had been right: he had been well and truly scatterbrained when it came to a sense of direction. The London addresses were mostly restaurants and parking garages. One turned out to be Holmes' solicitor, whose assistant checked for Arthur and told him that the professor had not visited on the twelfth. Another, in NW1, was for a Christopher Westley, a name he didn't recognize but who turned out to be Holmes' nephew, a young man who kept him on the line for a while reminiscing.

The Devon and Cumbria numbers were for a small hotel and a bed and breakfast. With considerable persuasion as to the importance of the matter Arthur was able to learn that Holmes had not visited them in the recent past.

The Warwickshire address was 6 Miller's Lane, Monks Kirby. The name that popped into the reverse-lookup box made him catch his breath.

Elizabeth Malory.

A Malory. From Warwickshire. The ancestral shire of Sir Thomas Malory.

Leaping up, Arthur bounded the stairs to the closet in the spare room where he kept boxes of his father's belongings. In a few minutes he was leafing through his father's old address book, filled with Malorys. But there was no Elizabeth Malory and no Malory in Monks Kirby.

Downstairs he dialed the listed number and waited as the ring tones droned on. He was about to give up when a small elderly voice answered by repeating the number, a quaint custom he remembered from his youth.

"Oh, hello," Arthur said. "I'm terribly sorry to bother you. Is this Elizabeth Malory?"

"Yes it is."

"My name is Arthur Malory, spelled the same way but that isn't why I'm calling."

"Are you the young man I read about in the papers? The one who donated a treasure to the British Museum?"

"Yes, actually, I am."

"Well, I though that was marvelous. I wondered if we might be related but I hadn't gotten around to checking the genealogy. I really should."

"I know this is an odd question, but would you happen to know a Professor Andrew Holmes from Oxford University?"

"Why yes, I do. He recently came to visit me. Let me check my calendar. Yes, here it is. He came to Monks Kirby on the twelfth of March."

Out of office. GQ.

Arthur pictured Holmes making the notation on his calendar and smiled.

GQ. Grail Quest.

Monks Kirby was a pretty little village in Warwickshire, a dot on the map with a population under five hundred. Arthur had been near the village before, he was sure, though he'd never been through it. Newbold Revel was close by. No self-respecting descendant of Sir Thomas Malory could possibly have eschewed a tour of Newbold Revel, the knight's ancestral home, though it was now the HM Prison Service College.

During his visit some years earlier, Arthur had talked his way into an audience with the director of the Prison Services Museum located on the grounds of the college. Once he declared his historical connection to Thomas Malory the director rolled out the red carpet and took him on a private tour of the manor house. The mansion bore no external clues of the fifteenth-century house that Thomas Malory had known. It was remade time and time again, particularly in the Victorian era where heavy cornices and balustrades were added.

Winding through the college's reception halls and classroom wings, the museum director showed Arthur the secret house within, the original medieval footprint of thicker walls and ancient hearths laid out in a symmetrical *H*. He couldn't help but to point out the irony that the boyhood home of the knight who spent so many years imprisoned by the king, writing *Le Morte D'Arthur* in captivity, should now be a crown jewel of the modern prison system.

Elizabeth Malory lived in an isolated property off Miller's Lane not far from St. Edith's Church. Arthur climbed from his Land Rover and stretched while admiring the ample Tudor thatched cottage, its plaster painted petal pink, its exposed timbers dark, almost black with age. Aromatic wood smoke rose from the chimney and mingled perfectly with the bouquet of the country air. The garden shed had an overhang protecting a large stack of split firewood. Neatly pruned rosebushes were laid out like sentries along the path to the front door, with more of them surrounding the house. Arthur regretted not having come in the summer; surely then the garden at peak would be awash in brilliant color.

The woman who appeared at the door perfectly matched the voice on the phone—frail, elderly, formal. She was dressed in a floral-pattern dress and thin sweater done up with misaligned buttoning, off by one. (Throughout his visit, Arthur wrestled with the idea of pointing this out, but in the end he kept it to himself.)

The cottage lacked central heating but Elizabeth Malory seemed tough and resilient as she fed the fire and organized tea and biscuits in the sitting room.

"I'm eighty-three years old," she told him over tea. "Guess how long I've lived in this house?"

He politely gave a try.

"No, a bit longer than that," she said. "It's eighty-three years! I was born in the dining room. Right over there. Why my poor mother wasn't allowed to deliver me in her bed I don't know; I suspect it was too cold upstairs.

"I did my research, or I should say, my father did the bulk of the research years ago," she announced. "And I'm pleased to tell you that we are, indeed, related and we are both assuredly descended from Sir Thomas Malory."

She launched into a lucid explanation. The missed buttonhole was a red herring. She was sharp; all her faculties. According to her recitation, Thomas Malory married a woman named Elizabeth, perhaps Elizabeth Walsh from Wanlip, in the 1440s, around the time he was knighted. They had two sons, Thomas and Robert, but the bloodline ran through Robert, as Thomas died in childhood. Robert Malory married another Elizabeth, who bore Nicholas, who in turn married Katherine Kyngston.

"Now Nicholas was the Lord of Newbold Revel, Winwick, and Swinford," she said. "As you may know, the official genealogy has it that Nicholas sired two daughters only and that the Sir Thomas Malory bloodline ran out before the sixteenth century."

"But that's not correct, is it?" Arthur said.

"No. Otherwise you and I wouldn't be enjoying our tea together, would we?" A smile creased her face. "Birth records were kept by the church, of course, and there was a fire at the parish church at Winwick in the early 1600s which destroyed the records."

Arthur nodded. "But in the 1930s a researcher from Leeds found some marriage records in Coventry which indicated that Nicholas fathered a boy too," he said. "John Malory."

"That's your lineage," she said. Then she added gleefully, "My lineage comes from another son, Thomas. You see, Arthur, my father was something of a genealogist himself and he dug and dug until he discovered Thomas's existence as well. He always suspected we had the blood of knights flowing through our veins and I'm proud to say he proved it. I must add, however, that he was always cross about assertions made by certain scholars over the years that Sir Thomas Malory was more of a brigand than a knight. Some say he was a thief and even a rapist. He did spend many years in prison. What do you think?"

"I don't accept that he was a common criminal," Arthur said flatly. "This would have flown in the face of all his chivalric principles. I think there are alternative views. He had enemies, especially the Duke of Buckingham. These enemies may have had reasons to put him behind bars."

"Well, he certainly had a colorful life."

Arthur agreed. "So there's a whole other branch of the family tree which I've been ignorant of." He rose to kiss her cheek. "Hello cousin."

She loved the gesture and despite her age blushed like an ingénue.

"I never married," she said, "so I'm afraid my line dies with me. But you are another story. May I ask if you're married?"

"I'm not."

"Well, you're young. There's plenty of time for that. More tea?"

He held his cup while she poured. Her arm had a fine tremor, which she volunteered was early Parkinson's disease. "The local quack wants me to take tablets but I don't believe in that. Once you start with these medicines it tends to be a self-fulfilling prophesy, doesn't it?" She sat back down in her chair. "It is really lovely to meet you, Arthur. From what I read in the newspapers I suspected you were a fine young man and now I've confirmed it with my own eyes."

"Thank you. It's really lovely meeting a relation, particularly from a branch of the family I didn't know existed." He didn't feel at all impatient but he asked, "Can you tell me how you and Professor Holmes came to meet? Did you contact him or was it the other way around?"

She had a letter on Oxford stationery and showed it to him.

> Dear Ms. Malory,
>
> By way of introduction I am the Professor of Medieval History at Cambridge. I am endeavoring to contact as many possible descendants as I can of Sir Thomas Malory, the fifteenth-century knight who wrote the seminal English account of King Arthur, *Le Morte D'Arthur*. I realize it is very much a shot in the dark but if you are a descendant and if you are aware of any documents or manuscripts in your family possession pertaining to Sir Thomas which may not have previously come to light, I would be most grateful to hear from you. I am writing a book on Malory and any new material and original insights would be manna from Heaven.
>
> Yours truly,
>
> Prof. Andrew Holmes

Arthur put it down, eyes moist.

"Are you all right?" she asked.

"Yes, I'm fine. I don't know if you saw it on the news but Professor Holmes was killed last month."

"My God," she said. "How ghastly. What happened?"

"It was a home invasion. Terrible business, I'm afraid. Anyway, I'm trying to piece together the last bits of his research. I feel I owe it to him to complete his last work in progress."

"Yes, of course. He was such a lovely man."

"So you replied to his letter, I take it."

"I did. I rang him straight away."

"You possessed relevant documents?"

"I did. In a trunk in the attic. Shall I tell you about them?"

As a girl she had been fascinated by the old trunk. Had the attic not frightened her so, with its wasps and mouse droppings, dust and spooky shadows, she might have played with its contents more. There were, she told him, silver candlesticks and plates and desiccated articles of clothing, an old bible or two and a short stack of papers tied with a ribbon. Her father had always said that the chest had been passed down from generation to generation, from Malory to Malory, and contained remnants of the family's illustrious past. She hadn't examined it for many years. In fact, she could no longer navigate the attic's steeply pitched pull-down ladder. The only time she had ever untied the ribbon to inspect the papers was a half century ago, after her father died and she was making a survey of her inheritance. She had trouble deciphering most of the documents, as they were written in Middle English in dense curlicue scripts. She suspected her father too had been unable to read them; but as far as she could tell they seemed to be a collection of deeds, legal documents, and letters. One letter in particular had stayed in her mind because it was clearly signed by Thomas Maleoré, knight, the same way he spelled his name in his notations within *Le Morte D'Arthur*. And she recalled two words she could make out in the body of the letter that she now whispered to Arthur with genuine excitement: *Excalibur* and *Graal*.

Thomas Malory's signature on a document was rare though not extraordinary—but as far Arthur knew, there were no known letters written in his hand. Add to that a mention of the Grail! He wished Andrew Holmes was at his side.

"I have no heirs, Arthur. I plan to donate my house and all its possessions to St. Edith's Church. The vicar is from Uganda of all places but he's such a lovely man and he and his wife have been so very good to me. But I'd like to give you the chest. All you need to do is carry it down from the attic and it's yours to take today."

He was more than eager to accept her bequest and rush headlong upstairs but he respected her pacing. First they had to finish their tea. Then she had to carry the tray back to the kitchen and refresh the firewood. Again she vigorously refused any help. He watched her slow, deliberate attendance to chores with admiration and hoped he'd be as capable at her age.

When she was done she led him up the stairs and down a chilly hallway past three bedrooms, all neat with made beds. At the end of the hall a rope with a polished wooden handle hung from the ceiling. She had him tug on it and at once he understood her difficulty. The hatch yielded only with a fair amount of force. After several tries it finally swung open, exposing a folded ladder that he grabbed and extended.

"There's a light at the top," she offered, and he climbed up into the dark, cramped space. "You'll see the chest halfway down on your left, by the wall."

The attic was just as described, with thick dust everywhere and countless carcasses of wasps and flies mixed with rodent droppings. The roofline was steep and he could stand upright only down the center. When he spotted the chest, tucked into the angle of the roof amid a jumble of furniture, he stooped then crab-walked until he could touch it.

It was filthy but despite thick layers of cobwebs and dust its antiquity was obvious. Yet something else caught his attention first: clear footprints leading up to the chest and handprints on its top and sides. They appeared recent. The prints were large, certainly not Elizabeth's. Holmes' shoe prints, like ghostly apparitions. It was so very sad.

The chest was walnut, about four feet long, roughly made with iron strapping and hinges, a sturdy and utilitarian medieval storage chest. He slid it away from the wall and lifted it. It was manageable. The only difficulty sliding the chest down the ladder was the cloud of dust that fouled his throat and made him cough.

"Sorry for the mess," he said, back in the hallway. "Shall we clean it off here?"

"No, just bring it down to the lounge. I'll get some tea towels to set it down."

Elizabeth insisted on wheeling out her Hoover to clean the heavy stuff off the chest again, refusing to allow Arthur to lift a finger to help. When she was done she did let him run some paper towels over the surface to finish the job. He tossed the towels into the fire as she sat down in her chair to watch him lift the lid.

The clothes were on top. He carefully extracted each of the items, laying them out on the floor. There was a pair of old leather boots, flat as pancakes, impossibly dry and cracked. A folded and unidentifiable leather garment—leggings, perhaps, and a ratty velvet vest of some sort, possibly a doublet. Some folded pieces of linen, yellow as tobacco-stained teeth. Then the two bibles, fat with fairly good bindings. A quick glance at their frontispieces revealed them to be sixteenth and seventeenth century, respectively. Underneath the bibles were the silver pieces. The candlesticks were generous in size, primitive in design, and lacking in ornamental flourishes. The plates, however, were a different story and their engraved decoration sent Arthur's juices flowing: the Malory coat of arms, a chevron against a ground of ermine tails.

Arthur tapped the center of one of the plates and said, "We're getting closer to our man."

From her chair Elizabeth asked, "Can you see the papers?"

The packet was near the bottom of the chest, a collection of creamy parchment pages tied with a faded and brittle-looking ribbon the color of a robin's egg. He carefully lifted them out.

"Shall I have a look at them here?"

"I wish you would," she said. "See if you can find the one I told you about and make some sense of it."

He thought the ribbon might disintegrate in his fingers but it stayed intact with careful untying. The stack of parchment felt dry and crinkly. He crouched beside Elizabeth's chair so she could follow along with him. His time as a Grail Loon well prepared him for the obscurities of the medieval hand. As he scanned the pages, he found most of the scripts florid but generally decipherable, though some tightly packed words flummoxed him. The archaic Middle English characters were far from second nature and dramatically slowed his comprehension. Most of the pages appeared to be deeds, bills of sale, and feoffments signed by men other than Thomas Malory. But half-way through the stack he uncovered what looked to be the letter and said softly, "I think this is it."

She glanced over and said, "Oh yes, that's the one I let him photograph."

It was undated, written in a loose, flowing manner with an ink turned coppery with age. The large confident signature at the bottom of the page was just as she had described: *Thomas Maleoré knight.* As marvelous as it was to set eyes on this rare holograph, it was the recipient of the letter who attracted Arthur's attention. It began, *My Dere Waynflete.*

Could this be William Waynflete, the bishop of Winchester? Arthur, a student of all things Thomas Malory, remembered that Waynflete was said to have been a confidant of the knight. And it was historical fact that the only known copy of *Le Morte* in Malory's own hand was found—by a scavenging academic in 1934—within a locked cupboard in the bedroom of the High Master of Winchester College.

He told Elizabeth who this Waynflete might be, then continued to glide through the letter as quickly as he could. And there it was: a reference to a sojourn to Winchester and time spent with the bishop. After some additional pleasantries, however, the letter took a dark turn with mention of a great danger. A scroll delivered to him in Normandy at a place he called *Maleoré Sur Seine*, which Arthur imagined might be the modern La Mailleraye-sur-Seine. Evil men in pursuit—*Qem*, he called them—and a treacherous journey to a cave; a sword. Excalibur!

This was the letter Holmes had planned to show him, which perished in the fire.

Arthur must have looked quite peculiar because Elizabeth at once put her hand on his shoulder and asked if he was ill.

"I can't believe it," he uttered, with the off-kilter look of a man beset with sudden vertigo. "Let me read this to you and try to modernize the language on the fly, if I can. Malory writes, 'It gladdened my heart to see you, dear Bishop, and share the astonishing truth that my blood derives from the blood of King Arthur. He too was a proud Maleoré of Norman stock. He too had the noble thirteenth rib. To honor the great king I do swear to you that I will write of his noble deeds and his glorious death in a book I will call *Le Morte Darthur*. Moreover, dear Bishop, you know I have found the great sword of Arthur and with it the heavenly prize is within reach, the holiest of all things known to man, namely the Sangreal of our Christ. Now with your help I better understand the meaning of the sword and I will endeavor most ardently to find the Graal, though I pray I will not be thwarted in my task. To stop all enemies from learning the secret I have heeded your advice and hidden the sword anew. For without Excalibur the Graal cannot be discovered. If I am defeated in my quest, I will endeavor to leave a trail for a Maleoré who descends from me. May that man possess virtue and be worthy of the prize. Pray dear bishop that my quest is successful and pray that I may deliver unto the church of Rome the Holy Graal."

Elizabeth saw that Arthur was rubbing the tender left side of his chest.

"Are you sure you're all right?"

"It's just my extra rib," he said. "All the Malory men have one."

Elizabeth smiled. "My father had one as well."

Arthur rose from his crouch and absently began putting the contents of the chest back together as though in a trance. "And so did King Arthur," he said. "Imagine that, Elizabeth. We're descended from Arthur, the once and future king!"

9

NORMANDY, 1450

Twenty years was a long time, for many a lifetime in this war- and plague-ravished world in which he lived. Twenty years earlier he had been a soldier in his prime, his battle sword light in his hand, his armor no more than a nuisance. Twenty years ago he had been a captain in the army of King Henry V, racking up victory after victory against the French at Caen, Cosne-sur-Loire, and Meaux where his beloved king had died of pleurisy at the tragic young age of thirty-five.

Now Thomas Malory was fifty, a far greater age than he imagined he would ever reach, and his battle gear felt weighty, like the yoke on an ox. He rode slumped in his saddle, desiring only to dismount and have a night's rest somewhere safe from the Comte de Clermont's archers.

The days of the English as lords and masters of Normandy were nearing an end. He knew it and so be it, he had come to believe. For reasons beyond his ken it seemed God's will. As a young soldier he had helped achieve the prize of Normandy heralded by the stunning victory against the French at Agincourt on that bright Saint Crispin's Day.

Now, as a knight of the realm, he was a reluctant witness to the unraveling of it all. It had been only a week since their humiliating defeat at Formigny, where five thousand Englishmen met five thousand French. Malory had commanded a large company of men that day and owing to bad luck, bad geography, and a sudden rush of Breton reinforcements the English were scattered and their commander killed. With ignominious defeat weighing heavily upon Malory, he and a few able-bodied soldiers led a party of wounded men, oozing blood and pus through their bandages, on to the sanctuary of Calais. If they could survive the northward march, then it would be back across the channel and home for them. Little more was to be done in this land. Caen and Cherbourg would certainly fall, their English defenders, sacrificial lambs. Once Calais was gone, so too all of Normandy.

Malory would not have returned to France had it not been for the entreaties of Richard Neville, the earl of Warwick, who, though only twenty-three, was Malory's good lord to whom he owed fealty. When the young king, Henry VI, had asked Neville to field a fresh force to hold off the insurgent French in Normandy, the earl pressed Malory into service, plucking him from his comfortable and prosperous life as a knight and member of Parliament and sending him back to the realm of powder, blood, and death.

Malory's page, a once healthy teenager, now sallow with chronic dysentery, pointed at the darkening sky. "Look, my lord, chimney smoke."

Malory straightened in his saddle. He still cut a fine figure: tall, well-muscled, the body of a fighting man with the composure and intellect of a gentleman. His face was lined with fatigue and worry and his beard and hair had lost its youthful color, but it was a kind face, not a bellicose one.

"We should be there by dark," Malory said. He turned and called back to the column of men behind. "Do any of you know which village is ahead?"

One answered, "Maleoré. I've been there. There's water. It's on the river."

Malory grunted and held his tongue. His father and uncles had always said that Maleoré was the ancestral home of the Malorys. He had long chosen not to reveal to his men the inconvenient fact that he had Norman blood. After four centuries in Warwickshire, the Malorys were as English as the next but there was no reason to sow doubt over his allegiance. Despite the king's claims to Normandy this land felt like foreign soil. He was an Englishman.

Malory's path to this day had begun with a privileged childhood in Newbold Revel, a veritable nursery of chivalry, where as soon as he could walk he was placed on a pony and taught to ride with one hand on the reins and the other on a tiny wooden sword. Growing up, he was tutored in Latin and Greek in the morning and hunting and martial arts in the afternoon. The household chaplain took on the task of teaching him religious observance. His mother and aunts taught him manners and to respect and admire women. His father and uncles schooled him on the principles of a chivalric life. By the time he was ready to become a page he had been imbued with these notions: he must care for his lands and his tenants, defend women at all cost, be just and merciful in his dealings, counter wickedness by guarding ordinary people against oppression, protect his faith and his church, and above all else support his lord in battle with courage and unfailing devotion.

Young Thomas matured quickly. By age twelve he was legally responsible for his actions. At fourteen he was eligible to be called upon as a man of arms and that is what occurred. In 1414, shortly after this milestone birthday, he was consigned to the Normandy invasion force of King Henry V and found himself battling for Calais as an esquire and lancer in the retinue of Henry Beauchamp, the previous earl of Warwick, at campaign after campaign that year and into the next. He learned what it felt like to kill a man and to see comrades fall in violence. But he also had time during interminable sieges to follow gentler pursuits and during these years he learned to read French.

In October 1415, he was at Agincourt where, against a superior French force, the English longbow won the day. And two years later he was at the siege of Caen, one of the last of the great Normandy strongholds to fall to the English before the victory was sealed by the Treaty of Troyes. It was at Caen that he heard about a noble's library containing fine volumes being crated for the English king's pleasure. The king, by way of reward for his good service, bade Malory to take his pick of the volumes and it was here that Thomas had his first long drink of King Arthur when he claimed a fine illustrated copy of de Troyes' *Perceval, le Conte du Graal.*

The war over, Malory was released from service. He returned to Newbold Revel to help his father with the management of their holdings but country life was short-lived. A treaty, Malory learned, was only a piece of paper and fighting erupted in Normandy anew. Once again he donned his plate armor and joined the fray on French soil. This time, again in the direct service of Beauchamp, he was a captain commanding a company of lancers, archers, and axmen. He was at Cosne-sur-Loire when the king died and he remained in charge of the garrison town of Gisors while Beauchamp returned to London to take up the guardianship of the new infant king, Henry VI. And Malory was at Rouen on Christmas Eve, 1430, when the young peasant warrior, Joan of Arc, was delivered to the English, sold for 10,000 livres tournois by the Burgundians, who had seized her in battle.

Beauchamp had asked Malory to accompany him to see the petite lass in her dank cell in the tower of Bouvreuil. She was shivering, a little mouse in irons, but proud and defiant beyond belief. Another English noble was there that night too, Humphrey Stafford, an arrogant young man who would become the earl of Buckingham. It was then that Malory and the future Buckingham became sworn enemies.

In French, Beauchamp asked the prisoner, "How are you being treated, Mademoiselle?"

Joan was mute with anger.

Beauchamp repeated the question, this time emphasizing his concern for her health.

She answered. "Your guards are pigs! They put their filthy hands on my body. Did you know that?"

Her impudence enraged Stafford, who swore at her in the foulest language, called her a liar and drew his dagger as he approached. Malory could scarcely believe what he saw and heard. Under any circumstances to do violence upon a shackled prisoner was beyond the pale but to do so to a woman was inconceivable. He rushed forward to place himself between Joan and the charging Englishman and when

Stafford tried to push him aside Malory seized his wrist and gave him a sharp, backhanded blow to the cheek.

On Beauchamp's orders the guards separated the men and Stafford withdrew in a fury. As the French girl looked on gratefully Beauchamp said, "You did the right and honorable thing, Thomas, but know this: you've acquired a powerful enemy on this day—and no ordinary one."

"How so?" Malory asked, breathing hard.

"It's said he dabbles in dark arts."

"What sort of dark arts?"

"Alchemy."

As they approached the outskirts of Maleoré, Malory's page asked apprehensively, "Will they fight?"

"Most of these villages have sent their men into the field against us. I don't expect we shall encounter any but women, children, and the aged. But soon we shall see. Be at your ready."

"Will we burn them?"

"If they treat us fairly we shall treat them fairly. There is little profit in destroying a place such as this. Our task is to reach Calais as quickly as we are able."

They entered the town at dusk. The rutted street was deserted save for a boy standing at the door of a cottage glaring at Malory's motley column. Malory rode at the front, followed by a small contingent of soldiers on horseback, then the walking wounded and the litter-bearers. An arm quickly snatched the boy inside and the door was slammed.

"Be at your guard," Malory commanded the soldiers. As a precaution he had his page give him his shield that was emblazoned with his crest, a red chevron over an array of brown ermine tails.

To their right, every hundred paces or so, were narrow lanes that led down to the dark river. Fetid smells wafted up the lanes and they could hear the gentle sound of flowing water.

"Where shall we stop?" his querulous page asked.

"Not here," Malory said. "These meager cottages will do us little good. We seek substantial shelter. There will be a manoir."

Soon enough, on a hillock overlooking the town, Malory spotted a stone manoir, a generous structure commanding a good view of the surrounding countryside and river. There was still enough daylight to find the path up the hill and Malory brought the column to a halt on the flat grassy piece of ground that led to the manoir's massive oak door. Like most of the great houses in this region the structure was built for defense, with sparse narrow windows and archer slits. Malory searched for signs of life but no livestock were about and the house appeared dark. He scanned the ramparts against the blackening sky but they were empty. It began to rain.

"Will you dismount, my lord?" his page asked.

"I will."

The page unstrapped a mounting box from the packhorse and took Malory's reins as the knight swung his leg over the saddle.

A sound.

Malory heard it and held his breath: the unmistakable whisper of airborne death.

The arrow caught his page in the tender space between eye and nose and buried itself deeply enough to kill instantly.

Before Malory could utter his first command he heard a wail from within the manoir, a man crying out, "*Non!*"

"Fall back!" Malory shouted, flipping his visor down. "Out of the archer's range. Be quick. Set a line, well-spaced."

There was shouting from the manoir, then a bloodcurdling scream. Malory's archers nocked their arrows. Then the huge door slowly opened.

"Await my command!" Malory shouted to his men.

The body of a young man, no older than the page, fell from behind the door and lay crumpled at the threshold.

A man called out in French through the opening. "I have slain the wretch. I bade him not to shoot. I am coming out to reveal myself."

"Men, let not your arrows fly!" Malory yelled, turning to make sure his archers understood.

An old man emerged, holding a torch that illumined his emaciated face. He was dressed finely in a loose gown. There was no sword in his hand, nor one on his belt.

"Englishmen," the old man announced. "I am the Baron Maleoré. This servant did not obey me and now he is dead. Did his arrow find its mark?"

"My page is dead!" Malory roared back in French.

"A thousand apologies!" the baron cried. "Though we are enemies, I am grievously dishonored by this act."

"We did not come to your village to do you harm but as punishment for the murder of this lad I will have my revenge," Malory bellowed.

"I beg of you, dear knight," the baron implored. "Let me feed you and your men this evening and provide you with shelter. Let us drink together and talk as men. In the morning you may do what you will do."

The great hall was largely barren. There were padded chairs by the hearth, a few rugs on the floor, and a few sideboards and cabinets against the stone walls. Lying near the hearth was a pile of broken-up furniture. Malory understood. War had taken its toll. With few able-bodied men about, their store of seasoned wood had dwindled and the baron was reduced to burning household possessions.

Malory's men found places on the stone floor of the hall. Some groaned in pain, others muttered their thanks for being out of the rain that night.

"Do you have any honey for their wounds?" Malory asked the baron.

"Some, perhaps. I'll give you what we have."

"And clean linen to bind them?"

"My daughters and nieces will cut our bedsheets and tend to the men as best they can. Come by the fire, if you please." He called for his manservant to bring wine.

Malory automatically looked for his page to help him remove his armor, remembering that at that very moment he was being placed into the ground by a burial party.

The baron's servant assisted Malory with the task. Unburdened by the weight of the plates, the knight sat down and drank from his goblet.

"What was the name of your page?" the baron asked.

"It was John. He was the son of a dear friend who lives not far from my estate."

"The Lord works in strange ways." The old man sighed. "My young archer was called Jean. A Jean for a John. Will you tell me your name, Monsieur?"

"I am Sir Thomas Malory."

The old man's eyes widened and he set his wine down. He repeated the name slowly, mimicking the English pronunciation. Then he said, "Maleoré," the French way.

Malory nodded his head. "I come from Norman stock, Baron. It is within the traditions of my family that our kind may have come from this region, perhaps even this village. In past campaigns on Norman soil I had not the occasion to stop here. Now I have."

The baron's face was stiff. "Before we go any further, I must ask you a question. Do you possess the Maleoré rib?"

Malory smiled and tapped his side over his liver. "Would you like to feel it?"

The baron rose briefly, as if confused or excited; Malory could not tell which. He sat again. "My God! A miracle! We are kin and yet …" he began.

"… We are enemies," Malory finished.

Behind them the women of the household were tending to the wounded, and the baron's stone-faced servants were laying out trays of bread and wheels of cheese for the hungry soldiers.

The baron turned his head at the scream of a man whose caked bandage was being removed by a young, homely woman. "My daughter, Marie, is the most skilled in my family. When my middle son, Phillipe, came back from Paris with a festering wound after an English cannonball took his leg it was Marie who nursed him for the time before he died."

"I am sorry," Malory said. "What of your other sons?"

The baron sighed. "I do not know. Perhaps they are dead. Perhaps they are prisoners. Perhaps they fight on. Tell me, Thomas Malory, what will you do with us tomorrow?"

Malory gazed into the fire. “I do not know.”

The baron leaned forward. “If I show you something astonishing which concerns the Maleorés and therefore concerns you, will you spare me and my village?”

Malory chortled. “It depends how astonishing, Baron.”

“It is about the Grail of our Christ.”

Malory resisted the urge to speak his mind. Grail fables abounded. If he had a coin for every tale, his purse would be too heavy to carry. “If I am sufficiently impressed, then perhaps it will temper my anger and alter my intentions.”

“In the morning then. It will take time to retrieve a scroll from its hiding place. In the meanwhile my servant has prepared a bed for you, the only one on which linens remain.”

Malory felt a tinge of guilt lying in a comfortable bed while wounded men slept on the stone floor. His last thought before sleep was of his page lying dead in the grass but it would not be his only glimpse of death that night. An old dream returned to haunt him. He was back in the market square of Rouen on a sun-drenched morning. It was May, 1430. He was in the crowd of catcalling Englishmen as the toothless executioner, Leparmentier, adjusted the ropes that bound Joan of Arc to her stake. That day Malory had been anonymous but in the dream she always looked straight and unflinchingly into his eyes as the flames leaped to the height of her breast. There was no anger in those eyes, no fear, no suffering. It was said that at the moment of her death a white dove emerged from the flames and took to wing. In truth he had seen no such thing but in his dream the dove was there and it circled overhead three times before it soared heavenward.

In the morning, the baron’s own manservant attended Malory and helped him dress. His men seemed content and well fed. Only one had succumbed from his wounds during the night. The baron was waiting for Malory by the fire, dressed in a finer, more formal costume than the previous day.

He pointed to a tray. “Come, have some food, some drink.”

“Show me this scroll of yours. I have a decision to make and I must resume my march.”

"To Calais?" the baron asked.

"I will not say."

"Ah, a secret. I understand. Yet, some of your men told their nurses of your defeat at Formigny and your withdrawal. I cannot say I am unhappy that our land is finally being returned to our king; so much more the pity that you should instigate a final act of violence against our poor village. I pray this scroll will help change your mind."

He handed Malory an ancient piece of vellum that had been rolled up for so long it did not require a ribbon or seal to hold its shape. It was burnt orange with age. Once he unrolled it he had to hold each end firmly to prevent it curling back on itself.

Malory moved to the hearth for better light. Within a few moments he erupted in frustration. "I cannot make anything of this! What language is written here?"

"It is Celtic. I thought Englishmen could read your own ancient tongues."

"Well, I am sorry to say I cannot, Baron. You will have to tell me what it says."

The baron looked alarmed. "I know what it concerns, as it has been passed down within my family by an oral retelling, but I cannot read it myself."

Malory let the scroll curl. "Then I am done here. Your oral tale will hold no weight with me. Your hospitality has been admirable but I do not think you have moved me from my need for justice. I will spare your castle but I will burn the village."

"Wait! Please!" the baron cried desperately. He turned to the soldiers spread out in the great hall and called to them in his best English, "Pray, men of arms, is there one among you who can read the ancient Celtic writing?"

A silence fell over the hall.

Then a thin voice could be heard from the rear. "I can."

"Stand up!" Malory commanded.

"I cannot."

Malory and the baron sought out the man and found him lying on a litter, the new linen bandages swaddling his belly already stained through with fresh blood. He wore the clothes of a lancer.

"What is your name?" Malory asked, standing over him.

"Godfrey, my lord."

"Where are you from?"

"I am Cornish," the man answered weakly. "I am from Penryn."

"How were you wounded?"

"A French sword. I think I am killed, my lord."

"You do not know that. Only God knows."

"I will not quarrel with a knight but I am certain I will never see Penryn again."

"We shall see," Malory said. "How do you come to read the Celtic writing?"

"Before I took to soldiering I was a monk novice at Saint Michael's Mount at Bodmin. I learned Latin … and the old Celtic prayers. I can try to read what needs to be read if it pleases my lord."

"Tell me, Godfrey of Penryn, why did you leave the monastery?"

"I was … cast out for excessive fornication, my lord."

Malory fought a smile and held out the scroll. The baron called for a candlestick to aid the man's sight.

Godfrey unrolled the scroll and studied it. "Maybe not all the words but the most of them. I *can* read it, my lord."

"Proceed," Malory said. "Make a translation as you go—but keep your voice low so none other may overhear."

Godfrey began, haltingly and softly but clearly enough. "I Gwydre son of Arthwyr who doth rule the Britons as their King thusly offer unto God my true and complete testament. I have been grievously wounded. I will surely die before I can return to my home and I desire to be buried at Castle Maleoré where my father was born. My bones will be witness to my noble birth. Those who examine them will find my royal ribs which number two more than mere men and the same number as King Arthwyr. I did as my father commanded and rode off to foreign lands as the knight Gwalchavad had done before me. He was not able to bring home the Gral of the Christ and owing to treachery alas neither was I. Yet I did see the Gral with mine own eyes and thus know that the words which have been carved upon the sword of my father are true. I will not live to see the King again and he may not live to see the Gral for himself. I pray my brother Cyngen will find it. If he does not I leave this parchment for the heirs of Arthwyr. May it be found if it pleases the Lord. To find the Graal first find the sword of Arthwyr hidden at the castle of Tintagel which was the castle of Uther Pendragon father of Arthwyr. Arthwyr did bury it deep within the great sea cave near the sign of the cross. May a worthy and noble man of royal blood find the sword and thus find the Graal. May God make it come to pass."

As Godfrey read from the scroll, the baron nodded vigorously as if remembering the tale he had been told as a child. For his part Malory stood like a marble beside the wounded soldier.

When Godfrey was done Malory took the scroll from him and said, "You must never speak of this. Do you understand?"

In response Godfrey sounded a dolorous note. "Like this Gwydre, I too am dying, my lord. I will not live to see Penryn nor even the crossing. My tongue will be silent soon enough."

Malory nodded and touched the man's hand in gratitude. Then he and the baron withdrew to the hearth where Malory shocked the old man by tossing the scroll into the flames.

"But why?" the baron asked.

"No one else needs to see it. The man whom Gwydre sought has arrived. I am that man. My veins and yours course with the blood of kings and no ordinary king. To think! Arthur, the greatest king of all! You knew of this?"

The baron nodded solemnly.

Malory quickly added, "Tell me, Baron, did any of your ancestors ever attempt to journey to find the sword?"

"None that I know. If it exists, it is within the strange and faraway land of our enemies. If any Maleorés had tried, I think they surely would have failed."

"It is my land," Malory said. "To me it is neither strange nor faraway. I will not fail. I pray I may be able to find the sword and with it, the Grail. It will be my quest, like the ancient knights who came before me." He took the old man's hand and said, "We will go now,

Baron. I will spare both you and your village. Let us hope your sons return to you soon. I leave in peace."

The old man's eyes welled up. "Fate brought us together, sir knight, and I pray with every fiber in my body that you will succeed in your quest, for the greatness of the Maleorés and the greatness of God."

10

Arthur returned from Warwickshire and pulled into his drive as dusk was descending. He was about to get out to remove Elizabeth's old chest from the back of his Land Rover when he noticed someone seated on his front steps, a young woman with feathery auburn hair, perhaps in her early thirties.

Their eyes met. Hers were large and searching, and when she stood and gathered her unbuttoned raincoat as a shield against the evening chill he caught sight of tight jeans and a clingy sweater.

When he climbed out she called over to him. "Excuse me, you are Arthur Malory?" She had a French accent.

"I am." Somehow it felt rude to ask who she was.

Her demeanor could not have been more serious. "My name is Claire Pontier … I wonder if I may speak with you?"

He didn't know why but he found himself smiling at her. "About what?"

Her eyes scanned the road. She looked frightened. "I'm here to warn you. Your life is in danger. There are people who wish to kill you."

His smile evaporated. He didn't want to leave the chest in the car but he didn't want to produce it in front of a stranger, either. Reluctantly, he locked the car and said, "Why don't you come inside?"

He took her coat and asked if she wanted a drink.

"A tea." She shook her head. "Or maybe a whiskey, if you have it."

"How about both? Tea, then whiskey."

"Why not?"

He spied on the woman from the kitchen. She sat on his sofa with legs tightly crossed and arms folded across her bosom in a defensive posture. He could tell she was reading the spines of books on his shelves. Her thin cashmere sweater was like a second skin, her shapeliness so revealing it almost made him self-conscious to be alone with her.

He came back in bearing a tray of tea. Claire sipped hers unembellished and smiled a bit as he loaded his with milk and sugar.

She seemed to wear little or no makeup, and he couldn't help but notice other than perhaps a natural gloss because her lips were quite moist for a dry, windy day. A short green scarf the color of her eyes settled into her cleavage. The tea or tea ritual seemed to relax her. She uncrossed her legs and settled back into the cushion, about to speak when there was crashing glass and a blinding hot flash.

Arthur and Claire sprang from their seats, spilling their tea as they retreated from spreading flames. The Molotov cocktail had entered through the front bay window and immediately set the curtains and rug afire. In a few seconds the sofa on which Claire had been sitting was alight.

"This way!" Arthur shouted, yanking her arm and dragging her to the rear.

He pulled her through to the kitchen where he grabbed his briefcase, then back to the front hall where they were temporarily spared from fast-moving flames that now had engulfed the sitting room. Claire snatched her handbag and coat while he flung open the front door.

At once, he noticed a black Vauxhall stopped in front of the house. His first thought was that a Good Samaritan had stopped to lend assistance—but then he saw a gun pointing from the half open driver's side window.

In the next instant came a muffled noise and the light fixture over the entrance exploded, showering them with glass. Claire cowered and screamed but Arthur had the presence of mind to pull her down the stairs to the cover of his Land Rover.

A next-door neighbor appeared from his house and shouted that he'd called the fire department. Just then the Vauxhall sped off.

"We're okay!" Arthur yelled to his neighbor. "No one's inside." Then he fumbled for the car keys and said to Claire, "We mustn't stay here."

She didn't require persuasion. They leaped into the Land Rover. Arthur threw his briefcase into the back and slammed it into reverse.

"Yes, move it away from the house!" the neighbor shouted, but when he saw them driving off he called after them in confusion.

Arthur was breathing hard.

"Jesus, my house … Are you okay?"

"Yes. I think so. Where are we going?"

"I don't have a clue."

"They tried to kill us …" She started to shake violently.

Arthur reached for her arm and gave it a squeeze.

"We're all right now. Let me just think for a minute."

The London Road was coming up and he had to make a decision. East made as much sense as west and he turned toward Bracknell.

"Who are they?" he asked.

"What?"

"You said *they* were trying to kill us."

"I don't know who they are."

"But you came to me to tell me …"

"It's not something I can explain quickly."

Something caught his attention in the rearview mirror. He swore.

"What is it?" she asked, frightened.

"The Vauxhall's behind us."

She turned to look and mumbled something in French. It sounded like a prayer.

Arthur accelerated and moved to the right, overtaking a chain of slower cars.

The Vauxhall did the same, keeping pace.

Arthur's old Land Rover rode high and with every sharp move of the wheel he and Claire strained against their seat belts. The A329 was well-trafficked with evening commuters but cars were moving at speed. Arthur tried to get some separation from the Vauxhall by weaving lanes, drawing honks and irate hand gestures as he cut drivers off.

"My phone's in my bag," Arthur said, knuckles tight on the wheel. "Can you use yours to dial nine nine nine?"

"I used up my battery waiting for you," she said, looking behind. "Do you want me to climb over and get yours?"

"No! Stay belted. It's too dangerous."

"What do you have back there?"

"Just an old chest."

"No, the machine."

"It's a metal detector."

Arthur kept weaving for the next two miles, pegging the speedometer at 70 plus whenever he had a clear stretch. With a couple of perilous overtakes he managed to get two car lengths ahead of the Vauxhall, all the while checking the mirrors.

"I want you to take down his license plate number but I can't make it out. Can you see it?" Arthur asked.

She turned. "The car doesn't have a front plate."

"Christ."

In two minutes the Skimped Hill Roundabout came into view. Only one car now separated the Vauxhall from the Land Rover.

"Hold on," Arthur said. "Local knowledge."

At the roundabout Arthur signaled and moved right and the Vauxhall did the same.

Then Arthur cut hard to the left, narrowly missing the trailing car, which began furiously honking its horn. The Vauxhall had neither time nor room to make the left exit. As Arthur accelerated, he saw it behind him in the rearview mirror relooping the roundabout.

The entrance to the Odeon Cinema was coming up on the right and Arthur screeched his tires turning into the car park.

He raced into the first space he could find and killed the engine.

"You like movies?" he asked.

"Yes. Especially now," she said.

He opened the back of the car and threw an old blanket over the chest and metal detector and took his briefcase with him. Then the two ran into the cinema and grabbed tickets to the first movie on the roster. Inside the dark theater they sat near an exit and tried to compose themselves. The film was already playing but didn't register. Instead of looking at the screen Arthur watched for the driver but no one else entered. He glanced at Claire who sat stiffly. He leaned over and whispered, "This feels like the worst first date in history."

Either she didn't understand or didn't think it was funny because she kept staring straight ahead.

They waited a tense hour before Arthur tapped her shoulder and the two slipped out. They moved cautiously through the car park until Arthur could get eyes on his vehicle. He scanned the area for the Vauxhall then waited another several minutes before they got back into his car.

Arthur started the engine. "We need to go somewhere to talk."

She looked at her watch.

"I was planning on taking the Eurostar back to France tonight."

"I don't think you'll make the last train."

"Where should we go?"

"I don't think I have a house anymore. Let me call the police first. I know somewhere we can get a bite and talk."

Arthur fished DI Hobbs' card from his wallet and rang the mobile number. Hobbs picked up. From the background noise it sounded like he was in a pub.

In a torrent he told Hobbs what had happened. Hobbs asked if he was all right and said he needed to make a call.

Arthur began driving, heading back toward Wokingham.

"What did the police say?" Claire asked.

"Nothing, yet."

Hobbs rang back before too long. "I've had a word with The Fire and Rescue Service. Apparently, a passerby called in a report of a gas smell a few minutes before the explosion. They're treating it as a gas explosion. Leveled your house, unfortunately. Have you had a problem with any of your gas appliances?"

"No! Look, someone threw a Molotov cocktail through my front window! I'm sure the fire inspector will find evidence for an accelerant."

"If I recall, Mister Malory, you had a kerosene lamp in your front room."

"That may be but someone shot at me! Someone followed me."

"There were no reports of gunfire."

"He probably used a silencer."

"Very cloak and dagger."

"I don't appreciate your sarcasm, Detective Inspector. Someone followed me.

"Did you get the plate number?"

"It was a black Vauxhall. Fairly new. There was no front plate that I saw."

"I see. Why don't the two of you come in and make a statement? I can meet you at the Reading Police Station."

The question jolted Arthur. "I didn't say I was with anyone."

"Didn't you? I thought you did. Well then, why don't *you* come to Reading, Mister Malory."

Arthur immediately hung up and switched off his phone.

"What's the matter?" Claire asked.

Arthur kept driving, his hands tight on the wheel. "Something's not right. Not right at all."

Ten minutes later he pulled into the grounds of the Cantley House Hotel in Wokingham. He had used it for company meetings and knew the place well. It was an old converted country house tucked away in leafy parkland and its seclusion felt right.

The hotel was lightly booked and he had no trouble arranging accommodation without a reservation. He asked for two rooms.

Claire whispered in his ear, "I'd rather not be alone tonight." When he looked at her quizzically she added, "Don't think … I'm feeling a bit nervous, that's all."

He changed the request to one room with two beds and arranged for some toiletries to be sent up.

He left her alone in the room and came back with the old chest. He heard the water running in the bathroom. When she came out she asked about it.

"I didn't want to leave it in the car."

"What's inside?"

"I think we both have long stories to tell each other," he said. "Are you hungry?"

"Yes, very."

The hotel restaurant was nearly empty. They sat at a table for two against a rustic brick wall. They ordered their dinners and Arthur had the server bring a decent bottle of red. They drank the first glass as if it were medicine.

"I'm sorry you lost your house. How terrible."

He drank some more, the reality settling heavily onto his chest. "My books … the family photo albums … my father's papers … it's—" He caught himself before losing his composure in front of her. "I'm sorry."

"No. I can't believe you're so calm. I'm a wreck and I didn't lose my house and my possessions."

"Okay look," he said, sucking it up. "Why don't you tell me why you're here?"

She seemed hesitant. "This isn't easy," she began, looking down. "I don't do this type of thing ordinarily."

"You mean come to England, meet a total stranger, get firebombed and shot at then chased down the London Road? I should hope not."

That finally elicited a half smile. "Okay. Here it is. I have a boyfriend—well, an ex-boyfriend now. Maybe he doesn't know he's an ex but he is."

"Poor chap."

"I was suspicious of him. He's usually quite open. He always spoke with his friends in front of me, didn't log out of his e-mail accounts or delete his call logs. And I'm the same with him. We've been together four years. A good relationship, I'd say. This changed two weeks ago. He began to get calls which led him to go into another room or go outside to talk. He religiously started logging out of his personal e-mail account when he was done. His mobile call logs were empty."

"You know because you checked."

She thrust out her chin. "I'm not a snoop by nature. It's not like me but it was such an abrupt change for Simone. Also he became more distant, preoccupied; maybe a little angry. He wouldn't talk about it. So, I assumed he was having an affair. It happens. It's human nature but I wanted to know. I never want to be in a triangle. It's not my nature."

"I could have sworn you were French."

Her laugh sounded like a bar of music. "This indifference about affairs—it's a stereotype. Like the English and their stiff upper lips." She became serious again. "For some reason I had more nerve to spy on him at work than at home. So last week I did it."

"You work together?"

"Yes, we're both at Modane."

"I'm sorry?"

"You wouldn't know about this place. I sometimes make the crazy assumption that everyone I speak with is a physicist."

"You're a physicist?"

"Yes. Does it surprise you?"

He wasn't the least sexist but he realized his question came off as just that. "Well, no. Well, maybe it does."

"Another stereotype? A preconceived notion the way a woman physicist is supposed to look?"

"Actually, for me it's a conceived notion. I work with a lot of physicists and none of them look like you."

"Are *you* a physicist?" she asked, tossing the question back at him.

"I'm a chemist by training but I work at a physics company. Neodymium magnets."

"Ah, practical physics. At the Modane Laboratory we do impractical physics, particle physics."

"You were saying you spied on him last week."

"Yes. I knew his password because I'd seen him enter it so many times. It's my name, which isn't so good for security reasons but was a sweet gesture. Anyway I got into his e-mail account while he was in a meeting and I had a quick search for the other woman. I didn't find her. I found a man."

"I'm sure you didn't come to tell me your boyfriend is gay."

She ignored him. "This man—do you recognize the name Chatterjee?"

He didn't.

"This man forwarded him an e-mail from another person whose name I don't remember. The e-mail contained your name, address, phone number, passport number and car registration number."

Arthur put his glass down, any amusement wiped from his face. "What else was in the e-mail?"

"This is from memory. The only thing I wrote down was your name and address after I read it. It said something like, 'Arthur Malory is engaged in a credible pursuit of the Grail based on information obtained from Andrew Holmes.' I may have gotten this name wrong, I'm sorry."

He felt a soft lump forming in his throat. "No, go ahead."

"The message finished with 'We are tracking Malory and will deal with him at the appropriate time.'"

Though the dining room was warm, Arthur suddenly felt chilled. He poured more wine and had another gulp.

"Did you ask your boyfriend about the e-mail?"

"I couldn't, could I? I had no right to read it. All I could do was—I don't know, monitor him, for lack of a better word; evaluate him in a different light. Was there something about him I didn't know, some affiliation?"

"Had he ever talked about the Grail?"

"No, never. As far as I knew, he wasn't so interested in history. He's certainly not religious."

"He's French?"

"No, Italian."

"And that was it? That one e-mail?"

"Two days ago Simone went shopping. He left his laptop in the flat. I checked his e-mails again. There was a new one from this Chatterjee again marked urgent. I clicked on it and it was in a code, just symbols. It needed to be decrypted, which I couldn't do. So I left it alone and restored it as a new message. But I couldn't let it rest. I Googled you. You seemed like a good man what with this treasure you donated—so I felt compelled to warn you."

Arthur wondered if Chatterjee was one of the "interested parties" invoked by the man with a gun.

"Why didn't you just ring me?"

"You don't deliver this kind of news by the telephone."

"Why deliver it at all? You don't know me."

She shrugged. "I couldn't live with myself if I could have prevented something terrible and I didn't."

"You didn't tell him you were going to see me, did you?"

"Of course not. We had an argument over the way he's been behaving, something on the surface not related to these e-mails but to me completely related. I told him I wanted to take a break, to see my parents in Toulouse. I took some vacation days. I came here."

"I'm sorry you were put in danger tonight."

"Well, it wasn't so nice. But it happened."

Their food arrived.

When the server left them Arthur said, "I've never been to Modane."

"It's very small, out of the way, quite picturesque because of the Alps. Even in the summer they have these beautiful pure white peaks. But I'm only there because of the lab."

"Sounds like an odd place for a physics lab."

"No, no, it's a perfect place. You see there's a tunnel eighteen hundred meters below the summit that passes through the Fréjus Mountain between France and Italy. The lab is burrowed into the mountain near the middle of the tunnel so it's naturally almost completely shielded from cosmic rays, which are the biggest enemy in the search for rare subatomic particles."

"Like neutrinos? Those sort of things?"

"Yes," she said. "Exactly those kind of things. Very good."

"As I said, I'm a chemist, but Harp Industries being a physics company—I pick up some of the journals lying about. What's your area?"

"Me? I'm a dark matter person. Simone and I are on the EURECA team, an experiment to look for dark matter."

"I've heard of it," Arthur said, "but I can't say I know what it is."

"Actually, no one knows precisely what dark matter is but maybe I'll have a chance to explain. It's not a casual discussion."

"But you haven't found it yet, right?" he asked.

"Not yet but soon, I hope."

"And what will you do when you succeed?"

"Probably get quite drunk. But …"

"But what?"

"This problem with Simone. It's a complication. I don't know how we can keep working together. I don't even know who he is."

"I wish I could give you advice," Arthur said.

"I'm sure it will work out. Tonight, why weren't the police helpful?"

"I don't trust them. I'm in the middle of something complicated."

"Does it involve the Grail?"

"It does."

"That chest too?"

"Yes."

"I told you my story," she said. "Will you tell me yours?"

11

Back in the hotel room Arthur sat on one of the beds, Claire on the other, each nursing a Scotch from the minibar.

She had asked for "his story."

As he searched her pale, expressive face he asked himself why on earth he should tell it. He'd only known her for a few hours. She was as close to being a stranger as one could be. Other than spending a few hours together in the hot crucible of danger, what did they have in common? Who was she? Why would anyone be so altruistic that they would travel hundreds of miles to warn a stranger about a threat contained in an intercepted e-mail?

I would, he thought. That's exactly how I'd behave if I found myself in her position. Was he staring into the face of a like soul?

He began telling her about his last few weeks. It all came out in a clear, linear fashion. When he gave presentations at his company and at conferences he had always owned the room and he certainly owned this one. Claire seemed rapt as he told her about the Grail Loons, the break-in at Andrew Holmes' house, his sense of being followed and targeted, the maddening unhelpfulness of the police, his unfair dismissal for inadvertently belittling his chairman, and how he had made his discovery in Warwickshire earlier that day. In the course of telling the story he found that Claire had read *Le Morte D'Arthur* in school and as a girl once had a passing interest in the world of King Arthur, but that her fascination with science had left the King of Britons in the dust.

Finally, he said, "Well that's it. That's all there is."

"It's really incredible," she said. "Our lives, well, we had nothing in common, and suddenly we have this connection around something as crazy as the Holy Grail."

"It is pretty wild." The minibar Scotch was finished so he moved them onto the two small brandies.

"I have to check the train schedule," she said. "I need to go back tomorrow."

He ignored the comment and lifted the old chest onto his bed.

"What do you say we have a look?"

He saw her eyes light up at the prospect.

He opened the lid and carefully laid the contents on all the flat surfaces in the room. The clothes, silver objects, and bibles were banished to the chairs and end tables. The parchments got pride of place on the bed.

He found the Waynflete letter and read it out loud for Claire's benefit. He had thought about the letter all the way back from Warwickshire.

He was more than a descendant of Sir Thomas Malory. If the letter could be believed, he was also a descendant of King Arthur himself! The chain of revelations was dizzying. No wonder Holmes had sounded so excited. Most serious scholars thought the evidence was tenuous at best for King Arthur being anything other than mythological, a character invented out of whole cloth to suit the needs of medieval popular culture. For if there was a real King Arthur living during the sixth century or thereabouts, there was no mention of him by name in the writings of the few near-contemporaneous historians: Gildas in the sixth century, Bede in the eighth century, Nennius in the ninth century. A King Arthur did not rear his head in the pages of recorded history until Geoffrey of Monmouth wrote in 1136 in his *Historia Regum Britanniae*, "And even the renowned King Arthur himself was mortally wounded; and being carried thence to the Isle of Avalon to be cured of his wounds, he gave up the crown of Britain to his kinsman Constantine, the son of Cador, Duke of Cornwall, in the five hundred and forty-second year of our Lord's incarnation."

He explained the implications for Claire: in one fell swoop, here was a degree of confirmation that King Arthur was indeed real, and with it came the rudiments of a genealogy that placed not only a fifteenth-century Thomas Malory in his lineage but also a twenty-first-century Arthur Malory.

If Arthur could have one wish, it would be to speak with Holmes about the letter. Holmes had sounded so confident on the phone. Yet there was nothing in the Waynflete letter to give any comfort that Arthur's sword let alone the Grail could actually be found.

Arthur put down the letter and began paging through the unexplored part of the stack. The results were disappointing. Parchment after parchment were drab legal documents pertaining to sixteenth and seventeenth century Malorys—deeds, wills, land transfers and the like.

Then with the turn of a page everything changed.

"Well, here's something," he murmured.

Arthur immediately recognized Thomas Malory's distinctive crowded scrawl from the Waynflete letter on not only the sheet in his hand but also the next.

"It's a second document in Thomas Malory's hand."

He apologized for his need to remain silent as he scanned the parchment. It took only a few minutes to understand what he had discovered.

Malory's book, *Le Morte Darthur* (this being the Middle French spelling he had employed), first had been published by the London printer William Caxton in 1485, some fourteen years after Malory's death. Caxton, it was thought, had obtained a manuscript in Malory's hand or that of a scribe—perhaps a collection of Arthurian tales—and stitched them into a single volume to which a preface had been added, presumably written by Caxton himself. The preface had long been considered an unusual document: after explaining the necessity for extolling the virtues of a great Christian such as King Arthur, Caxton then launches into a detailed and wholly unnecessary description of how many chapters are contained in each of the twenty-one books of the volume.

Since the Winchester manuscript of *Le Morte Darthur*—the only know copy in Malory's hand—lacked this introduction, one could reasonably assume the preface had been authored by someone else, most likely Caxton.

Arthur suddenly said, "I need a copy of *Le Morte*." He pictured his own book as a small pile of ashes.

"Maybe they have a computer downstairs," she said. "You can get it online, I'm sure."

"I've got my laptop in my bag."

He sprung from the bed and sputtered when he found the laptop out of power. He plugged it in and purchased a day of Wi-Fi access from the hotel.

Arthur clicked on the first full-text copy of *Le Morte* in his search and went straight to the preface.

He read it aloud. *"I have divided it into twenty-one Books, and every book chaptered, as hereafter shall by God's grace follow. The First Book shall treat how Uther Pendragon gat the noble conqueror King Arthur, and containeth twenty-eight chapters. The Second Book treateth of Balin the noble knight, and containeth nineteen chapters."* And on and on until the last sentence: *"The sum is twenty-one books, which contain the sum of five hundred and seven chapters, as more plainly shall follow hereafter."*

He turned to the parchment again. Here, in an undated block of script, was the peculiar book and chapter enumeration in Malory's own Middle English penmanship.

> *And for to vnderstonde bryefly the contente of thys volume I haue deuyded it in to xxj bookes and euery book chapytred as here after shal by goddes grace folowe. The fyrst book shal treate how Vther-pendragon gate the noble conquerour kyng Arthur and conteyneth xxviij chappytres. The second book treateth of Balyn the noble knyght and conteyneth xix chapytres.*

Arthur scanned back and forth, comparing the first parchment to the Caxton preface. "It's virtually word-for-word identical. This means that it's likely that Malory, not his publisher, wrote the preface."

"Is this important?" Claire asked.

"I'm not sure. At a minimum it's historically interesting."

Arthur turned to the next sheet of parchment and this one delivered the payoff.

He read the letter out loud for Claire but he imagined that Holmes was listening too.

"Alas my enemies, these unholy men who call themselves the Qem have succeeded in preventing me from making the journey to find the Graal. I am now old and too feeble. Yet by placing me in prison all these years they have given me the benefit of time and I have been blessed by God with the ability to well and fully chronicle the tales of my noble forebearer the great and noble Arthur King of the Britons. I pray that a Maleoré who comes after me will find this parchment and take up the quest for the Sangreal. To find the Graal that man must first find the sword of Arthur which I myself have found and which I myself have well hid to keep it from evil hands. The finder of the Sangreal must be keen of intellect virtuous and pure of heart. The hiding place of the sword can be found within the preface to *Le Morte Darthur* in companionship with the tale itself provided one is as mindful as priests who mind the Sacraments of the green acres of Warwickshire which were chronicled in the *Domesday Book* written during the realm of King William I. I have conceived this puzzle to make the quest indeed real for an heir who comes to possess this very tract and who has the temperament and the grace of God to find the holiest of holies to wit the Graal of our Christ."

Arthur placed the pages onto the bed and stared into space.

This was what Holmes had meant.

"It's almost like he's speaking directly to you," Claire said softly.

He saw it clearly. This was *his* quest now. It had been from the moment he fought back against the intruder with a gun.

"I need to make a call," Arthur said.

He rang Tony Ferro at home, apologizing for the lateness of the hour.

"Tony, you won't believe what I've stumbled upon up in Warwickshire—or rather, what *we* stumbled upon."

"We?"

"Holmes was there first."

Tony was a serious academic who clearly would be reserving judgment until he examined the documents personally. He drifted into a story about an elaborate medieval manuscript fake that had cost a trusting and gullible colleague her job. Yet two Tonys were on the line: one, an eager boy who wanted to jump at the news, the other, a credible historian with a reputation to protect. By the end of the conversation, the boy won out.

"Can you come down to UCL tomorrow? I mean, for God's sake, Arthur, can you imagine what this means if it's authentic? Not only a stiffer measure of confirmation than has ever previously existed for the existence of King Arthur, but a concrete nexus—not a mythological one—to two vital elements of the Arthurian tales: Excalibur and the Grail itself. I need a stiff drink to calm myself."

While Arthur had been on the phone, Claire had been lying on her side, watching him from her bed. She looked sleepy. After he hung up, he took a moment to consider something.

"Can you get a later train tomorrow?"

"Why?"

"I'd like you to meet Tony Ferro. Come with me to the university first. It's near St. Pancras station."

"Okay … why not?"

Her answer made him feel lighter.

His cell phone rang. It wasn't a number he recognized. The call was short and tense and when he was finished she asked who it was.

"It was the fire brigade. They want to speak with me. I'm not sure how they got my number. I'm not keen to go back but apparently I don't have a choice."

"Shall I go with you?"

"No, stay here and get some sleep. I'll be back."

Arthur knew perfectly well what he'd find when he returned. The fire services were still there, hosing down the blackened, collapsed walls. Still, it was surreal and profoundly mournful seeing the artifacts of his life in cinders and ashes.

Arthur made himself known to the deputy brigade manager, who berated him for leaving the scene. He made up a cock-and-bull story about fleeing in a state of panic, having a few drinks and some food at a friend's house to calm down.

"It's a good job you agreed to return, Mister Malory, or you would have had to face some serious inquiries. Did you smell gas before the explosion?"

"No."

"Any problems with your gas cooker?"

"None."

"I see. A passerby called in a report of the strong smell of gas coming from your house."

"So the police told me."

"So you've spoken to them?"

"Yes, I rang them."

The fireman pulled out a card and handed it to him. "A DI Hobbs was here earlier. He had your mobile number. He said he wishes to interview you."

"As I said, we've already talked."

"My investigator found preliminary evidence of a kerosene-like residue in the area of your front room. Can you shed any light on this?"

"Did Hobbs say anything about it?"

"As a matter of fact he did. Seems he's been here before. He said you had a kerosene lamp."

If Hobbs hadn't mentioned the Molotov cocktail, he wouldn't, either. Arthur didn't want anything more to do with the police. How had Hobbs known he was with someone? There could be only one way: Hobbs had been there watching. *Interested parties* had gotten to him. The lackluster investigation into the Holmes's' murders now made sense.

"I did have a lamp," Arthur said dully.

"It wasn't in use tonight, was it?"

"No."

"Well then, thank you for making yourself available. We may wish to ask you additional questions. And I'd suggest you call the emergency number of your home insurer to get the ball rolling there. You're a lucky man, Mister Malory. This could have ended much, much worse."

When Arthur returned to the hotel the room was dark. Claire was asleep on her bed. By the light of his mobile phone he saw every stitch of her clothes in a neat pile. He undressed to his boxers and climbed into his bed, and for the few moments before sleep overtook him he preferred to think about the naked woman a few feet away rather than the ruins of his blackened house.

Tony Ferro's office at the Department of English Language and Literature was located within the labyrinthine complex of University College London in Bloomsbury. In size it was more of a closet than an office and the ample man looked comically shoehorned behind his desk.

Arthur introduced Claire and in typical Tony fashion, the large man asked, "Why don't I ever get attractive French women falling from the sky onto my doorstep? The world is simply not a fair place. Well, let's see the parchments"—he began clearing things off his desk—"I hardly slept."

Arthur and Claire watched in silence for a full ten minutes while Tony read each and every line, eyeballing the documents through a magnifying glass. When he was done, Tony looked up and stared at Arthur gravely.

"Well?" Arthur asked.

Tony tapped his folded reading glasses on the desk and exhaled deeply. Arthur hadn't noticed he'd been holding his breath for a good while.

"This is the greatest moment in my life," he said quietly. "Perhaps I should have said *in my academic life* to be politically correct, but between you and me, it's better than the birth of my children, which were messy affairs. I think these documents are absolutely authentic—without question. The paper is correct, the ink is correct, the grammar and syntax are correct. I've had the occasion to study Thomas Malory's signature on the Winchester manuscript and this signature on the Waynflete letter is identical. My only regret is that Holmes isn't here to share this with us."

Arthur nodded. "I feel the same way."

Tony choked back a tear. "I had no idea you were a mutant."

Arthur raised an eyebrow.

"An extra rib? Stand up and let me have a feel."

"Oh, that. Really?"

"Absolutely. Consider it primary research. Pull up your shirt. You may avert your gaze, Ms. Pontier,"

Ferro said with a twinkle.

Exposing his flank, Arthur joked, "What if someone comes in?"

"I'll tell them I love you."

"Other side." Arthur pointed. "Still a bit tender."

Tony reached over his desk and palpated on the left over Arthur's liver. "It's a little stubby affair. Rare, is it?"

Arthur sat back down. "So I'm told."

After a pregnant pause, Tony told him, "We've got to publish this, you know. It's imperative. The journal Sandy edits would be the most logical place. We'll need to bring her and Aaron into this ASAP and the rest of the Loons, of course."

Arthur shook his head. "Slow down. We'll publish—rather, *you'll* publish—in good time. This is your career, not mine. You can have the limelight to yourself, Tony. I just want to have the time to look for the sword and the Grail in peace."

"Of course!" Tony exulted. "You'll have all the time you need. The academic wheels, they do turn slow. When the time comes to write the paper I'm putting Holmes down as the first author. This should have been his coup. But don't delude yourself into thinking that you'll be able to scurry off into the shadows, my boy. You're already a media darling just for being a good bloke. Can you imagine what's going to happen when the world finds out that King Arthur was likely real and that you're a descendant, complete with a royal rib? You'll be canonized, mate. We'll probably live to see your mug on postage stamps and tea towels!"

"Christ, Tony, I'm just not going to worry about all that now. I'm going to run with this. I'm going to run like hell before the murderer shows up again."

"I'm worried about your safety," Tony confessed. "Strange things afoot. Awful about your house."

"I'm trying to be careful."

"The police aren't being helpful?"

"It's worse than that. I can't prove it but I think they're in on it. I've broken off contact."

Tony shook his head gravely. "Not good … *at all.* If you need a place to stay—"

"Thanks but no."

"Have you made any sense out of Malory's clues? The *Morte* preface? The *Domesday Book*?"

"Not yet. Early days. I need a copy of the *Domesday Book*. Got one handy?"

Tony had a couple and lent Arthur a fat paperback the weight of a brick.

"Well, use me as a sounding board. And the other Loons," Tony offered. "Consider us your brain trust."

"I will. Can you believe it, Tony? A real-life Grail quest."

"It is unbelievable but it's true, isn't it? Holmes was right, Arthur. It's your quest. Can I run off a copy of the letters so I can study them some more? I'll keep them close to the vest."

The three walked to the empty copy room down the hall.

"What do you make of these *Qem* that Malory mentions?" Tony asked, gently flattening the first parchment against the copier glass.

"Never heard of the term. You?"

Tony retrieved the first copy. "After you mentioned the word yesterday I did a quick search of related homonyms, *Q-E-M, Q-U-*

E-M, K-E-M, K-H-E-M and *C-H-E-M*. Khem is Egyptian for black, that's all I came up with. There's no record of anyone or anything by that name in my medieval history databases. Intriguing, though, in light of Malory's legal woes. I mean, the man certainly had enemies."

"So what's your role in all this going to be?" Tony asked Claire.

"My role? Well, I don't know. I have to go back to France."

"Pity," Tony said.

Outside in the sunshine, Arthur and Claire started walking toward St. Pancras.

He'd been waiting for this moment, thinking about what he was going to say all morning and it came out in a hurried rush. "I know it's a lot to ask but I'd like you to stay. For a little while. I could use your help, someone to bounce ideas off."

"Arthur, I—"

He wouldn't let her finish the sentence. "Claire, we hardly know each other. But I don't want to let you go so easily."

She inhaled sharply, and looked down, her cheeks flushing.

He kept pressing. "This feels awkward. It's not exactly like asking someone out on a date. I'm asking you out on an adventure. Will you stay a couple of days? If there's even a hint of danger again I'll send you packing."

"But I don't even have any clothes."

"That makes two of us," he said.

She looked up. Her answer was yes.

The simple word lifted his heart and posed a small, happy quandary. Should he shake her hand? Touch her shoulder? Kiss her? None seemed quite right so after a mumbled "terrific" he immediately changed the subject to shopping.

In the Marks and Spencer at Covent Garden, Arthur quickly assembled a serviceable wardrobe and trappings for himself and looked for Claire in the women's wear department. He hung back, as men do, as she shopped for intimates then drew closer when she turned to other clothes, shoes and outerwear. She chose things breezily, making swift decisions, playfully holding items up to see if he approved. He did, every time, signaling his assent with a nod and a smile, a thumbs-up.

He enjoyed the interlude, as carefree an hour as he'd spent in a long while, watching her slap like a pinball between the racks.

At the cashier he insisted he pay for her items and she reluctantly agreed. As an afterthought, they stopped in the luggage department and bought a couple of roller bags for easier carriage.

They wheeled the bags to the car park in Bloomsbury and drove back to the hotel, Arthur nervously checking his mirrors for suspicious vehicles. Claire sent an e-mail to her boss at Modane requesting some vacation days. At Cantley House she changed into a new top. When she exited the bathroom he picked up a whiff of spicy perfume. He hadn't seen her purchase any so he assumed she had a bottle in her handbag all along and was delighted she had decided to break out the arsenal.

He ordered sandwiches from room service and they got down to it, Arthur retrieving the key documents from the chest and both of them taking their positions on the freshly made beds. He read aloud again what he considered to be the most important section of the most important parchment:

> *To find the Graal that man must first find the sword of Arthur which I have well hid to keep it thus from evil hands. The finder of the Sangreal must be keen of intellect virtuous and pure of heart. The sword can be found within the preface to* Le Morte Darthur *in companionship with the tale itself provided one is as mindful as priests who mind the Sacraments of the green acres of Warwickshire which were chronicled in the* Domesday Book *as written during the realm of King William I.*

"So, are you keen of intellect, virtuous, and pure of heart?" she asked.

"Maybe two out of three."

She smiled. "Which are you lacking?"

"You'll have to be the judge. What do you know about the *Domesday Book*?"

"I've heard of it but I have to say it wasn't included in the French curriculum."

He picked up Tony's copy. "Catch."

With a grunt she caught the heavy book cleanly, opened it to a random page and read for a few moments. "My God, is it all like this? This is surely the most boring book ever written."

"It's pretty dry, like reading a company's accounts."

"Except these are the accounts for an entire country, no?"

"An eleventh-century country where you could reasonably tote up all the pigs, cows, and plows."

Arthur reclaimed Tony's book, hardly knowing where to begin. It was 1,500 densely packed pages in a font that strained even his young eyes. Claire used his laptop to find an online version.

The book was the brainchild of William the Conqueror, who in 1085 decided he ought to know the precise wealth of his kingdom. To accomplish the task he sent his royal commissioners and clerks throughout England to record how much land was held in each shire, how much land and livestock the king himself owned, and what annual dues were rightly his. It was a meticulous process done quickly and efficiently and collated and transcribed into two great parchment volumes, *Great Domesday* and *Little Domesday*, by a single scribe in Winchester who wrote in a stylized and abbreviated clerical Latin. The survey was said to be so thorough that not even a single ox or one cow or one pig escaped notice of the king's auditors.

The manuscripts were taken with utmost seriousness by the king and before long they began to be called *Domesday Books*, a reference to the awesome Final Judgment Day when Christians learn their fate. Then, as now, death and taxes were certain. Indeed King William learned that his was a prosperous country with vast land holdings and that his barons and archbishops owed him a large income every year.

Arthur absently opened to a page and settled his eyes on the entry for the village of Malden in Surrey. He read it to Claire then said, "Gripping stuff, this."

> Robert de Watteville holds of Richard OLD MALDEN. Hearding held it of King Edward. It was then assessed at 8 hides, now at 4. There is land for 5 ploughs. In demesne is 1 plough; and 14 villans and 2 bordars with 4 ploughs. There is a chapel and 3 slaves, and a mill rendering 12s and 4 acres of meadow. From the herbage, 1 pig out of 7 pigs. Of these hides a knight holds 1 hide and 1 virgate, and there he has 1 plough and 1 villan and 1 bordar and 1 acre of meadow. The whole TRE was worth £7; now £6 12s.

After some glossary work he deciphered the entry to mean that Robert de Watteville, the Saxon holder in 1086, worked the land in Malden in an undertenancy of Richard Hearding, the tenant in chief who held it under Edward the Confessor, the king until the Norman invasion of 1066. The Malden holdings previously had been assessed at 8 hides of land (about 120 acres) but were now only 4 hides. Watteville owned his own single plow and the labors of 14 peasants. Two small-holders possessed some land themselves and had their own plows and pigs, one of which was owed to Watteville annually. Malden had a chapel and 3 landless villagers. There was a mill that paid Watteville 12 shillings a year in rent and 4 acres of grazing land. An unnamed knight controlled a little more than a hide of land and had some laborers. The value of the holdings in Malden had been £7 in 1066. It was assessed in 1086 at £6 12s.

Arthur paged through the book reading village by village entries and soon was snowed by the blizzard of dry facts and figures. How were they to make sense of it? Why had Thomas Malory decided to use this book as a vehicle for concealment? And how had he gained access to it? After a generation or two within the treasury at Winchester, the *Domesday Book*, housed in an iron-studded chest, had been transported to Westminster Palace by King Henry II and for the next 600 years there it lay. So Malory would have had to have been granted permission to view it from a high official in the court of King Henry VI.

Claire put down the laptop and asked for the parchment. She read it to herself, her eyes narrowing thoughtfully then said, "Look, this guy, Thomas Malory, I'm sure he was quite intelligent to write a beautiful book like *Le Morte D'Arthur* but as far as we know he wasn't a mathematician or anything like that."

"Your point?"

"My point is that I'm sure his puzzle or his code or whatever it's best to call it isn't so amazingly complicated. There are only two elements, the preface and the *Domesday Book*. The most important thing is to know that both are required. This letter, which is basically addressed to you across time, says this."

"Okay," Arthur said, "but where to start? The preface or the *Domesday Book*?"

"That I don't know."

Arthur and Claire remained planted for the rest of the day and well into the night reading the *Domesday Book* and *Le Morte D'Arthur* and rereading the parchments. Arthur filled up his spiral copybook with notes and both of them tried to form connections but all their work led to dead ends. Fatigue finally overtook them. They returned to the hotel restaurant for dinner then worked for a few more hours until they were numb from it all.

While Claire was in the bathroom getting ready for the night Arthur undressed and got into his bed. He pretended not to look at her when she emerged, dressed in a plain, short nightgown, very schoolgirlish. She gave him a quick, almost embarrassed smile and slid between her sheets. With the lights out, he thought about her lying there close to him but soon he drifted away into a maze of dreams, a weird jumble of Arthur's Camelot, William the Conqueror's *Domesday Book* and his own burning house.

12
ENGLAND, 1451

Thomas Malory parted the curtains in his bedroom and let the sunshine flood in. His wife, Elizabeth, was still asleep but she stirred at the brightness and pulled the fur bedclothes over her eyes.

"Is it fair or foul?" her small muffled voice called out.

"Most fair," Malory said. "Shall I call your ladies to attend you?"

"In a moment. There is no need for haste. I did not sleep well."

"I did. Most deeply."

Her head appeared slowly, much like a badger tentatively emerging from its sett. "In any event I do not wish to see the boys too soon. They are so taxing before they have been dressed and fed."

Her long black hair was stuffed into an unattractive sleeping bonnet, which made her look too matronly for his liking. Malory had a mind to fling it off and ravish her but with more pressing matters on his mind he began to sweep out of the room to summon his dresser.

"Must you leave today?"

"I must."

He had made the transition from a military to a country life many times, as there seemed no end to conflicts between England and her neighbors. Yet never had he found himself as weary of war as he was now. True, nothing could equal the thrill and emotional release of a battlefield victory, but such pleasure was brief, akin to the crescendo of a carnal union. At his age he much preferred gentler pursuits as a prosperous knight in Warwickshire over the dreary slogs and periodic bloodfests of a Norman campaign. Today, he would embark on a journey that would straddle both worlds. He did not expect bloodshed but he hoped for exhilaration.

Dressed in his short doublet, breeches, a cloak, and soft leather boots, Malory bounded from his private chambers to the public rooms of his manor. The floors of the grand house were flagged with plaited rushes that had been dampened by the servants to refresh them. They gave out a scent of newly scythed hay, a smell he had dreamt about in France amidst the stench of his siege camps.

Malory could not pass through the public rooms of his manor without attracting the attention of members of his household. His estate accommodated over a hundred outdoor and indoor servants, agricultural laborers, yeoman, husbandmen, and various tenants as well as two gentlemen and their extended families. His groom wanted a word about the readiness of his horses, his brewer offered to have him sample a new barrel, and his chaplain wanted instructions concerning his departure mass.

Malory dealt with them in haste and made his way to his tapestry-draped library where two of his retainers awaited him. Robert Malory was one of them, a distant cousin from Radclyffe-on-the-Wreake, one of the gentlemen who resided at Newbold Revel. The other was John Aleyn, a loyal soldier who had campaigned with him in Normandy and was now a handy man of arms in his domestic service.

Malory greeted them cheerfully and bade them sit with him at the table nearest the hearth. An attentive servant quickly appeared with a tray of carved pork and cold roasted potatoes. The men set into their breakfast with their belt daggers and washed down the food with weak ale. Robert was his usual talkative self, launching into a drawn-out and largely boring story about his previous day's boar hunt in the forest near Coombe Abbey. He was younger than his knight cousin, a fleshy fellow with a thick waist and a limp from a Norman arrow taken to the hip years earlier. A more eager soldier might have shaken off the injury and returned to battle when he had healed but Robert mustered out of his company and returned to a comfortable life of wenching, hunting, and drinking.

John Aleyn was a different sort. He was a hard man, all lean and gristle, who lived for service. He led an acetic existence in a tiny one-room cottage—really more of a hut—on the edge of the estate. Malory could not remember ever seeing him either in the company of women or drinking to the point where his fighting skills were compromised. He was, in short, the perfect man for certain jobs.

"Are you ready for our journey?" Malory asked, spearing the last potato.

"The packs are ready. Say the word and I'll dress the horses," Aleyn replied.

Robert Malory gulped messily from his flagon and wiped ale from his chin. "My hip's sore as a whore's cunny from the hunt but if you say it's time to ride, I'm ready enough, coz."

"Yes, it is time. The priest will send us on our way with a mass. We'll depart immediately thereafter," Malory told him. "Bristol is a five-day ride. From there, perhaps another five days to our destination." He smiled at the word; he might just as easily have said *destiny*. "From the day I returned from Normandy six months ago I have had little time for this journey but have kept it foremost in my mind. Today, thoughts turn to action."

When Malory returned to Newbold Revel from his recent foray into Normandy the affairs of his estate were badly in need of attention and he found himself drawn into a number of compelling obligations. It was a time of turmoil. Malory and other loyalists had long suspected that the death of his first lord, Warwick, Henry Beauchamp, had been unnatural, and in their minds a trail of poison led directly to the loathsome earl of Buckingham. Beauchamp's death had hit Malory hard. Though the young man was Malory's lord and retainee, Malory was his mentor. He had taught the idealistic youth swordplay and archery and had regaled him with tales of his own exploits in France and Turkey and Arthurian tales of romance and adventure.

Beauchamp had absorbed the lessons learned at Malory's knee and applied them in his own role as the principal mentor of the child king,

Henry VI. The king had rewarded Beauchamp's attentiveness by naming him as the first earl of England with precedence over all other earls. Beauchamp's allies well imagined that his influence with the king was a problem for one man and one man only: Buckingham, who saw his primacy diminished by the royal dependence on Warwick.

Before Beauchamp's death, the two powerful earls had clashed in Parliament over matters of state, and Buckingham had irritated Beauchamp no end by acquiring Maxstoke Castle in Beauchamp's own shire. The proximity of Maxstoke to Beauchamp's Warwick Castle put the retinues of both earls, Malory included, in frequent contact and conflict, further stoking the fires of feud.

Following Beauchamp's untimely death, Malory was now in service to the new earl of Warwick, Sir Richard Neville. Fortunately for Malory, Neville was an extraordinary man, every bit as fine in character and intellect as Beauchamp. Buckingham did not share the admiration. To him Neville was merely another Warwick to despise and crush.

Since the death of Beauchamp, Buckingham had consolidated his power at court, seeking to shape the attitudes and policies of the impressionable young king to serve his own rapacious goals. Those who opposed Buckingham whispered that he practiced the dark art of alchemy. Some claimed he sought and others that he already had obtained the Philosopher's Stone, the legendary alchemical substance that could turn base metals into gold.

Clearer thinkers dismissed the notion that his wealth was a result of the mysteries of alchemy. The enormous inheritance gained at the death of his mother, the dowager countess of Stafford, explained his bulging accounts easily enough. There was not, however, a mote of dispute about Buckingham's character. All agreed he was an unimaginative and unlikeable man with a harsh and vindictive streak who, at a moment's notice, could veer into the most abject cruelty. One London wag who wrote anonymously of Buckingham that he was fat and full of grease found himself hauled off to the Tower when his identity became known.

Malory had only been back from France for a month when he came into conflict with Buckingham in the Coombe Abbey woods on land bordering Newbold Revel. John Aleyn had gotten wind of a raiding party of Buckingham's men intent on causing mischief or worse, Malory being a softer target than Warwick, principle object of Buckingham's ire.

The alarm raised, Malory organized a party of some two dozen supporters to ride out from his manor and take up positions in the forest. At dusk the keen-eyed Aleyn pointed into the gloom and alerted Malory to the approaching raiding party. Buckingham's men crept forward on foot and when they drew closer it was clear they were carrying fatted torches on long handles, useful for tossing from afar to set ablaze just such a house as Newbold Revel.

Malory surprised them by ordering a charge from the front and both flanks. The marauders turned heel and retreated so fast that casualties were light on both sides. Yet, in the heat of pursuit, Malory swore he saw the blue-plumed coronet of Buckingham bobbing above a black stallion before horse and rider disappeared into the darkness.

The abortive attack and its aftermath absorbed much of Malory's attentions. Without prisoners he was unable to prove that Buckingham was behind the outrage, but he worked the backrooms of Parliament where he served as MP for Great Bedwyn, recruiting wavering parties to take his side against he who was fat and full of grease.

Then another distraction prevented Malory from undertaking his quest. In his youth, Malory had served as a Knight Hospitaller in Turkey, and one of his comrades-in-arms against the Moors was a gentleman, William Weston, from a village near Newbold Revel. One day Weston came to Malory desperate for help. His sister Joan, a prosperous woman in her own right, had married Hugh Smith of Monks Kirby, an intemperate brute who beat her and forced himself upon her in a manner unsuitable for a gentleman and a husband. Malory had known Joan fondly from childhood and was persuaded by Weston to help rescue the unfortunate woman from her woeful circumstance. His desire for Excalibur was eclipsed by his moral imperative to help a damsel in distress.

The raid took some planning but went off without confrontation or violence. Joan gathered up her own marital possessions into a chest and Malory, Weston, and their party spirited her away to one of Weston's properties in Barwell. There, Joan and Malory, flushed with the thrill of the exploit, fell into a night of passion. Malory, ever the gentleman, regretted the lapse as soon as it happened and later would come to regret it even more.

When this affair was settled and London politics had quieted, Malory finally could turn his attention to Excalibur and Tintagel.

The journey to Cornwall was long but not particularly arduous. The weather was mainly fair and Malory's party of five that included his cousin, John Aleyn, and two squires, made their way west unimpeded by brigands or highwaymen. They slept under the stars, though on occasion Malory and his cousin were given a mat by a hearth in a roadside cottage. Though none of them had ever been to the Cornish coast, they learned the way from the archbishop of Taunton, who gave the gentlemen overnight accommodation in his priory house. On the last day of their journey they suspected they were close when they smelled the sea, and they knew they had arrived when they heard waves crashing against the rocky coast.

Malory, tall in his saddle, saw it first and shouted, "Look, there!"

Robert Malory, under the weather the past few days from some stomach disagreement, nodded limply; but John Aleyn shared his knight's excitement.

"It's a beauty, isn't it?"

Out of deference to Robert's delicate state they chose not to end their trek in joyous gallop.

The castle was perched at the edge of the cliffs. They would not appreciate how high and steep the rock face was until they were upon it. It sat on a promontory joined to the mainland by a narrow spit of land. The cliffs below faced the full force of an unforgiving ocean. The fortress, erected in 1233 by Richard, earl of Cornwall, had been built upon earlier and ancient structures, some as early as Roman days. Richard was all too aware of the Arthurian heritage of the site.

It was common knowledge passed down the generations that some seven centuries before Richard's time a long-forgotten Cornish castle had occupied the land. That fortress was said to be the place where Uther Pendragon seduced Queen Igraine and sired a baby who was to become Arthur, King of the Britons. Richard capitalized on the Arthurian connections for his own prestige and deliberately built his castle in the style of antiquity, low and squat with thick walls. Now, three hundred years hence, Richard's castle was itself wrecked and abandoned, the casualty of sacking by a Cornish warlord a century earlier.

The five travelers dismounted at the foot of the highest standing wall and tied the horses to scrub. The castle was a place of palpable solitude. Not a soul was to be seen nor a sheep grazing on the plain. Malory walked the sort distance to the precipice over coastal meadowland and peered hundreds of feet down to the churning surf. The sky was becoming as gray as the sea. Though anxious to proceed, Malory said, "Let us set up camp for the night. At first light we will find the way down and then we will find our cave."

Buckingham was a man who felt comfortable in the dark. He had sensitive eyes that stung and watered in the sunlight so he ordered all the drapes permanently closed at his country manors and London palace. Besides, the darkness had always vitalized him more than daylight. Like a nocturnal animal his senses were more acute when the sun had set. His unhappy wife called him a bat to his face; behind his back she called him worse.

So it was with profound irritation that he emerged from his candlelit London study to meet with his colleague, George Ripley, and examine the amazing scroll laid out on his sunlit dining room table.

Ripley was even fatter than he. Buckingham squinted at the man's huge face and said, "Does it need to be so bright?"

"I beseech you to look quickly, my lord, and then we can retire to a more comfortable room to discuss our affairs."

Their affairs, as Ripley put it, were Buckingham's most private ones—and well hidden from public view, though it was whispered in gossip and rumor that Buckingham was a disciple of the alchemical arts. While not an avid practitioner like Ripley, Buckingham's vast wealth put him in position to be the leading patron of the dark science. As such, his influence stretched across the channel, throughout the continent and into Asia.

Even within the secretive and rarefied world of alchemy Buckingham's interests were rather more rarefied. While most alchemists devoted themselves to finding the secret of manipulating cheap base metals into gold, Buckingham had a loftier goal. He was a member, indeed the leader, of a loosely affiliated group of worthies who followed in the footsteps of the great alchemists of the past, tracing their lineage to the greatest of them all, Nehor, son of Jebedee, cast-off disciple of Christ.

Ripley was the newest member, recruited to take the place of a Spanish alchemist who had died from inhaling mercury vapors. Ripley, a Yorkshireman, had inherited a considerable fortune and used it to indulge his passion for the natural sciences. When tapped by Buckingham to join the secretive Khem he was midway through his twenty-five-volume alchemical treatise, *Liber Duodecim*, which already had brought him fame for his progress in finding the Philosopher's Stone.

Ripley recently had concluded the production of an elaborately illustrated scroll cryptically and enigmatically laying out in Latin the steps necessary for the acquisition of the Philosopher's Stone and there it was, all eighteen feet of it, unrolled on the long banqueting table. Buckingham walked its length, shielding his eyes with one hand, gesticulating with the other.

"These illustrations are by your own hand, Ripley?"

"They are, my lord."

"I had no idea you possessed this talent. And who might this be?" He was pointing at the image of a large bearded man in a robe and headdress clutching an egg-shaped vessel to his chest.

"Why it is Nehor, of course."

Buckingham was about to order a servant to close the curtains when he remembered he had shooed the butler away. He angrily performed the chore himself.

"I do hope that among all this nonsense you've made no mention of the Grail."

Ripley looked crestfallen. "I did no such thing! I would never venture into forbidden topics. And I would hardly refer to my text as nonsense."

"Not nonsense, eh? Tell me, Ripley, have you or have you not actually found the Philosopher's Stone?"

Buckingham's eyes were adjusting to the low light. He saw beads of sweat forming on Ripley's forehead.

"I would say that I have made great strides, my lord."

Buckingham laughed and made for the door. "Just as I said, Ripley, *nonsense*. Now come with me to talk of more substantive matters."

Ripley joined him in his windowless lair, which was strewn with books, quires, and maps. The fire had gone to embers and the only light came from a few candles.

The men sat and drank a port wine.

"Sir Thomas Malory," Buckingham said. "Have you ever heard of him?"

Ripley had not.

"He is a small player on a large stage, a Warwick toady and member of Parliament who has been a thorn in my flank from time to time. But his politics are not what concerns me today."

"I see."

"I have a man close to him who is my spy. I have learned of late that Malory is not altogether as ordinary as I had thought. Indeed he well may be a descendant of King Arthur, as incredible as that might sound. It seems he is on a journey to Cornwall to find Arthur's sword and from there the Grail itself."

Ripley's eyes, already wide from the darkness, grew larger.

"If he is successful, Ripley, then we must seize the sword and find its secret before Malory is able to do so himself. Your Philosopher's Stone is but a child's plaything. The Grail is the one true object of our desire. With it, kings and queens and popes will be as insignificant to us as flies to be swatted and swept away."

Malory awoke to the sound of surging waves striking the cliffs. Aleyn had already managed a small fire and was roasting the last of the rabbits he had snared the previous night. The others gathered around and they ate just enough meat to quiet their bellies. A sea mist dampened their clothes but not their spirits as they made their way to the cliffs to find a way down to the beach.

The cliffs directly below the castle were sheer. Only a madman would attempt a descent at that point. Malory led the group away from the mainland over an expanse of meadowland that inclined sharply toward the sea and before long he identified a more favorable approach. Though treacherous, the climb down, he reckoned, would be safe enough.

His cousin rubbed at his hip as he looked over the edge. "I would hate to impede your progress, coz. Better I should wait here and guard the horses."

Malory grunted and took the first step toward the sea.

The four men made easy enough work of their descent. The two squires were youngest and fittest and were the ones with heavy picks and shovels slung over their backs. Halfway down they paused on a narrow ledge and debated whether the tide was coming in or out. Malory hoped the waters were ebbing since a flooded cave would be a danger but the men concluded that the tide was against them.

"Let us make haste," Malory said. "We are almost there and I will not wait another minute to fulfill my destiny."

"Come hell or high water," one of the squires said to the other.

Malory was the first to step on the beach, a narrow strip of wet sand that he figured would be under water before very long. The sea was dark and roiling. Swooping gulls seemed to mock their efforts with their cries. Malory made heavy footsteps in the sand and pointed with excitement. There were two caves, one with a huge mouth, the other smaller by half.

"Which one, my lord?" Aleyn asked.

"A great king would favor a great cave," Malory reasoned. "This one I say."

The large cave beckoned; stepping in felt like entering the gaping mouth of a sea monster. The floor was the same soft sand as the beach but strewn with smooth rocks washed in by the tide. The black walls of the cave rose high above their heads, forming a massive arched gallery that dwarfed them.

Malory looked out into the sea. The mouth of the cave was the shape of a great clasped fist. The tide would not be their ally. "Make fire and light the torches," he commanded. "Quickly."

His squire took a pouch from his belt and went to work sparking flint onto a heap of dry cotton threads and brittle wood chips. When a spark caught, the other page held a greased torch to the flame until it was lit then used that to light another. Malory took one and led the way, casting light onto the wall, looking for the symbol and praying it was there. A few hundred paces in he once again saw daylight and exclaimed that the cave went all the way through the head of land to the other side.

John Aleyn was marking Malory pace for pace on the opposite wall of the cave when he soon cried out, "Here, my lord!"

Malory ran to his side and saw what John pointed to, etched into the rock face at chest level. Only the size of a man's hand, a simple cross—the cross of Christ. Aleyn looked down and stepped away as though he were treading on forbidden ground.

"Dig there," Malory ordered his squire, "in the marks made by John Aleyn's feet."

There was no need for the pick so the young squire used only the long-handled shovel to scoop at the heavy sand. As the squire dug, Malory crouched and held the torch above. As the hole grew deeper, Malory prayed that something might be found before the water rushed in from the bottom. He had sent the other squire back to the mouth of the cave and now the young man was calling out, "The tide is at the entrance. We don't have long, my lord!"

The hole was knee deep and nothing thus far but sand and stones. Then the iron of the shovel made a satisfying clunk on something hard. Malory shooed the squire out of the hole and stepped in himself, using his dagger and free hand to probe deeper.

"Hand down the torch!" he called, planting the flambeau in the corner. "I am certain there is something here, something made of metal."

"Hurry!" Aleyn said. "The tide is rising, my lord. It will be upon us soon."

Malory would not be rushed. He dug and probed, scraped and threw handful after handful of sand over his shoulder. Finally, with the sound of the surging sea in his ears he rose from his haunches cradling something between his palms.

Aleyn held up the other torch. There was no mistaking it. It was a sword. The blade was long, thin, and irregularly scalloped, corroded by black masses of rust, a shadow of its former glory. But the guard, hilt, and pommel were as pristine as the day they had been fashioned.

Malory stepped from the hole and told his squire to wet a cloth in seawater. The squire ran toward the mouth of the cave and returned with the washcloth he always kept in his tunic. Malory washed the grit from the sword handle. The gilded silver gleamed in the torchlight.

"Behold! Excalibur!" he exclaimed.

Malory strained his eyes to inspect the heavy guard, a slab of silver forming a cross with the corroded blade.

"What is it, my lord?" Aleyn asked.

"It is some sort of writing, though I cannot make sense of it. But this much I do vouch. I believe it to be a message sent to me o'er the ages from the great and mighty Arthur, King of the Britons."

13

Over breakfast Claire sipped at her coffee and said, "I was thinking in the shower."

Arthur put down his newspaper, smiling at the image.

"It seems to me that one should always start with the simple and progress to the complex," she continued. "It's a good approach for math, it's a good approach for physics; it's probably a good approach for this too. The simpler of the two documents is the preface. The book is a bit like a nightmare."

"All right, I'll go with that," he said. "Let's start with the basic facts. We have every indication that the printer, William Caxton, wrote the bits about putting King Arthur into a grand historical perspective. The part we know Thomas Malory wrote relates to the peculiar laundry list of books and chapters." He referred to his notes. "The last sentence of the preface says, 'The sum is twenty-one books which contain the sum of five hundred and seven chapters, as more plainly shall follow hereafter.' So if there's a clue that links to something in the *Domesday Book*, we have twenty-one books and five hundred and seven chapters to sift through. How the hell do we know where to start?"

Claire stood up and began pacing, sending a drift of perfume through the room. "Once again I'd come back to the principle of simplicity. Instead of dealing with this entire book maybe we should see which of the twenty-one books concern themselves with King

Arthur's sword. Then, which is the most important book—and when we think we know this we have a number. Then we see which *chapter* is the most important in the book, and we have another number. Then maybe we can take these numbers and apply them to the *Domesday Book*, which is a book of numbers." She opened the *Domesday Book* to a random page, "Like here, this village has twenty plows and thirteen villans and eight bordars, whatever these things are."

Arthur nodded in agreement. "I think you're onto something. It's always been a sore point at my company but maybe physicists *are* smarter than chemists."

She delivered an insouciant Gallic shrug. "Of course. This isn't in question."

It was pointless to wait for a declaration that she was joking because clearly she wasn't. He let it pass. He'd dealt with physicists for years.

He opened *Le Morte* and turned to the preface. "All right, let's do it," he said. "Let me see which books deal with the sword."

After a while he made a face.

"What?"

"None of them. Malory doesn't mention Excalibur in the preface at all."

"But it's talked about in the book, no?"

"All over it. Dozens of mentions, probably. But not in the preface. I can do an online search and find each book and chapter where Excalibur is mentioned if you think it'll be helpful."

"I don't think so. At least not now. That would violate our principle of simplicity."

"Okay …" He looked to her for their next move but he beat her to an idea. "We're looking for the sword but the sword is only a means to an end. What we're really seeking is the Grail."

She pointed at him with a playful smile. "So, chemists can be reasonably clever too. See what the preface says about the Grail."

In a short while he had the answer. "This is more promising. Listen to this: 'the thirteenth book treateth how Galahad came first to King Arthur's court and how the quest for the Sangreal was begun and containeth twenty chapters. The fourteenth book treateth of the quest of the Sangreal and containeth ten chapters. The seventeenth book treateth of the Sangreal and containeth twenty-three chapters.'"

"That's it?" she asked. "In the preface he talks about the Grail in just three books?"

"I think it's mentioned all over the place but it's the main subject of these three books, yeah."

She asked for his pen and a pad and had him repeat the relevant numbers. "Okay, assuming we're on the correct path we've got three pairs of numbers to look at, three sets of book and chapter numbers. It's thirteen and twenty, fourteen and ten, and seventeen and twenty-three."

"But that's too complicated, according to your hypothesis," he said.

"Yes, so I'd ask you to tell me which pairing is the most important."

"How can I do that?"

"For the Grail, which book is the most important one?"

"I'm going to have to read them again."

"Okay. You read and I'll make some calls to my parents in the lobby. Then maybe take a little walk in the garden."

"Where do they live?"

"Toulouse. My mother and father like to hear from me. I'm an only child."

"I was too," Arthur said.

When she returned he shot her a thumbs-up. He'd made progress. By way of context he explained that in the Arthurian tradition multiple knights had sought the Grail. Five of them—Percival, Gawain, Bors, Lancelot, and Galahad—achieved some sort of mystical vision of the Grail. Three of them—Percival, Bors, and Galahad—actually attained true sight of the holy object.

Thomas Malory in *Le Morte* had highlighted Galahad's quest. Galahad was the illegitimate son of Lancelot and by all accounts was the better of his father in valor and piousness. When he was reunited with his father, Lancelot brought him to Camelot where he was taken to the Round Table and bade to sit at the Siege Perilous, an unused chair kept vacant for the only person capable of succeeding in a Grail quest. Yet anyone who sat in the chair not worthy of the quest died instantly. Galahad survived the test and King Arthur, much impressed, gave him another test. As Arthur had become king after removing a sword from a stone, likewise Galahad became the greatest knight of the Round Table by removing a sword from a stone in a nearby river. Soon afterward Arthur set Galahad on his Grail quest.

Although Galahad set off on his own, smiting enemies along the way, he was reunited with Sir Bors and Sir Percival. Percival's sister showed them the way to a Grail ship that took them to a distant shore. Percival, Bors, and Galahad pressed on and eventually found their way to the court of the holiest of rulers, King Pelles, who was the keeper of the Sangreal. In a room in the castle Galahad was allowed to see the Grail and was asked to take it to the holy city of Sarras. He was so overcome by the heavenly splendor of the chalice, however, that Galahad asked the holy king if he might die at the time of his choosing; and in Sarras, after an ethereal visit by Joseph of Arimathea, Galahad was overcome with rapture and there he made his request to die, and it was granted. Witnessed by Bors and Percival, Galahad was carried to heaven by angels and the Grail disappeared with him, never to be seen again by man.

"Book thirteen describes the beginning of Galahad's quest," Arthur elaborated. "Book fourteen, despite Malory's preface, has very little to do with the quest. Book seventeen is the other meaty one. This is where Galahad finds the Grail and dies."

Claire retrieved the notepad and crossed out the middle pair of numbers. "So it's two pairs of numbers to consider: thirteen and twenty, and seventeen and twenty-three."

"Still too complicated?" he asked.

"I think so. It should be only one pair. Which is more important to a story, the beginning or the end?"

"You can't have one without the other."

"Here's the way I see it," Claire began. "One of the pairs is important, the other one is irrelevant. Either way, I think this may be a simple chain of numbers. The first number points to the second number, the second to a third. If you want to call it a code, it's a very primitive one."

"So let me understand what you're suggesting. The book number leads to a chapter number and the chapter number leads … where? There's no third number."

She picked up the *Domesday Book*. "Here. This is where it has to lead. Malory says so in his letter. The sword can be found in the preface, taking into consideration the green acres of Warwickshire as written in the *Domesday Book*. Something like that, no?"

"Close enough."

"So either the number twenty or the number twenty-three is our key. We don't know which so we'll have to follow both of them into the pages of the *Domesday Book*." She opened it to the back cover and sighed. "All fourteen hundred and thirty-six pages of it."

In the last light of a warm and windless day Lake Geneva looked still and purple like a sheet of Murano glass. On the second floor of a grand building on the Quai du Mont-Blanc, a group of men sat in a semicircle of club chairs positioned to take in the water view over the pollarded London Plane trees lining the avenue. It was a private room in a private club and they waited for the tuxedoed server to hand out their cocktails and leave before speaking of anything but the weather.

When the nine were alone, all eyes turned to their leader, if a somewhat rudderless group such as this could be said to have a leader. He lifted a glass of wine by the stem and said, "Gentlemen, a toast."

Their response wasn't in unison. They weren't a disciplined and drilled lot. But they managed a scruffy reply, "To the Khem."

"To the Khem," the man said.

Stanley Engel wasn't a drinker. The rumpled academic from the University of California at Santa Barbara vigorously stirred the ice in his ginger ale with a swizzle stick and piped up, "So tell me why I had to schlep over here?"

"It was encouraged, Stanley," the man said. "None of this is mandatory. As you can see, some weren't able to come."

"I'm a team player," Engel said, but his colleagues weren't buying it.

"Since when?" Raj Chatterjee asked, his bushy eyebrows rising. "Even when you're my bridge partner I have the feeling you're playing against me."

Andris Somogyi, thin in a vested suit the color of his gray hair, didn't join in the levity. He was the oldest, in his eighties, and he had been the one who had championed this putative leader. "None of us are team players. It is not in our nature as individualists. We are in this group because we believe it is important to do so and we all have a sense of purpose arising from history."

"Well put, Andris," the man said. "It's a good message for our newest member to hear." He was looking directly at Simone Guastella, the youngest in the room by a decade. "How long did it take you to get here from Modane, Simone?"

"Only two hours by car, sir."

"He's so new he still calls me sir."

Simone gave a tight-lipped smile and nodded. "Sorry. I'm just happy to be here."

Li Peng, a bespectacled man in his forties, had come farthest, from Taiwan. "And I'm happy I'm no longer the new boy."

"Well, that makes me an old boy," the man said. "Simone's been fully vetted and fully indoctrinated by myself and others in the room. Choosing a new member is always a tricky business but it's nothing that hasn't happened many, many times before. Khem have dealt with ensuring the organization's perpetuity for over two thousand years. Bad choices were made in the past—men who were indiscreet and unreliable—and those men were dealt with harshly and permanently. Fortunately, there have been no transgressions in the modern era and I'm certain that given Simone's stellar sponsorship, he will keep our traditions proudly moving forward."

There were murmurs of assent around the semicircle.

"I'll do my best," Simone said soberly.

"Now as all of you know, everyone here shares two passions," he said. "We are all scientists and we are all seekers of the Grail. Our knowledge of the Grail comes to us through oral history which, as you know, can be fraught with distortions and inaccuracies. But our oral historians, the Khem who came before us, were not ordinary men as we are not ordinary men. They were the clearest thinkers and greatest scientific minds of their generations in a golden chain going all the way back to Nehor. First came alchemists. Then chemists. Now physicists. A logical evolution.

"As science and mathematics have evolved so has our understanding and beliefs of the unique properties of the Grail. When—not *if* but *when*—we find it we will be in the best position to study it, exploit it, and harness its potentially vast power. And after two millennia of search I believe we are the closest we have ever been to finding it. That's why I asked you to come here in person. This is not the kind of topic one discusses via e-mails or phone calls or Skype. I want to brief you on what we know about a man we have talked about briefly in the past, Arthur Malory."

"He's in the Loons, right?" Engel said. "The guy who may be related to Thomas Malory?"

"Correct," the man answered.

"We didn't have anything to do with Andrew Holmes's death, did we?" Peng asked.

"I'm afraid we did. It was an operation that went wrong. It arose from our routine phone-bugging of the Loons and a burglary I initiated to obtain certain interesting documents. It's on me." The man ignored the looks of concern that flashed among the assembly and carried on before he could be interrupted. "I want to tell you what we have done to date with Malory. Warts and all. And I want to discuss various scenarios. Should Malory succeed in finding the Grail, as I hope he will, we will need to be ready, willing, and able to take it from him."

"And then do what with Malory?" Engel asked.

"We would deal with him in an appropriate way," the man answered. "Then toast his memory with some good champagne." He smiled broadly at his own thought. "Perhaps we would even make him a Khem. Posthumously."

14

ENGLAND, 1451

On the journey back to Newbold Revel Malory carried the sword tucked in his saddle pack, slept with it under his blanket, and unwrapped it each morning before the others rose so he could study the indecipherable language on its hilt. He ran his finger over the incised letters and pronounced the strange words as if doing so would unlock their meaning. There was only one word he could understand and that was the most tantalizing of them all.

Gral.

None of his fellow travelers had a facility with ancient languages, of course, and he could hardly trust Cornish strangers. So the rest of the message remained elusive. Yet he had succeeded in the greatest part of the challenge: finding the sword. Learning the meaning of the inscription would come. Then, perhaps, so would the Grail.

He endeavored to keep his return to Newbold Revel understated, with no feasts or celebrations. He dismissed the squires with coin for their service and their silence, clapped John Aleyn on the back, permitting him to return to the solitude of his cottage, and invited Robert Malory for an intimate dinner much to the chagrin of both their waiting wives.

Over a steaming plate of lamb and turnips Malory told his cousin, "Thank you for your support, Robert. We have achieved a great prize."

"What will you do now, coz?" Robert asked.

"I must find a man who knows the language of King Arthur. Without that I have a relic and nothing else. Without that I cannot find the Grail."

"Any notions who this man may be?"

"I will consult some learned friends—discreetly, of course."

"Of course."

Malory wagged his dagger at Robert. The chunk of lamb skewered on the tip made the gesture less threatening than pointing naked steel. "And it goes without saying that I can be assured of your absolute discretion."

"It does go without your saying, Thomas. I will refrain even from uttering a word to my good wife in our bedchamber where I intend to retire presently, having had my fill of male company. Tell me, coz, where will you keep the sword?"

Malory frowned at the question. "Somewhere safe."

Robert lifted his ale and buried his face in the goblet. His lips wet with drink, he speared a turnip and added to his cousin's cagey reply, "A great treasure demands a great hiding place."

Coombe Abbey, the large Cistercian monastery in Warwickshire, possessed substantial land holdings abutting Thomas Malory's estate. Malory had always maintained cordial relations with the abbot of Coombe, Richard Atherstone, a priest as much businessman as man of God. There was brisk commerce in livestock and produce between Newbold Revel and Coombe, and the cellars of Malory's estate were filled with ale, wine, and mead crafted by the monks. There was a good library at the monastery and several scholarly clergymen employed in the scriptorium; and for that reason and one other, Malory rode alone through his forest and crossed the Smite Brook onto abbey land.

He was met by a young monk outside the abbot house who took the reins of his horse and offered to watch over the corded iron chest tied to the saddle.

"I will take that myself," Malory said.

Atherstone was dressed in an ermine-trimmed cloak reading accounts at his desk. At the announcement of Malory's arrival he sprang up and bounded over to greet his neighbor.

"Ah, Sir Thomas! You've returned home, hale and hearty I see."

"It was neither a long trip nor an arduous one—at least not compared to my last campaign in Normandy."

"Come, sit. Drink with me. I've a new wine I'd have you sample. If you like it, I can give you a very good price on a barrel or two. Or three!"

Atherstone was portly with a fine head of hair for a man of his age and a neatly tonsured circle of pink scalp at the crown. He personally poured the wine from a fine silver decanter and watched for Malory's reaction.

"I *will* have a barrel," Malory said, approvingly.

"Excellent! Tell me how I can assist you, Sir Thomas."

"Are there any monks in your service who can read the ancient Cornish writings?"

"Cornish, you say?"

"Aye."

The abbot closed his eyes and mumbled various names, dismissing each with a *no* or a grunt. "No. I'm quite certain no one here possesses this facility. Why do you ask?"

"I have a brief passage whose meaning I need to know."

"What is this passage? Can you show me?"

Malory shook his head. "No, but I'll speak it." He said the words that he had committed to memory by uttering them so many times.

Atherstone shrugged. "Means nothing to me. A guttural tongue if ever I heard one. If it were Latin or Greek or Hebrew—or even Gaelic, as we have Brother Bruno from Ireland—then we could assist you. Alas …"

"I'll look elsewhere then," Malory said. "Could you do something else for me?"

Atherstone opened his arms in a gesture of yes.

Malory pointed to the chest at his feet, which the abbot had been glancing at throughout their conversation. "Could you take this chest and keep it safe?"

"May I ask what it contains?"

Malory smiled diplomatically. "One day I hope to tell you."

"I've heard a rumor, Sir Thomas. One must always discount the value of a rumor but it comes from a man close to Buckingham."

Malory bristled. "Which man? What did he say?"

"I cannot in good conscience reveal him but he suggested he had heard that on your travels of late you recovered a relic of old. Something which may have belonged to a king."

Malory rose and spat vehemently, "I have nothing to say on this but the hearing of it redoubles my notion of keeping my valuables at a distance from Newbold Revel. Will you take my chest into your possession for safekeeping or will you not?"

Atherstone rose too and waved his hands in conciliation. "Of course, Sir Thomas, of course! I will place it in my privy chamber inside my own chest of valuables. I see there is a lock."

"And I have the only key," Malory said. "You must tell no one of this."

"I swear to you before God that I will not. You can trust me absolutely to do your bidding."

Malory bowed his head. "Thank you, your grace. On reflection, perhaps I will take three barrels of your wine."

Malory returned to his estate riding slowly through the verdant forest, the sound of humming insects in his ears and venom in his mind.

Who is the traitor?

It certainly could not be John Aleyn—as loyal a man as could be, he'd stake his life on it. Likewise, his squire was the son of a comrade-in-arms from the old Normandy campaigns and he implicitly trusted the lad's innocence. What of his cousin's squire? A possibility, he supposed, but what access would such a youth have to Buckingham's camp? And would he risk his life for a traitorous act? He thought not.

That left Robert.

His cousin was not Malory's sort of man. He was wanting in courage and valor and fortitude, traits which any knight would value more than any other in one's estimation of character. But he was blood. And blood didn't sell out blood. He had trusted him enough to bring him on the expedition. Had his trust been misplaced?

The answer came soon enough.

That night, while Malory sat drinking by the fire, his sleek dogs lounging at his chair, John Aleyn came to the manor house.

"Sorry to bother you at the late hour, my lord."

Malory poured him some strong ale. "I have not seen you of late."

"Been to Coventry."

"Oh yes?"

"Whoring and drinking for the best part of the week. At the Blue Boar."

"Well-deserved after our journey, I would say. Absent obligations I reckon I would have done the same."

"I saw something there."

"I am quite sure you saw many things."

"I saw your cousin, Robert."

Malory stiffened. "And what was he doing there?"

"He was meeting up with a man. I saw him but he did not see me. The fellow was someone I have seen before. Richard Humphrey, he was, one of Buckingham's men."

"I know him, a brigand, no better than shyte on your boot. Could you hear what they were saying?"

"Not a word, but I saw your cousin waving his right arm about as if he had a sword in his hand."

Malory exhaled in sadness and anger. He could almost hear Robert, drunk on ale, sweating like a pig, bragging about finding King Arthur's sword as he pantomimed brandishing Excalibur in his warm chubby hand.

Soon afterwards Malory rode south with a small entourage, leaving John Aleyn at Newbold Revel to be his eyes and ears at the estate and protect his interests. There was urgent political business at Parliament and urgent personal business at Winchester. As it happened there was a connection between the two enterprises in the form of William Waynflete, bishop of Winchester.

Waynflete, one of the most learned men in England, had met Malory a decade earlier in Windsor in a meeting arranged by Thomas Welles, a gentleman who managed Waynflete's episcopal estates. Welles, an acquaintance of Malory, thought that Waynflete, then headmaster of Winchester College, would enjoy Malory's company and he had been correct. Though not a scholar, Malory impressed Waynflete with his keen mind, political savvy and his righteous character, which the headmaster believed was a perfect embodiment of the best of the code of chivalry. Through Waynflete's influence, Malory was named as a member of Parliament for Great Bedwyn, a wool town 80 miles from Newbold Revel, with a seat that Waynflete happened to control. A decade later the two men remained close, allied by a common desire to serve an increasingly unstable King Henry VI to their utmost.

Malory spent less under a fortnight in Westminster participating in a fractious parliamentary debate on allocating funds to assist in the defense of Bordeaux, one of the last French towns loyal to the English. Parliament was dismissed, however, following an explosive proposal by a loyalist that the duke of York be recognized as the heir to the throne after the king's five childless years of marriage.

Malory, disgusted by Parliament's inability to support the stranded English troops, happily left his rooms in Whitechapel for the journey to Winchester.

William Waynflete was a man of great physical as well as mental stature. He greeted his old friend Malory with a bear hug, almost lifting him off the ground, then treated him to a lavish feast accompanied by some of the finest wine Malory had tasted since his days in Paris.

Over a platter of venison chops they caught up on the intrigues between the Yorkists and the Crown until Waynflete changed the subject.

"You know, Thomas, I have a treat for you. I have secured the loan of the most important nonecclesiastical book in England. The

Domesday Book. I petitioned the Crown to return it to its original home in Winchester on the occasion of the three-hundredth year since it was removed from the old royal treasury in the city on the orders of King Henry II and taken to Westminster Palace. It is being kept at the college for the tutors to study and the pupils to marvel at. Would you like to see it?"

"I would indeed, your grace. It would be a marvelous thing to behold."

"Tomorrow then. Now, enough of my concerns. You said you wished my help with a matter."

"I do, your grace. I seek a learned man who can read the ancient Cornish writing."

"I sense you have a marvelous tale behind this request, Thomas, and I am most anxious to hear it."

"It is a marvelous tale, your grace, and you shall be the only man beside myself who knows the full extent of it."

The *Domesday Book* was on display within the Master's Library at Winchester College. It was surely the most prodigious book Malory had ever seen, so great, in fact, he was dubious its pedestal could reliably bear its weight. After a small discourse on its history and import, the master of the college, William Yve, a rodentine fellow in an overly long robe once having belonged to a predecessor but never altered, assisted Malory in finding the section of his home shire and with a brief lesson on deciphering the black and red text.

"Did the scribes write in code?" Malory asked.

"Not code; they employed a method of shortening the words to fit more on each sheet. Otherwise the book would be even more unwieldy than it is."

When the headmaster had finished the lesson he left Malory alone with the great book, informing him that the linguist the bishop had requested would be arriving before too long.

As Malory thumbed through the parchments, which were surprisingly supple for their antiquity, the words his friend Waynflete had uttered to him the previous night came back to him. "Keep your secret close, Thomas. If anyone with a black heart were to learn of your royal lineage and the clue you possess to the Grail carved upon that sword, then your life would surely be in grave danger. *You* may trust the abbot of Coombe Abbey but I have met him and I do not. The riches he has amassed are well beyond the needs of his community and a cleric who cares more for gold than for God rouses my suspicions. Find a better place to hide the sword: that is my advice."

A notion began to take shape in Malory's head.

The list of towns and villages of Warwickshire contained in the pages of the *Domesday Book* whet his memory of the haunts of his youth. Though the words before him were dry recitations and ledgers of commerce, many of the places evoked pleasant memories of wenching, drinking, fairs, and jousting.

One particular village caught his eye and he read and reread its account with fascination, committing the entry to memory. Shortly thereafter, a man entered and announced himself as John Harmar, the scholar commanded by the bishop to assist the visiting knight.

Harmar was young, with the smooth skin of a boy and no eyebrows. Malory surmised he was one of those rare hairless men who would survive better teaching school than soldiering among hirsute warriors.

"The bishop sent word you required a man with an aptitude in old Cornish," Harmar said, his hands clasped at his waist.

"I do. I have a short passage I wish to understand."

"May I see it?"

"I did not travel with the text. I can say it for you." He spoke the words as slowly and carefully as he could.

Harmar furrowed his brow and sat at one of the library tables nearby. From his shoulder bag he removed a quire of blank parchment, a quill, and a small pot of ink.

"My lord, please say the words again."

He wrote down what he heard and showed it to Malory and asked him if the words matched the ones he had seen. Malory thought there was a close resemblance.

"Can you make sense of it?" Malory asked.

"Indeed I can, my lord. It is a strange instruction, wholly obtuse to me but perhaps it will be meaningful to you."

On his return to Newbold Revel Malory hardly had time to reunite with his wife when John Aleyn announced he had urgent business with his master. A spy at Coombe Abbey, a young monk who worked in the brewery and the son of Malory's loyal butcher, reported that two days earlier he witnessed a meeting between the abbot and one of Buckingham's men, who placed a heavy purse in his palm.

"He's sold us out, John," Malory said, his face drooping with the weariness of a traveler who had hoped for expected rest.

"There is more, my lord," Aleyn said. "Word spreads that Buckingham has procured a warrant for your arrest. I had it best from a bailiff in the employ of Sheriff Mountfort."

"A warrant? On what charges?" Malory bellowed.

"Diverse, I hear. Remember that skirmish last year with Buckingham in the Coombe woods? He claims you assaulted his men."

"Me? It was he who was preparing an assault on the manor!"

"You are also to be charged with the theft of livestock from Coswold."

"For the love of Christ! I delivered six cows to Giles Dowde and he never paid me for them. All I did was to reclaim my property."

Aleyn hung his head. "And there is to be one other charge."

"Go on …"

"They are saying you raped Joan Smyth."

Malory collapsed onto a chair. He had saved her and in gratitude and lust she had slept with him. Now the foolish act was coming to haunt him. Rape! Was there a worse charge to sully the name of a knight of the realm?

A footman knocked and entered bearing a letter. "My lord, this arrived with a rider from Coombe Abbey."

Malory seized the letter and ripped off the wax seal. When he had read it he tossed it upon the floor in disgust.

"It is from the abbot." Malory grimaced. "He informs me that hearing I am an accused criminal, he took it upon himself to break into my chest. He suspects Buckingham will pay handsomely for it. He wants to know if I will pay more."

"The bastard," Aleyn spat.

"Where is my cousin?" Malory asked, pushing himself up from the chair.

"He left the estate while you were in the south."

"By God, I will find him and I will kill him with my own hand. But more pressing matters first: saddle my horse and yours. We must be off to the abbey."

Aleyn was cinching the saddle of Malory's steed when men approached, riding hard. Aleyn swore and called furiously for his lord and when Malory appeared with a small coterie of household men he and Aleyn exchanged glances and fingered the hilts of their swords. Then Malory shook his head. It was pointless to die in battle over an arrest warrant. His mission was to live to find the Grail.

"Stand down, men," Malory commanded. "Sheriff Mountfort is not our enemy. I will yield to him."

Mountfort rode at the head of his column of sword- and pikemen, an elderly gentleman kitted out for battle, stiff in the saddle with the plaintive look of someone reluctantly doing his sworn duty.

The old man spoke from his horse. "Sir Thomas Malory, I arrest you in the name of the Crown for diverse serious charges relating to your conduct. You will leave your sword and dagger behind and come with me."

Malory turned to Lady Malory, who was weeping at the doorway, hugged her and told her it was a trifle and promised her he would return in a paternoster while. Then he mounted his horse and sidled up to Mountfort, an old family friend.

"I am sorry," the man said. "Buckingham is behind this."

"Be assured, I do not fault you," Malory replied.

"He wanted you to be taken to his castle at Maxstoke or the jail in Coventry but I am taking you to my house in Coleshill. You will be most comfortable there while you await your appearance at court."

Malory thanked him and received permission to have a word with his man. He instructed John Aleyn to journey to Coombe Abbey and to inform the abbot that he was prepared to pay whatever he asked for the chest. Then he tugged at his horse's reins and rode off with the sheriff as a prisoner.

Malory had visited the moated manor house at Coleshill many times and on this occasion Mountfort accorded him the same hospitality. His room was large and comfortable, a manservant attended him, and his first night he ate at the sheriff's table while the sheriff's own men camped rough beside the barn.

While the household slept Malory did not.

His door was unlocked and he only had to tiptoe down the corridor, past the sheriff's own bedchamber and down the back stairs to the pantry. He slipped out a back door and crept around the house to a point farthest away from the barn.

The moat looked like a black void. He pulled off his boots and threw them across, unhappy with the thuds they made, but when no one sounded an alarm he slowly settled himself into the cold water and swam across with a quiet breaststroke. His boots retrieved, he made his way across a field into the forest.

A rider was coming. Malory crouched low behind a large tree and waited until the horse passed him by. By the light of the rider's torch he saw it was friend, not foe.

"Here!" he whispered loudly.

John Aleyn turned the horse and smiled down at him.

"You said you'd be back in a paternoster while. Takes you a good while to say the Lord's prayer, I see. I have a horse for you a short way from here."

"Bless you, John. Let's get the men assembled and ride to Coombe."

After a tumultuous and sleepless night, Malory rode alone over wild countryside as far from the traveled roads and lanes as he could. The raid on Coombe Abbey had been swift and loud. In the dead of night, Malory's men battered down the gates and doors of the monastery with wooden rams. Once inside they made their way to the abbot house where the abbot was rudely rousted from his bed and his toad of a prior was kicked in the arse a few times. Malory personally used a pry bar to thwart the lock on the abbot's treasure chest and retrieved his own strongbox. He left it to his men to decide if they wanted any of the abbot's loot and of course they did, helping themselves to gold and silver rings, bracelets and necklaces of coral, amber and jet. With a snort Malory reckoned that none of these pieces were essential to the service of God.

It was a fine morning and butterflies passed close by his face. He made good time to his destination, his iron chest wrapped in a blanket to stop it abrading the horse's hindquarters. In Winchester, while immersed in the *Domesday Book*, a better hiding spot had come to his mind, wholly fitting the sword's valiant history. In the French prose poems that Malory knew so well, King Arthur, mortally wounded in battle, bade his knight, Sir Griflet, to return Excalibur to the Lady of the Lake. Malory would do the same. He knew of a water source, a lovely place where he had frolicked and fished as a youth. It was broad but not so deep. The sword could lie undisturbed there until it was safe for him to reclaim it.

And when he arrived at the beautiful, isolated spot, full of wildlife but free of men, Malory wept, as Griflet must have done, when he flung the chest into the murky water.

Now he was in prison again—a proper prison this time, with iron bars and few comforts.

When Malory returned to Newbold Revel, Buckingham had been personally waiting for him with a party of two hundred armed men.

Malory then was taken to the Priory of Nuneaton, a short distance from Buckingham's Maxstoke Castle, where justices and jurymen were summoned by the duke to effect his indictment on the very charges that John Aleyn had heard were forthcoming.

After brief and stormy proceedings in which Lady Malory wept and Sir Thomas shouted his innocence, branding the charges as preposterous, Malory was taken to a disused nun's cell converted for his benefit into a temporary jail. A key rattled in the door and in came Buckingham, fat and smug.

"I have you where I want you, Malory," he said.

Malory stayed seated on the mattress. "And where is that, my lord?"

"At a disadvantage."

"For the moment, perhaps. What is it you want? Surely these ridiculous charges were meant to serve some larger purpose."

"I want something you have. I want it badly."

"My manly physique? Perhaps you should ride more?"

"You are in no position to make jests. I want the sword. I want the Grail."

"Through the ages many men have sought the Grail, Sir Humphrey. For them it has been a holy quest to honor the greatness of God. Yet I fear your interests are not so pure and spiritual."

"My reasons are not for your ear. They are for me and my associates."

"Your associates? Some unholy cabal, I should think."

Buckingham ignored him. "If you tell me where you secreted the sword, the charges will be dropped. If you do not, you can expect to spend a very long time in prison serving at the pleasure of His Majesty."

Malory shook his head and lay down facing the opposite wall. "I will fight your charges and if I lose, I will serve my time in jail honorably. What I will never do is let you get your greasy hands on that noble relic."

Malory was remanded to London to stand charges at a Crown Court and found himself in the custody of the Marshal of the King's

Bench and locked away in Marshalsea Prison. It was a rank, pitiless prison but as a knight Malory was afforded a level of accommodation not available to the general population. He had a room with a window and ample candles. Family and friends could visit freely and his good wife had already made the journey to London to see to his well-being. His servants from Newbold Revel had delivered a cart loaded with furnishings, plates, a cask of wine and, most importantly as far as he was concerned, ink, quills, parchment, and a crate of books, his collection of Arthurian tales.

As he settled into what would turn out to be almost two decades in prison for crimes he did not commit, Malory was visited in Marshalsea by his faithful ally, John Aleyn, who shed tears at the sight of his master in captivity.

"I am glad you came again, John."

"I would change places with you, my lord."

Malory went to the door and peered through the barred window. "They let you enter without a toady to accompany you inside."

"I did as you said, my lord, and bought along a small cask of wine. They set upon it like flies to dung."

Malory smiled. "I need you to be my eyes, my ears, and on occasion my voice to the world outside these prison walls. I want you to keep close to those who know Buckingham's affairs and favor my plight. I want to know of his associates—not the usual ones at court, but others who might have an interest in the sword. I desperately need to know who these men are and what their intentions."

"Surely no one can find the sword. You alone know where you hid it."

"And that is why I can sleep peacefully at night, even in such a place as this. When my day of freedom arrives I will use the knowledge the sword holds to find a much greater treasure."

"What treasure is this?"

"A spiritual one, John, worth more than all the silver and gold in the realm. One day I hope to tell you. Perhaps we will go on the quest together. For now, I have a letter I would have you send to Waynflete, bishop of Winchester. It is most sensitive in nature. Show it to no one. Do they search you when you leave me?"

"They do."

"Do they make you strip off your garments?"

Aleyn shook his head. "If they did, they would have to hold their noses."

"Good. I will fold it well. Place it behind your man sack."

Aleyn snorted. "Twin sentries."

"Do not take it from here to Winchester directly. I would not have you followed and Waynflete brought into this affair. I know it is circuitous but return to Newbold Revel first and sally forth from there at night. If something prevents you from delivering it, burn it or hide it somewhere safe, as it must not fall into Buckingham's hands. Do you understand my instructions?"

Aleyn took the folded letter and tucked it into his trousers. "I do, my lord. Have faith in me as I have faith in you."

The two men hugged.

Aleyn noticed a small stack of parchments on Malory's writing desk.

"You have been writing something, my lord."

"Indeed I have, John. I feel that God intended me to be freed for a time from my household and parliamentary duties so I could accomplish something more important. I have started a book, a grand book I am calling *Le Morte Darthur*, my own telling of the life and death of Arthur, the greatest king this land has ever known."

15

Arthur and Claire spent the entire day poring over the *Domesday Book*. They broke for meals in the restaurant and walks in the garden until another day had passed and they were punch-drunk with mind-numbing statistics.

Claire went into the bathroom to brush her teeth.

"Can you stay longer?" he asked through the door.

"It's difficult," she said. "I have to go back to work soon."

"I think we're making progress."

"Yes, maybe; we'll see how we do tomorrow."

She emerged in her nightgown and got into her bed, turning to face him in his.

"The past two days have been surreal," he said, lying on his side, his head propped in his hand.

"Yes, not ordinary days, for sure."

"Hiding in a hotel, working on a five-hundred-year-old puzzle."

"I have to say, it appeals to me intellectually. It's very different from my usual work. It's quite romantic."

"I've been feeling guilty."

"Why?"

"I don't want you to get hurt."

"That's very sweet. But I feel very comfortable with you. Very safe."

She switched off her bedside light. He thought about going to her but resisted. The last thing he wanted was to tip the scales and drive her away. So he turned his pillow to the cool side and went to sleep.

In the morning Arthur awoke first and had a sly look at Claire's bed. She was partly under the sheets with a long bare leg showing.

As quietly as he could, he loaded grounds into the room's coffeemaker and sat watching the carafe slowly fill with steamy liquid, drip by drip.

At once he was struck by a glimmer of clarity that had eluded him during the long preceding day.

Claire awoke to see him rapidly paging through the *Domesday* text.

"You're already at it," she said.

Arthur looked up, excited. "It came to me, Claire. Your principle of simplicity. Malory was a Warwickshire man. He specifically mentions Warwickshire in the letter. I think we can filter out over ninety percent of the book. We only have to concentrate on one county. So we should keep going along the lines of yesterday, looking for mentions of the numbers twenty or twenty-three."

She caught his excitement and sat up in bed. "Didn't he use the word *acre* with Warwickshire?" she asked, recalling it now. "The *green acres* of Warwickshire? Maybe we need to find the village with either twenty or twenty-three acres of land."

They poured themselves coffee and she joined him on his rumpled bed so they could read the text together. If he weren't so focused on the book, the sight of her bare legs and arms might have derailed him. He opened the book to the first page in the Warwickshire section and both furiously began to scan the dense text. It was like a race. Arthur could tell from her laser-like squint and coiled posture that she was competitive—and she confirmed his suspicion by triumphantly calling out, "Here! This place has twenty acres!" She was pointing at the village of Harborough, where, it was written, *There are 4 ½ hides. There is land for as many ploughs. There are 4 villans and 4 bordars with 1 plough. There are 20 acres of meadow.* "This could be the hiding place. Do you have a map?"

"Hold on," Arthur said. "Here's another one with twenty acres of meadow."

On the very next page were three more villages that fit the bill: Leamington Hastings, Mollington, and Binton; and in time they had added Newnham Paddox, Wolverton, Oxhill, Weddington, Hodnell, Nuneaton, and Stoneleigh to the list—a total of eleven towns and villages in Warwickshire with twenty acres of meadowland. Yet there was only a single village with twenty-three acres of meadows: Stretton-on-Fosse.

"So it's quite clear," Claire said. "If our hypothesis is valid, then Thomas Malory must be pointing with the number twenty-three to Stretton-on-Fosse. It's a very clean result, unlike the twenties."

Arthur went online to get a Warwickshire map and frowned at Stretton-on-Fosse. "I don't know. It's quite a bit south of Malory's home in Newbold Revel." After a quick online search on the village he added, "And it's never had a significant manor house or castle, so he wouldn't have had a noble connection to the area."

"It's speculation, no? How can you be sure of that?"

"I can't." He studied the list of places and picked up the parchment again. "You know, I think we're missing something just keying in on twenty or twenty-three acres. There's another phrase here that's peculiar, maybe intentionally so. Remember, he writes that the sword can be found within the preface, and I quote, in companionship with the tale itself provided one is *as mindful as priests who mind the Sacraments* of the green acres of Warwickshire. As mindful as priests. Why is he saying that? It's an unnecessary embellishment. What is it about priests?"

She grabbed the book from his lap, brushing his crotch with an apologetic giggle. "Yes! Remember this? In Leamington Hastings, in addition to the twenty acres of meadows it's written there are fifteen slaves, thirty-three villans and a priest! So we have to see if this is the only one which satisfies both conditions."

She reread the twelve flagged locations out loud, raising her voice for emphasis on Stretton-on-Fosse again, as there was also a priest in that village; then nothing until the last village, Stoneleigh—where again she raised her voice. "This one had two priests."

Arthur mapped out Leamington Hastings and Stoneleigh while Claire insisted that all signs pointed to Stretton-on-Fosse. "Leamington's also not very close to Malory's home but at least it's on the way to London," he observed, "and we know he was a member of Parliament so it might have been on a familiar route. Stoneleigh is closer, just south of Coventry, more his stomping grounds." He did another search and declared, "There was a significant Cistercian Abbey there in the fifteenth century, which is interesting."

Claire rose to stretch her legs. "Look, we could be completely wrong with the entire premise but if we're on the correct path, there are three possibilities: Stoneleigh, Leamington Hastings, and Stretton-on-Fosse, which is my favorite. How do we narrow the search? I mean, even if we knew that one of these was the place Malory meant, where would we look? These are entire villages!"

They took a stroll before breakfast. It was cloudy and when they were at the farthest point on the grounds the skies opened with remarkable ferocity, soaking them as effectively as if someone had sprayed them with a garden hose at arm's length. Laughing like school kids, they ran back to their room and, dripping wet, shucked their coats and kicked off their shoes.

"I've got to change," she said, working the top button of her blouse and moving toward the closet.

He followed her, unbuttoning his shirt and she suddenly turned to face him. He kissed her—tentatively at first, to see how she would react, then harder when he could tell she was willing. They moved in lockstep onto her unmade bed and in a succession of unbuttonings, undrapings, and unclaspings they were naked.

Everything seemed right about her—her smell, her taste, her small murmurs, her beautiful body; and when they were done, gasping at the unexpectedness of it all, she seemed as happy as he was.

He had no idea why the thought came to him just then but with a hurried apology he reached for his laptop and one of the parchments.

She didn't seem at all upset by his postcoital manners and pulled back the covers so both of them could get under the sheets.

"That was amazing, by the way," he said, "but we missed this. I missed it." He pointed to a section in the parchment. "It's this part: the sword can be found *in companionship with the tale itself.* That's got to be the other critical part to finding the sword."

She put her hand on his chest, as casually as if they had been lovers for some time. "I'm sorry, I don't see."

"As he lay dying, King Arthur orders Sir Girflet to return Excalibur to the enchanted lake from which it came. Girflet reluctantly complies and a lady's arm emerges from the lake to catch it and carry it under the water. This has to be what Malory means—in companionship with the tale itself. He must have tossed the sword into a lake. That's where he hid it. All we need to do is find out which of the three villages has a lake."

"It's quite brilliant."

He kissed her. "For a chemist?"

It only took a couple of minutes on Google Earth to get the answer and it was a crushingly disappointing one. Leamington Hastings, Stretton-on-Fosse, Stoneleigh—none of them had lakes or even ponds. The River Avon ran through Stoneleigh but that hardly counted. He shut his laptop with a frustrating slap.

"Now what?" she asked.

He shrugged and turned to face her. "There's only one thing to do," he said, sliding onto her again.

Arthur and Claire arrived early at the Mortimer Arms Pub on Tottenham Court Road but Tony Ferro was already there polishing off his first pint. He was chatting with a man whom Arthur presumed was Jim Mawby, the UCL geologist Tony had mentioned over the phone earlier in the day.

Tony waved them over to their table and again made a fuss over Claire before introducing them to Mawby. Arthur had called Tony to bring him inside the tent on the new developments and it was Tony who suggested Mawby. "Can a lake disappear in five centuries?" Tony had repeated Arthur's question. "Damned if I know but there's a chap at UCL who'll be able to tell us." Tony bought a round and sat back down, resuming his fawning over Claire.

Mawby had dry, sun-wrinkled cheeks from years of geological fieldwork in Africa. He quietly took in the banter while making a dent in his second pint. Finally, he seized on an opening and said, "I read about you and your Suffolk treasure hoard, Malory. You're an interesting bloke. Do you mind telling me why you want to know about vanishing lakes?"

Arthur was uncomfortable being evasive but Tony jumped to the rescue. "We could tell you, Jim, but then you'd have to disappear for a very long time. Would that be all right with your missus?"

Mawby laughed. "I expect she would be forever in your service. Okay, understood. Need to know and all that. I won't pry. Keep feeding me pints of best bitter and I'll behave. Want me to dive in, if you'll excuse the pun?"

"Please do," Arthur said.

"Lakes disappear for a host of reasons. Sometimes it can happen in the blink of an eye, sometimes over eons. The most common scenario is when sediments get deposited and the lake gradually turns into a swamp or a marsh. Then peat forms and the zone becomes a fen. In the last stages trees start growing, turning the wetland into a forest."

"This can happen in five hundred years?" Arthur asked.

"That would certainly be on the quick side. More like thousands of years. Now some lakes disappear seasonably but these so-called ephemeral lakes usually are in very dry places like Death Valley so they're not relevant here. Very rarely a lake can disappear in a matter of minutes. This happened only recently in 2005 in Russia when Lake Beloye vanished like magic. We think there was a seismic shift in the soil underneath the lake, allowing it to drain through channels leading to the Oka River."

"So that's a possibility here?" Claire asked.

"Possible but not very likely. There's no historical record of something like this happening in Warwickshire over the last five hundred years and no cartographic indication I could find that there were ever lakes in Leamington Hastings, Stretton-on-Fosse, or Stoneleigh. Just to be complete there's also the phenomenon of so-called murdered lakes where feeding rivers are diverted by man for irrigation and the lakes are starved of water. But this also isn't relevant to Europe."

"So we're left with nothing?" Tony asked. "Good beer money down the drain?"

"My alimentary canal is hardly the drain," Mawby huffed. "But one other thought. Must your elusive body of water be a lake? Could it not be a river?"

Arthur shook his head. "The historical document we're chasing up clearly states a lake."

"Sometimes rivers can bulge out quite dramatically and these sections can appear very much like lakes. The wider the bulge the harder it is to appreciate the current."

Arthur pushed out his lower lip. "Stoneleigh has the River Avon running through it but we didn't see any bulging bits on the maps. It looks like an ordinary not-so-wide country river."

"Ah," Mawby said, pausing to gulp some more bitter. "I may be earning my beer after all. Look here." He pulled a satellite map from his bag and pointed to a stretch of the Avon where the river forked around an island. "This land mass in the center of these diverging and converging branches of the river near the old Stoneleigh Abbey: it's called a river island. I won't bore you with the hydraulics behind it but suffice it to say that channel geometry, fluid mechanics, sediment transport all play a role. I think that this river island could well have formed in the span of hundreds of years. No problem with that. Now for a moment, imagine it wasn't there. The bulge would be a good one hundred meters wide and five hundred meters long at this point. It would appear very much like a small lake. Well, anyway, that's the best I can do for you. Hope it helps." He looked at his watch. "I'm not lecturing for another hour and a half. Fetch me another pint, would you, Tony?"

When the four of them left the pub a man was watching from a nearby bus kiosk. Griggs pulled his cap over his eyes and stubbed out a cigarette. He had to decide which pair to follow when they parted company and in the end he took a few discrete photos of Ferro and Mawby with his mobile phone and set off after Arthur and Claire.

"Well?" Claire asked, placing her hand into Arthur's.

"Can you stay another day?"

"Okay," she said after a pause lasting only a second but seemed much longer. "Yes."

"What do you say we visit Stoneleigh?" He squeezed her hand. "A relative of mine may have left something there for me."

16

ENGLAND, 1471

Thomas Malory was old and broken. The years of cold and damp had ground him down. When he awoke, shivering under his blanket, his knees and hips were as stiff as planks and rising from his bed to use the chamber pot was achingly slow and painful. As simple an act as grasping a cup was difficult until the morning stiffness ebbed and his joints regained a tolerable fluidity.

Twenty years in and out of prison! Twenty years of the exultations of being granted bail or release and the despairs of rearrest and remandment.

Marshalsea Prison, Colchester Gaol, the Tower of London, Ludgate, Newgate—Malory, abandoned and without further resource, was resigned to serving at His Majesty's pleasure in his worst hellholes, all the while dreaming of his comfortable life at Newbold Revel, lost.

Where was the justice?

A knight of the realm had been cast into a sea of iniquity like a piece of flotsam—over false accusations. Common theft? Rape? The idea that a man who had served his king on the field of battle as a knight, a man who immersed himself in the chivalric virtues, who was a descendant of Arthur, King of the Britons—that this man would have committed these ignoble acts beggared belief. Yet the charges, kept alive by powerful enemies who stirred the pot of a corrupt judicial system, were enough to keep Malory in captivity when most men of his age and station were whiling away their time drinking by the fire with hunting dogs dozing at their feet.

During his first decade of captivity Malory had at least kept up hope that his plight would end soon when King Henry came to his rescue. But Henry had other matters weighing heavily on him. His ambitions to end England's interminable war with France had produced a schism among his lords and created a formidable rival out of the powerful duke of York. When the king slipped into a catatonic melancholia after being cuckolded by his pretty French wife, York rushed into the void and seized the reins of power from the House of Lancaster. Though the king eventually would regain his senses, two decades of teeter-tottering clashes between the House of Lancaster and House of York wreaked havoc on the land, occupying the full attention of the crown and marginalizing the travails of one poor imprisoned knight.

All the while Malory pickled in his juices, shuttling from court to court and prison to prison, some bleak, some like Marshalsea, at least hospitable. Sometimes months would pass, sometimes a year or more before Buckingham would make an appearance. His offer was always the same.

"Tell me where I may find the sword and you will be released."

John Aleyn and other trusted associates had been able to ferret out pieces of information about Buckingham's cloaked pursuits. There was talk of a network of men scattered throughout Europe and Asia called the Qem, alchemists bound together not by allegiance to any crown but to a darker commonality. There was another Englishman, Ripley, who was rumored to be as deep in the muck as Buckingham. Buckingham and Ripley, it was said, owed loyalty to these other men who collectively shared a desire to find the Holy Grail, not for the sake of the glory of God but for some whispered base and demonic purposes.

So every time Buckingham appeared with the key to unlock the cell and put forward his proposition, Malory would offer the same response. "My lord, you will not have the sword and you will not have the Grail. The Grail is meant for goodness and light and you, I fear, wish to use it for evil and darkness. I will die a happy man knowing that you shall never possess it."

While politics and war swept England into a vortex of violence, the rhythms of Malory's life in captivity, thus shielded, were slow and repetitive. On a good day, when illness was at bay and provisions were acceptable, he might even admit to a certain enjoyment of his gentle pursuits.

After a lifetime of battle and blood, the solitude of writing and of precious books was quietly comforting. Often he would begin his day with a letter to his dear wife or a loyal friend but then he would settle into his chapter of *Le Morte Darthur* and lose himself in a description of a great battle, passionate love affair, or noble quest. He would write for hours upon hours and thereby transport himself to the windswept hills of Camelot and the vibrant court of Arthur, his king, his inspiration, his ancestor.

Buckingham, a thorough man, took a keen interest in what Malory wrote and had a literate man read his letters and pages of his manuscript for possible hidden messages concerning the location of the sword but they found no such thing.

For a prisoner, Malory was kept well informed and up to date by his gaolers and visitors, and within a week of the Battle of Northampton in July 1460, he had heard the news at Newgate Prison. The duke of York had scored a stunning victory against King Henry's 10,000 men on the grounds of the Delapré Abbey. The king was captured and quickly agreed to a short-lived accord by which he would retain the throne for life though the crown would pass to York and his heirs. But more importantly for Malory, Buckingham was dead!

Buckingham, every bit the schemer and an opportunist, had played the York side when the pendulum of the War of the Roses had swung in their direction, and the Lancastrian side when the king was in ascendency. Unfortunately for him, on that day in Northampton, he was commanding the Lancaster forces for King Henry and was piked clean through by a Yorkist Kentishman.

Malory, rejoicing at the news, petitioned the crown and waited. Finally, weeks later, without the noxious interference of Buckingham, he was released to the waiting arms of his wife and his faithful man, John Aleyn. It was like a dream. Back in Newbold Revel, his meadows green and plantings ripe for harvest, he began to slowly restore his health following a bout of summer dysentery that had nearly killed him.

He ate what he could and walked his land trying to regain his strength. All the while he planned and plotted. The sword could remain a while longer in its watery resting place. He would dearly love to have it again, to treasure it, to pass it to his heir but there was no need for haste; Excalibur was safe. He sat on a bench beside the grave of his eldest son, Thomas, who had died of the pox two years earlier while Malory was rotting away at Newgate. His remaining son, Robert, was a good lad, not yet thirteen but already noble and brave; in time, Malory knew, he would be an able steward of the family lands and treasures. Yet he would not imperil Robert by informing him about the sword or the Grail, for that was dangerous knowledge. The quest was his and his alone.

The manuscript for *Le Morte Darthur* now lay in a box in his library, half finished. Its completion would have to wait. There was more urgent business. He knew the inscription on the sword by heart and, more importantly, its translation. When he was strong enough, perhaps in the spring, he would mount a small party of loyal men, including John Aleyn, to secure a ship and provisions. Their journey to a distant land would be arduous and the outcome uncertain but there was a chance—a glorious chance—that at journey's end he would hold the holiest relic on earth in his trembling hands.

The awful reversal came a few months later and arrived just as the winds of winter began to blow. It was a hard, crushing blow to be arrested once again on the same tired charges and sent to Marshalsea Prison. Malory demanded to know who was behind it. The answer came like a hand from beyond the grave. A man he did not know appeared in his cell one day and bade his forgiveness for the interruption.

Malory looked up from his desk. Though bitter, he had resumed work on his manuscript and was deep in thought about Lancelot and

Guinevere. The man at his door was enormously fat and, judging by his fur-lined robe and jeweled rings, also enormously wealthy.

"Who are you, sir?" Malory asked.

"I am George Ripley. Perhaps you've heard of me."

Malory smiled. Here was another of Buckingham's lot. "I have indeed."

"Good, then perhaps you know why I'm here."

"Sit yourself down, Ripley. Marshalsea does not provide the best accommodations but I daresay you won't be here long enough to be bothered."

Ripley grimaced as he squeezed his rump into a narrow chair.

Malory rested his quill in the inkpot. "Why don't you tell me about the Qem?"

If Ripley had been surprised, he didn't show it. "We are students of natural philosophy, curious men; gentlemen. That is all."

"You are alchemists."

"Indeed we are. I and others fervently believe that alchemy is a noble pursuit. You would agree that understanding the hand of God is a noble pursuit, would you not?"

"Why do you want the Grail?"

"Why do you, Sir Thomas?"

"For the glory of God."

"And that also is why we want it."

"I have heard otherwise."

"I cannot and will not comment on the depraved and scandalous accusations of unknown men."

Malory rose painfully, rubbing at his hip. "Yet here am I, sir, unlawfully imprisoned because of the depraved and scandalous accusations of unknown men! It was you who put me back in gaol, was it not? I thought a Kentish pikeman had finished Buckingham's interest in my poor soul but methinks I am wrong. The Yorkists are now in charge. Does your influence extend to them?"

"Our influence extends to diverse places. Buckingham, may God rest his soul, found himself on King Henry's side at a most inauspicious point in time. Now that the duke of York and his heir, Edward of York, are in ascendancy, my own influence is perhaps better placed. The duke has placed certain aspects of Edward's education in my hands: if I were to whisper, for instance, that a certain knight ought again to be confined, then perhaps my will would be done. And if perchance I were to plead that just such a knight should be released, then likewise perhaps my will would also be done."

"I encourage you to whisper away, then."

"I will do just that. All you need do is to tell me where I may find the sword."

Malory hobbled around to the other side of the desk and leaned hard against it. "Ah, there it is again, that infernal proposal. I will tell you what I told Buckingham many times over. I will never tell you. You may sully my name, I will not yield. You may torture me, I will not yield. You may take my land, kill my family, I will not yield. The Qem may be powerful, you may be powerful, but no man is more powerful than my iron will—fortified by the certain knowledge that what I protect I protect for God. Now, fine sir, if you are able to extract your nether parts from that chair, then I will bid you a good day."

For the next decade Malory's shuttle from prison to prison continued, punctuated by brief periods of bail and pardon; but it was almost as if he could hear the whispers from Ripley's fat lips. He heard them in his dreams. *"Snare the rabbit. Yank him from his happy hole. Put him back in his cage. He's mine. He's mine. He's mine."*

The War of the Roses dragged on but Ripley's influence at court only grew. The duke of York perished at Pontefract but his nineteen-year-old son, a magnificent specimen of a man at six foot three inches, took the throne as Edward IV. Nothing could stop Ripley now. Openly serving as court alchemist, his whispering continued—directly into the ear of a king.

Once a year on New Year's Day, Ripley visited Malory in prison to offer him a conditional release, and once a year Malory refused. That day was chosen, Malory suspected, so that he might all the more painfully reflect on his fate.

On the first day of 1471, Malory dismissed the fat man and poured himself some poor ale. The warden of Newgate Prison had sent him extra rations the night before. Malory had squirreled away a better than usual piece of venison and a nice slab of bread for his New Year's supper. He sat at his desk, chewing slowly and reading the last page of *Le Morte Darthur*, completed only that morning. Here was two decades of work, a labor of love and devotion, crowned by this dolorous and personal lamentation.

> *Here is the end of the book of King Arthur, and of his noble knights of the Round Table, and when they were whole together there was ever an hundred and forty. And here is the end of the death of Arthur. I pray you all, gentlemen and gentlewomen that readeth this book of Arthur and his knights, from the beginning to the ending, pray for me while I am on live, that God send me good deliverance, and when I am dead, I pray you all pray for my soul. For this book was ended the ninth year of the reign of King Edward the Fourth, by Sir Thomas Maleoré, knight, as Jesu help him for his great might, as he is the servant of Jesu both day and night.*

Pray for me while I am on live.

He wiped away a tear and finished his crust of bread.

It was curious to feel one's existence slowly draining away like water from a bucket with a tiny hole. His manuscript was done and so perhaps was his life. King Edward, guided by Ripley, no doubt, had granted a general pardon to prisoners a few years earlier and had excluded only eleven men, Malory being one of them. Even if the king were to reverse himself and free him, it was too late now to pursue the Grail. He was frail and infirm. An overseas adventure was out of the question. All he could do was pray that an heir might pluck the battle standard from his dead hands and sally forth for the honor of the Malorys and the greatness of God.

A fierce storm dumped a foot of snow onto London. From his high window, Malory watched it accumulate on the prison grounds and smiled as the warden's children threw snowballs at one another. How marvelous it would be to ride his horse through the drifts, to feel the cold flakes against his face. He wondered if it was snowing up in Warwickshire. Elizabeth would be rising from her bed about this time and see the snow falling through the small panes of their bedchamber. She too was old but still beautiful.

He sighed pitifully and returned to his desk to complete his legacy. The parchment quires of *Le Morte Darthur* were tied with a ribbon into a thick stack. He had written the preface the night before, thus fulfilling the promise he had made almost twenty years earlier in his letter to Bishop Waynflete. A worthy man, hopefully a descendant, could now marry knowledge of *Le Morte Darthur* with that of the *Domesday Book* to find the sword Excalibur and, God willing, the Grail. All that was left to do was to pen a message to the ages in the hope that a Malory would find it. Perhaps it would be his son, Robert, or perhaps his son's son; or a more distant Malory.

He wrote,

Alas my enemies, these unholy men who call themselves the Qem, have succeeded in preventing me from making the journey to find the Graal. I am now old and too feeble. Yet by placing me in prison all these years they have given me the benefit of time and I have been blessed by God with the ability to well and fully chronicle the tales of my noble forebear the great and noble Arthur King of the Britons. I pray that a Maleoré who comes after me will find this parchment and take up the quest for the Sangreal.

He finished the letter shortly before John Aleyn arrived for what would be their final visit. As usual, Aleyn bribed the sentries with wine to allow him to speak to his master alone. Aleyn was himself stooped with age. He had a shuffling gait and a tremor in his hand but he managed, as always, to show his master a measure of good cheer.

"The cold has turned my balls to brass, my lord," he said, warming his hands by Malory's fire.

"What need have you for balls, old man?"

"Little need, my lord, though I pray my wenching days are not completely done for."

"How is Elizabeth? And Robert?"

"She is well. No ailments of which I am aware. Robert is north, heading to St. Albans with a company of King Edward's men to fight the last of the Lancasters. Queen Margaret and her son are making their last stand, I reckon."

"I pray he survives. John, I would ask you one last favor."

Aleyn grimaced at the words but stayed silent.

"Carry this book of mine to Bishop Waynflete in Winchester and ask him to set a scribe to copy it. The gaolers will let you take it. They have read it and care not what I do with it. Bid Waynflete to have the copy delivered to William Caxton, the London printer. I know Caxton from years past. From Calais."

"I remember him, my lord. A wool merchant in those days. Turned to printing, has he?"

"Apparently with great success. And one more thing: this letter." He slipped it deep inside the pages of the book for safekeeping. "Bring it back to Newbold Revel and place it inside a locked chest with various and sundry documents and belongings of mine. I would have Robert find it, or his son or some future Malory. It is made of words but it is surely a treasure map. Keep it safe. I will say no more."

When it was time for his visitor to leave they clasped each other hard.

"Take care, my lord," Aleyn said. "I have heard that Ripley intends to do you harm."

"What harm can he do beyond what has been done? I am ready to accept my fate, eternally hopeful that one who follows me will fulfill the destiny which has eluded me."

Aleyn departed with letter and manuscript in his cloth satchel. He would go to Winchester and place the book into the bishop's own hands. And the bishop would give Aleyn for safekeeping the letter Malory had written him twenty years earlier. Aleyn would return to Newbold Revel and place the old letter and the new one into a sturdy locked box for safekeeping for his master's heirs. Robert Malory would emerge from the Battle of St. Albans with a head wound that left him incompetent. He would die in 1479, a year before his mother, never to open the locked chest. The map of words Malory had produced would be ignored and overlooked for the next 543 years.

On a cold day in March, Ripley appeared in Malory's cell with some rough men and a bag of implements. He announced the end of his patience. He would test this old knight's assertion that he would not reveal the hiding place of the sword even under torture. After all, what had he to lose? Reports from Newgate had reached him that Malory was losing the last of his strength and that he would likely not live to see the flowers of May.

Malory's hands were crushed by their vises, then his feet. Hot irons were pressed against his chest and thighs and finally his privy parts.

Though he screamed like any man would, he ignored Ripley's exhortations and uttered not a word. As he took his last breaths he was blessed with a vision, not unlike the visions of Arthur's knights—Percival and Gawain, Bors and Lancelot, Galahad. The stone walls of his prison cell gave way to a bright blue sky and there in the heavens was the Grail, a glowing chalice radiating beams of light, as beautiful a sight as he had ever seen.

His quest was over.

17

The Stoneleigh Park Lodge was only a few minutes' drive from the river island in the Avon. Arthur and Claire checked into the hotel and climbed back into the Land Rover. The back of the vehicle was packed with his last possessions, metal-hunting gear, some good flashlights, and a pair of army surplus night-vision goggles that he had purchased years earlier but had rarely used.

Venturing from the cocoon-like safety of Cantley House was weighing on him. Arthur obsessively checked for any signs of being followed. He was reasonably sure they were in the clear.

As Jim Mawby had pointed out, the island lay on the grounds of Stoneleigh Abbey, which had settled into a modern purpose far removed from its ecclesiastical roots. Henry II had founded it in 1154 and it thrived as a Cistercian monastery for four centuries until Henry VIII swept the bricks and mortars of Catholicism from his realm. The buildings and land were handed over as a plum to Henry's chum, Charles Brandon, duke of Suffolk, and the old abbey stayed in private hands, undergoing waves of renovations and additions until 1996, when it passed to a charitable trust. Along the way it was the country seat of the Leighs, Jane Austen's ancestors, and the house served as inspiration for her novels *Persuasion* and *Mansfield Park*. It was now a museum and banqueting hall and when Arthur and Claire pulled into the sunny car park a catering firm was offloading a large tent for a wedding. At the visitor's center they bought two tickets for a garden tour and Arthur chatted up the ticket girl to learn about the wedding. It was an evening affair, 350 guests, a fairly big one.

At the garden entrance, Arthur asked Claire, "Do you want to be friends of the bride or the groom?"

He heard a *"Mon Dieu!"* under her breath before she said, "I don't have the right clothes."

"Plenty of time to go shopping later."

The abbey grounds were seven hundred acres of parkland and formal gardens laid out along the Avon but Arthur was only interested in the river island, accessible via a footbridge from the manicured lawn adjacent to the abbey's orangery. The island was flat and grassy with only a few trees, crisscrossed by a couple of brown, worn walking paths. Arthur's heart sank. There were at least two acres of ground to cover; and judging by the grade of the banks and what Mawby had told them about the depth of the Avon, an object thrown into the ancient river could be up to two or three meters below the surface. Even if the sword were here—a very substantial *if*—finding it would be exceedingly difficult.

Arthur kept his reservations to himself: no sense in discouraging Claire. They were the only walkers on the island and he threw his hand over the idyllic expanse of green. "All right … say you're Thomas Malory standing on one of these banks. You want to heave a sword into something that all the world looks like a lake. Do you aim for the middle so it's hardest to find, or near one of the banks so it's easier to retrieve?"

Claire put her hands on her hips and looked through her sunglasses. "I'd compromise: far enough from the bank so a fisherman wouldn't notice the glint of metal but not all the way to the deepest part. He did want it to be found one day by the right person."

Arthur nodded. "I'll buy that. Hopefully he was as smart as you."

The evening was turning cool. The wedding reception was to begin at seven-thirty and sunset would be in an hour. That afternoon

Claire had bought a long, gauzy dress and a shawl. Arthur made do with the sport coat he'd packed. After seeing no one checking invitations, they mingled with a knot of arriving guests and made their way to the tent where they helped themselves to hors d'oeuvres and glasses of wine. They quickly decided that the safest maneuver was to keep floating away from the tables and stick by the dance floor and thereby never once had to claim to be Jason's friends from school who were so very happy for him and Roz.

Claire declared that Arthur was a pretty good dancer for an English chemist and he countered that she was *pas mal* for a French physicist. During a slow dance he held her tightly, feeling her breasts against his chest.

"It's a good night to start a quest," she whispered in his ear.

He pointed at the dais. The father of the bride was standing up and motioning to the band.

"That's the bloke we should be careful about. He's paying for our food and drink tonight."

They stood on the sidelines while speeches were made and cakes were cut and first dances were taken and then when it was quite dark they slipped away to the car park. Opening the trunk, Arthur retrieved a duffel bag and slung it over his shoulder.

A glowing half moon provided just enough light for them to wend their way across the lawns and onto the island footbridge without a flashlight. From the island the band sounded dreamy and far away, and had it not been for the task at hand Arthur would have desired to pull her down onto the cool grass. Instead he unpacked his metal detector, powered it up, and set its sensitivity for a large, deep object. No time to waste on coins or the odd piece of lost jewelry.

Excalibur or bust.

Mindful of Claire's opinion that Thomas Malory would have tossed the object not too close and not too far from the bank, he stashed the duffel bag by a tree, donned the earphones and began a pattern of concentric circles around the island. He started at the footbridge and headed clockwise until they returned to the starting point.

On each circuit he did a full sweep to his left, followed by a complete sweep to his right, about a six-foot swath, before taking another long pace. It was close to 10 P.M. when they began. Though they walked together, it was a solitary pursuit. He listened for just the right tone; she looked at the moon and stars and listened to the band and distant laughter.

The first circuit took an hour. Arthur removed his headphones.

"You okay? Want my jacket?"

"I'm fine." There was no wind and if anything the air was warmer than when they started. "Have you heard anything?"

"The good news is we haven't been slowed down by garbage hits. The bad news is we haven't had any hits."

"That's okay. Sounds like a good signal-to-noise ratio."

He'd almost forgotten that the beautiful woman following along in a filmy dress was a scientist.

"At this rate it might take all night."

"I don't mind. It's lovely out here."

An hour passed, then two more, and suddenly the music stopped. The wedding party was over. There were drunken shouts from the car park and the tent eventually went dark. The night sky clouded over, the wind picked up a bit and Arthur insisted Claire take his jacket. Once the caterers and event staff were done for the night the abbey went completely dark too and only then did Arthur feel comfortable breaking out a flashlight. With headphones off and the countryside empty they could both hear the river's gentle flow. On the next circuit Claire shined a beam past him, illuminating the way. He figured they would be making their final tight circuit around the center of the island in some five hours' time.

"Okay, let's do another circuit," he said.

Two men sat inside a dark vehicle parked at the abbey car park. Griggs had a night vision scope that he kept trained on the two glowing ghostlike figures a long distance away.

"Walking in bloody circles," he muttered.

The other man checked his glowing watch. "Looks like we're going to be here all night." Hengst was former SASS, the South African intelligence agency. He was a good ten-years younger than Griggs.

"You should be kissing my ass that I took you off gatehouse duty."

Hengst puckered up. "Pull your trousers down and let me have at it. This is more my line."

"Lot of surveillance work in the SASS?"

"Bread and butter."

Griggs reached over to the backseat and tugged a tactical bag onto his lap. He unzipped it and pulled out a compact sniper rifle.

"Let's have a look," Hengst said.

Griggs passed it to him and the younger man gave it a practiced once-over.

"Like it?" Griggs asked.

"Sweet. What is it?"

"American. Desert Tactical SRS. Twenty-two-inch barrel, eleven pounds, titanium suppressor, Moro Vision sniper scope with night sights, Barska laser."

"What's it chambered in?"

"Three thirty-eight Lapua Magnum."

"Fuck. Elephant gun. What'd it cost?"

"Fully kitted? Six thousand."

"He let you buy that?"

"Absolutely."

"I want one too."

"Dream on, mate."

Griggs took it back and removed the lens covers on the scope. He opened the car window halfway to allow him to point and rest the barrel and adjusted his aim until Arthur's head filled the optics.

"Target acquired."

"What's the distance?"

"About two thousand feet, maybe eighteen hundred. No wind. I could make the shot nine times out of ten."

"He'd have your scalp."

"Fuck him."

"Nice way to talk about a bloke who bought you a six-thousand-quid toy."

Griggs came to a boil fast. "Malory didn't see his face that night and he didn't see yours. It's my neck's on the block. There's only one way to make sure Malory never fucks me over."

"I'm getting the distinct impression you got reamed out for killing those two."

"Are you telling me you never had an op go wrong in the SA-fucking-SS?"

"Fucked up with some regularity, truth be told. But I always covered my tracks, something you obviously didn't do with metal-detector-boy out there."

"Only thing that's saved my neck. If I'd put a bullet in his head rather than letting him burn, I expect you'd have gotten the job to put a bullet in my head."

"What's so important about the Grail anyway?" Hengst asked, lighting a cigarette.

"He won't talk about it but the Swiss bloke I worked for before he hired me was chattier. They both belonged to some kind of Grail group. He told me the Grail had certain—what was the word he used?—*properties* they wanted to control."

"Control for what?"

"Fuck if I know. He never said."

Hengst took a hard drag. "These rich bastards have too much bloody time on their hands."

Arthur began another rotation and on his third sweep to the left he thought he heard something. It wasn't so much a recognizable tone than the sense that there was a sound. It reminded him of getting his hearing tested as a child by an audiologist who kept dropping the decibels until he could make out only a ghost of a tone.

He swept right and there was nothing. Back again left and there was the same faint perception. He took a half pace forward and repeated the sweeps: something, perhaps, to the left; nothing to the right. The instrument's display screen showed nothing on the Target ID cursor. Progressing a half step at a time, Arthur crept forward until the indistinct tone, if that what it was, disappeared.

He pulled off his headphones.

"Anything?" she asked.

"Maybe yes, maybe no. Something really faint but nothing on the display."

"What do you want to do?"

"Go with my gut. I'm going to dig a little. Stay here, I'll get the shovels."

They were at the end of the island closest to the abbey about fifty feet from the nearest bank. Arthur returned with his duffel bag and pulled out a spade.

He began slicing through the lawn at the first spot where there'd been the hint of a tone, careful to preserve the sod for re-laying. Under the beam of Claire's flashlight he cleared out a meter square and dug it down a couple of feet. The soil was moist and firm and his steel cut through it cleanly. When he was done he lit the screen of his metal detector and put the scanning head into the hole.

There was a clearer tone and the detector registered a fairly durable signal in the nonferrous range. Gold. Silver. Bronze. Good metals.

He kept digging and as the hole progressed he had to widen it half a meter in all directions to make the digging easier. The deeper he got the louder the tone. It was now a strong single midtone with a reading of 70 on the discrimination scale. There was one object down there either of gold, silver, or bronze. He dug faster despite his aching rib. Dawn wouldn't wait.

Two meters down the soil was getting wet and hard to handle and Arthur wished he had made the trench longer and wider. The walls seemed unstable and there were small cave-ins. There was no time to fix the problem. Climbing out of the trench without a ladder was going to be tricky. Come time to exit, Claire would have to shovel dirt back in to give him enough height to pull himself out.

The sky was losing some of its inkiness. He worked faster, pain be damned. Claire used the other shovel to keep the growing pile of refuse from sliding back into the trench. Both she and Arthur were smeared with dirt and muddy to the ankles.

The tone in his ears was almost painful.

He called for his trowel and when Claire handed it down he dropped to his knees and began scooping away at the slop.

Something caught the trowel blade and a dark object rose from the mud. Later he would tell Claire it reminded him of an arm rising from the mire, like that of the Lady of the Lake, who was said to have caught Excalibur and carried it down to its watery resting place.

He couldn't make out what he had. It was metal, a little over a foot long.

"Give me your light," he called out, trying to rein in his excitement. "I think there's a water bottle in the duffel bag. Drop that down too."

He held the flashlight under his chin and doused the piece of metal with water, cleaning it as best he could with his fingers. There was a glint of silver.

It was unmistakable. It was the hilt of a sword with a guard, a grip, and a pommel. There was no blade, just a rough nubbin of corrosion at the base of the guard.

"Is it?" Claire called down.

"It is," he said. "By God, it is."

She began sending earth back down and he built himself an escape ramp. Once free of the hole, he wrapped the hilt in her shawl and began back-filling the trench as fast as he could. The sky was getting pink and he feared that early morning dog walkers might descend on them. As he labored away, Claire packed everything but the spade in his hands into the duffel bag and took them back to the car park to wait for him, unaware that two men were hunkered down low in one of the few other parked cars.

Dripping with sweat, Arthur stamped on the soil to firm it up and placed the pieced-together sod. As dawn broke he inspected his work: it didn't look pretty but didn't flash neon either. In the distance he saw a man with two dogs coming his way. He thought better of carrying a spade past the fellow so he tossed it into the river, pleased with the symmetry of the gesture.

At the hotel they showered together but didn't make love, both too eager to clean the sword. Wrapped in a bath towel, Arthur brushed his teeth then used his toothbrush to scrub the hilt under the tap.

The silver looked as fresh and proud as the day it was fashioned. The heavy guard was a good ten inches long, five inches on both sides of the blade. If the blade had still been there the sword would have resembled a cross. And as Arthur scrubbed the silver guard, letters emerged under the bristles.

Claire leaned in. Her towel slipped off but she made no attempt to cover herself. Together they mouthed the words phonetically.

"Eni Tirro Euric Nemeto Ouxselo Brunka Kanta Cristus Ke Wereo Gral."

"What language is this?" she asked.

"I've no idea. But this word is the one we wanted to see: *Gral.* This inscription is about the Grail!"

He stood to face her and smiled at her nakedness. Then he was seized by an urge he didn't quite understand. He curled the fingers of his right hand around the grip, and when he raised the hilt high over his head triumphantly, Claire took a step forward and pulled away his towel.

18

BRITANNIA, A.D. 498

Arthwyr of Maleore, King of the Britons, Lord of the Isle of the Mighty, tested the heft of his new sword and sliced the air appreciatively with his powerful right arm. The blade was the finest Damascus steel forged by Cedwyn of Camlan, the greatest swords maker in the realm. The hilt was fashioned by Morien of Glastonbury, the ablest silversmith in Britannia. The sword felt at once heavy and light and with that paradox Arthwyr could tell its balance was perfect. His last weapon had shattered against a Saxon axhead and though he had been wielding a fine borrowed blade, he felt bereft without his own.

In a rush of exultation he raised the new sword high over his head.

He was the champion of the battle of Mynydd Baddon, where thousands of Angle, Saxon, and Jute invaders had been slaughtered by his warriors. For the first time in memory Briton was largely free of foreign rapists and pillagers. His father, Uther Pendragon, had been beloved by the people; but Arthwyr had risen to another level. He was Godlike.

He was in his throne room in his fortress castle built on a high flat-topped hill in Gwynedd. It was summer and he was dressed lightly in a sleeveless cloth tunic, leggings, and boots. The wide leather belt, cinched tight around his slim waist, accentuated a powerful torso. His hair was long and flowing, the color of molten gold, and he wore his beard close-cropped as his father had done, kept short by a manservant adept with a flint blade. He was not yet fifty and had accomplished everything in life he had ever strived for, save one.

"Will you give it a name?" The question came from his queen, leaning languidly on her padded throne chair, a smaller version of Arthwyr's own. Gwenhwyfar was such a wisp of a woman, it was deemed a miracle by her ladies that she had been able to pass children through her narrow hips. Her hair was as dark as Arthwyr's was light, and Arthwyr always told her that their hues reflected their dispositions. Hers was gloomy, of the night, whereas his was of the day, filled with optimism.

"I will call it Caledfwlch," he said. "That which cleaves stone. For if it can cleave stone it will cleave a man with ease."

"Do you never grow weary of killing?" she asked. Her cupbearer, a young girl, hovered by her side and filled the goblet Gwenhwyfar held in her thin outstretched hand. The queen wore two white ribbons in her hair to mark her mourning of the knight, Llych Llenlleawg.

"My lady, I will never tire of killing heathens, invaders and nonbelievers. It is the duty of a Christian king to protect his subjects and defend Christ."

"You have driven out the invaders. Will you now follow them back to their own lands? Can we not live in peace for a time?"

Arthwyr saw his younger son, Cyngen Maleore, playing by the hearth with one of his cousins. The boy was only three, a miracle child, if ever there was, born late in life to a king and his queen. His other son, Gwydre, was a full eighteen years older and he would certainly be king one day, though it comforted Arthwyr no end to have Cyngen in reserve. A warrior king always favored reserves. The king called Cyngen over to show him the sword and laughed when the boy could not lift its tip off the ground. Arthwyr dismissed the towheaded lad, handed the sword to his page, took his place by the queen's side and held out his hand. She knew to touch it.

"For your sake I will stay at court for a time," he said. "But my knights are hot-blooded young men who are not so easily shut in a pen. They will seek adventure and I will not stand in their way. But remember this, good lady, that peace is as permanent as a footprint in the sand. War will come again. It always does."

Gwenhwyfar sighed and drank more wine.

A swarthy man emerged from shadows behind the thrones. He was severe in his countenance, bald as a hen's egg, with a small rectangular Pharaonic beard that harkened back to his birthplace, in Egypt. His black tunic scraped the floor. He came forward just far enough for the king to be able to see he was in attendance then stopped, clasping his hands expectantly.

"What say you, Myrddin?" Arthwyr asked.

Myrddin answered, his accent exotic. "The hall is filled with supplicants, my lord. Now that your enemies have been driven from your realm, your people have turned their heads to dowry disputes and such matters as who is the rightful owner of this ox or that hog."

Arthwyr asked the same exasperated question he always did. "And why must a king decide these matters?"

"If not you, then whom?" Myrddin replied. "But before we begin the audience, one of your knights wishes to see you and ask that you grant him his desire."

"Which one?"

"Gwalchavad."

Arthwyr smiled broadly. It was wrong for a king to show favorites among a coterie of knights who all were as brave and loyal as a ruler could ever wish, but Gwalchavad was a special young man, eager as a pup, pious as a monk and the finest jouster in the kingdom. He was of royal blood. His mother was the queen's sister, his father the great knight Llych Llenlleawg, who had ardently desired the king's own woman but had settled for her youngest sister. Arthwyr had been painfully aware of the unrequited passion that burned so brightly between Gwenhwyfar and Llych Llenlleawg and used it like an implement to push his leading knight to greater and greater heights of daring on the battlefield. At Mynydd Baddon he had handed Llych Llenlleawg one of his wife's scarves and told him she wanted him to carry it, thereby inflaming the knight. Arthwyr never knew if the man was seized by ardor or embarrassment or pride but he fought like a madman and it took four arrows to bring him off his horse that day.

Gwalchavad was summoned, bounding into the throne room with all the energy and zeal of youth. He approached his king and fell to one knee before him, his scabbard clattering on the stones.

"Rise, Gwalchavad," Arthwyr commanded, "and speak your mind."

Gwalchavad rose to his full height brimming with the confidence of a man at the peak of life. The ladies of the court milling at the edges of the room looked on him longingly; and the men, Arthwyr's nobles, lowered their heads in envy. (Indeed one of them was Arthwyr's oldest son, Gwydre, who, true to form, became livid in Gwalchavad's presence. "I am his son, not Gwalchavad," he had complained only recently to his mother. "Why does he treat *him* like his heir and *me* like his dog?")

"Sire," Gwalchavad said. "I have come from Castle Caerlleon. I received word that one of the Saxon nobles I captured at Mynydd Baddon wished to see me to discuss a proposal for his ransom."

"Which prisoner?" Arthwyr asked.

"Sir Wallia, son of Ardo."

"An able knight. You cleaved him well. Has his wound healed?"

"He is well mended. Until we spoke I had not been made aware he was the nephew of King Euric."

Arthwyr frowned at the name. "Euric was a great adversary. I much despised him, though I much admired him too."

"Wallia seems a decent fellow," Gwalchavad said. "Though we have treated him with the respect his noble heritage deserves and have afforded him all reasonable comforts, he is restless after these many months in captivity and wishes to return to his own land."

"Then his people should pay his ransom!" Arthwyr bellowed.

Myrddin took a small step forward. "The negotiations are at an early stage, sire. These matters are delicate and take time, though King Cissa has oftentimes pledged to ransom his nobles without ever delivering the booty."

"Then we should take such time as is necessary," the king barked.

"With respect, sire," Gwalchavad said, "Wallia told me something that has quickened my heart. He swore to me on the honor of his ancestors that he knows where we might find the Gral of Christ, our Lord!"

The throne room erupted in murmurs, which Arthwyr silenced with a fierce wave of his hand. The quest for Christ's chalice had inflamed his mind ever since Myrddin appeared at his castle offering his services as a seer to the young king. Arthwyr's advisers, his father's men, had shunned the foreigner, seeking to discredit him at every turn; but Myrddin's counsel had been infallibly wise. He foresaw the best time to attack the enemy, the best time to retreat, the best time to sail the fierce channel to reach Gaul, the best time to bed a woman to produce a male child. In time, Arthur elevated Myrddin to become prime counselor to the king and Uther Pendragon's old guard was sent to pasture. And Myrddin, who had forsaken his ancient religion to embrace the teachings of Jesus Christ, had goaded his king at every turn to commit the prestige of his throne and the lives of his knights to finding the Gral. It was a quest, the Egyptian had insisted, that if successful would establish Arthwyr as the greatest ruler in all of Christendom. Finding the Gral was Arthwyr's one great unaccomplished goal.

"The Gral, you say?" the King erupted. "Is this the talk of a desperate prisoner who will lie to gain his release or the words of a truthful man?"

"I believe he is being truthful, my king," Gwalchavad said. "Here is his tale. He says it has been told by bards of his people that Joseph of Arimathea, the great saint who gave his own tomb so that our crucified Christ might be buried, came into possession of the Gral after our Lord's resurrection. Pursued by Pontius Pilate, Joseph fled Jerusalem and journeyed to the land the Romans called Tarraconensis. There he became a priest and founded an enclave to honor Christ high in the mountains where he and his followers might be safe. And it is there where he hid the Gral."

Arthur shifted in his throne with impatience. "We have heard tales such as this before and many a time have our knights braved the perils of foreign lands in search of nothing more than mist. Why should this time be different?"

Gwalchavad's confidence did not fade. "Has a man of honor ever before claimed to have held the chalice in his own hands?"

Arthwyr glanced at Myrddin before shifting his gaze back to his knight. "Has this man, Wallia, told you this?"

"He has, sire."

Arthwyr leaned forward. "And what did he say it felt like in his hands?"

"He said it felt as warm as the belly of a baby, as warm as blood. He felt its power."

Arthwyr leaned heavily against the throne and nodded. This was just as Myrddin had predicted. The Gral, he had said, would be the temperature of a beating human heart.

"What say you, Myrddin?" Arthwyr asked.

"When Sir Gwalchavad informed me of Sir Wallia's tale I fell to my knees in a prayer of thanks. There have been those who have whispered about the Gral being hidden in the kingdom of Euric and those who claimed that Saint Joseph found sanctuary in Tarraconensis with a precious relic. I believe we cannot ignore the claims of Sir Wallia."

"What does Wallia propose?" Arthwyr asked Gwalchavad.

"His demands are this," the knight answered. "He will tell me where this sanctuary lies and where the Gral is hidden within. If I return from my quest with the Gral, then we will promise to release him immediately, free of ransom, and give him and his comrades safe passage to Germania."

"A modest request for a treasure so great," Arthwyr said.

"Sir Wallia fears he will spend his entire life in captivity otherwise and die a wretched death," Gwalchavad continued. "He wishes to see his wife and children again. He knows the reputation of his own king in matters of ransom. I ask that you, sire, grant me the honor of leading a band of knights to find the Gral so I may lay it at your feet."

Arthwyr was not ashamed to openly shed tears. While Gwydre seethed in the shadows, Arthwyr replied, "Go, my brave and noble Gwalchavad. Fulfill my most fervent dream."

Myrddin had his own turret room high in the castle with rich furnishings, every bit as fine as the king's, silver plates and cups and wooden chests full of fur-lined garments. Mailoc, a hulking Gaul, and Kilian, a small strong Pict from the northern lands, sat by the hearth drinking Myrddin's wine and tearing off chunks of roasted gamecock with their greasy fingers. Myrddin showed little interest in food or drink. Instead he seemed drawn to the leaping flames and the tiny explosive pops emanating from his stack of cured, split logs.

Finally, he broke the silence. "Mailoc, I want you to accompany Gwalchavad on his journey. I will persuade Arthwyr that Gwalchavad needs to have a seer at his side to advise him by and by."

"Do you really believe this Saxon's story?" Kilian asked.

Myrddin shrugged. "It has the ring of truth but who can say? We Qem have been chasing after the Gral since the day Joseph of Arimathea stole it from us. I came to this desolate land twenty years ago because I believed that Arthwyr would become a powerful ruler and he has become that. I also believed I could influence a young king to dedicate the resources of his court and kingdom to help us find the Gral and I have done that. Perhaps this prisoner, Wallia, has knowledge of the relic, perhaps he is a scoundrel. There is only one way to know."

"And if I get my hands on it?" Mailoc asked.

Myrddin smiled. "If you do, I trust you will have the reverence to wipe the fat from your fingers first. Then steal it away from Gwalchavad and his party of knights. Kill them if you must. It matters not to me. After this, send word to me via messenger and take the Gral to Jerusalem where you will keep to yourself in the guise of a humble pilgrim. Wait for me there. If this is the true Gral then we will surely fulfill our destiny."

Gwalchavad led his small band of seekers across the black, treacherous waters separating Briton and Gaul and began his journey through the wild Gallic countryside, inching south to the land of

Euric, the land of Tarraconensis. A large force of knights and soldiers would have attracted the attention of hostile lords and their armies so a mere twelve men rode on.

There were two other knights of Arthwyr's court, Sir Jowan and Sir Porthawyr, both fine young men who were content to accept Gwalchavad's leadership. Myrddin had persuaded the king that Mailoc would be invaluable: he was a native of Gaul who knew their ways and could make a divination from the entrails of a rabbit as ably as he could thrust a dagger.

Seven squires and servants attended the entourage, riding the pack horses and tending to the party's victuals. The knights wore simple cloaks over their chain mail and swords. When approached by the local folk, Mailoc told them in their own tongue that these were tradesmen and pilgrims seeking relics of the Virgin Mary and the holy saints that they might sell to priests and bishops.

Wallia had told Gwalchavad that he should proceed to Barcino, the great Iberian port city in the heart of Tarraconensis. From there it was only a day's ride to the place the locals called the Mountain of Miracles where, it was said, the sick could be healed by bathing in the icy waterfalls that cascaded from its slopes. The journey to Barcino took two months—during which the travelers endured storms and bad food, insects and snakes, and a skirmish with a minor Gallic warlord who tried to rob them. The knights dealt harshly with the marauders and sent them to their maker with cold steel through warm flesh. In Barcino, a bustling city populated by merchants and mariners from a mélange of foreign lands, they were able to find good lodgings and rest their horses for the final push.

Gwalchavad was eager to complete the journey. He sensed a presence deep inside of something great and wondrous; how could that not be the Gral? Yet his knights and the others were anxious to stay for a time in the comfort of the portside inn to recover their strength. Gwalchavad was about to agree to a respite when Mailoc pulled him aside, to a corner of the barrel room, to convince him otherwise. As the two were downing their flagons of barley wine, the Gaul told the knight that he foresaw danger should they linger. He had seen a dead crow on each of three days, the last practically on the threshold of the inn. Here, in the city, was evil.

When Gwalchavad announced they would depart the next day the young squires ordered more wine for their table, then more, until they were well drunk. Had Gwalchavad or any of the knights heard Sir Jowan's squire pissing behind the inn and boasting to a stranger in his slurred Briton tongue about a Gral quest they would have throttled him on the spot.

The next day the pilgrims departed at dawn, their horses pointed toward the misty distant peak. The mountain loomed larger as the day progressed and by the middle of the afternoon they had to crane their necks to take it in. Throughout, Gwalchavad felt the urge to glance repeatedly over his shoulder but he saw nothing of concern. At the base of the mountain it took time to find the landmark Wallia had described: an enormous triangular boulder the color of watered-down wine. It was Jowan who first spotted it, letting out a triumphant cry. Beside the boulder was a worn path wide enough for one horse or man to navigate at a time. That was the path they took.

The path snaked up the mountain by turning back on itself over and over again. The result was a gentle grade that hardly taxed horse or rider but took several hours for the party to negotiate to reach the next of Wallia's landmarks: a wide clearing where the whole of Barcino was visible in the distance. Gwalchavad knew they were close, and just as Wallia had said, the path grew dramatically steeper—and littered with treacherous stones, as if to signal the final stages of the quest would not be easy. The horses whinnied and fought for their footing and Gwalchavad decided to send the packhorses and servants back to the clearing to await their return.

The men pressed on for another hundred yards before Gwalchavad concluded that their steeds could go no further. Everyone dismounted and the squires led the horses down to join the others. Gwalchavad instructed his squire to wait for them for up to one full day before seeking them out. Then the three knights—Gwalchavad, Porthawyr, and their seer, Mailoc—ventured upwards on foot.

The trail ended in a higher clearing, which they reached in the softening light of evening.

Then Gwalchavad pointed, fighting an urge to drop to his knees in thanksgiving.

"There!" he cried. "Just as Sir Wallia promised. We are close, my friends! We are close indeed."

19

"Come on, Arthur, let me see it. You can tell me all about your sleepless night later."

Arthur unzipped his shoulder bag and passed the sword, wrapped in a hotel wash towel, to Tony Ferro. Tony unbundled it slowly, clearly savoring the anticipation.

Arthur had phoned him early that morning and had driven with Claire directly to London from Stoneleigh to see him at the university. Tony's desk was awash in harsh light and when the sun first caught the silver, Claire and Arthur saw the large man's face soften like heated wax.

"My, my, my," he muttered, turning the hilt over in his hands.

"What do you think?" Claire asked.

"I think I want to blubber like a baby. I wish the hell we could show this to Holmes."

"Me too, Tony," Arthur said. "What's it telling you?"

Tony curled his hand around the grip. "First of all, they had smaller hands than we do today. I can't easily get both my paws around this but that's how it was used. It's a greatsword, meant to be wielded two-handed. Of course, it's a pity there's no blade. It would have been up to seventy-two inches in length. This hilt is about eighteen inches, so you'd have ninety inches—that's over seven feet of destructive power, the assault rifle of its day."

"What day is that?" Arthur asked. "Can you date it?"

"Well, not precisely, not without metallurgical analysis, but stylistically its certainly early medieval: fifth century, sixth, seventh perhaps. It's entirely consistent with our best guesses that a King Arthur lived in fifth-century Cornwall or Wales and that he was a renowned warrior who may have played a rather direct role in kicking the posteriors of the Angles and Saxons back to the continent at the battle of Mount Badon, among other venues. Look at this cross guard. It's almost a foot long. It's covered in silver but it surely has a steel core for strength. The silver veneer probably stopped it from corroding. Picture a long blade with this cross guard. What do you imagine?"

"A cross," Claire said. "A beautiful cross."

"Precisely that. The perfect implement for a king or a knight to take into battle. The power of Christ, the glory of Christ, all in one."

"There's no escaping it, is there, Tony?" Arthur said. "This is Excalibur."

"Arthur! I don't know if we can jump to that conclusion about its provenance and especially its name. Perhaps the little boy in me would like to go there but the stuffy academic I've become is far more circumspect. I mean, the moniker Excalibur first appears in the twelfth century in Chrétien de Troyes' *Perceval* as Escalibor before it mutated over time to Excalibur by the time of your Thomas Malory. Yes, the great lords and kings of the period did have a tradition of naming their weapons but this sword's name, if any, will be lost to time.

"This we do know: in his letter to Bishop Waynflete, Thomas Malory claims to have found King Arthur's sword. And in the other important parchment in the Warwickshire chest he laid out a rather elaborate puzzle. You two clever bunnies have solved the puzzle and here is that sword. It is undoubtedly a medieval sword. Does that make it King Arthur's sword? No. Does it make it a very important artifact? Yes, it does. Without too much more study it probably deserves its own pavilion at the British Museum."

"The inscription," Claire said. "Can you read it?"

"Yes, let's have a look at that," Tony said, rummaging for his magnifying loupe. He squinted through it, moving from left to right over the cross guard. Then he looked up. "Wow."

"Wow?" Claire repeated.

"Yes, my dear, *wow.*" He carefully wrote the inscription on a pad and read it out loud. "*Eni Tirro Euric Nemeto Ouxselo Brunka Kanta Cristus Ke Wereo Gral.* Not only is the message shockingly provocative but this goes a long way to helping date the sword."

"You're killing me," Arthur pleaded.

"Hang on. First of all, there's the language. This is Proto-Celtic, also known as Common Celtic. This is the predecessor language to modern Celtic. More specifically it's late Proto-Celtic, which began to seriously disappear by the fifth and sixth centuries in favor of the modern Celtic variants. Putting that together with the morphology of the sword, I'd say that we can reasonably date the artifact to the late fifth to early sixth century."

"But that's not the wow," Arthur said.

"No. It's the translation. Here it is: 'In the land of Euric on a sacred place on high lie before Christ and find the Grail.' Do you know what this means?"

Arthur and Claire looked at each other in incomprehension. "No!" Arthur exclaimed. "I don't!"

"The key is Euric. In the land of Euric. Euric was King of the Visigoths, the fellows who ruled a good bit of Gaul and Hispania in the early Middle Ages—that's France and Spain, Claire, in case you only took mathematics and physics in school."

She forced a smile.

"Euric died somewhere in the 480s—I'd have to check my references to be more precise—and here we again have a degree of triangulation on dates. What's really intriguing is that he and an Arthur-like foe were at loggerheads for much of his reign. It's said that he defeated a push into Gaul in 470 by a Briton king, sometimes referred to as Riothamus—who some scholars, Andrew Holmes included, thought might be Arthur. It's also believed that he may have been the invader in Briton defeated by an Arthur-like foe at the battle of Mount Badon. So this is all tantalizing stuff."

Arthur now was on his feet, his hands thrust in his pockets, looking for somewhere to pace in the tight space. "I'm sure the dating is important, Tony. But it's the message!"

"Indeed. *In the land of Euric on a sacred place on high.* Hispania was the land of Euric. Put that together with the twelfth-century letter which Holmes found in a certain mountaintop monastery library and what does that tell us about the location of the Grail?"

Arthur immediately thought of the twelfth-century letter Holmes had found.

"Montserrat."

Arthur and Claire checked into the Cantley House Hotel for one more night. There was no other place he could think to go.

"You don't have to come with me, you know," he told her.

"Don't you want me to come?"

"Of course I do. But it could be dangerous. And I don't want you to lose your job."

"I'll call my boss. I'll tell him I need more time to take care of some personal things. I'm in good standing so it shouldn't be a problem."

He was on his laptop. "We could go tonight but we'd need a hotel. It's just as fast to fly out early tomorrow."

"What about the sword?"

"We can't take it with us. We'll do what Thomas Malory would have done. We'll bury it in the garden tonight. I'll come back for it later. It can spend another few days in the wild before the British Museum gets it."

"We can visit it there. Maybe together …"

He sighed. "Look, I'm concerned about you."

"And I'm concerned about you. You were the one who was attacked."

"I'm prepared to take the risk myself but I'm not prepared to put you in danger."

She sat beside him on the bed and took his hand.

"I know what it's like to be on a quest, Arthur. It's what I do every day as a physicist. It's thrilling. It's wonderful. I haven't found new subatomic particles yet so I'm already a little impatient and frustrated by my quest. Your quest, well, it's tangible. In a short time you've made so much progress."

"We've made progress."

"Yes, you, we. This is too fantastic. I've never had this kind of adventure and I don't want to turn my back on it and then wonder about it for the rest of my life. And there's something else, of course."

"And that would be … ?"

She put her hands around the back of his neck and kissed him. That was her answer.

Tony spent the rest of his day juggling various obligations—a faculty lunch, a two-hour lecture, papers to mark, a tutorial with one of his graduate students—all the while returning again and again to the silver sword. It wasn't until after 6 P.M. that he had the solitude necessary to home in on that sweet topic.

He'd taken some pictures of the hilt with his mobile phone and as the sun went down he studied them on the screen of his laptop. *Euric.* He zoomed in on the engraved name until it almost filled the screen.

He went to his bookshelves, drew down some volumes and before long he'd refreshed his memory. Euric of the Balti Dynasty, King of the Visigoths, son of King Theodoric, father of King Alaric. Powerful foe of the Britons. King Arthur would have woken at night, cursing this Euric, damning him to hell. By the time of the Visigoth's death he had consolidated his dominion over most of Spain and a third of modern France; but Britannia was not to be his, thanks, perhaps, to Arthur.

The land of Euric.

If this was Arthur's sword, then what greater tribute to an adversary could there be than to call Hispania the land of Euric?

Tony wanted some hard copies of the photos so he sent them to the shared departmental printer then pushed himself from his chair to retrieve them. The hall was deserted, the other offices dark. Tony had unlaced his shoes for comfort as he often did late in the day. Rather than relace them he walked in a shuffle, his laces trailing behind, and marched down the hall like a large penguin.

In the copier room he snatched the pages from the printer and turned at the noise of a footstep.

Griggs was filling the doorframe, his silver and black Bersa in his gloved hand, a silencer, longer than the gun, threaded onto the barrel.

Tony's first reaction was indignation. "What's the meaning of this?"

"Let's quietly go back to your office, Professor Ferro."

"How do you know my name? What do you want?"

"I just want to talk."

"About what?"

Griggs looked at the printouts in Tony's hand. "Let me have those."

Tony looked perplexed. "These? You want these?"

Griggs nodded, stepped forward and held out his free hand. Tony passed them over.

"Any more on the printer?"

"No."

Griggs stepped away to clear the doorway. "Okay, back to your office. After you."

"May I tie my shoes?"

"No."

In the office Griggs shut the door, which had a large panel of frosted glass. With Tony reseated behind his desk Griggs switched on a desk lamp and flicked off the brighter fluorescents.

"Arthur Malory visited you today." Griggs waved the printouts. "Was this what he found last night?"

"Who the hell are you?"

"I'm nobody. But I work for somebody interested in the Grail."

Tony's indignation returned. "Then perhaps we'll have him join our discussion group. Barging in with a weapon like a thug is unlikely to get your Mister Somebody what he desires."

"Did you take any other photos of this? Did you take any notes on what Malory talked about when he was here?"

Tony instinctively glanced at his desk, so obliquely another man might not have noticed but Griggs was observant. Pointing the gun he used his free hand to gather up all the papers on Tony's desk.

"Any others?" he asked.

"No," Tony said quietly.

"What did you use to take the photos?"

"My cellular phone."

"Give it here." Griggs saw the photo of the sword hilt on the laptop. "The computer too."

"What does your Mister Somebody want with the Grail?"

Griggs ignored the question. "Where did Malory say he was going next?"

"I think he was off to the pub. I would've joined him if I didn't have a busy day."

"All right, fine," Griggs said. "It doesn't matter what he did or didn't tell you. We've got it covered."

Tony looked at the gun and sighed loudly. "Andrew Holmes," he said.

"What about him?"

"You killed him, didn't you?"

Poof. Poof.

Griggs put two rounds through Tony's heart, removed a plastic carrier bag from his coat pocket and put the computer, phone and papers inside. Then he turned off the desk lamp and quietly left.

20

BRITANNIA, A.D. 499

A lesser man, a man with lower resolve, who was not a knight of the court of a beloved king such as Arthwyr, might not have finished his journey; but Sir Jowan was cut from a finer cloth than most men. He endured isolation and deprivation, instances of kindness from strangers, and treachery. The seasons changed and the last months of his passage were done in the winter. His wounds drained then healed then drained again and his finely muscled body slowly melted away.

When finally Jowan appeared at Arthwyr's court at Gwynedd he was not recognized until he stumbled into the arms of his own cousin, a knight named Morgant, and carried off to bed to be fed and have his putrid wounds cleaned.

Word was sent to Arthwyr's bedchamber where he had been bedridden for a month with fever and a swelling in his jaw. The painful affliction had rendered him weak as a girl, and though he demanded to be taken to Jowan's sick chamber immediately, the king was persuaded by the queen and his caregivers to remain in his own bed.

"He was alone?" Arthwyr asked.

Yes, he was told.

"Did he have it? Did he have the Gral?"

No, he was told. He had nothing but the tattered clothes on his back.

On hearing of Jowan's return, Myrddin rushed to the room where he had been taken and barged in while the women were washing his wounds. Though the stench in the room was sickening and the women had wrapped their faces with their scarves, Myrddin hardly flinched. He pushed the ladies aside and fell to his knees so his ear would be close to the knight's mouth.

"Did you find the Gral?"

Jowan nodded.

The Egyptian's eyes blazed. "Tell me where it is?"

Jowan tried to speak but his lips were too cracked. Myrddin ordered the closest maiden to give the man some water.

Jowan finally was able to rasp, "It is … where Sir Wallia … said it would be."

"Then why do you not possess it?" Myrddin almost screamed.

When the knight began to tell the tale of what had transpired on that faraway mountaintop Myrddin ordered the women out so none but he might hear the knight's words. Though crushed with fatigue and wasting away from malnutrition and gangrene, Jowan imparted every detail from the moment they scaled the mountain to the instant he fled for his life.

Alaric's men were lying in wait. How they knew the Britons were coming Jowan did not know. Moments before the attack began, Gwalchavad had found the Gral! He had actually held it in his hands before reluctantly putting it down to draw his sword.

Though the Britons were outnumbered five to one they fought valiantly and smote many enemies. Porthawyr died from a blow to his neck and Mailoc took a thrust to his belly through and through. Gwalchavad fought on and he alone killed seven men before he was pierced through the chest. Jowan received a heavy slice to his upper arm and a lighter one to his brow, and when he saw he was the last Briton alive he fled down the steep mountain path to rally the men who had waited in the clearing—but to his horror found all of them dead. He whistled for his horse and using his good arm, managed to mount it and begin the long and mournful return to Britannia.

"I would have climbed back up the mountain to fight and die with my brothers," Jowan avowed, tears streaming, "but I believed I had a higher duty to return to my king's court and let him know that the Gral exists. I pray that other knights might succeed where I have failed."

"I say this," Myrddin demanded, "tell no one else what you have told me. I will inform the king myself."

The knight nodded weakly. "Sir Wallia must be freed," he implored. "Though we failed in our quest, everything he said was true. I have thought about him and his plight during many a lonely night."

Myrddin responded with a grim smile. He had personally had Wallia killed three seasons earlier. A cell door deliberately left unlocked, a desperate knight who craved his freedom, it had been a facile claim that Wallia had been slain while escaping. One Gral tongue had been silenced and here now another. But before he could take the pillow from under Jowan's head and press it against his face, the royal surgeon entered with his apprentice.

Thwarted, Myrddin proceeded to the king's chamber, hatching a plot. The great leader was moaning under his pile of bed furs. On seeing his seer Arthwyr propped himself on an elbow and spoke, his mouth distorted by the grotesque swelling of his mandible.

"You spoke with him?"

"I did, sire."

"Tell me everything he said."

Myrddin complied. He had no choice but to be forthcoming. For all he knew, Arthwyr might rise from his bed and visit the stricken knight at any time and learn the truth himself. The seer could not risk being caught in a lie or half truths. He asked, though, that all of Arthwyr's attendants leave the chamber first; the fewer who knew, the better.

Arthwyr listened intently, thrilled by the revelation that the Gral had been found but saddened to the quick that it had been lost again and that his fine knights Gwalchavad and Porthawyr had perished.

"We must mount a new expedition," Myrddin said.

"Yes," Arthwyr agreed. "Not a small band of men, as we have done, but an army. We will take the Gral by force, King Alaric be damned. I defeated his father and I will defeat the son."

"It will be done," Myrddin said.

Arthwyr began to rise from his bed. "I would command this army myself…"

"Here, I do not agree," Myrddin objected. "You are afflicted, weakened. It is winter and the crossing of the sea will be perilous. With respect, you would slow down the advance of your army. I will go in your stead and bring you back the holy object."

Arthwyr rubbed his throbbing jaw. "No, I need your counsel here. I will send my son to lead the army. Sir Morgant will be at his side. Send for Sir Gwydre so I might speak with him."

Myrddin knew that once the king had set his mind, nothing would change it. Gwydre was summoned to Arthwyr's chambers and the king bade Myrddin to repeat Sir Jowan's account of Gwalchavad's noble and tragic quest. Then it was Arthwyr's turn to speak. When it was apparent that he would have his eldest son lead an army to recover the Gral, the young knight fell on his knees, his yellow hair spilling over his brow. He took his father's hand and kissed it in gratitude.

"Make your preparations in haste," Arthwyr told him. "Though snow does fall and the wind howls, you cannot wait until springtime. We know where the Gral was the day Gwalchavad died. Perhaps it has already been moved. Perhaps it will be moved soon. We cannot bide our time. Go to the land of Euric, defeat Alaric if you must, return to the holy mountain and find the Gral. You are my son. Bring it to me before I die."

Myrddin grasped the young man's sleeve. "But tell no man what you know of how to find the Gral. There is too much room for treachery—even among those as noble as your father's knights."

Arthwyr dismissed everyone and summoned his queen.

"You honored your son and by so doing you honored me," Gwenhwyfar said.

With her help Arthwyr downed a portion of mead but some of it ran out his swollen mouth onto his shirt. "He is not Gwalchavad but he will be king, and now is his time to prove himself."

"It will be dangerous."

"I know. Keep Cyngen safe, my Queen. Make sure your ladies give him the freshest food. Have them take care he does not climb to the parapets. If Gwydre should come to harm, then young Cyngen will be king."

She kissed his forehead and with a cloth tenderly wiped his face clean.

"Leave me now and send to me Myrddin and Gwydre," Arthwyr said. "Should Gwydre fail and I should die I must ensure that Cyngen might find the Gral when he is of age. My quest will be his quest."

To Myrddin he said, "Send my sword to the smithy. I want him to engrave words on its guard."

Myrddin furrowed his brow. "What words, sire?"

"These words: In the land of Euric in a sacred place on high lie before Christ and find the Gral."

Gwydre asked, "What is the purpose?"

"So that your brother, Cyngen, might find it one day and resume the quest should our present efforts fail. Only you and I and Gwydre will know that place, Myrddin. If any of us should die the others will tell Cyngen where to look when he is older. Will you pledge that?"

Both Gwydre and Myrddin agreed.

"Father, where will you hide the sword?" Gwydre asked.

"In a place that is sacred to me. Though I was born across the sea in Gaul, my boyhood home was my father's castle. It was there, listening to the sea, that I learned how to be a king and it is there where I will hide it."

Weak and in pain, Arthwyr was determined to fulfill his own quest, though it was not as perilous as Gwydre's. Soon after Sir Jowan lost his battle with gangrene and Sir Gwydre's army departed for faraway Euric, Arthwyr's personal guard and entourage left Gwynedd Castle for a three-day journey to Dumnonia. Though swaddled in hay and fur inside a covered wagon, Arthwyr remained dangerously feverish.

Nevertheless, when he arrived at the abandoned castle that had been the court of Uther Pendragon, his father, Arthwyr insisted on standing alone and walking to the edge of the cliff. There he filled his lungs with the briny sea air and felt for a moment like a boy again on the verge of a great adventure.

He squinted up into the cold bright sun. The castle had fallen to ruin only a few decades after it had been vacated. After Uther's death, Arthwyr had no reason to keep it occupied. His realm had grown and Tintagel was too far to the west to be practical. Gwynedd Castle was a better place to rule the Britons and counter invaders from across the sea. Perhaps a quarter of the castle stones were gone, looted, he supposed, by local tribesmen. He hoped that some of the blocks had at least made their way into churches and chapels.

With strong young men ahead and behind to catch him if he fell, Arthwyr slowly made his way down the steep cliff. The weather here was milder: on the coast there was no snow. In his youth the path had been well-worn but it was overgrown now and at points only barely visible. A soldier hacked through thick tall grasses with a short sharp sword until the party reached the beach.

The tide was going out and the sand was wet and dark. Myrddin bore the king's greatsword. He took the shovel from a squire and sent all the men back up the cliff to await his summons. Then he walked beside Arthwyr, ready to lend an arm, as the king trudged to the larger of the two sea caves.

At its mouth, Arthwyr said, "This was always a magical place. I heard voices inside, the voices of my ancestors. Here, my voice will call out to my descendants. Come, let us do the deed."

The cave passed through one side of the cliffs to the other and received light from both mouths. At the halfway point, Arthwyr stopped and gestured.

"Dig there," he commanded his seer. "Dig deep."

When the hole was deep enough for water to just begin to rise, Arthwyr took his engraved sword, kissed it and wrapped it in his cloak. His knees indented the sand as he placed it lovingly into the trench. In short order Myrddin had filled the hole and stamped the sand firm.

Arthwyr pointed to a spot on the cave wall above the buried sword. "There," he said, handing Myrddin a smooth hammerstone. "Take your dagger and chisel the sign of the cross on the rock. It will be a beacon to Cyngen, though I pray he never needs it, for I would dearly love to see the Gral myself in my own lifetime."

The route Gwydre took to Barcino was the same that Gwalchavad had taken—but with three hundred men, a full hundred of them men of arms and knights, they had little trouble with brigands and local warlords. Instead, their enemy was the winter weather that plagued them until the end of the journey when spring began to warm the southern climes.

Myrddin had made sure that his man, Kilian, was part of the troop but Gwydre had no affinity for him or his advice and marginalized him on the march and at camp. Sir Morgant was his true friend and confidant and the two young knights led the column, inseparable.

Their only battle of significance was near Tolosa, the seat of King Alaric's Visigoth kingdom. Gwydre gave the city a wide berth to avoid meeting a much larger army but about a hundred of Alaric's soldiers came upon them on the old Roman road and a fierce skirmish ensued. Gwydre had been itching for a fight to relieve the months of tedium and the Britons fought with ferocity— not a single Visigoth survived the bloody day. Gwydre lost only thirty men and gave thanks to God for a great victory. Kilian was in his good graces that night, proclaiming that he had seen a celestial sign: the Gral, reflected in puddles of enemy blood.

In time, they reached their destination without further engagement by Alaric. To be safe they forewent the comforts and pleasures of Barcino and proceeded directly to the Mountain of Miracles. The mountain trail was just as Jowan and Wallia had described. Armed with the knowledge, Gwydre and Morgant conferred and decided it would be best to station the army at the trailhead to prevent a sneak attack by Alaric from the rear. A small party of the best knights would accompany them up the mountain.

Twenty men began their ascent in the early morning. First on horseback and then on foot, they encountered nary a soul; then, at the high clearing Jowan had described, Gwydre was overcome with joy.

"Go with care and secure the Gral," Morgant told him, "while I seek out the monks."

Spring turned to summer and summer gave way to autumn. Arthwyr had recovered his health after his surgeon removed an abscessed tooth. He took his recovery as an auspicious sign that Gwydre had been successful. Myrddin, for his part, kept analyzing the entrails of goats, though he did not require divination to have certain knowledge that Arthwyr would never see the Gral. He waited hopefully every day—not for Gwydre's return, but for a messenger to tell him that the Gral was in Jerusalem and the Qem were awaiting his arrival there.

Finally, on a bright crisp day, men on the ramparts saw a column approaching and the king and Myrddin were notified.

Both men rushed to the inner courtyard of the castle, joined by the queen and all the nobles to await the entry of the column through the portcullis.

The first knight to appear was not Gwydre. Instead, Morgant rode into the courtyard slowly, his head bowed in despair.

Arthwyr ran to his horse and took its reins. "Where is my son?" he asked.

"He is dead, sire. It was a magnificent death from a wound sustained in battle. He fought like a lion and killed many men before he was dishonorably struck from behind."

Hearing this, the queen began to wail and Arthwyr's knees buckled.

"What of the Gral?"

"Treachery," Morgant said, dismounting. He stared at Myrddin. "Gwydre succeeded! He had it in his hands! I saw it. Then there was a cowardly sneak attack. We were overwhelmed by men who lay in wait. They knew we were coming. Gwydre fought ferociously, like the son of a king. We smote them to a man but the Gral disappeared during the battle and to my everlasting lament I could not find it again. Monks were on the mountain. Perhaps they knew where it was—but even under the harshest treatment I might deliver unto them, they would not say."

"Was it Alaric?" the king demanded. "Was he behind the cowardly adventure?"

"It was not Alaric, sire."

"Who then?"

"Myrddin!" Morgant cried, pointing at the dumbstruck seer. "Kilian named him. This is what Kilian said to the attackers: 'For the Qem! For Myrddin! Kill them all!' I know no more, as I smote Kilian after he uttered these foul words."

"Wretched knave!" Myrddin screamed. "How dare you defame me?"

The king's face turned hateful. "Silence!" he bellowed. "Where is my son's body? What became of him?"

Morgant drew close to the king so he alone could hear his words. "I endeavored to bring him back to you alive, sire. We bore him on a litter across foreign lands for two full months until we could bear him no further, his condition so terrible. We made it to a safe haven in northern Gaul to Castle Maleoré where your mother, Queen Igraine, bore you while Uther Pendragon was warring in those lands and where Uther named you Arthwyr of Maleoré. The lord of the manor received us warmly and gave us food and shelter and his ladies attended to Gwydre. A Norman surgeon declared that his royal rib had saved him from instant death and opened the wound to allow foul humors to escape more easily. That act improved your son to the point where he was able to take some food and drink and regain a measure of strength. It was during this period that he was strong enough to ask for quill and parchment. I know not what he wrote though he was despairing most grievously at the loss of the Gral. His parchment was to be kept at the Castle Maleoré in case treachery or misfortune caused us to fail to return to your court. Alas his fever returned and he could not be saved. By his wish he was buried at the Castle Maleoré." Morgant raised his voice now for all assembled to hear. "With a most heavy heart I rallied the men for the crossing and made way back to your court, driven by my desire to avenge Gwydre's death and see the traitor Myrddin pay for it."

Myrddin had been watching the two men whisper to each other with fear in his eyes. There was nowhere to run so he held his ground, trembling with rage. "Come here, Morgant," Myrddin seethed, "and call me a traitor to my face."

Morgant strode forward, his jaw thrust out in anger, until he was standing toe to toe with the Egyptian.

It happened so quickly Morgant was powerless to act.

Myrddin slashed at him with a concealed dagger and severed his throat, releasing a torrent of red.

As the knight dropped to his knees clutching at his gaping wound, Arthwyr raged, "A sword!" to no one in particular, to everyone.

A nearby knight drew his and gave it to his king.

"What say you, Myrddin, before I kill you?"

Myrddin looked like a trapped animal. As he backpedaled, men made a cordon to hem him in. He made quick little slashes with his knife to hold them at bay.

"The Gral is not for mere kings," he railed, his voice dripping with poison. "It is for men such as I—who know what to do with it."

Arthwyr advanced step by step. "And what would you do with it?"

Myrddin spit onto the dirt. "You are not meant to know these things. Though you may be a king, you are but a lowly creature." Then he cried out, dropping his dagger, "You call this the land of chivalry! Will no man give *me* a sword?"

When none appeared, Arthwyr shouted, "A sword for this swine!"

One was thrown out, clattering at Myrddin's feet. He picked it up and assumed a fighting stance.

Arthwyr charged with a bloodcurdling scream and Myrddin did the same. It was as if two bucks had rushed headlong and crashed antlers.

Both survived the vicious collision and each backed away to regain a good separation.

Then they rushed each other again but after this clash the fight was over.

Both men had succeeded in impaling the other through the chest.

Arthwyr's sword punctured Myrddin's great artery. He died without a word, staring wide-eyed at the sun.

Arthwyr lingered long enough to hear Gwenhwyfar's sobs and feel her lips upon his.

He tried to speak but blood filled his lungs and bubbled out through his mouth.

He *had* to speak.

How else could he tell her where he had buried his sword?

How else could Cyngen undertake the quest when he was a man?

Yet he could not speak. As his life slipped away, the tide was high at Tintagel and the cold waves were lapping onto the sign of the cross over the burial place of a king's great silver sword.

21

When they arrived in Barcelona, Arthur and Claire rented a car at the airport and drove directly toward Montserrat. Unlike the tentative weather in England the spring in Catalonia was full-throated, almost summerlike, and they peeled off their outer clothes and drove with the windows partly down.

It was not a long drive. The monastery was only thirty miles from the airport and as they passed through suburbs then countryside, the sprawling city receding behind them, the landscape took on a dramatic flair. At each leg of the journey, from their morning ride to Heathrow to the Spanish highway, Arthur scanned the environs for any signs of being followed and finally was beginning to relax.

At the first sight of the looming mountain Arthur took one hand off the wheel and touched Claire's hand.

Arthur had spent the previous afternoon planning everything for Spain: flights, car hire, and gathering information about Montserrat. He had decided that a simple day trip to the monastery would be inadequate. The clue they possessed was only reed-thin so he imagined they'd need at least a few days on the mountain to explore the complex.

He learned there were three types of accommodation at the monastery: a three-star hotel, the Hotel Abat de Cisneros, adjacent to the religious buildings but technically outside the grounds; the Celdas

Abat Marcet, a short-term-stay apartment complex, also outside the grounds; and forty-eight pilgrim's rooms within the monastery itself.

The choice was clear.

He had called the monastery's reservation center and was soon talking to a woman who spoke excellent English and who informed him that a single pilgrim room was available.

"I'm not at all sure of the protocol here, but I was rather hoping to stay with my fiancée. Are these rooms for men only?"

"No, we accept couples."

"Even unmarried ones?"

"Yes, unmarried couples are okay. We only ask that all our visitors conduct themselves with modesty."

"Think we can be modest for the next few days?" Arthur had asked Claire afterward.

"I'm not so sure," she'd said with a laugh, "but we can try."

At its peak the mountain stood 4,000 feet over the Plane of Bages, though it appeared higher and more imposing because it stood alone, rising almost vertically from the Llobregat River with no other mountains challenging it for attention. It was a vast labyrinth of pastel limestone with heaps of fairy-tale conical peaks, some with such fanciful names as The Mummy, The Cat, The Pipes, The Pharaoh, The Death Head.

There was a good paved road leading up the mountain and when Arthur rounded the last curved section the monastery revealed itself.

"Would you look at that?" he said quietly.

It seemed natural to keep one's voice down for there was something ethereal about the sight of it, as though a loud noise or sharp movement might cause it to fly up and disappear. The basilica and surrounding structures seemed magical, built as they were on a narrow 2,500-foot plateau sandwiched between a sheer drop into the valley on one side and towering peaks on the other. The buildings were fashioned from the same pink limestone as the mountain, and though they owed their existence to the labor of men, they appeared to have arisen from the same forces that shaped the mountain.

Arthur parked the car in one of the designated areas and he and Claire made their way through the crowds of day trippers who had arrived on tour buses or the funicular railway. It was hot and sunny. The low-lying clouds had already burned away and the views into the valley seemed to stretch to infinity. They announced themselves at the visitor's center and sat on a bench, their small bags at their feet, affixing guest badges to their chests and waiting for one of the monks.

Brother Oriol arrived quickly and in passable English apologized for whatever wait they had encountered. He was tall and youthful, no more than thirty, with a thick brown beard and glasses. He wore the black robe and black hooded scapular of the Benedictines, and treaded silently on crepe-soled shoes.

The monk asked where they were from and made small, friendly comments about England and France as he led them inside the complex. On learning this was their first visit he asked for their initial impression of the monastery. He seemed to like the way Claire gushed over the natural beauty of the place and launched into a discourse on the importance of Montserrat to the Catalan people.

"It is a deep part of our heritage. The people of Catalonia venerate Our Lady of Montserrat in a special way as their own mother and patroness. Yes, we have tourists and pilgrims from all over the world but the local people—well, many of them—regard at least one visit a year to the Shrine of the Black Madonna as an obligation not to be overlooked and one which they fulfill faithfully as a ritual."

"The statue is in the basilica, yes?" Arthur asked.

"Yes, but right now the lines will be very long. Since you are staying you can visit at a quieter time in the late afternoon or early morning and spend more time seeing the Madonna."

He led them through an arched passageway overlooking a lovely green cloistered garden and through the so-called Gothic Chamber, which had a fine corbelled ceiling and walls lined with medieval tapestries. Up a flight of stone stairs they entered a more modern building, which, the monk explained, housed the guest rooms for pilgrims, the monks' quarters, dining facilities, the library, and the chapter house.

The abbot had his apartment in the adjacent building. There were sixty-eight monks at the monastery, mostly Catalan men.

The guest room floor looked very much like a modest hotel. Brother Oriol unlocked the door to Room 13 and showed them in. The quarters were tiny and basic. A table with three Catalan books: the New Testament, the Bible, and the Rules of St. Benedict; a bed, a chair, and a lavatory with shower.

"The bed is quite small," Brother Oriol apologized.

The window looked as though it hadn't been washed in a long while but through streaks the tourist-filled courtyard of the basilica was visible.

"If you can leave your bags, I will show you the dining hall."

The monk took them to the nearby dining room, which was being prepared for a buffet lunch by two laywomen. Then he showed them a small lounge with a few books and some reading chairs and that was the extent of the tour. They were free to wander in all the public areas of the monastery but were prohibited from entering the private areas reserved for the monks. If they needed further information, there was a sheet in their room with the times of masses, several books in the lounge, and more in the gift shops.

Arthur thanked him for his time and added, "You must be quite busy here."

"We have much to occupy us. We pray five times a day, we receive and counsel visitors, we work in many vocations, the one best known to the outside world being our choir school, *L'Escolania*, one of the oldest boy choirs in the world."

Then with a bow, Brother Oriol politely explained he had to be on his way.

They took a walk in the sunshine, mingling with the polyglot tourists, and then went to the shops to buy some English-language books on the monastery. When it was time for lunch they returned to the guest dining room now filling with earnest-looking middle-aged and elderly visitors, most of them men. Perhaps because they were new to the group and were youngest, they attracted attention and conversation. The guests were from all over the world, many of them avid monastery travelers who liked to "pray and stay," as they put it. For their part, Arthur and Claire told their companions that they too were interested in a few days of quiet prayer and contemplation in this beautiful spot.

At 12:30 the diners began to disperse to attend midday mass in the basilica. Arthur and Claire were told they absolutely must attend since the famous boy choir would sing some hymns.

As they were heading back to their room, Arthur's mobile phone rang from a UK number he didn't recognize. It was Sandy Marina calling from Oxford. She sounded peculiar and somber.

"Are you on the continent?" she asked.

"Yes, Spain."

"I could tell by the dial tone. It probably explains why you haven't called. You don't know, do you?"

"What's happened, Sandy?"

She began to cry. "It's lightning striking twice. It's Tony. I'll just come out and say it, Arthur. He's been killed."

She told him how he'd been found that morning, in his office at UCL, shot dead. His wallet was missing, his watch. It was thought to have been a robbery. There'd been some drug-related crimes in the area of late.

Claire saw his ashen face and asked in a whisper if something was wrong. He nodded and she unlocked the room door.

He sat on the bed and heard Sandy say, "First Holmes, now Tony. It's too much to bear. It's almost as if our little group is cursed."

"I saw Tony yesterday morning, Sandy. I was at UCL showing him something. I found what Holmes found."

"What was it?"

"I'm not going to tell you. It's too dangerous. These people who want the Grail are killers. They killed Holmes and they probably killed Tony. They're after me too."

"Surely the police will believe you now."

"I can't trust the police."

"Jesus! Are you on the hunt? In Spain? Arthur, are you in Montserrat?"

"Please don't ask me more questions. I'll tell you about it when I get back. Until then, just tell the Loons I'm far away and can't get back for the funeral. Christ, Sandy, I wish I could give you a big hug right now."

Claire had heard enough of the conversation. She looked scared.

He held her and murmured, "It's going to be all right … no one knows we're here."

"How can you be sure?"

"No one followed us from baggage claim to the rental car. No one followed us from Barcelona. No one followed us up the mountain."

"What should we do?"

"Let's go to the church and say a prayer for Tony."

The basilica was cool and dark, a Gothic jewel sparkling with gilded wood and gold-toned mosaic. High above the altar through an open balcony the gilded Black Madonna of Montserrat—a virgin and child with faces blackened from ancient ebony-toned wood—gleamed in a shaft of light that pierced the church through a towering window.

Arthur and Claire sat in a middle pew in sad contemplation as one of the priests celebrated mass in Latin and Catalan. Then the choir appeared, boys in white scapulars, marching into position, flanking the altar. Their choirmaster conducted them through three hymns, sweet soprano voices melding and soaring through the cathedral, bringing Claire to tears.

The mass over, the crowd began leaving, some exiting to the sunlit courtyard, others joining the queue to climb a narrow stairway to see the Black Madonna. Arthur and Claire blinked at the sunshine.

A large man with a beard and a wide-brimmed tropical hat held back, lurking in the shadows inside the cathedral entrance. When he saw Arthur and Claire cross the courtyard and enter the dormitory building Griggs stepped into the light, slipped on sunglasses and calmly sauntered toward the Hotel Abat de Cisneros.

22

In the dormitory Arthur heard footsteps from behind. He nervously looked over his shoulder to see a monk overtaking them. He had a smooth youthful face and a serious expression and he apologized for the narrow corridor. Arthur recognized him as the choirmaster.

"Your choir was beautiful," Arthur said.

The monk stopped to thank them, taking notice of their guest badges and Claire's tear-streaked face.

His English was even better than Brother Oriol's. He introduced himself as *L'Escolania*'s headmaster, Brother Pau.

"You're crying," he said to Claire. "I didn't think the boys were that good today."

She wiped her eyes. "We just learned that someone we know died. We're still in shock."

"I'm very sorry to hear that. Tell me your friend's name and I will pray for him."

"Tony," Arthur said.

"Very well, I will pray for Tony's soul."

Arthur shook his hand in thanks.

"Are you doing something just now?" Brother Pau asked. "If not, perhaps I can show you a few special places. I have a free half hour before I have to teach."

"You're very kind," Claire said, and when she smiled the serious young monk smiled too.

He escorted them on a brisk tour of the ornate chapel house, a capacious vaulted room with seating in the round where the monks prayed together, listened to their abbot read from the St. Benedict's Book of Rules, and discussed community matters. A large mural that depicted the monks of Montserrat being martyred during the Spanish Civil War loomed over them. The library was on the floor above guest quarters, its central room an achingly beautiful two stories with an open gallery and skylights set into a barrel-vaulted ceiling. The library, which housed some 300,000 books and manuscripts, was built in the nineteenth century—though, according to Brother Pau, there was some evidence of a library here as far back as the eleventh century.

Arthur seized on the opportunity to ask questions. The quest was more urgent than ever. He imagined Tony and Holmes urging him on.

"Everything I've read about Montserrat suggests the earliest structures were from the early part of the tenth century. Is it possible there were even earlier religious communities here?"

"It is difficult to say," the monk answered. "There are no documents to shed light on this. My own belief is that this was a holy site from almost the time of Christ. If there were hermitages here going back centuries before the accepted dates, it wouldn't surprise me at all."

"The basilica isn't very old, is it?" Arthur asked.

"Not so old, late nineteenth, early twentieth century. The original Romanesque church was lost to fire during the Napoleonic Wars."

"The crypts below the basilica aren't old then?"

"No, they are relatively recent, though quite interesting. You may visit them on your own."

"What are the oldest remaining parts of the monastery?" Claire asked.

"There is a small twelfth-century crypt, the Crypt of the Clericates, adjacent to the music library inside the choir school; and, of course, the Hermitage of Sant Iscle, a chapel that is mentioned in a ninth-century text."

Arthur had been gazing at the spines of ancient books. At once he looked up. “Could it be older?”

“It is possible, at least the foundation, but this has never been studied. Let me show you some fascinating nineteenth-century photographs we have on display in the next room.”

As they walked, Arthur asked more about the collection. “I imagine you have some important ancient manuscripts and letters here?”

“Indeed yes. Some of the earliest Catalan texts in existence, though I am sorry to say much material was lost when the monastery was burned by Napoleon.”

“I apologize for that,” Claire said.

“This is not your cross to bear, I think.”

Arthur continued, “A friend of mine, a professor of medieval studies, recently was permitted to do research here.”

“Ah, yes, we have scholars visiting from around the world.”

“He found a twelfth-century letter concerning the Holy Grail.”

“Always an interesting topic,” the monk said, checking his watch. “I have time to show you one more room, the sacristy. Come along.”

The sacristy was adjacent to the basilica, a frescoed vault with rich mahogany cabinetry for sacramental vestments. While Brother Pau was describing the architectural details, Arthur’s eye was drawn to a fresco on the far end of the long room, a depiction of the Last Supper. In it, a rather young and handsome Jesus had his left hand on a loaf of bread and his right hovering over a large simple chalice.

Arthur pointed to it. “That’s quite beautiful.”

“Yes it is. The mural is by Josep Obiols.”

“The Grail is painted quite prominently. Tell me, what do you think about the legends that say the Grail is here at Montserrat?”

The monk seemed irritated by the question. “You know, this is a tiresome subject for us. There is no basis for it. It has no relevance for us. You are not a Grail tourist, are you, Arthur?”

“I don’t know what a Grail tourist is but I don’t think I’m one of them,” Arthur said as dismissively as he could.

The monk must have realized his sharp tone because he then said apologetically, “I have to return to the school now. You may walk with me if you wish.”

The choir school was in a long rectangular four-story building at the far end of the complex. As they made their way, Brother Pau told them about the school and a recent tour they had made to Russia that was a great success and had yielded their latest music CD. His pride was palpable and on Claire’s prodding about his own background he revealed that in his youth he too had been one of the choirboys. At the entrance to the school he wished them well then pointed toward a walled garden lined by needle-thin Italian Cypresses.

“The old chapel of Sant Iscle is located down there.”

“May we see it?” Arthur asked.

“I’m afraid not. It’s private, for the monks.”

In the afternoon they visited the crypt under the basilica and satisfied themselves that it was a relatively modern affair with no relevance to the early medieval period. The nineteenth-century basilica wasn’t even built on the original site of the Romanesque church; even if one could take a jackhammer to its floor, they likely would find nothing of importance.

The queues now thinning, they ascended with the faithful onto the balcony to see the Black Madonna. Although there were perhaps thousands of such statues worldwide, either blackened with age or deliberately by the artist, none were more revered than the Madonna of Montserrat, which had become a cultural symbol of Catalonia.

According to legend, the statue had been found a short distance from the monastery when shepherds saw celestial lights and heard heavenly music, which led them to a mountain cave. The bishop of Manressa was summoned and suggested moving the virgin and child to his church on a pallet; but as the villagers progressed down the mountain trail, the pallet grew heavier and heavier until they reached the site of the old hermitage, whereupon they could move it no further. Thus the Madonna had shown her insistence to remain at Montserrat.

Now at the top of the narrow stairs, Arthur watched Claire drop to her knees before the statue. Claire began to silently pray until a glance at those behind her in the queue prompted her to rise and move along.

That night they ate communally, read their guidebooks in the guest lounge and made plans. Others chatted amiably, worked on jigsaw puzzles, and read the Bible—gentle, contemplative pursuits perfect for the time and place. Claire briefly excused herself to call her parents and when she returned declared that all was well on the home front.

They were tired. It had been only two days since their all-nighter in Stoneleigh and they hadn't yet caught up with their sleep; and Tony's death was a heavy yoke. They retired at nine.

The bed was indeed narrow. They lay on their sides facing each other, inches away.

"You seemed taken by the Black Madonna," he said.

"It was very beautiful."

"You're Catholic?"

"Of course. I'm French."

"I watched you pray. You seemed, well, ardent."

"A good word for it. I am ardent. I believe in God without reservation."

"You must be in a minority: physicists who are believers."

"Maybe, but a minority in good company: Max Planck, Arthur Compton, George Lemaître—who was a priest, you know; Werner Heisenberg, Freeman Dyson, Christopher Isham, many others. Even Einstein, who maybe didn't believe in a personal God, thought a non-created universe impossible. Tell me, Arthur, what are your beliefs?"

"We Church of England types are a bloodless lot when it comes to religion. We don't wear it on our sleeves. But I believe more than I don't believe, if that makes sense."

"Yes, it makes sense … and if you find the Grail? Will that change anything?"

"Well, it would be a tangible connection to Christ, but a connection to a man named Jesus, not necessarily the Son of God."

"You don't believe in the Resurrection?"

"Do you?"

"Yes, absolutely."

"And how does the physicist in you explain the phenomenon?"

"There's a lot we don't understand. I'm not sure that physics and spirituality are incompatible."

"I'd like to hope your faith is well-founded. I'd like to believe that Tony Ferro and Andy Holmes are having a celestial pint together around about now. Listen, Claire, I've been thinking about this all day. I think you should go back to France tomorrow. I'm worried about your safety. I've got to do this but you don't."

She leaned forward the small distance that separated them and kissed him. "The answer is no. I feel perfectly safe with you. Now tell me, what time are you setting the alarm?"

He returned the kiss. "Two A.M."

Griggs lightly tapped the door of the adjoining room at the Hotel Abat de Cisneros. Hengst opened it. He was dressed in black like Griggs.

Hengst saw that Griggs had his tactical bag. "What do you need that for?"

"I don't want to leave it in the room."

Hengst shrugged at the explanation. "What makes you sure they'll go roving tonight?"

"I'm not. But they might."

The two men crept across the deserted moonlit plaza and took a position a hundred yards away from the dormitory doors behind a parked utility van. Griggs unzipped his bag and removed the rifle.

"What are you doing?" Hengst whispered.

"Relax. I'm just using its night scope."

"Tell me why I should believe you."

"Because I'm your boss."

"He gave specific orders," Hengst said.

"I've been following those orders. I could have killed him in Wokingham but I didn't, did I?"

"Maybe he was too fast for you."

Griggs was steaming up. "Your balls aren't in a vice. Mine are. I've done three for him now. How many have you done? That's right, zero. So zip it. I'm tired of being second-guessed, mate."

Arthur's phone alarm beeped them awake and they groggily dressed in the lamplight. They dressed in their darkest clothes and pocketed small LED flashlights.

The mountain air was sweet and cool. The monastery grounds and surrounding buildings were dark and empty. Guests, monks, and choirboys were all asleep. Under a moon three quarters full, they were easily able to find their way into the walled garden.

The twin rows of Italian Cypresses were like runway lights to a pilot. They followed the cloistered strip of garden directly to the wooden door of the small stone chapel.

The chapel was simple and ancient, no bigger than most sunrooms attached to suburban homes. It was made of irregular, roughhewn limestone blocks at one time plastered over, though much of that plaster was gone. A gently sloped tile roof and small open belfry was topped by a diminutive cross. The brown door was arched and decorated with wrought iron scrolls. There was no visible lock.

"Here goes," Arthur said, giving it a push. He had hoped he wouldn't have to force the door and he didn't. It swung open and they were in.

They both clicked on their flashlights and explored the space. It was a single rectangular room with an apse at the farthest end. A chunky limestone altar, within the apse, stood on a platform of the same blocks as the chapel walls. The altar was flanked by pair of chest-high candlesticks, and above it stood a very simple, very ancient black iron cross. The walls were plastered, pale green and unadorned. One modest grated window graced the apse. A modern space heater was against one wall, unnecessary now but no doubt welcome on a winter day. The floor was fashioned from large stone tiles smooth with antiquity and mostly covered by a sisal mat so the monks could prostrate themselves without too much discomfort.

It was an uncomplicated room.

"This is our only shot," Arthur said. "If it's not here, there isn't any other place around conceivably from the fifth century."

"Then let's get to work," Claire said.

They started with the altar, searching behind it, pushing and pulling at its limestone slabs but it was solid and weighed a ton or more. The walls were next. The two spent the better part of twenty minutes meticulously rapping at the plaster with their knuckles, trying to detect a hollow.

When they'd exhausted that they turned to the floor.

"Help me roll up the rug," Arthur said.

As they knelt, their backs to the altar, Griggs rose up and spied them through the grate in the window then quickly dropped from sight.

Claire lightly tapped the tile stones while Arthur stood back, taking a longer view, sweeping the stones with his light.

Hers went out and she swore. "I broke it."

He laughed. "What did you think would happen?"

As he bent to help her up, he pulled back his hand and shined his beam on a spot.

"Look!"

She saw it but he'd already found another and then two more.

Four shallow indentations in two adjacent tile stones.

"Lie before Christ and find the Grail," she whispered.

"Hand- and footholds," he said, breathing faster. "Take my light and shine it there."

He had a ballpoint pen in his pocket and he used it to probe the mortar between two tiles. Then he scraped at another stripe separating two different stones.

"The first one's softer, more crumbly. Let me give it a go."

He flopped on his belly and felt the coolness of the stones through his shirt.

The altar and cross were before him.

He felt for the grooves with his feet and found them, bearing down with his toes.

Then he grasped the handholds.

"They would have been shorter," he complained.

"You want me to try?"

"I think I'm stronger."

He held his breath and bore down, pulling with his fingers while maintaining a counterforce with his toes.

Nothing happened.

Grunting, he tried again.

Was there a faint cracking sound?

He doubled his effort, feeling his face flush and ears burn.

There was movement—a small movement of one of the tiles.

One more.

He'd lifted weights when he played rugby. As he had always done while pressing out the last implausible rep, he gritted his teeth. An animalistic growl emanated from his core.

Suddenly the stone under his torso shifted then fell away, partly dropping into a void.

Claire shouted out in surprise, "Are you all right?"

Arthur found himself angled downward, his head below the surface of the floor. Startled, he scrambled to his feet.

"The light," he said. "Shine it down there!"

He saw the way the simple trapdoor had been constructed. The stone, which slid back, had been resting on a half-inch lip: once the false mortar gave way, it moved a little more than half that distance until it dropped down.

He got Claire to help him lift the stone clear of the hole. They propped it against the rolled-up mat.

The hole under the stone was only large enough for three shoe boxes.

Shining his light on it, he felt bitter disappointment welling up. It was empty.

He swore.

"No wait," Claire said, pointing. "Look."

Then he saw it in the corner, a small yellow square of paper.

He reached for it and unfolded it.

There were three words, a florid signature, and a date.

Ho he trobat!
A Gaudí, 1883

"What does it mean?" Claire asked.

"I don't know but let's hurry up and get this floor put back together."

They maneuvered the tile back in its place and lowered the stone back onto its lip, snatching away their fingers lest they be crushed.

As they worked, Griggs watched them through the grated window.

Arthur cautiously went outside for a handful of dirt to replace the pseudo-mortar.

A soft rustling gave him a start but he thought it only the trees, swaying in the freshening wind.

The patch job done, he stamped on the cracks and declared it as good as they could make it. They unrolled the mat and left the chapel and now stood under the towering cypresses, their tops painted yellow by moonlight.

Arthur had a translation app on his mobile phone and typed in the three-word message.

It was Catalan.

I have found it!

Arthur whispered, "It was here!"

Griggs had withdrawn about sixty yards to higher ground, propping himself against a waist-high wall at the boundary of the monastery.

He raised his rifle and sighted through the sniper scope. With small, practiced movements Griggs clicked on the laser and clicked off the safety.

Hengst appeared at his side. "What the hell are you doing?"

"He found something," Griggs said.

"Is it the Grail?"

"I don't care. It's time to put him down."

"Not unless we're sure it's the Grail."

Griggs placed his finger on the trigger. "Fuck off."

Arthur and Claire were outside the chapel whispering to one another when suddenly she gasped at the red dot dancing over Arthur's temple.

Before she could react, Hengst grabbed the stock of the rifle and pulled it from Grigg's cheek. The sound of the suppressed shot was imperceptible but the heavy bullet crashed and sparked into limestone.

"Get down!" Claire cried, reaching for him.

"What was that?" Arthur said, falling to the grass with her.

"There was a laser on you!"

Griggs maintained a hold as Hengst lunged, using the butt of his rifle to deliver a blow to the other man's face. Hengst grunted and crumpled to the ground.

Repositioning himself further along the wall, Griggs started to reacquire his target through the scope.

"Where the hell are you?" he muttered.

Arthur and Claire were near the door of the chapel, shielded from Griggs by the building.

"If we try to get back to the dormitory, he's going to have a clear shot at us," Arthur said.

"We can't stay here!"

"I've got to go for him," Arthur insisted, panting.

"No!"

"Here. Take the note and the car keys. If I don't come back, get away from here tonight. Go back to France. Forget this ever happened."

"Arthur …"

He got up into a crouch, felt her hand dropping off his shoulder and moved to the corner of the chapel. Then, after a few bolstering breaths, he sprinted toward the perimeter wall.

Griggs continued scanning the walkways from the chapel to the buildings. He was just about to make a move toward the chapel when Arthur spotted him twenty-five yards away, silhouetted against the moonlit sky. Arthur found an egg-sized rock and threw it into the darkness. It landed with a thud to Grigg's left, drawing his attention.

Arthur ran toward the sniper as fast as he could, his mind icy, in survival mode.

Griggs heard him a moment before Arthur was on him and wheeled his rifle around, a fraction too late. Arthur rammed a shoulder into the man's hard gut, the momentum from the charge toppling him.

Arthur heard cursing. With balled-up fists he tried to pummel the man on the ground into some kind of submission but Griggs wasn't going down so easily. He still had a hold of the rifle and with a sharp upward jab thrust the mounted scope into Arthur's tender ribs.

As Arthur gasped and doubled over, Griggs started to his feet. If he rose it was over. He would have pushed the barrel against Arthur's head and jerked off a fatal round. Arthur scrambled up first and desperately swung his fist into the side of the other man's head.

His hand exploded in pain. It was like punching a brick wall and didn't seem to stop Griggs from rising. Arthur half expected the fellow to shake off the punch and laugh but something different happened.

Griggs stopped moving. His rifle slid from his hands. Without uttering a sound he teetered and fell backward over the wall, tumbling five hundred feet down the mountain, his lifeless body coming to rest in a dense thicket of forest.

Arthur heard tree branches snapping. He peered over the wall, seeing nothing but a chasm.

He ran back to the chapel where Claire met him with frantic sobs.

"Thank God! I was so scared."

"Come on," he said, pulling her toward the dormitory. "We've got to get out of here."

Hengst rubbed his swollen cheek and walked over to the wall where Griggs had gone over. He holstered his pistol, its suppressor still warm from the 9 mm round.

Grigg's sniper rifle was lying in the grass near the wall. Hengst picked it up and put it on safe.

"Sweet."

The man was awakened by his encrypted mobile phone at 3 A.M. He clicked on the bedside light. His wife was in a separate room in another wing of the mansion. They both preferred the arrangement.

"Yes?" he answered hoarsely, confused by an interrupted dream and muddled by the brandy still in his system.

"I'm sorry to wake you but there's been a development."

"Who is this?"

"I'm sorry, it's Peter Hengst. Griggs tried to kill Malory. I had to shoot him."

"Griggs, you shot Griggs?"

"Yes."

"Is he dead?"

"He is."

"And Malory is all right?"

"Yes. Freaked out I'm sure but none the wiser, I reckon."

"I knew I couldn't trust Griggs to stand down. Bastard. Where are you?"

"Still in Montserrat. I think Malory found something. In a small chapel on the grounds."

He closed his eyes tightly and asked, "Was it the Grail?"

"I don't think so. I heard Malory say something like, 'it was here.'"

The man opened his eyes in disappointment. "Okay, clean up any mess. You know what to do. Keep following them. I expect you know what this means?"

"No sir, what?"

"It means you're promoted."

23

They drove in stunned silence, the dark mountain receding in the rearview mirror.

Finally, Arthur said, "I killed someone."

"You had no choice."

"I didn't think I hit him that hard."

He gripped the steering wheel so tightly it hurt his bruised hand.

"Do you want me to drive?" she asked.

"I'll be okay. I need to focus."

"Was it the man who killed your friends?"

"I'm not sure. It was dark. It could have been."

"Then maybe he was the one who killed Tony too."

"Maybe."

"Then I'm glad he's dead. Hopefully, that's the end of it. Hopefully, you won't be followed anymore."

"Interested parties," Arthur said in a monotone. "That's what he said that night. This isn't over, Claire. There's more than one of them. It won't be over till we find the Grail."

As he drove along the deserted highway, he tried to put the thoughts of the tumbling man out of his head and concentrate on what they'd found.

Antoni Gaudí.

He knew little of the man beyond the barest of bones. He was an architect; the genius behind some of Barcelona's most important buildings.

I have found it!

They'd have to go to Barcelona.

The road was clear. It seemed sure there was no one following them. But he'd been sure that they weren't followed to Montserrat.

He passed Claire his phone. Its screen glowed in the dark as she read out descriptions of centrally

located hotels in the city. Arthur chose one and Claire rang the hotel. A night clerk told them they could check in before dawn.

They arrived at the Gothic Quarter just off Las Ramblas. The Hotel España had struck Arthur as an auspicious choice since, by its description, it had been designed by one of Gaudí's contemporaries, Lluis Domènech.

Arthur went to the ice machine down the hall from their room and iced his swollen hand.

"Do you think it's broken?" Claire asked.

"I doubt it. I've broken bones playing rugby. As a rule of thumb, if it's not sticking through the skin it's not that bad."

They were too tired to undress. For the next five hours they slept deeply and, were it not for Arthur's phone alarm, would have slept well into the afternoon.

When they awoke they asked the concierge where they might find a good bookstore in the area. The Librería La Central del Raval was in a refurbished seventeenth-century church a short walk from the hotel. It was spacious, with a generous selection and a bustling café but after several minutes of futile browsing they decided they needed help navigating the Catalan.

The manager, who looked like a bushy-haired academic, offered to escort them to the Gaudí material.

"On his work, his architecture, we have this selection here translated to English. The best, in my opinion, is by the Gaudí scholar Esteve Vallespir, maybe not the best pictures but the most profound analysis. This one here has the best photos. It's quite beautiful but it's more of a coffee table book, not something to carry around."

Arthur took both while Claire added, "We also need books on his life. We want to understand him too, not just his buildings."

The manager nodded appreciatively. "Biographies, yes, this is the right approach to completely understand Gaudí. I think you're not ordinary tourists. I have only two biographies in English. This one, written in English by a Dutch author, is quite excellent; and this older one, translated from Catalan, also has some useful insights I think."

As the manager was ringing up the purchases, Arthur said, "You've been very helpful. Beyond the books, could you possibly steer us to someone in the city, a curator, a professor, someone we could talk with to get some questions answered?"

The young man scrunched his forehead. "Well, the one I can contemplate is the librarian at the Enric Casanelles Library at the Gaudí House Museum. It's not open to the public but maybe you can place a call there."

"You wouldn't have the number, would you?" Claire asked.

"Maybe, somewhere," he said, looking a bit harried.

"Do you think they speak English?" Claire smiled at him very sweetly.

The manager sighed. "Would you like me to speak to the librarian for you? She's been to our store many times. I know her."

"You're amazing!" Claire said, making him blush.

In a few minutes the manager returned from his office smiling. The librarian, Isabella Bellver, would see them in the afternoon as a favor.

At the hotel they flopped on the bed, ordered some coffee and divided the books between them, spending the next couple of hours reading passages to each other.

"Gaudí was born in 1852, so in 1883 he was thirty-one."

"After he graduated from the Architectural School in Barcelona he fell in with a group called the Modernists, who searched for the cultural identity of the Catalans through architecture."

"It says that Gaudí discarded traditional architectural building blocks—cubes, spheres, and prisms—and replaced them with the geometrically warped shapes of things in nature such as flowers, bones, the stems of plants."

"Listen to this. In 1883, he was recommended for a project to build a cathedral to honor the holy family, the Sagrada Família. Gaudí didn't want to do it at first. He resisted taking it on but for some reason he changed his mind and worked on it until the day he died, forty-three years later. Work has been continuous since that time and it's still going on. It won't be finished till 2026, believe it or not."

"1883. You think it's a coincidence?"

"Who knows?"

"Also about the same time he essentially became the family architect for Eusebi Güell, a rich industrialist, and he designed buildings and gardens for the family his whole career. We're going to Parc Güell this afternoon. Gaudí and Güell lived in houses next to each other for a time. Gaudí's house is the museum now."

"After Güell died in 1918, Gaudí took no more outside commissions and worked exclusively on Sagrada Família. He eventually moved into his studio at the cathedral and lived there till his death."

"In 1926, he was walking from Sagrada Família to take mass when he was hit by a cable car. The police thought he was a vagrant at first and took him to a charity hospital where he died a few days later. His funeral was one of the largest Barcelona had ever seen. There was a debate where he should be buried and in the end he received a special dispensation from the Church to be interred in the crypt in Sagrada Família."

"In 1936, during the Spanish Civil War, his workshop and archive at Sagrada Família were ransacked and most of his personal papers, architectural plans, and scale models were destroyed."

When they were done they had extracted the essence of his life as if it were juice from a lemon; but it was merely a collection of facts, bringing them no closer to *I have found it!*

After lunch they flagged a taxi and headed north to the hill of El Carmel. Their appointment with the librarian wasn't for an hour so they thought they might get to Parc Güell early and have a look around first.

At once, Claire grasped Arthur's arm and pointed. The spires of Sagrada Família had come into view.

"Can we go there first?" she asked.

"We've got time for a quick look around but no more than that."

The taxi driver let them off in the square beside the cathedral's Nativity Façade and they arched their necks in wonder.

It was almost impossible to fathom the scale and complexity and audacity of Gaudí's cathedral. Eight of the planned eighteen towers soared to dizzying heights against the pale blue sky, exceeded only by the construction cranes that rose higher. The Nativity Façade and its bell towers, the first section completed, was both familiar and alien at once. They seemed hard as the stone from which they were fashioned but soft as a confection melting in the sun.

Though the cathedral was as rooted to the earth as any man-made structure could be, it also appeared to be growing right in front of one's eyes. From every column and arch and spire dripped the most intricate symbologies, drawn from the natural world: turtles, chameleons, oxen, mules, snakes, birds, eggs; the signs of the zodiac. Then there were the plants: leaves, fronds, branches and stems, entire cypress trees. And a human statuary that seemed without end. Musician angels. Adoring shepherds. The three kings of the Orient. Mary, crowned by Jesus, as Saint Joseph looks on. And despite the density of detail, no one element ever competes with another: all harmonize, like the myriad instruments in a symphony orchestra.

Arthur and Claire walked its circumference, weaving through crowds of tourists, taking in the Passion Façade to the east and the incomplete Glory Façade to the south. Claire took pictures with her mobile phone. They stayed silent, tacitly knowing that simple words of surprise and delight might trivialize the experience.

Only when they climbed into another cab did Claire exclaim, "My God! Did a man build that? What kind of a mind could conceive this?"

24

BARCELONA, 1883

He cut a rather imperious figure, this thirty year old, a man finding his stride in the hard, competitive world of professional architecture in a city that defined itself as Europe's architectural jewel.

He already had a reputation as a rising star and carried himself erect, head up, shoulders back, and legs striding purposefully. Though far from tall and not at all handsome, he had a way of turning heads. It was his confident demeanor, his reddish hair, imposing beard, and his glorious blue eyes.

He left his apartment building, savoring the warm autumn air with its aromas of baked bread and roasted meats, and began walking down the narrow carrer del Call. He had an hour until his appointment in the Eixample district, and set a moderate pace to keep on time.

"Good day, Senyor Gaudí," a tailor called out from his open-fronted shop.

He had been lost in thought and he replied with a start. "Good day. Yes, it is. A fine day. Not a cloud in the sky."

He had much on his mind. In the five years since receiving his qualifications, new architectural commissions were coming in fast. One was a workers cooperative, La Obrera Mataronense; another, Casa Vincens, a large private residence in the Gràcia district; and a hunting pavilion for an influential industrialist, Eusebi Güell, who hinted that there could be more family projects if things went well. Today's meeting was something of a nuisance. A book dealer named Bocabella, whom he had never met but who was widely regarded as a flagrant eccentric, had begun a personally financed ecclesiastical project: a new cathedral in a city that already had one, the venerable Cathedral of the Holy Cross and Saint Eulalia.

Apparently, there was a problem with the first architect hired for the project. Francisco de Paula del Villar had lasted only a year, throwing up his hands in frustration over his dealings with Bocabella. Juan Martorell, one of Gaudí's old professors and a champion of the young man's enormous talents, had put him forward, and Gaudí, only out of respect, agreed to take a meeting with the bookseller.

Approaching the building site just north of the carriage-laden and fashionable Avinguda Diagonal, Gaudí saw the better part of a hundred workers milling around a large scrubby lot. A partial foundation had been laid but it was impossible to ascertain any specific design. He had heard vague talk about a neo-Gothic structure but hadn't given it a thought; he had his own projects to worry about.

Bocabella spotted him first and rushed over to greet his visitor.

From a distance he shouted, "You must be Gaudí—I was told you had red hair and you are the only red-haired man I see!"

Bocabella had a shock of white hair and a bushy white mustache. He was twice Gaudí's age but moved like a much younger man, with small quick steps and seemingly boundless energy. When he was within hand-shaking distance he pulled up and stared.

"This is Providence, Senyor! There is no other explanation. Just the other night I dreamed that the man who would come to save my project, which this scoundrel Villar has tried to destroy, would have blue eyes! You have the bluest eyes I have ever seen!"

Gaudí did not know how to respond other than simply to say, "Well, I am pleased to meet you, sir. Your work and your philanthropy on behalf of the church are well known to me."

Bocabella was the founder of the Asociación Espiritual de Devotos de San José, a group dedicated to honoring Saint Joseph, whom they believed had never received the same level of respect as the Virgin Mary. "The whole family is important!" Bocabella would fume. "This is not to diminish in any way the Holy Mother and the Holy Child. But Joseph was Mary's husband and nothing is more important than the family in our Christian way of life. It is especially important for the poor and unfortunate among us. This will be a temple for the poor!"

His church would be called Basílica i Temple Expiatori de la Sagrada Família, although everyone called it by its shortened name. Work had begun in 1882. Villar had conceived the church to be in the Gothic revival tradition, done in a standard cathedral form.

Gaudí was taken on a tour of the construction site. He peered into the excavated shell of a crypt, inspected the foundations and noted the desultory working habits of the stonemasons.

"Yes, Senyor," Bocabella agreed. "The men are like a ship without a rudder. I cannot supervise them. I know books. I know nothing about stones."

Gaudí reviewed Villar's architectural plans and silently dismissed them as ordinary and uninspired. Gaudí already had formed a strong esthetic style, embracing the possibilities of modernism and venturing beyond it to incorporate ever more naturalistic features. He couldn't walk through a park without plucking a tulip to examine its stem or come upon a dead bird without studying its wings. A physician friend once ushered him into the anatomy suite of the medical school to witness a human skeleton stripped of its flesh.

At the end of the tour, Bocabella impetuously offered him the commission on the spot.

"You are the man for this, Senyor Gaudí. I have no doubt. Will you take on this temple? Will you help me create my vision?"

Gaudí politely answered that he would consider the offer but advised Bocabella that he was extremely busy and not at all sure he could do a project of this size and scope the justice it required. He made it clear, however, that in the unlikely event he were to accept, he would not be a slave to Villar's design. He would have to have complete architectural control.

Bocabella eagerly nodded. "When will I have your answer?" he pressed.

"I am off for a brief respite to Montserrat," Gaudí answered. "You will have my reply when I return."

"Montserrat!" the bookseller exclaimed. "My dear Gaudí, I knew you were the right man! I make many pilgrimages every year to Montserrat, and it was during such a pilgrimage that I gazed on an image of the Holy Family in a painting and had my revelation—that I must build a temple in their honor. Go to Montserrat and pray. I am sure you will have good news for me."

Gaudí packed a small knapsack for his trip. After a half-day carriage ride and long hike up the well-traveled mountain trail, he found himself at the monastery where the abbot, Miguel Muntadas, greeted him warmly. Muntadas was as ancient as the sanctuary, he liked to say. He'd been abbot for thirty years, a visionary with a strong sense of how to rebuild from the destruction wreaked upon Montserrat by the French. Napoleon's army had burned it down and blown up a group of buildings in 1812, leaving the shrine in ruins. Years earlier, Muntadas had learned that this avid young pilgrim was an architect and he had bent his ear and picked his brain during each of Gaudí's visits.

Before Gaudí could even put his backpack down and have a drink of water, the abbot, who was sprightly for his age, pulled him by the sleeve to show him the new plans. Here, a rack railway to ferry pilgrims; over there, the new basilica.

"I have been told that Pope Leo is opening his purse for us," the abbot said happily. "A committee has been formed. The choice of the architect for the basilica is to be Villar. I suggested you but they wanted someone more seasoned, I'm afraid. Do you approve of Villar?"

Gaudí grunted. "He'll do a good job."

"Maybe when we dig a great hole for the crypt of the new church we will find the Holy Grail!" the abbot said, repeating an oft-made jest.

Though most pilgrims were made to pitch tents and shift for themselves, Gaudí was afforded the privilege of his own cell in the monk's dormitory, where he now unpacked his few belongings and laid on the mattress to rest.

To his chagrin he found himself crying. He willfully staunched the flow of tears and clenched fists at his own weakness.

He had to get over her—to purge her from his mind!

He had always been introverted, a poor conversationalist, someone more comfortable reading and sketching than talking to another. And he was certainly no ladies man. In fact, he had never been with a woman. Yet his perspective on life changed when he became the protective uncle of his little niece, Rosita, and the notion of female companionship and forming a proper family entered his mind.

A friend, Salvador Pagés, of Mataró, had made him an introduction in that town to a Senyor Moreu, who had two single daughters. There he met Josefa, a slim beauty who went by the nickname Pepeta. Gaudí was smitten. Pepeta had fine features and reddish-gold hair, almost mahogany in color. She sang, played the piano, and was sporty with a love of swimming in the sea, daring for a girl, some said; and she was a freethinker who even read Republican newspapers!

Though massively timid, Gaudí eventually plucked up every ounce of courage to propose marriage—only to learn she was already engaged to another, a successful wool merchant. Devastated, he retreated to his inner world to sort through his grief and through intense prayer he scourged himself, not with nettles or whips but with mental admonition.

He was not worthy. If Pepeta rejected him, then he would reject women. And he would go further. He would adopt the life of the leading Spanish mystics, who were espousing the Living Flame of Love, the spiritual path leading one toward God through denial of the flesh. He would eschew the companionship of women forever. He would fast and deny himself meat. He would purge himself with copious water. Most of all, he would work!

And when tears would well up over a love lost or a road not taken he simply bore down and cut off these thoughts.

He climbed off the bed and knelt and prayed.

In the quiet of the late evening, after taking evening prayer with the monks in their makeshift church, Gaudí took a small walk in the refreshing air. Strolling through some wild greenery on the edge of the grounds, he mused over the abbot's flippant remark about the Grail.

That Montserrat long had been touted as one of the possible resting places of the Grail was no secret. In fact the monks and even the abbot had slyly capitalized on the notion to increase pilgrimages and donations. Gaudí made a mental note that indeed he should return to the mountain when the excavations began so he could peer into the ground.

His ramble took him to the Chapel of Sant Iscle, one of his favorite spots on the mountain. He found the little structure perfect in every way, a primitive piece of architecture that had one purpose it fulfilled brilliantly: to create a simple space to glorify God and be one with prayer. He knew he would have the chapel to himself since the monks soon would be retiring for the night. Before he entered, he stubbed out his cigar and left it on a flat rock.

It was getting fairly dark so he fumbled in his pocket for matches and struck one to light a candle. As always, there was no place to sit. The monks would kneel and prostrate themselves in front of the altar on a reed mat and he would do the same. But the mat was rolled up and standing against one of the walls and he could see why: one end was singed and partially burned through, a casualty, he suspected, from a tipped candle. One of the benefits of an all-stone structure is that there is precious little to burn.

He lit the altar candles and admired the primitive simplicity of the large iron cross. There was nothing here to distract from one's devotions, not even the image of the Christ suffering for one's sins. He decided to perform more personal prayer. Having allowed Pepeta to creep into his thoughts he felt particularly weak and in need of a bracing dose of spiritual fortitude.

Lowering himself to the cool stones, he bowed his head, yet before he could say his first Hail Mary he was distracted by something. The fingers of his right hand had sunk into an indentation in one of the stone tiles, and when he raised himself to have a look he saw a similar groove by his left hand.

Out of curiosity he stood, and his keen eye immediately spotted two more indentations a body's length away from the altar on the adjacent stone. He plucked one of the altar candles from its holder and held it beside each of the grooves as he probed them with his finger. These were clearly man-made, precise, chiseled, smoothed.

Then another anomaly caught his eye. He was a master of color, a master of texture, exquisitely schooled in construction techniques. The mortar in between the adjacent stones didn't seem right. It was coarser than all the other lines of mortar and half a shade lighter. He put the candle down on its base, took out his penknife and used the small blade to scrape at the mortar stripe. It was crumbly and came up in dollops. The line of mortar to its right was as unyielding as the stone itself.

He stood again and folded the knife.

He stared at the grooves and when the epiphany struck he went to the chapel door and looked out to make sure no one was coming.

Lying upon the stones, he found the indentations with each hand and foot. Then he yanked his arms down hard as if pulling himself up to the top of a cliff.

He felt the mortar crack and pulled harder. The stone nearest the altar began to slide and at once one end dropped with a loud thud into a cavity, tipping him headfirst down an incline.

Startled, he pushed himself up and grabbed the candle.

A rectangular hole!

With all his strength he lifted the stone tile away and slid it to one side.

He reached into the hole and touched something smooth, something warm, warmer than the surrounding stones, warmer than his own hand. He pulled it out and placed it on his lap, lifting the candle to it.

Instantly, he knew what it was.

What this had to be.

"My God," he sobbed. "My God, my God, my God."

He was breathing so heavily he thought he would pass out.

He struggled to compose himself, struggled to decide what he should do.

As though by instinct, he ripped out a sheet from his omnipresent pocket notebook and wrote some simple words, folded the paper, and placed it in the cavity. Then he replaced the stone tile and using his skills, scooped up the remnants of the ersatz mortar and blended it with some of the sandy soil from outside the chapel, mixed with some saliva. He smoothed the new mortar with his penknife, put the bowl under his jacket, and practically ran back to his cell.

He would spend a lifetime of penance for what he did that night. It was not his to take or his to possess but alone in his simple monk's cell he sat all night staring at it and marveling at its extraordinary properties.

Was it an accident he had found it?

Or was it divine providence?

No sooner had his Bocabella approached him to do what no modern man had done—build a new cathedral—than he had found it!

Surely he was being called to a higher purpose.

25

High on a hill overlooking the city, Parc Güell would have been rural in Gaudí's day, but now it was contiguous with Barcelona's sprawl. Walking uphill from the taxi stand into the park, Arthur and Claire found the breezes a little stiffer and the air a little cooler.

The museum was the house where Gaudí had lived with his niece for twenty years. It was pink and tropical with lime green shutters and a churchlike spire adorned with a cross. The house was small compared to Eusebi Güell's nearby residence and stood alone with expansive views down to the sea. The park was one of Güell's few unsuccessful commercial ventures: planned as a housing site intended to lure wealthy city dwellers to sixty luxury houses, there were no buyers. Even the pink show house went unsold, and Güell ultimately persuaded Gaudí to buy it at a knockdown price.

They had a few minutes, so Arthur and Claire took the ground-level tour of the living quarters and found it beautiful in a spare and ascetic sort of way, the walls adorned by crucifixes. At the appointed time, they presented themselves to the woman at the reception desk and were directed up the stairs to the archive.

Isabella Bellver was alone in the Gaudí library. Glass-fronted white bookcases on every possible vertical surface cut into the already small space. If it weren't for a high-beamed ceiling and glorious city view, the room would have been claustrophobic.

The librarian, in her sixties with white hair clipped into a ponytail and wearing a fashionable dress, seemed agreeable enough receiving visitors but made it clear that last-minute appointments were not how things were done.

"Ordinarily, we get formal requests by letter or our website well in advance, outlining the specific reason a scholar or researcher needs to use the archive. We like to approve all reasonable requests, of course, but as you can see, our space is quite limited so we must control the visitation."

"I completely understand," Arthur said, flashing his best smile.

The librarian softened. "Alvar at the bookstore is a nice man so I did him a courtesy. Fortunately, there are no researchers here this afternoon, as you can see. Tell me, how I can help you?"

Claire had the folded note in her purse.

"We have a document," Arthur began. "We think it's signed by Gaudí and we were hoping to authenticate it and try to learn more about it."

With raised eyebrows, Bellver took the paper, unfolded it and stared.

"How extraordinary!" she exclaimed. "This is certainly his signature. Do you know how unique this is? We have his own writing on only a handful of documents, as his papers were lost during the Civil War. Where did you get this?"

They had a constructed story that bore no resemblance to the truth. She seemed to accept it without question.

"Well, 1883 was an important year for Gaudí but whatever could this be referring to—'I have found it'?"

"That's what we are trying to understand," Claire said.

"We were hoping to read through whatever papers of his you have and see if we can find any reference to this note," Arthur added. "Any context."

"We have not a single one of his handwritten papers here," she explained. "I can show you some reproductions as they appear in several books but I can assure that none of them will cast any light on your document. There are so few I know them all. There is his signed entrance pass to the 1888 Barcelona Exhibition, a limited collection of his school projects and reports when he was a young architectural student, a very small number of personal letters which deal with completely inconsequential matters, some business letters referring to changes to plans, payments owed for various building projects and, near the end of his life, a bequeathment in honor of his mother and a last will and testament leaving all his assets to the archbishop of Tarragona and the rector of Riudoms. I'm afraid that's all."

"Where are these documents kept?" Claire asked.

"Various archives: some at the national library, the Biblioteca de Catalunya, others here and there." She sighed. "I'm afraid I haven't been very helpful. As I said, I have reproductions of some of these letters here and I can help you with the translation if you don't read Catalan."

"That's very kind," Arthur said. "But it doesn't sound like it's going to be all that productive. Can you think of anyone, anywhere, who might be able to shed any light on our note?"

She sighed again, this time much more heavily. "I'll tell you what. I'll make you a deal. I'll try to pull in a very big favor from a good friend of mine who probably won't be such a good friend after I call him. This man, Esteve Vallespir, is the leading expert in the world on Gaudí."

"We bought one of his books today," Claire said.

"Yes, he's written many books. He's very old and doesn't like to see people anymore but I think he'd be interested in your document. I'll try to get him to see you."

"You said *a deal*," Arthur said.

"I want to purchase your document. I don't know how much it's worth or how much I can pay but I want the chance to buy it if it's for sale."

Arthur extended his hand. "I promise we'll come to you first."

The Escola Tècnica Superior d'Arquitectura de Barcelona at the Universitat Politècnica de Catalunya was, the librarian had told them, one of the preeminent architectural colleges in Spain and it was no wonder that Gaudí continued to be revered and studied there.

Vallespir's building at the college, in north Barcelona along the busy Avinguda Diagonal, was low, modern, and quite undistinguished for an architecture faculty in such an architecture-mad city as Barcelona. A student pointed the way and they found his office on the second floor.

Vallespir was there on his own, no secretary, no assistant—an old, stooped man in a ridiculously cluttered office. In a way he resembled how Gaudí himself looked in some of his photos near the end of his life. He had an unruly white beard that had not been trimmed for some time, drawing attention away from a scaly bald scalp. His twill trousers were too short, his white dress shirt threadbare at the collar, his bow tie crooked.

Vallespir spoke authoritatively in heavily accented English. "I did not want to see you. Frankly, I do not want to see most people these days but Isabella is persuasive. Come in. I'll give you five minutes. I'm going home soon. I'm not well, you see."

"We're very sorry to intrude," Arthur said. "We'll try not to take much of your time. We're trying to get some answers about a Gaudí document we found recently."

"Where did you find it?" the old man demanded.

Claire delivered their falsehood. "I was going through my grandmother's books and a letter was inside a book on Modernista architecture."

"Which book?"

"I don't recall the title offhand," she said, squirming a little. "It was quite old, a French title."

"France?"

"Yes, she was from Toulouse."

The professor shook his head. "Gaudí had no connections with Toulouse. Let me see the paper."

As Vallespir read it, Arthur searched the lined and sagging face for a reaction but the old man was impassive.

"I have found it," the professor said. "I have no idea what this means, though I can vouch that this is, in fact, Gaudí's true signature. Toulouse, you say?"

Claire nodded.

Vallespir repeated that Gaudí had no known interactions with people from Toulouse or that region of France and handed the document back gruffly, saying he couldn't help them.

Arthur thought quickly. They had an audience with the world's greatest authority on Gaudí and the audience was about to end. If this was a dead end, they would have nowhere else to go.

"Professor, I'm sorry, but we didn't tell you the real story. It's a little more controversial."

Vallespir's eyebrows rose. "Go on."

"We found this at Montserrat."

The old man stiffened and a look of outrage overtook him. "How does one find something like this at Montserrat?"

"I can't really say at this point."

"Who are you? Did you steal this? Was it from the monastery library?"

"We just want your help to understand it," Claire said evenly.

"I should call the police. Would you like me to do that?"

"We read that Gaudí was very religious," Claire continued, in an obvious attempt to diffuse his anger. "Did he make pilgrimages to Montserrat?"

The question had the desired calming effect. "Yes … Montserrat was a special place for him. He ventured there many, many times as a young man … when he was older … his entire life. It is a special place for all of the Catalan people."

"What do you think he could have found there, professor?" Arthur asked cautiously.

The old man sighed. "I'm sorry. I really don't know what your intention is or who you are. Are you scholars? Are you with a university?"

"I'm a descendant of Thomas Malory, the man who wrote *Le Morte D'Arthur.*"

"And you?" the professor asked Claire.

"I'm here offering my moral support. I'm a physicist."

Vallespir opened his arms in a gesture of confusion. "What does a descendant of Thomas Malory have to do with Antoni Gaudí?"

"To be perfectly frank, professor, I'm interested in the Holy Grail."

The old man checked his watch and pushed himself off his chair. "This is not a subject of mine. I am an architect and an architectural historian. Perhaps you want to speak with someone in our medieval history or religious studies faculties. Now my wife is expecting me home."

"Can I give you my mobile number in case you think of something that might be helpful?" Arthur jotted the number on a page from the hotel's notepad.

Vallespir looked at it. "Ah, this hotel was designed by Domènech. Now that's something I know about."

Arthur and Claire returned to the hotel, dispirited; then meandered to Le Boqueria market for lunch. Two metal stools opened up at the crowded Pinotxo Bar and they had tapas and talked, oblivious to the lunchtime bustle, a man and a woman at the end of an exhausting adventure.

"It was quite a ride," Arthur said.

"Are you sure it's over?"

"For now. I'll go home—well, first I need to find a home. I'll try to do more research on Gaudí. But if the number-one Gaudí authority in the world has nothing to offer us, then I've got to accept that we may have gotten as close to the Grail as we're ever going to get."

"Do you think you'll be left alone?"

Arthur shook his head. "I don't know. I hope so. But I killed one of them, Claire."

"I suppose I'll be going home too."

He touched her knee with his. "The most important thing is that you'll be safe."

At the hotel they booked flights to the UK and France. Then they packed their bags and called for their car.

Arthur paid the bill. As he was slipping the bellman a few euros, a woman from the reception desk came outside and waved at them.

"Excuse me, Mister Malory, but someone has just arrived to see you."

Arthur looked up, alarmed. "Who?"

"A woman. I'm sorry but I didn't get her name."

Claire got out of the car and both of them reentered the lobby.

A stylish woman in her sixties was at the front desk. Arthur saw her arrive as they were leaving but hadn't paid her any mind. The receptionist pointed at Arthur and said something in Catalan to the woman.

She stepped forward and said in good English, "My name is Elisenda Vallespir. You visited my husband this morning. Can we talk somewhere?"

Arthur tried to keep his excitement in check. The hotel bar was empty. "Maybe we can go in here."

They sat and ordered coffees. Arthur introduced Claire.

"Yes, Esteve told me about both of you. He was quite agitated when he came home."

"I'm sorry we troubled him," Arthur said.

"He's easily troubled, I'm afraid. He has never been an easygoing man. Now that he is ill his fuse is ever shorter."

"I feel bad we upset him," Claire offered.

"The problem with my husband is that he treats Gaudí as though he were still alive. In this city you are constantly reminded of Gaudí. To see a Picasso or a Miró you must enter a museum or a gallery. To see a Gaudí you merely have to walk down the street. Esteve worships the ground he walked upon and is fiercely protective of his legacy and his reputation. It's not that I don't share this respect; I was Esteve's architectural student before I became his wife and research assistant. It's been a ménage à trois, always living with Gaudí. But my husband has cancer. They haven't given him long."

"I'm sorry," Arthur once more said.

She nodded. "I know why he turned you away but I don't agree with him. There is no reason other than his stubbornness for him not to help you. I asked myself: What purpose would be served by letting him take this to his grave?"

Arthur stopped himself from interrupting—better to let her talk.

"Gaudí was very close to a priest. His name was Mossèn Gil Parès. He was the first parish priest of Sagrada Família. He ministered to the workers and their children. Gaudí personally financed and built the famous Escuelas for the children, which you can see today next to the temple. The two of them, Gaudí and Parès, constructed a sort of utopian Christian community there. When Gaudí died in 1926, Parès was executor of his estate. After the dictatorship of Primo de Rivera, Parès was stripped of his post for his Catalan sentiments. Unfortunately, he was murdered in 1936 during the Civil War, together with twelve other martyrs of the Sagrada Família. Recently, his body was buried in the crypt of Sagrada Família near his friend Gaudí, and the Vatican has begun the process of his beatification."

She paused to clear her throat just as the coffees arrived. Claire poured her some water.

"The reason I am telling you this," she continued, "is that we possess a letter which Gaudí wrote to Parès in 1911. Gaudí had contracted brucellosis and was very seriously ill. He was not expected to survive. His physician and friend Dr. Santaló sent him to the Pyrenees to convalesce for several months. It was a miracle he lived and was returned to health. This letter I have is written on the stationery of Gaudí's hotel."

She pulled it from her bag and removed it from its envelope.

"Let me be clear about this," she said, fixing Arthur then Clair with an emphatic stare. "Esteve never published this letter. It came to him many years ago from the estate of Gil Parès' brother. It was written in the form of a confession. I believe that Parès took Gaudí's confession often and from his presumed deathbed in the Pyrenees, Gaudí wished to unburden his soul one last time. We never understood the subject matter of this letter. And here is the issue. My husband's reverence for Gaudí has always been such that he really and truly felt that it would be a violation to betray his written confession, even so many years after the deaths of both parties. To me this sentiment violates fundamental scholarship but, well, Esteve has always been the boss. But the document you discovered at Montserrat is like finding a missing piece to a jigsaw puzzle, and with it, perhaps a picture can be properly formed. That is why I decided to come here."

She began a search for her reading glasses in her handbag. All Arthur could do was exchange glances with Claire, control his breathing and try to stay still.

"There are some incidental sections. I'll only translate the relevant part … Here it is, on the second page. 'You know, dear friend, what I speak of, for I have revealed all in the confessional and if I could be with you now I would ask you to take my confession one last time. This letter will have to suffice. You know I found it. And you know I stole it, which is a great sin I have carried like a heavy weight, though in all my times of trouble I have drawn infinite comfort from it. I have dedicated my life to it and I pray I have honored it. I have discussed with you many times what I desire in death. You alone can make it happen. Your eternal friend in Christ, A. Gaudí.'"

Claire whispered, "My God."

Arthur had grabbed a pen and had been furiously jotting notes on the back of his hotel bill. "Could we have a copy of this?" he asked quickly.

"I've made one for you." She reached into her bag again. "Please do not publish it without my permission."

"Of course not," Arthur assured her. "I don't know how to thank you. I wish I could thank your husband too."

"Well, don't think about him. Think about this quest you seem to be on. Tell me," she asked with a cracking voice, "this object Gaudí found. It now seems certain it came from Montserrat. Do you think, Mister Malory, it could be the Holy Grail?"

26

BARCELONA, 1926

The last of Gaudí's close friends had passed six months earlier. The sculptor Llorenc Matamala died at Christmas, 1925, but as his health was failing he made a final visit to the Sagrada Família to goad Gaudí's priest to action.

"He hardly sleeps, the only time he's not working is when he's making his daily treks to and from St. Felipe Neri, and all he eats is almonds and raisins! Isn't there anything you can do to make him slow down a little, act his age, eat a good meal and maybe take a small holiday, father?"

The priest, Mossèn Gil Parès, shrugged at the notion. "He's set in his ways like one of your plaster casts. Anyway, you're one to talk, Matamala. You almost worked yourself to death, of your own accord."

Matamala had been Gaudí's principal collaborator, the sculptor who had turned the architect's concoctions into clay and plaster models for forty-three years. The partnership had begun in 1883 when Gaudí said to him, "Come and work for me in the temple, Senyor Llorenc, and you will have work for life."

Their collaboration had come to an end less than a year earlier when Matamala's facial cancer invalided him from work. Making what would be his last visit to Sagrada Família, Matamala had buttonholed the priest to plead his case, his words slurred by a distorted tongue as he mopped at his drool with one of many handkerchiefs he carried.

"Nonetheless, try to reason with him. Someone has to take care of him, father. Use your influence. I'll wait for him in the workshop," the sculptor said, dabbing at his chin. "I don't know if it's just the way I look at things with my life coming to an end, father, but progress on the temple seems slow."

"You know what Gaudí always says, Llorenc," the priest told him. "My client does not have a deadline."

Gaudí had wept at Matamala's funeral and now, in the summer of 1926, he was an old man of seventy-three, alone in the world, finding comfort in a routine as regimented as the workings of a clock.

Only a year earlier, Gaudí had moved from his home in Parc Güell to a makeshift bedroom near his studio at Sagrada Família, though he already had devoted himself exclusively to the temple since the death of his patron, Eusebi Güell, in 1918. He rose at dawn every day to toil nonstop in his small studio, pausing only to nibble on nuts and berries and scoop milk with lettuce leaves, chosen because they made excellent natural spoons. Every evening he made the forty-five-minute walk to St. Felipe Neri Church for mass, followed by the same journey back to his studio. Walking was painful due to arthritis in his legs but he was too stubborn and impecunious to use streetcars. And every night, prior to going to bed, he would summon Father Parès from his nearby house to take his confession—though both men would have to admit that for an ascetic such as Gaudí fresh sins of deed were virtually nonexistent and any sins of thought on the mild side. Yet Gaudí, like a reliable grandfather, confessed daily to a sin more than four decades old, the theft of a sacred object from his beloved shrine of Montserrat.

When Gaudí first confessed to his sin Parès struggled mightily. This theft of the Grail was not so small a sin. He urged Gaudí to consider the consequences, to return it to the monastery; but Gaudí refused, arguing that he was certainly chosen by God to honor the artifact. The act, however, weighed heavily on the architect and he insisted on daily confessing the sin.

Their exchange typically went as follows: "If it troubles you so much, Antoni, why don't you return it? Far from being angry with you, the abbot, I expect, will be delighted to possess the greatest relic in Christianity."

"You don't understand," Gaudí would reply. "It was divine providence! I was presented with the commission for Sagrada Família. I did not wish to take it on; then only days later I found it. It was meant to be. God was telling me to build the temple. He was telling me to build it to honor Christ and the Holy Family. He was telling me to honor the Holy Grail. I am the Grail's guardian, father. I was given the responsibility by God and I will not turn my back on my divine obligation. You have your vows, I have mine."

"I am a priest," Parès would say with a sigh. "The confession is sacred. I have no choice but to carry your burden as if it were my own."

Now, after so many years, on hearing Gaudí's confession, Parès would only wearily say, "Say ten Hail Marys," and follow this by telling him, "although God has already forgiven you, Antoni, and if I've said it a thousand times, I will say it again: You have honored Him with your life and your work in a fashion that few men can match."

"Remember what I asked of you," Gaudí would reply.

"Yes, of course, I remember. But you are not ready for that yet. You have more work to do on this earth."

Work on the temple progressed; and day by day, week by week, year by year Gaudí's vision shaped itself in stone and glass. The crypt had been completed, the Nativity Façade nearly done, with four circular campanile towers slowly rising above it. The interior space was roughed out, although existing mainly on paper and worked into models, and the school for the worker's children was built. It was perhaps twenty percent on the way to completion. Others would have to carry the task forward long after he was gone.

Work continued amid grave political and social tensions. Anticlerical sentiments that fueled the death and destruction of Tragic Week in 1909 persisted, making fund-raising for the temple a challenge. Yet Gaudí surely was grateful that the Sagrada Família had been spared the mayhem of the riots. A growing movement for Catalan independence fueled general strikes. Social unrest boiled over but was brought to a swift end by Primo de Rivera's successful coup d'état in 1923. From his dictator's perch in Madrid he sent edicts and soldiers to suppress the Catalan independence movement and ban the Catalan tongue.

Gaudí, for the most part, kept his head down, sticking to his routine while the troubles of the world swirled around him. And when the good people of Barcelona saw him coming toward them on the sidewalk often they would cross to the other side, as he was apt to beg them for a few pesetas to help him meet the payroll of his masons.

Enrique Sánchez Molina was never at ease in Barcelona. Born and bred in Madrid, he resented that he felt like a stranger in what he believed should be one unified Spain. No politician, he nevertheless belittled the Catalan separatist attitudes, preferring to leave those messy issues to others; he had his own concerns.

He was a physicist and these were heady times for the discipline. A professor at the Universidad Central de Madrid, Molina was one of the leading Spanish researchers in experimental physics and he had been the honorific host to the great Albert Einstein during his visit to Spain in 1923. After centuries of darkness, Einstein's theory of general relativity was finally bringing the universe into the light.

It was a propitious time to be a Khem.

Molina waited within the cavernous Estació de França for the train from Paris and when it arrived he surveyed the arriving passengers, looking for a familiar face. Before long, Gustav Ergma, the great Estonian physicist appeared, a ferret-like man dressed too warmly for a summer day, sweating and scowling.

"Molina, take me someplace cooler, for God's sake," he said in their only common language, English. "That train was impossibly warm."

"Perhaps you might begin by removing your coat, Gustav," Molina said. "Come along, we'll get a cold beer into you for a start."

A sleek white and black Hispano-Suiza roadster was waiting at the curb and the two physicists climbed into the spacious rear seat while the driver secured the luggage.

"I have rooms for us at the Majestic," Molina said. "We'll be there in no time."

Ergma pointed to the driver's back. "Can we speak in front of him?"

"Carlos is pure muscle. Plus he doesn't understand a word of English. So speak freely."

"I'm a busy man, Molina, but I felt compelled to heed your telegram and make the long journey. We have had a very long dry spell. Since I assumed the leadership position within the Khem I have not had one single piece of credible information on the Grail to act upon. How good is your intelligence?"

"I don't want to overplay it, Gustav, but it is intriguing and I would have been terribly remiss not to pass it along for your consideration. It seems that last Christmas a man died from cancer at one of the hospitals here. His name was Matamala and he was a well-known architectural sculptor. Before his death he was administered radiation emanation therapy for a facial cancer by a Doctor Simó, one of the few practitioners of the art in Barcelona. Last week this Simó came to Madrid to participate in a conference on the use of radium in the clinic and I gave a talk on the physics of radiation. Afterward he sought me out in the bar and we had more than a few drinks. He was a jovial sort. Well, it seems this patient of his, this Matamala, under the influence of heavy doses of morphine for his pain, babbled to Simó about some relic which the architect Gaudí possessed. He said he had found a wooden box one day in Gaudí's workshop with a carving on its lid of Montserrat mountain. Without permission he opened it."

Ergma perked up at the mention of Montserrat. "What was in the box?"

"Apparently, in his drugged state all he said was that it was as warm as human flesh."

Ergma's thin eyebrows arched. "He said that?"

"So I was told."

"Have you approached this Gaudí?"

"No, I was waiting for your arrival. I've heard he's a real eccentric, a misanthrope, a difficult man. I thought we might have only one chance to get him to talk and I thought you would want to be personally involved in, shall we say, an interview."

"Good. You made the correct decision, Molina. What is your intention?"

"Tomorrow, we will pick him off the street. He has a predictable routine. We'll take him to Carlos's garage. He has car batteries there. Electricity applied to a man's tender areas loosens the tongue, or so I've been told."

On the evening of 7 June 1926, Gaudí put his drafting pencils down. It was 5:30 and time to leave for his three-kilometer walk to mass at St. Felipe Neri. Though it was a fine enough evening, owing to his state of emaciation, the old man shivered as he always did out of doors.

Shuffling in his bedroom slippers bound with elastic to keep the soles attached, he made his way down carrer de Bailén to the broad avenue of the Corts Catalanes.

A car was parked on the avenue near the intersection, a white and black Hispano-Suiza.

"That's him," Molina said from the backseat.

"Really?" Ergma exclaimed. "That man? He's old and weak. We hardly need Carlos's help to do the job."

When Gaudí began to cross the Corts Catalanes the burly driver got out, looked for traffic and approached him as he was reaching the median.

"Hey, Senyor, let me speak with you."

Gaudí kept his head down and ignored the ruffian.

"Hey, come here."

Carlos grabbed him by his coat sleeve and gave him a tug but was surprised at how violently and forcefully the old man reacted.

Though Gaudí did not utter a word, thoughts exploded inside his head at the affront.

Leave me alone! Unhand me! I am on my way to mass!

Carlos had a generous handful of coat sleeve in his hand and despite the old man's resistance he was not about to let go. One more hard yank would do it but the fabric was so threadbare it ripped in Carlos's hand, sending him backward a step and launching Gaudí forward.

Just at that moment, the Number 30 tram clattered by. The driver was unable to apply the brake in time to avoid the old man who had stumbled onto the tracks. Gaudí was thrown to the ground and lay there immobile, blood pooling from his ear.

Some pedestrians ran to his side and Carlos looked helplessly at Molina, who motioned him back to the car.

"Drive," Molina commanded.

"He looked bad," Carlos said, pulling away.

Molina shook his head. "I'll have his quarters searched. Maybe we'll be able to find it without him."

Ergma's face soured like a bowl of curdled milk. "Tell me Molina, when is the next train to Paris?"

Gaudí was presumed to be a homeless tramp. He had no papers on him. His pockets were greasy with nuts. His clothes were filthy and patched, his shoes a disaster. His legs were bound with old bandages to combat arthritic swelling. No one knew he was one of the most admired men in all of Barcelona.

The ambulance crew took him to the hospital for the poor, the medieval Hospital de Santa Cruz, where he was diagnosed with fractured ribs and a cerebral contusion. Placed in Bed 19 in the public ward, he spent the night going in and out of consciousness very much alone.

Father Parés would find him later that night and stand vigil at his bedside.

Gaudí was moved to a private room and by the following day the hospital corridors were lined with bishops and politicians and poets and architects.

And then he would die two days later, his body passing on a horse-drawn cortège from the hospital to the Sagrada Família; the people of the city lined the streets in an outpouring of grief and respect.

As he had lain dying, his brain swelling from trauma, his thoughts had been mad and fragmented—but in those rare, lucid, heaven-sent moments Gaudí believed he saw the Grail, black as night, warm and glowing, floating over his bed; and he had not been the least afraid of death.

27

He was walking his land with his estate manager when his mobile phone rang. It was planting season and they were trying out a new strain of barley. He had been peppering his man with questions about its disease-resisting qualities As he answered he watched his dog squat in the rectangular depression in the field. He grimaced and made a mental note to have his man do a better job filling it in.

He excused himself and trudged several yards away to take the call. It was Andris Somogyi.

"It's Somogyi. Is it a good time?"

"Yes, Andris, of course."

"I happened to speak with Stanley Engel on an academic matter. It wasn't a secure line so he would only say there had been some interesting developments and that I should ring you."

"Yes, good, I was going to call you. Malory has been industrious and, I would say, productive. It's almost—and I emphasize, almost—a shame we have to kill him."

"As you know, Stanley is squeamish about that."

"Stanley is squeamish about many things. Where do you stand, Andris?"

"I stand with you. Give me the details."

"Malory and Pontier are in Barcelona right now hopefully making solid progress. I'm told they've been meeting with some experts on the Spanish architect, Antoni Gaudí."

"Has Gaudí ever been on our radar screen?"

"It's an interesting question. I've been thinking about it quite a lot the last day or so. It's one of the problems with the Khem. We've always relied exclusively on oral history. We can't just go to the shelves and pull down a reference book. Remember old Professor Hoyt from Oxford?"

"Of course."

"He was my mentor's mentor."

"Roy Higgins."

"Yes. Hoyt nominated Roy to become a Khem and Roy brought me in. I recall having a drink with Roy in his club a good long time ago. He was already retired and was in failing health. It was somewhat poignant. He knew he'd never live to see the Grail but told me it was all right because at least he'd been a link in a two-thousand-year chain which would eventually lead to its discovery. Anyway, I'm telling you this because if my memory serves, he did say that he had heard from an older Khem that there had been some suspicion in the 1910s, 1920s maybe, that a Spanish architect knew something about the Grail."

"And?"

"Nothing came of it, apparently. I'm actually surprised I remembered the discussion. It was minor, a small footnote."

"Mind like a steel trap."

"I like to think so. Look, Andris, I think we may be at a critical junction. The trail will, I expect, soon get either very cold or extremely hot. If it's the latter, we need to be prepared to travel to Jerusalem at a moment's notice for the greatest moment in history since the resurrection of Christ."

Arthur and Claire had rebooked their same room and now lay on the bed facing one another. Elisenda Vallespir had left them no answers but at least they had hope.

"It looks like our adventure's going to last a little longer," Arthur said. He reached for his notes. "Here's the key part of the letter. Gaudí wrote, 'I have discussed with you many times what I desire in death. You alone can make it happen.' What does someone desire in death?"

Claire crinkled her face. "Well, to be honored, to be remembered, to be written about. A favorable legacy."

"Gaudí seemed too modest for that. Look, this guy, Father Parès, was his friend but he was also his confessor. You tell your confessor secrets. What do you think Gaudí's greatest secret was?"

"The Grail, of course. You think he told him about the Grail?"

"I'll bet he did."

"If you're right, then maybe what he desired in death was for the Grail to be put somewhere safe, somewhere appropriate. Maybe he asked that it be returned to Montserrat."

Arthur shook his head. "If that were the case, Parès most likely would have put it back in the chapel where Gaudí found it. Or the monastery would have built a chapel for it. We know that didn't happen."

"Well, maybe he wanted the Vatican to have it."

"Don't you think we'd have known about that? The Vatican would have made a huge deal over it. It would be in St. Peter's now behind glass. It would be the holiest relic in their possession."

Arthur got off the bed and retrieved Vallespir's copy of Gaudí's letter. It was two pages long on small-format Hotel Europa stationery. The section Vallespir's wife had read them was on the second page. He regretted not having a translation of the first page. Perhaps there was something of significance she hadn't appreciated. Turning to the signature page, he noticed a marking and made an obviously curious face.

"What?" Claire asked.

"Have a look at this, over the Europa letterhead. I thought it was a doodle but it's not. It's letters."

AΩ JHS

"Let me see," Claire motioned, and he rejoined her on the bed. "Yes, for sure," she continued, squinting at the scrawl. "They are letters.

The first two are alpha and omega, the first and last letters of the Greek alphabet. The last three are *J-H-S*."

"Someone's initials?" Arthur wondered.

"Maybe. What if this isn't some random notation, Arthur? What if it was meant as part of the message to Father Parès? To reinforce what Gaudí desires in death."

Arthur nodded. "Maybe. *J-H-S*. We need to find out who that is."

Claire's face crinkled again and Arthur watched as she leaped off the bed for her shoulder bag. She came back with her phone and began fiddling with it.

Asked what she was doing, she shushed him.

At once he heard her cry out "Oui!" and she thrust the phone in his face. "I thought I remembered seeing this. Look! It's one of the pictures I took yesterday at the Sagrada Família."

Arthur let out a triumphant yell.

High on one of the façades of the cathedral, flanked by two angels and beneath a white pelican feeding her young, was a large Greek cross emblazoned with J-H-S.

Arthur pounced on their stack of Gaudí books, tossed them onto the bed and both of them dove in, flipping pages.

"Here it is!" she said, showing Arthur a page from a chapter on Gaudí's use of symbols. "It says here that *J-H-S* stands for *Jesus Hominum Salvator*. Jesus Savior of Humanity. The cross is Greek because with four equal arms it's the best to symbolize the conjunctions of opposites in the earthly world. And Arthur, look at these pictures. You couldn't see it on mine. On the two ends of the cross the Greek letters—alpha and omega."

Arthur got up and began pacing kinetically.

"It all makes sense, Claire. Gaudí initially turned down the Sagrada Família commission in 1883. We also know he finds the Grail in 1883 and he changes his mind. He decides to take the project. Here, in his letter, he says, 'I have dedicated my life to it and I pray I have honored it.' Maybe that's the way he decided to honor it, by designing the most magnificent tribute to Christ since the time of the great medieval cathedrals."

Claire shook her head in agreement. "He spends the later years of his life living at the cathedral. And where is he buried?"

"In the cathedral," Arthur said looking Claire squarely in the eyes. "He was reminding Father Parès, pleading with him that he wanted to be buried there. It wasn't a done deal. It wasn't preplanned. When he died the only one already in the crypt was Bocabella. The bishop was persuaded to let Gaudí be buried there too. Who persuaded him? I bet it was Gil Parès."

"He wanted to be buried next to it," she said, almost whispering.

Arthur began slipping on his shoes. "We've got to go to the crypt."

They waited under a threatening sky for over half an hour to buy their tickets to enter Sagrada Família. Perhaps it was the impending rain that made so many tourists flock to the cathedral so late in the day. They finally passed through the turnstiles at 6:30 P.M. Closing time was at 8. Arthur was carrying a small backpack. Even if there had been heavier security—metal detectors, bag searches—his belongings wouldn't have attracted attention. Two small flashlights, a multitool, a couple of bottles of water, a few chocolate bars.

On entering the interior of the church, both of them were transfixed by its expansiveness and nearly insane complexity. There was such a density of detail that it was impossible to focus on one piece without being drawn to another. It was laid out, as most Christian cathedrals, in the form of a Latin cross representing a human figure with legs together and arms extended as crucified. Gaudí had said he wanted the interior of the temple to be like a forest and he had achieved that vision. Peering upward in the main nave was akin to looking through the canopy of a mature forest to the heavens.

The columns of the nave resembled massive palm trees soaring forty-five meters high but rather than forming any kind of expected ceiling they branched into a kaleidoscopic array of twisting geometric forms. Nothing was flat. There were no right angles or even conventional arches. Everything was a dizzying array of soft and hard shapes and angles no less complicated than the stalks of a plant or the longitudinal section of a seashell.

It was almost possible to ignore that the church was also an active construction site. While tremendous progress had been made in recent years with the interior structures, still there was much to be done: scaffolding and interior lifts abounded, cordoned off with yellow tape.

Their first destination was the apse and they wandered in that direction with necks craned and eyes open in awe. To get there they passed under the vault of the crossing, which was higher than the nave, rising sixty meters. The vault above the apse was the highest at seventy-five meters. It had been Gaudí's intent for a visitor entering through the main entrance to see the vaults of the nave, crossing and apse rising in graduated grandeur.

As dazzling as the vault of the apse was, Arthur and Claire looked downward because the central area of the apse incorporated the ceiling of the crypt. And here Gaudi's genius shined as profoundly as anywhere in the basilica. The vault of the crypt was surrounded by glassed and arched windows that penetrated the floor of the apse rising within the presbytery to the height of a man. The design allowed worshipers to gaze heavenward to the light-filled vault, the place where God resided, but also to gaze down into the crypt, the place of death and human repose.

Arthur spoke for the first time since entering. "There it is. Let's go down."

Searching for access to the crypt, they passed a guided tour in English and slowed to a crawl to soak up snippets.

"Although it is designed as a cathedral and most call it a cathedral, it is not actually one as far as the Church is concerned since it is not the seat of a bishop. That honor belongs to Barcelona's Cathedral of the Holy Cross.

"The basilica was consecrated in 2010 by Pope Benedict before a congregation of 6,500, including the king and queen of Spain. That allowed it to be used to conduct religious services, which continue to this day principally in the Chapel of the Assumption of Mary within the crypt.

"Follow me to the workshop area now where we will see how Gaudí used lattices of hanging strings and wires to conceive of his geometric forms and how the craftsmen of today use computer-aided design and manufacture to continue his legacy in the twenty-first century."

They peeled off from the tour. A broad spiral stone stairway led down to the crypt. Here were far fewer tourists than on the ground level and no attendants.

Arthur was almost lightheaded with excitement. Gaudí's tomb was tucked away in a nook but they resisted the temptation to go there directly. Instead they walked the perimeter of the crypt in the opposite direction, saving his tomb for last.

The central space of the crypt was dominated by the Church of the Assumption with a beautiful altarpiece sculpted by Josep Llimona. Flanking the altar were four chapels: one—housing Gaudí's tomb—dedicated to Our Lady of Carmen; one dedicated to Jesus Christ; one to Our Lady of Montserrat; and one to the Holy Christ. The latter chapel housed Josep Maria Bocabella's tomb. Three other chapels ringed the perimeter, bringing the total to seven.

They came upon a nook bearing a wall plaque to mark the resting place of the martyred priest Gil Parès; then completing the circle, they were back to the chapel housing Gaudí's tomb.

It was, perhaps, the simplest, least adorned space within the crypt or indeed the entire church. A raised white marble platform, ankle-high, on which lay a slab of gray granite with a surround of rose-colored marble. The granite was engraved with Gaudí's epitaph. The slab lay perpendicular to a wall of large limestone blocks. On each side of the wall were two similar walls joined at oblique angles, drawing the eye to the grave. Low to the ground was a ribbon-like surround of wrought iron rails designed to hold votive candles, now bare. Instead, a single row of red candles burned brightly at the foot of the tomb. Above it, on a small pedestal, was a graceful statue of the Virgin Mary, holding the infant Jesus. Against the limestone walls, four pedestaled columns rose to the apex of the crypt, framing three tall arches that poked into the apse above.

The granite tombstone was garlanded with bouquets of fresh flowers carefully placed so as not to obscure the inscription, which read in part, HINC CINERES TANTI HOMINIS RESURRECTIONEM MORTUORUM EXPECTANT RIP.

Arthur heard Claire reading the dedication aloud then translating, "From the ashes of so great a man look for the resurrection of the dead. Rest in peace."

A tear ran down her cheek.

He touched her hand then began to study every inch of the simple tomb, his thoughts in overdrive, but became distracted by a group of Japanese tourists who encircled them, talking loudly and flashing photographs. He nudged Claire and they withdrew.

It was 7 P.M., an hour until closing.

They needed a place to hide, ideally within the crypt itself since he had no idea whether the entrances leading to it were locked at night.

Yet the crypt was wide open with few points of concealment. There was only one door within it, a large gilded portal that led to the sacristy. While Claire watched for prying eyes, Arthur tried the door but it was locked.

They walked the perimeter again. The only possible place for concealment was one of the seven chapels: the Chapel of Saint Joseph.

Its design was identical to the one with Gaudí's tomb: a three-walled nook, a stone platform, and, best of all, a copious altar made of solid marble that offered them clear access. Again with Claire as lookout, Arthur quietly hopped onto the platform and snuck a peek behind. Here, between altar and wall, was just enough space for two people to hide. Now they had a plan.

With an hour to kill they returned to ground level and blended with the tourists, strolling through the workshop space and museum displays, and used the lavatories for the last time perhaps until morning. At 7:45 they returned to the crypt, milled around until they were the very last two, then slid their bodies behind the altar of Saint Joseph, Bocabella's inspiration for the stunning cathedral that soared magnificently over their heads.

28

Hengst felt his chest fluttering.

His targets had disappeared.

He'd been following at a perfect distance, not too close, not too far, dressed in a camouflage of sorts: blue jeans, polo shirt, sunglasses, and an American baseball cap. He was certain he hadn't been made.

When Malory and Pontier went back down to the crypt he had waited a couple of minutes before following, out of concern the thinning crowds would be a problem. But when he did go downstairs the crypt was empty, so he assumed they had ascended the other stairway.

Yet there was no sign of them on the ground level and he was forced to retrace his steps over and over without regaining eyes on them. Finally, back in the crypt just before closing time, he tried the sacristy door in the event they had gone inside but it was locked. A guard making his last sweep of the crypt pointed to his watch. He had to leave.

On the plaza, Hengst watched the last of the tourists depart and the entry gates close for the night. He made a circuit around the cathedral and placed a difficult call, and with no small anxiety he informed his boss he'd lost Malory.

First the lights went out in the crypt, then throughout the basilica. Claire and Arthur weren't entirely in the dark because the emergency exit signs glowed red. Their legs were cramped from crouching in the space behind the altar but for a full hour they dared not move until they were confident they were indeed alone. Claire trembled in the subterranean chill and Arthur held her until the shivering stopped.

Arthur rose and peered over the altar. He tapped on Claire's head to let her know it was safe.

"Do you think there's a night guard?" Claire whispered.

"No idea," Arthur said. "Hopefully not, but we shouldn't assume anything."

They crept past one of the stairways between their hiding place and Gaudí's tomb, listening hard for any footsteps. The crypt was dead silent.

Arthur passed Claire a flashlight and they began a visual dissection of the tomb, keeping their beams narrowly aimed. Stray light from the crypt shining through the arched windows would be visible to anyone patrolling the grounds.

"If it's here," Arthur finally said, his voice low, "it's got to be either under the floor or in the walls."

Claire pointed her beam fleetingly on the statue of Mary. "Or behind the statue?"

"It's flush to the wall."

Claire aimed her light at the tomb. "The crypt was finished in 1891. He died in 1926. He would have had to have hidden the Grail long before his coffin was lowered into place. So it can't be above the coffin. And besides, we know that the tomb was desecrated in 1936 during the Spanish Civil War and that the mob may have even gotten to his bones. Obviously the Grail wasn't found."

"If it's buried under whatever structure the casket is lying on," Arthur said, "we're out of luck. We'd need heavy equipment to get to it."

Nevertheless he tried sliding the granite slab and its marble surround with curled fingers but the effort was ridiculously futile.

Claire didn't bother to help. "If you're right, the only place which could be accessible to us is the walls."

He picked himself up and massaged his tender fingertips.

"I agree."

"Think about it," she continued. "He hides it, maybe in the 1890s when the crypt is being built, but how does he know he won't have to move it? Maybe the project collapses from lack of funding. Maybe there's a fire. He'd want a way to save it."

The limestone blocks that formed the walls of the chapel were rectangular but not uniform. The largest were the size of microwave ovens, the smallest, half as long. All of them were perfectly flush with one another and the joins were tight with the thinnest of mortar lines.

Arthur used the butt of his multitool to tap each block, starting low to the floor and moving as high as he could reach. As well as he could hear, the timbre of each rap was the same as the next, although tapping the blocks, which had iron candleholders affixed, caused faint metallic vibrations.

He stepped back and again beamed his flashlight. Each of the three converging walls that defined the chapel nook was about five feet wide, and each row of masonry comprised of two, three, or four limestone blocks.

"I'm trying to see if there's a pattern," he said.

"You mean of the blocks?"

"Yeah. When you step back can you see any pattern emerging?"

She shook her head. "It seems random."

"To me as well. All right, what about these iron candleholders? They're unique."

"Well, I agree they're very nice, the way they're made to look like ribbons. I haven't seen anything quite like them before; but there are a million things around the Sagrada Família I've never seen before. Gaudí's tomb isn't the only one with these candleholders. The tomb we were hiding behind has them too."

Arthur grimaced. "Too bad. I hadn't noticed. Probably not the answer then." He shined a light on the iron fittings pinning the candleholders into the limestone. "Unless …"

29

The candle rack on the oblique walls to either side of the granite slab of Gaudí's tomb was a double row of ribbons with evenly spaced cups for candles. The rack on the middle wall perpendicular to the slab was a single ribbon pinned to the wall by a thick rod at each end.

Arthur finally said, "Look at this row of blocks behind the ironwork. It's made of three blocks rather than two or four. The largest one is in the middle, and see here and here? The spikes are pinned to the smaller ones flanking it."

"Are you thinking what I'm thinking?"

"Can you move the flowers?"

With the flowers set aside, Arthur was able to stand between the granite slab and the wall and firmly plant his feet. He wrapped his hands around the right side of the candle rack nearest the anchoring rod and pulled against it.

Nothing moved.

"You're going to have to do better than that," she said, eliciting a frown.

He grunted and pulled again, without effect.

"I thought you said you played rugby?"

"All right, now you've got me mad."

He braced his feet against the wall and with a fresh new grip he pushed off with his hips, straining so hard he could hear blood pulsing in his ears.

Again nothing happened except for his beet-red hands going into spasm. He peeled off his jacket and wrapped the iron in cloth before trying again, groaning mightily at the exertion.

Something gave, accompanied by the small but satisfying sound of stone scraping upon stone.

He released his grip and stood back.

"Look," she said in a whispering shout. "The block moved a little!"

He bent over to look closer. She was right: a fraction of an inch.

"It's clean. There isn't any mortar," he said. "It's just stone on stone. Let me try the other side."

The left side of the candle rack was anchored to a smaller block and when he wrapped his hands and put his back and hips into it that one slid even more than the other.

With mounting anticipation he concentrated his effort on the right anchor and when that had moved a bit more Claire stepped in and gripped the left with his jacket. He clenched and unclenched his cramped hands then again grabbed hold of the right.

With a coordinated one-two-three they pulled together with all their might.

The candle rack moved dramatically, a good four inches, carrying the right and left blocks with it.

"Jesus," Arthur said when they stopped to inspect their effort.

"This has to be intentional," Claire said. "It *has* to be."

"Okay," he said, breathing hard. "If we pull it out all the way, it's going to be really heavy. If we can't control the weight, the blocks are going to fall and chip or maybe shatter. So the next pull has to be toward us then up as soon as they're free."

"Ready?"

"I'm ready."

They coordinated one great heave and the blocks came away, still firmly attached to the rack, but the construction of iron and stone was surprisingly light. They were able to lift it easily away and gently place it down on the marble platform.

"They're half blocks!" Arthur exclaimed. "They're only about five inches deep. The whole contraption was designed to be pulled out relatively easily."

"I don't think it was so easy."

Arthur pointed up toward the nave and spires. "There's a lot of weight above us. A lot more than when the crypt was first built."

The wall now had two voids on either side of the third and largest block in the row. Claire put her hand into the left void at the same time Arthur probed the right.

They both felt an angular iron strut pinned to the back of the large block and realized simultaneously that it wasn't a block at all but a slab, only two inches thick.

The voids were too small to poke in one's head or to shine a light at a useful angle so they kept feeling with hands and fingers.

"It's a false front, Claire. I think these struts are hinged. There's definitely something that feels like a hinge."

"I feel one too."

"The top of the slab doesn't have any fittings."

"So we should pull from the top and it should drop down."

"Exactly. All set?"

With a good bit of pressure the top of the slab moved forward, exposing its upper surface. It was ingeniously constructed, designed with a sharp, chiseled angulation so that it would clear the block above it yet still appear flush when in place. It was indeed hinged and lowered like a drop-leaf table, exposing a long black rectangular void in the wall.

"Do you think it's there?" Claire whispered.

"Only one way to find out."

He shined a light in and saw it.

A box. A wooden box.

He was surprised how calm he felt reaching in and pulling it out.

It was the size of a large cigar humidor, made of polished rosewood, chocolate brown, richly hued and veined. The lid had a beautifully carved relief of Montserrat with an inscription below it.

Gràcies a Déu

"Thanks to God," Claire whispered.

Arthur placed the box onto the granite slab directly above Gaudí's bones and without hesitation opened the lid.

There it was.

The Grail.

The bowl was snug in a cushioned satin depression.

It was jet black, polished to a gloss with thick rounded edges, a bowl of the simplest possible design meant to be lifted to the lips with two cupped hands.

But they were transfixed by its other attributes.

Surrounding it, conforming to its shape, was a circumscribed zone of invisibility, the width of a finger.

"My God, look at it, Arthur. Look at it!" Claire whispered.

Arthur felt paralyzed by the enormity of it all.

A two-thousand-year quest was over.

A quest that had consumed the likes of King Arthur and his knights, Thomas Malory, writers and bards; Andy Holmes, Tony Ferro should be here, he thought. A poet should be here to describe the moment.

I'm just a simple man.

Why me?

Claire broke the spell and said, as if reading his mind, "You found it. You're the one who found it."

"I'm sorry," he said suddenly.

"Why are you sorry?"

His eyes were wet. "I'm sorry, Senyor Gaudí," he said, speaking to the earthly remains of the genius. "This is a violation. I'm truly sorry."

"Pick it up," Claire urged. "Do you want to be first?"

"No, you. Go ahead."

She gently lifted and cradled it, her fingers partially lost from sight by its strange, ethereal halo. "It's warm," she said. "The stone looks so cool but it's warm, like holding a person."

She lifted it to her eyes. He saw that she was going to cry. It started quietly but soon her chest was heaving.

"Arthur … it's not any substance I know."

He swallowed.

"It doesn't come from the earth."

They spent the night sitting against the wall of the St. Joseph's chapel, ready to hide themselves behind the altar if a watchman came down to the crypt.

It had been an easy job replacing the candle rack and limestone blocks and when they were done Gaudí's tomb looked untouched.

They stayed silent for much of the night, both of them lost in their thoughts. They would wait until the Sagrada Família reopened in the morning and tourists came down into the crypt before finding the right moment to mix in with them and leave.

But throughout the long, dark night they passed the Grail between them, holding it to their chests for warmth.

30

The rosewood box distorted Arthur's backpack to a square shape. The zipper wouldn't close completely so he covered the gap with an unfolded map. With the nervous demeanor of a couple escaping from the scene of a crime they climbed into a taxi on the Avinguda de Gaudí and returned to their hotel.

Hengst was waiting near the hotel entrance, lurking in the doorway of a body piercing shop on the carrer de Sant Pau. He held a newspaper to conceal his tired eyes and ragged scowl. He had called up to their room several times and was satisfied they hadn't returned all night. So all he could do was pace the narrow deserted street in a testy nocturnal vigil.

As Arthur and Claire hopped from their taxi and disappeared into the lobby, Hengst exhaled in relief and placed a call.

In their room, Arthur put the backpack on the armchair and both sat on the bed, staring at it.

After a long, seemingly endless interval, he finally said, "Now what?"

She didn't answer.

He felt numb. The elation had been short-lived. The quest was over.

Now what?

The words came out robotically, a weary stream of consciousness, his eyes fixed on the prize. "I want to tell Andy and Tony about this.

But they're dead, aren't they? They were killed because of it. They'll want to kill us too. Claire, you should go home, get away from it, get away from me. You should leave now. Will you?"

She was bone-tired too. "I don't know."

"I don't think we were followed but maybe we were. Why do they want it so much, Claire? It's got to be more than its monetary value."

"I don't know. The stone has unique properties."

"What kind?"

"I'm so tired. I need to think, okay?"

He nodded wearily. "I really don't know what to do. The quicker we go public the safer we'll be. Should we give it back to the Sagrada Família? To Montserrat? To Spain? To the Vatican? Stupid, isn't it? I don't even know how to call a press conference. I've dreamt about this moment my whole life. Finding the Holy Grail …" His voice trailed off. "What do you do when you've achieved the ultimate? What do you do with the rest of your life?"

He felt his hand being squeezed hard.

"All I want to do right now is take it to the Bear, order a round of beers and show it to Sandy Marina and Aaron Cosgrove and the rest of the Loons. I want to put it down on the table next to Andy's cane. Then I'll figure out the rest, I suppose."

"Why don't you sleep for a little while?" she said tenderly. She peeled down the bedspread. "I'll take a bath. Then I'll join you. Afterwards, things will be clearer."

He agreed, took off his clothes, slid between the sheets.

In the bathroom, Claire undressed and while waiting for the tub to fill she switched on her mobile phone, which had been off for the night. There were multiple missed calls, all from her parents' number.

Alarmed, she called them back.

In fifteen minutes she came out, toweling her hair.

Arthur was still awake. "Everything okay? I heard you talking to someone."

She looked worried. "It was my mother. My father had some kind of a spell. Dizziness. They went to the hospital. They tried to call me. But it's all right. He's home now."

"What was it?"

"Maybe a ministroke. He's going to have more tests."

"I'm sorry. Do you need to go home?"

"They didn't want me to come."

She climbed beside him and wrapped her arms around his waist.

"In the bathtub, I was thinking … we should try to understand the Grail, its properties. The effect on light, the heat it's producing. As a physicist, I want to know more, learn from it. Don't you think we should study it first before you have your press conference so we can describe it properly?"

"Study it how?"

"I can do some tests in my lab. In Modane. It's Friday today. We can drive there this afternoon, stay in my flat, go to the lab tomorrow. No one will be there."

"What do you think it is?"

"I'm not sure. It's exotic."

"Let's sleep first," he said, his head drooping. "Then we'll talk about it."

A little more than an hour after leaving the hotel they were crossing the border into France. Arthur had agreed to spend the weekend in Modane, to try to get some understanding of the bowl's properties before showing it to the world. Besides, he didn't want to say goodbye to Claire. Not yet.

Claire sat beside him, cradling the rosewood box in a carrier bag on her lap. It didn't seem right consigning it to the trunk or the backseat. And she could feel a slight heat emanating from within that she said was unusually comforting.

31

They arrived in Modane in the early evening with only a short time to spare before the gallery of snow-peaked Alpine mountains disappeared into the night. Her flat was in an apartment block near the city center, small rooms, cheaply but appealingly furnished, a transitional kind of place more for a student than an adult.

They were tired. They stayed in, microwaved some frozen dinners and shared a bottle of wine. Afterward, she left him and called her parents from the kitchen. Through the thin walls he could hear her talking, not the words but the tones. She sounded upset and when she returned she looked worried.

"How is he?" he asked.

"He's fine. It's my mother. She doesn't handle these things well."

"Maybe you should you go to Toulouse?"

"There's no point. His tests aren't until next week. She won't worry less just because I'm there. I know her."

In her bedroom, she said, "I just want to see it before I go to sleep."

The wooden box was on her dresser. She opened the lid, stared at the Grail and touched it, watching her fingertip vanishing in its halo.

Saturday morning they awoke early but had to bide their time before leaving. The lab didn't open until 9 A.M. on the weekend.

At the mouth of the Fréjus Road Tunnel, the main commercial thoroughfare connecting France and Italy, they stopped at the administration building of the Laboratoire Souterrain de Modane.

Claire left Arthur in the car and returned a few minutes later.

"No one else has signed in. We'll be alone, at least for a while. It's usually not busy on Saturdays anyway."

"Don't I have to sign in too?"

"It's not so high security. I have a key card, of course, but if I bring a visitor, it's not such a big deal. I'm mainly glad that Simone isn't here."

Claire drove. The tunnel ran through the Col du Fréjus in the Cottian Alps between Modane and Bardonecchia in Italy. They entered it and went 6.5 km to its midpoint where they were 1,700 meters underneath the ground. She signaled and pulled off onto a well-marked turnout designated for the lab and took a couple of nylon mesh red vests from her bag and told Arthur to put one on. It was protocol, as they had to cross two lanes of high-speed traffic to get to the lab entrance.

Arthur did a double take: here was an entryway built into the belly of a mountain beside a major motorway. A truck rumbled past and for a moment the road was clear. Beside a larger vehicle entrance was a pale green door. Claire opened it with the swipe of her card and they were in.

The lab was not attractive, with little creature comforts. The floors and walls were poured concrete the color of cold oatmeal. Donning obligatory hard hats, they passed through an engineering room for fabrication and repair of instruments and entered the main hall: here were tanks, large and small, wrapped in piping amid a bulk of electronic gear. The largest tanks had catwalks for access. It reminded Arthur of a Bond film set, the underground lair of a mad nemesis.

Claire moved through the complex quickly, picking up tools as she went. He was at her mercy, in her world, and all he could do was admire her efficiency. His only job was to carry the Grail and he clutched the bag tightly.

They went as far as they could in one direction, entering a small chamber so packed with equipment that there was hardly room for a computer work station. The room was dominated by a large cylindrical copper vessel.

"Is this where you brew the beer?" Arthur jested.

"Hardly. Meet EDELWEISS-II. *Expérience pour Detecter Les WIMPs En Site Souterrain*. This is where I've lived for the past years. She's my baby."

"She?"

"Maybe it's a he; in any event, she's retired but not yet shut down. In the other wing of the lab, her successor is coming on line. It's much bigger, more detection power. It's called EURECA. Simone works on that project now; me too, mostly. We're going to use EDELWEISS. It's going to take an hour to power her up and do some calibrations. There's a chair. No coffee, I'm afraid. I should have bought a thermos. There's a toilet through there. That's it."

"I'll just have to watch you. Tell me what we're looking for."

She began to talk while she worked. "Astronomers know with almost complete certainty by observing galaxies and deducing the impact of gravity on them that ordinary visible matter—the stuff that makes stars, planets, trees, elephants, you and me—that this represents only four percent of the mass plus energy of the universe. So that leaves ninety-six percent to explain."

"You don't think the Grail is ordinary matter?"

"I don't know. That's why we're here. A force called *dark energy* represents seventy-three percent of the remainder of the universe. It's the property of empty space, Einstein's cosmological constant, the energy driving continual expansion of the universe. That leaves twenty-three percent. This is dark matter. It's almost too exciting to contemplate but I've been wondering if the Grail could have something to do with this substance. Dark matter as we understand it doesn't radiate detectable quantities of visible light or any kind of radiation. It's completely invisible."

"But we can see the Grail."

"Yes, but here's what I'm thinking: What if the Grail is made from material that was some kind of amalgam of ordinary and dark matter formed, perhaps, soon after the Big Bang—when temperatures were enormously high and various forms of matter may have interacted differently with one another than in a cooler universe? What if it came to Earth maybe billions of years ago as an exotic meteorite? Anyway, the point is, maybe we are seeing the stone's ordinary matter but not the dark matter."

"How do you explain the halo around it?"

"Maybe this is a gravitational bending of light at its surface, similar to the gravitational bending around galaxies that dark matter produces, which astronomers can detect with radio telescopes. It's crazy, I know, but we've never had dark matter to study before."

"Why not? If it's so common, why isn't it all around us?"

"Ah, it *is* all around us! We're showered by these dark matter particles, probably trillions and trillions every day. But they are also very difficult to find. I'll try to explain. Someone very clever once said that ordinary luminous matter is little more than a thin icing on a massive and dark cosmic cake. The dark matter is probably distributed throughout the universe, maybe evenly in some regions, maybe clusters in others. Soon after the Big Bang, regions that were slightly denser than others may have pulled in dark matter which clumped together and eventually collapsed into something resembling flat pancakes. Where these pancakes intersect you get long strands of dark matter filaments. Clusters of galaxies then formed at the nodes of the cosmic web where these filaments crossed. Anyway, like I said, dark matter is probably all around us. The problem is that it plays by different physical rules than ordinary matter. All the subatomic elementary particles which make up ordinary matter—you know, the leptons and quarks, et cetera—they're all bound together by the strong nuclear force. The candidate particles for dark matter are called WIMPs."

"Physicists come up with the best names."

She smiled. "Well, it's a field dominated by men. It stands for Weakly Interacting Massive Particles. Like ordinary matter these WIMPs have mass, they're acted on by the exceedingly faint force of gravity, but because they don't obey strong nuclear forces they almost never interact or collide with ordinary matter."

"They pass right through us?"

"They pass through everything we know and see. Their collisions with ordinary particles are so infinitesimally rare that they are almost impossible to detect. So in the last twenty years, laboratories all over the world have been looking for direct experimental evidence for WIMPs and trying to define them. This laboratory is one of them. All of the dark matter detectors have to be deep underground, built into mountains like Modane and Gran Sasso in Italy, and in mines like Boulby in England. The probability of a WIMP particle interacting with the proton or neutron in an atomic nucleus is so small, and the product of that reaction so tiny, that to measure it at all, all the background radiation that could mimic a WIMP collision and interfere with the calculations needs to be minimized. Deep underground we can greatly reduce cosmic rays, which bombard us all the time from space. Then the instruments have to be shielded from the natural radioactivity that comes from rocks. These instruments here are amazingly sensitive. They look for WIMPs by the scintillation—the ultra faint light—that's produced and the microscopic amount of heat that's made in a collision with ordinary particles."

"These WIMPs," he said. "Is there one candidate for dark matter or several?"

"The one that I'm betting on, and I'm not alone among particle physicists, is the neutralino. It's never been settled. Its existence has been predicted from mathematical models that arise from supersymmetry theory. We think its interactions would be really feeble—as we'd expect from a WIMP—and its mass would be very substantial: fifty to a few thousand times the mass of a proton. If I were a woman who liked to bet, I'd bet the Grail contains neutralinos."

"Why the warmth? Why is it putting out heat?"

"I've been thinking about this very hard. My honest answer is, I don't know. But everything could be explained by neutralinos. It also follows from supersymmetry theory that neutralinos are their own antiparticle. As particles and antiparticles collide, they produce energy. The models say that when neutralinos collide they would annihilate each other and produce another kind of particle, the neutrino. I'm going to be looking for neutrinos too."

She began to work on her instruments, keeping a running commentary going, letting Arthur know what she was doing and why. The biggest problem was to dumb the detector down, as she put it, to accomplish the opposite of what it was designed for—that is, to detect exceedingly rare collisions. She would need to see if it were possible to set the calibration to a coarse enough level so as not to be swamped by (what she hoped would be) frequent collisions.

EDELWEISS-II, she told him, had some limited success to show for its years of service. A handful of possible neutralino collisions had been detected—literally a handful. Five candidate collisions had been observed with a mass determination of approximately 20 GeV: the size of massive particles, about 25 times the mass of a proton. Unfortunately, this was somewhat higher than what the mathematical models had predicted and suggested contamination from background radiation. EURECA was designed to overcome the shortcomings of EDELWEISS. According to Claire, the true mass of a neutralino ought to be between 7 to 11 GeV.

The calibration took twice the time as expected and the two frequently looked over their shoulders in case anyone else came in. Claire had a story prepared that would convince anyone associated with the other projects but would, she conceded, be awkward if any WIMP people arrived.

"What about Simone?"

"Especially awkward," she said, keeping her eyes on the computer screen.

"It's hard for me not to see a connection here. Simone is working in this area too I suppose."

"Yes, he is."

"And he's communicating with a group of Grail hunters who are willing to kill for it."

She sighed deeply and painfully. "Yes."

"Then these people might have reason to believe that the Grail has something to do with dark matter," he said.

"I simply don't know the answer. I admit it's hard to believe this is only a coincidence."

Finally, she was ready.

She needed the Grail.

Arthur unboxed it and placed it gently on the lab bench. The first thing she did surprised him. She reached for a horseshoe magnet.

"About six percent of meteorites contain iron and iron-nickel alloys. I don't know what percentage of the bowl is ordinary matter versus dark matter but if there's iron it will create some problems with the detectors. I can correct for it, I hope."

She waved the magnet over the bowl and declared it iron free.

"Now … the tough part."

He saw what she was about to do and urged her to be very gentle.

"I need such a tiny amount of material. I think from the base, no?"

He agreed and sat beside her at the bench. She donned surgical gloves, opened a new petri dish from its plastic and had Arthur hold the bowl over it. Then she switched on a Dremel tool with the smallest cutting wheel and delicately skimmed the flat undersurface of the bowl, a task made difficult by its halo. She had to do it by touch and sound and when she thought she'd made contact she switched the tool off.

She slipped a black-covered notebook under the petri dish and they both inspected it. There were tiny flecks of opacity—minihalos—against the black background.

"Good, I think we have some," she said. "Now we're ready."

She pulled out an electronic module from an instrument attached to the large copper cryogenic tank. It was a bolometer, she told him, germanium crystals combined with an ultrasensitive thermometer, linked to a microprocessor. She placed the petri dish on the germanium plate, pushed the module back in and manned the workstation.

The screen came alive with dense plots of red and green dots.

"What do you see?" he asked.

She didn't look up. "Nothing yet! I need to do more calibrations."

"Sorry …"

Her fingers ran over the keyboard. Screen after screen of data zoomed by until all at once she clicked her mouse and leaned back.

She had frozen the screen on one plot. To Arthur it didn't look much different from the others but this was transfixing her.

"What?"

She put her finger on the screen over a mass of red dots. "Jesus, Arthur. This is it—an enormous spike of thermal and scintillation activity. At the lowest possible calibration, it's still almost off the charts. It's at 9.4 GeV. It's the neutralino, Arthur. It's dark matter."

He put his hand on her shoulder.

"And here, these green dots in the corner of the plot," she pointed. "These are neutrinos at 2.2 eV—a lot of them. It all fits."

She turned and buried her face in his shirt.

Arthur could only stand by idly while Claire raced to print out some key screenshots, clean the detectors, restore the default settings, and power-down the instruments before anyone arrived.

It took another half hour but they were done.

She switched lights off as they went along until only the engineering room was illuminated. As she walked into the light, she turned to tell Arthur she needed to sign out at the admin—

An arm shot out, grabbing her around the neck.

Arthur would never forget the look of fear on her face.

Hengst backed her up, showing himself in the yellow fluorescence. He had a pistol in his free hand and he pointed it at Arthur.

"Give it to me," he said.

Arthur's saliva tasted coppery. His skin prickled. He recognized him from somewhere.

Hengst moved the gun to her head. "Five seconds. That's all the time she's got."

"Arthur," she begged through her compressed larynx.

"Okay, I'm giving it to you."

"Slide it over."

Arthur put the bag on the floor and crouched to push it.

As it left Arthur's fingers Claire made a sudden move. With her right hand she reached behind her and grabbed Hengst's crotch, getting a tight grip.

He let out a primal grunt and let go of her neck long enough to deliver a roundhouse to her jaw.

As she fell to the floor Arthur charged forward, tackling the larger man at the thighs, binding him up then lifting and throwing him to the concrete floor. The black pistol hit and clattered away.

Hengst fought back, trying to buck Arthur off, slamming him with heavy fists. Arthur tasted blood but didn't let go, maintaining a hold while inching up, trying to bind the man's arms.

Hengst landed a blow to his temple, hurting him. Then Arthur took a knee to the groin. He groaned, broke his clench, and felt the man wriggling free.

Through the fog of pain he heard his name and saw Claire slide a large wrench across the floor. It came to rest against his leg. He grabbed it. As Hengst moved to his left to retrieve his gun, Arthur rose to his knees and swung it, hard.

The tool caught Hengst on the back of his head and showered the floor with a spray of scalp blood. He collapsed on his face, his body suddenly still. "We have to leave!" Claire shouted. "Now!"

Arthur kicked the gun under a workbench and fled with Claire, forgoing the urge to check on the man. He tried to remember where he'd seen him before and when he and Claire limped into the fume-filled tunnel it came to him.

The security man at the estate in Suffolk.

Jeremy Harp's man.

32

Claire was shaking too hard to drive so Arthur took the keys. When there was a large enough gap in the tunnel traffic he gunned the car out of the turnout.

"Are you okay?" he asked.

"Are you?"

He ignored the question. He hurt all over and suspected she did too. "We can't go back to your place."

"Do you think he's dead?" she asked, her body shuddering.

"I don't know. Maybe. I should have helped him."

"He was going to kill us."

He checked the mirrors. No one was following. "How did he get into the lab, Claire?"

"He must have had an access key. There's no other way."

"Where would he have gotten that?"

"Maybe he stole it. Maybe …"

"Simone?"

She began to cry.

"We've been followed," Arthur said. "Every step of the way. Stoneleigh. Montserrat. Barcelona. Here."

"What should we do? Where should we go?"

He tried to organize his thoughts but his mind was tumbling them around. "You checked into the lab, so the authorities will know you were there when he's found. So they'll be looking for you. Did you put down the license plate of the rental car?"

"No."

"Okay, there's that. Claire, there's something I need to tell you. I recognized him."

She looked shocked. "Who was he?"

"I don't remember his name but he worked as a security guard for Jeremy Harp. I told you about him."

"From your company. The man who had you dismissed for making him look bad."

He nodded. " The dinner I had with Harp the night before I found the treasure, he wanted to talk about the Grail. He'd said he'd read in our company newsletter that I was interested in it. He was knowledgeable, very knowledgeable. It surprised me. We talked about Andrew Holmes and Montserrat. He's a physicist too, like Simone. Jesus, Claire, Jeremy Harp wants the Grail."

There was a sign ahead in the tunnel: Bardonecchia 3 km.

In a flagging voice he said, "I suppose we're going to Italy."

Arthur and Claire drove the next hour mostly in silence. Driving aimlessly around Turin, he made the spontaneous decision to pull into the parking lot of a hillside hotel. He told Claire they needed to rest, to think, to come up with a plan and she wearily agreed. They checked into the Hotel Parco Europa. Passports were required. Reluctantly, they had to use their real names.

Their room overlooked a garden. Claire wanted a bath. He lay down weighing their options, the Grail under the bed.

He heard her phone ringing from the bathroom. She answered it. Alarmed, he opened the door. She was in the tub, holding the phone to her ear, half floating, skin pink from the hot water. She looked small and beautiful, like a water nymph.

She pressed the Mute button and told him, "It's okay. It's just my mother."

He left her alone and turned on the TV, looking for a news report about Modane but there was none.

She came out in a hotel bathrobe drying her hair.

"Is your neck okay, your head?" he asked.

"Yes, they're okay. What about *your* head. Let me see the bump."

"It's only a bruise."

"I'll find an ice machine."

"Don't bother, come here."

She lay beside him, both of them staring at the ceiling. She started trembling and he held her.

"Any change? With your father?"

"No, but my mother is making me crazy. It's too much, on top of all this. It's too much."

"I wish you hadn't gotten involved with me," he said sadly.

"Stop it. I love you."

They slept for an hour and when they awoke Arthur called down for coffee. They sat on the small balcony overlooking the garden.

"I know what I want to do," he said.

"Tell me."

"I want to go back to Spain. I'll call a newspaper, have them arrange a news conference. I'll talk about everything. The Thomas Malory papers, the sword, Montserrat, Gaudí, Sagrada Família. I'll come clean, give the Grail back. I'll surrender to the police for whatever crimes I committed in Spain. The Spanish can decide what happens to the Grail. It's theirs, not mine. I found it, now I'm done with it. Once everything's out they'll be no reason to have me killed. I'll have to figure out how to expose Harp's role in this but I'll leave that for another day."

"But there's more to the story than finding it!" Claire blurted out, suddenly animated. "It's more than a sacred relic. It's made of dark matter! Its scientific value may be even more important than its religious and cultural value. We can't just give it to some people who won't know anything about its properties. I need to be able to say what I know too."

"It's too dangerous. I don't want you to stay with me. We need to split up. You should go to Toulouse, be with your family. Get a lawyer, go to the police; tell them about being attacked in the lab by a stranger. Don't say anything about the Grail. It's the only way."

She was composed now, her old self.

"No, I'm sorry, but there's another way, a better way for both of us. We should stay together. I should be at your side at this news conference. I should explain what I know too, as a physicist. Maybe I'll be fired from my position for unauthorized use of the facility but it doesn't matter, it's too important. And I'll feel safer coming out into the public too. The Grail will be returned, both of our roles will be known, why would anyone try to hurt me then?"

He sipped his coffee and stared down at the rows of geometrically trimmed shrubs in the garden.

"Okay. We'll do it together."

"But we shouldn't do it yet," she said emphatically.

He put his cup down and stared at her. Her lips were firm and determined.

"Why not?"

"There's something you're not considering. You believe this is the true Grail. I believe it's the Grail. But why should anyone else believe it? It's circumstantial. Maybe King Arthur believed the Grail had been found but how did he know for sure? Maybe Gaudí believed he found the Grail but how did *he* know? They wanted to believe. *We* want to believe. But there's nothing, absolutely nothing connecting this bowl to Christ. We simply don't know it's the actual chalice that Christ used at the Last Supper, do we?"

"We don't, of course. It's conjecture. We'll lay out what we do know. Experts can go to town with it."

"Yes, conjecture. But we know with a degree of scientific certainty that it's composed of dark matter and that it emits neutrinos. What if we can combine the science with the biblical evidence?"

"How?"

"When I was at CERN in Geneva doing my postdoc, my professor and mentor was an Israeli particle physicist, Neti Pick. She's really brilliant and charismatic and, you know, as a woman, she was an inspiration to me. I mention her because of her interests outside of physics. She was an amateur archaeologist, very interested in biblical studies and bringing science together with the archaeological and biblical records. One of her real passions was the Shroud of Turin which we could even see today if we had the luxury of being tourists. She's one of the people who think the shroud is authentic."

"Really?"

"Yes. She served on a scientific commission organized by the Vatican and wasn't deterred at all by the carbon dating that suggested it was medieval. I don't remember the details of her argument but she believed the image on the shroud could have been formed by a neutrino burst at the moment of resurrection. It was all very hypothetical and she was dismissed as a crazy physicist but Arthur, with this object we believe is the Grail, we have a neutrino engine."

He leaned forward in his chair. "What are you proposing?"

"Let me call her. Let's go see her. She's at the Hebrew University in Jerusalem now. I want to show her the Grail, talk with her about the data, see if she can help us close the circle. We could take some instruments to the possible tombs of Jesus. Collect air samples, maybe some limestone samples to check for the lingering presence of neutralinos and neutrinos. If we're successful, it would connect the bowl to Jesus in the most definitive way possible. We'd prove it was the true Grail. No one could dispute it. It would be the most amazing announcement. All the ends tied into a beautiful bow. What do you think?"

"I don't know, Claire. I hear you but I think we should cut bait. Put a stop to the danger. I'd never forgive myself if you got hurt."

She frowned and nodded. "Whatever you say, Arthur, but I'm willing to take the risk."

They fell into a long silence. He studied her face. She seemed brave and determined. He could tell she wasn't ready to end the quest short of her notion of a finish line. He felt his resolve softening.

"Can you trust her to keep this secret?"

She smiled brightly. "Absolutely. She's like a second mother."

Jeremy Harp stood in the arrivals hall of Terminal 5 at Heathrow waiting for the passengers on the BA flight from Los Angeles to clear customs.

Stanley Engel finally emerged looking fed up, pushing his trolley.

"Stanley, welcome," Harp said. "How was your flight?"

"Long. This wasn't such a convenient time for me to be away from the university."

Harp waved over his driver, who took control of the luggage. The two physicists followed along to the car park.

"You didn't really have a choice, did you?" Harp said.

"Is it real? Is it found?"

"We need absolute confirmation but I truly think we are at that moment in time."

"Tell me what's going on."

"There's been a complication. My man, Hengst, followed them to Modane. Simone gave him an access card. Hengst waited until Pontier finished her analysis but when he tried to take possession of it there was a fight. Hengst was injured. Quite badly. We can't take Malory for granted. Simone found Hengst and took him to a hospital where he had emergency brain surgery. He probably won't survive, which is fine since it will remove the complication."

"Okay, okay. I don't care about your security guy. What happened to Malory and the girl? What happened to the Grail?"

"They got away with it."

"And?"

"Simone went back to the lab. He accessed the backup data on the EDELWEISS instruments. It's composed of neutralinos, Stanley. Neutralinos!"

"My God, just as we hypothesized. Were there neutrinos too?"

"There were. In abundance."

Engel pumped his fist. "Jackpot."

"Yes, jackpot."

"Now what? Do we know where they are?"

"Don't worry about that. We'll have the Grail soon enough. Then it will be on to the next step. Come, I've rented a house not far from here. Everyone's coming or already here. My jet's standing by. When it's time, we'll travel as a group and accept our destiny together."

At Milan's Malpensa Airport, Arthur ditched the rental car in a long-stay parking lot. He had come to his decision walking alone in the garden, gazing at jagged mountains against a magnificently blue sky.

He'd spent the afternoon planning things out. An online search pointed him to a prominent journalist at the Barcelona newspaper, *El Periódico de Catalunya*, who specialized in religious themes. She'd be the one he would contact from Jerusalem. He would invite all the Loons to the event. He'd dedicate it to Andrew and Tony.

Claire had assured him that since the Grail was nonferrous it would pass undetected through the airport magnetometers. He arranged for the hotel to mail the rosewood box to Sandy Marina, wrapped the Grail in his clothes and placed it in his backpack. Then he booked a flight to Tel Aviv from Milan leaving later that night.

Even with all their planning and forethought both of them were nervous wrecks throughout the check-in process in Milan. Had Hengst been found? Had the French police put out an alert for Claire?

It was only when the wheels went up and they were airborne that Arthur was able to relax a little, have a drink, and hold Claire's moist hand.

33

They arrived in Tel Aviv at 3 A.M. and by the time they emerged from customs, rented a car, and drove to Jerusalem the sky was already lightening. In a calculated move, Arthur had hoped that having a reservation at a top hotel might deflect suspicion away from their baggage, so he booked them into the King David where he'd stayed before on Harp Industries business.

The Israeli customs agent hadn't checked their bags. The Grail was back in Jerusalem.

"Welcome back to the King David, Mister Malory," the reception clerk said.

"It's good to be in here again."

When Neti Pick arrived later in the morning she proved to be a force of nature. She was short and stout, in her sixties with hair jet black and done in a youthful short cut. Her black dress was a good four inches above her bare knees. She wore bold gold jewelry hanging from her ears, neck and wrists. When she saw Claire across the hotel lobby she waved her arms and was soon delivering kisses to both cheeks.

"And you must be Arthur," she said with a thick Israeli accent, reaching for his hand and holding it in both of hers. Then she whispered, "Where is it?"

Arthur pointed to his backpack.

"Good. Please don't let it out of your sight. We should go somewhere where I can see it. Then we can talk a little."

They took her up to their room. Through the windows the Old City and the Mount of Olives was bathed in morning sun, a full palette of browns and yellow. Claire threw the bedspread on to give Neti a place to sit.

When Arthur placed the black bowl in her hands her face lit up in surprise and joy.

"Sweetheart," she said to Claire. "Get me some tissues to dry my eyes. I won't take my hands off this beauty."

"What do you think?" Arthur asked.

"What do I think? I think I died and went to heaven. It's as warm as a baby's bottom and look at the way it makes my fingers disappear. It's a treasure you found, the biggest treasure. And it's so simple. Just a small black polished bowl made of the most precious material on earth. Here, take it and keep it safe, Arthur."

He took it back.

"Okay, show me the data, Claire."

Arthur placed the Grail into his backpack and the two women sat side by side on the bed poring over the Modane printouts. Much of their banter was over his head but it was clear that the professor was in agreement with Claire's interpretation. The bowl contained some amount of dark matter. Their conversation veered off into additional experiments that needed to be done and Arthur went onto the balcony to search his mobile phone for any news about Hengst and Modane. Why was there nothing? Had he recovered from the head blow? Could he possibly still be on their trail? It was unsettling but at least he and Claire didn't appear to be international fugitives.

Claire called him back inside. "Neti has some ideas."

Arthur drew up the desk chair.

"Claire told you I have two passions," Neti began, "physics and archaeology. The first I got from my father, who was a great physicist, the other I got from my husband, may he rest in peace, but not complete peace because to tell you the truth he wasn't such a nice man all the time. He was an archaeologist at the Hebrew University who studied Jerusalem at the time of the Romans. So, it was natural that I picked up some of his subject matter and I got interested in applying some physics to what he did. For a Jew, I must say, he became pretty obsessed with the search for the tomb of Jesus and through him I got involved with the Shroud of Turin."

"Claire told me," Arthur said. "I thought the dating of the shroud some years back cast substantial doubt on its authenticity."

"There is no question," she answered, "that the radiocarbon dating done in 1988 under Vatican supervision came up with a date of thirteenth or fourteenth century but there's been a lot of criticism about sampling errors, contamination problems and even the possibility that they dated a piece from medieval patchwork. But there are other features, like the sewing technique of the linen and limestone particles embedded in the weave, which are the same as from Roman tombs, that all suggest a first century date. But from my point of view there is no convincing artistic technique that could have simulated this image of a crucified man on a piece of linen. The techniques weren't known in the first century, they weren't there in the fourteenth century, and I don't believe anyone could do it in the twenty-first century. That's why I think it's real."

"And you think neutrinos have something to do with the image formation?" Arthur asked.

"This has always been my leading hypothesis. In fact, I don't know what else could have made this image. You press a piece of linen against the corpse of a bloody man, you anoint him with oils, leave him in a hot place, a cold place, any place, and you're not going to get this kind of a perfect, almost photographic negative of a human body complete with the stigmata of the crucifixion spikes, the dumbbell-shaped scourge marks from the *flagrum*—the Roman whip—the blood and serum stains from where his lung was punctured by the spear."

"Neutrinos could produce an image on cloth?"

"Absolutely. A burst of neutrinos emanating from a body would oxidize the cellulose layer in linen and produce the precise negative image of the body upon the cloth. But neutrinos are very weakly interacting particles so nothing else would have been disturbed. Now here comes your Grail and here comes a possible explanation, don't you think?"

Claire nodded. "The mass of dark matter with its neutralino–antineutralino collisions is a continual source of neutrino production. If Jesus drank from the bowl and incorporated enough of these fundamental particles into his tissues, the neutrino release after death could explain the images on his shroud."

Neti agreed. "No need for dematerialization to explain the shroud."

"But his tomb was empty," Arthur said. "What about the resurrection?"

"You're not Jewish, are you?"

"Church of England."

Neti shrugged. "I don't want to interfere with your religion. Maybe the accounts of the Gospels were made up to promote a new religion. Maybe someone stole his body. Maybe the resurrection was real. All I'm saying is that my theory on neutrinos and the shroud mesh very nicely with your Grail. So I agree with Claire. The possibility exists to complete the picture."

"That's why we're here," Arthur said.

"I'll make the arrangements. We'll use my instruments at the most credible tomb sites in the Old City. If we detect neutralinos and neutrinos I'll go to Barcelona with you and the three of us we can give the most amazing press conference anyone has ever seen. Okay?"

"I'm tremendously grateful for your help, professor, I really am, but we've been followed the past week. Three people have been killed. This is dangerous."

Neti stood up and pulled down the hem of her dress. "Claire told me about all this. Yes, it is, but I'm too old and too stubborn to be scared. I'm not surprised there are people who want the Grail. It's a very valuable object which people have been looking for, maybe since the day Jesus became more than just a troublemaker who was executed. You two think about it. I've got to give a class. You'll call me in a few hours, Claire?"

"Absolutely."

Arthur was about to get the door for her when Neti suddenly said, "Tell me, Arthur, have you ever heard of a group called the Khem?"

34

Arthur was jolted by the question. "I *have* heard of the Khem."

"What do you know?" Neti asked.

"Only that a distant relative of mine, Thomas Malory, the man who wrote *Le Morte D'Arthur*, chronicled being hounded by men he called Qem—*Q-E-M*—in the 1400s. He was on the trail of the Grail and they were on his."

She sighed loudly and sat back down on the bed. "When I was a young woman and first introduced my husband-to-be to my father I remember listening to them talking and getting to know each other a little. My father wasn't so interested in archaeology, which he regarded as a very soft science, but when he found out that Ari was studying things related to Jesus of Nazareth and the Roman occupation of Judaea the subject turned to the Holy Grail. It seems my father knew a physicist when he was a student himself, in the Soviet Union. He said this physicist—whose name I can't possibly remember—had a great interest in the Grail. My father said he heard the man was a member of a secretive group who called themselves the Khem. They were all physicists and all Grail hunters and by the sound of my father's description, this was a bad fellow and these Khem were bad apples."

Arthur felt queasy. Jeremy Harp was a physicist too, as well as Claire's ex, Simone. "Did he say what they wanted with the Grail?"

"They called it the Resurrection Stone. That's all I know but this name for it suggested all sorts of possibilities for their motivation."

Arthur said numbly, "Jesus, resurrection …" As soon as he said it, the irony of the juxtaposition struck him.

"So, listen, Arthur," Neti continued. "If these Khem were around in the 1400s like you said and still strong in the 1950s like my father said, maybe they're here right now, today. I want both of you to be very careful. Claire is my little princess. I want you to protect her."

"I will."

"After my class I'm going to make some calls. I know all the groups that control the so-called Jesus tombs very well and I'll pull every string to get us after-hours access, hopefully starting tonight."

"How many sites are there?"

"Only two serious ones, the ones in which the real academics, including my husband, Ari, had any confidence: the Garden Tomb and the Church of the Holy Sepulcher. I'll get to work on obtaining permissions and preparing my portable instruments. You'll do this?"

Arthur and Claire both nodded.

"Until then you should stay in the hotel to be safe."

"Good advice, I'm sure," Arthur said.

"And if we go to a tomb tonight, take the Grail with you. Don't leave it in your room. Not even in the safe if it fits. It's not so hard to break into a hotel room. I don't trust anyone with something so valuable."

"Won't it interfere with your measurements?" Arthur asked.

"I love that he's so smart," Neti said, touching Claire's arm. "I'll bring a special box lined with lead to shield my instruments from it."

The Garden Tomb was in East Jerusalem, just outside of the Old City walls and the Damascus Gate. Neti picked them up in the hotel in her car and, true to her word, in the backseat was a lead-lined box for the Grail. Arthur let Claire sit in front, stuffing his Grail-filled backpack into the box and latching it. It was 10 P.M., short-sleeves warm, and the streets were largely deserted. In a few minutes they arrived. Neti pulled into a parking space reserved for the owners of the tomb, a Protestant charitable trust based in the UK. Arthur retrieved Neti's gear from the trunk and carried most of the heavy load. Claire took along the Grail box. Neti led the way with a flashlight and keys for the gate set into the walled compound.

Once inside, Arthur found the garden to be a tranquil oasis within the bustling city. There was a fragrance of trumpet lilies and a pleasant rustling of shade trees. In the darkness he couldn't well distinguish the outcrop of quarry rock above the garden, notable for a formation that very much resembles a human skull. It was precisely this deep-socketed natural sculpture that led Charles Gordon, a British general visiting Jerusalem in 1883, to explore the site further: as stated in the Gospels, of Jesus and the crucifixion, "And he bearing his cross went forth into a place called the place of a skull, which is called in the Hebrew, Golgotha" (John 19:17).

At the bottom of the quarry wall Gordon had found an ancient tomb chiseled into the limestone with a small entrance and groove cut into its base, which he thought surely was intended for the rolling stone that had covered Jesus' tomb. As far as Gordon was concerned, everything fit the biblical picture of this being the true tomb of Jesus, for John also had written, "Now in the place where he was crucified there was a garden, and in the garden a new sepulcher, wherein was never man yet laid. There they laid Jesus" (19:41–42).

Gordon established the society that owns the tomb to the present day, and since his time, archaeologists and biblical historians have avidly studied the site and debated its authenticity.

They stood before the vertical chiseled wall of the tomb that Neti now illuminated. A tall doorway leading to the so-called weeping chamber apparently had been enlarged at some more recent time: the original doorway was only a third the size and more compatible with biblical descriptions of both John and Mary Magdalene stooping down to look inside. To the right of the doorway was a *nephesh*, or soul window, through which, according to Jewish tradition, the spirit of the deceased departed after the third day in the tomb.

Neti entered first and set up a battery lamp that harshly lit the weeping room. It was small but large enough for the women described in the bible to have prayed and lamented over the body of Jesus. Through a low portal and down a single stone stair were four diminutive burial chambers including the longest in the northeast corner, the one said to be where Jesus was laid out.

Arthur bent over to enter and took in the burial chamber's stark simplicity: a hand-chiseled bench within a hand-chiseled room, a place to honor the dead, a place that might have served the needs of the most venerated soul in all of history. His reverie was interrupted by Neti's announcement.

"Okay," she said. "I don't know if this was *the* place but that's what we're here to find out. I want to put one detector right there on the possible Jesus burial niche and another one in the weeping room. Help me unpack everything and make the connections to the laptop."

"Where should I put the Grail?" Arthur asked.

"It doesn't matter. It's shielded. You can put it in the burial chamber."

The instruments were electronic boxes with hard-wired detector wands that Neti placed on small tripod stands. As they worked to set up the instruments, Arthur asked how they worked and was treated to a long, dense discourse from the professor about germanium wafers, palladium electrodes, ion fields and the like. When he rolled his eyes behind her back Claire smiled weakly and went on with her business at the laptop keyboard. Finally, Neti declared they were ready and took command of the laptop, which had been set up in the weeping room on a small folding table with a folding chair.

"How long will this take?" Arthur asked.

"Why? You got someplace better to be?" Neti answered.

"It should depend on the quantity of lingering neutralinos and neutrinos," Claire explained. "Maybe right away, maybe hours, if we find anything at all."

Arthur was concerned about Claire. She seemed listless, dragging. She had reasons enough—the stress, sleep deprivation, the blow she'd taken, her father. He'd asked if she was worried about him and she told him she was. As soon as Barcelona was over he vowed to take her to Toulouse to attend to her family.

They'd brought along a few water bottles. Arthur had some and offered Claire a drink. She gulped at it thirstily and wiped her lips with her hand.

A half hour passed, then an hour. Arthur had been told they were looking for red or green dots to appear on a computer plot but nothing was happening. He stood behind Neti while Claire crouched in the burial chamber.

After staying quiet for a long time, he finally asked Neti, "How strong is the evidence for this being the authentic tomb?"

"Well first of all, the site is clearly outside the walls of the Old City, which is where all the executions and burials would have been done in those days. The skull formation in the quarry makes this a good candidate to be the Golgotha in the bible and there's a lot of evidence that this quarry was a Roman execution ground, close to the city gate and near the main northern road. This would have been a very good place for passing people to see the crucifixions and get a lesson from their Roman masters. Now for the tomb itself, it certainly qualifies as a tomb made for a rich Jew like Joseph of Arimathea because it's got this very nice separate weeping room and the same kind of chiseling as many of the wealthy first-century Sanhedrin tombs in the Kidron and Hinnon valleys. On the other hand, some scholars think that some of the elements, like the multiple burial niches, make it more likely it's much older than first century, which goes against the idea it was a new tomb as the Gospels state. But then look at the Jesus niche: it's more finished than the other niches, which could mean that it was a new tomb when Jesus was buried here. And see how it's been chiseled and enlarged in the area where the head would have been? That's a sign the person who was put here was too tall for the original bench, and guess what? The length from head to toe is the same length as the image on the Turin Shroud. How about that?"

"Did your husband think this was the place?" Arthur asked.

"When I asked him things like that he'd always answer, 'I'm only an archaeologist. Make me a time machine and I'll get back to you.'"

The night droned on and the computer screen remained static. Arthur sat on the cool weeping room floor with his back against the rough wall. Claire stayed in the burial chamber seated next to the Jesus niche and the two kept eye contact through the portal, exchanging small gestures.

"So the Grail hasn't interfered with the instruments?" he suddenly asked.

"As you can see, no," Neti replied, pointing to the empty plot. "I'm not detecting anything I'd call our elusive particles."

"There was something you said this morning I've been thinking about."

"Oh yes? What was that?" the professor asked.

"You said that the composition of the Grail meant there was no need to invoke dematerialization to explain the shroud."

"Yes, that's true. The neutrinos—"

"That's not the part I was thinking about," Arthur interrupted. "It's the concept of dematerialization. Let's say that Jesus' body wasn't stolen by his disciples or anyone else. Let's say he really disappeared from the tomb. Is there any rational scientific basis to say that could happen to a body, his body?"

"Beyond *Star Trek*?" Neti joked.

"Real world, real physics."

"Look, a lot of interesting possibilities emerge from the recent work of theoretical physics. A lot of possibilities are lurking in the equations of supersymmetry models and string theory. I'm a particle physicist, an experimentalist, and some of the math is beyond me but I can see the shadows of what's possible."

"And what is that?"

From the burial chamber Claire answered, "Multidimensionality."

Arthur laughed. "Come on, really?"

Neti peered over her reading glasses into the burial chamber. "Claire can probably explain it better than I. It's a very modern theory and she's a young person who's closer to it, I'm sure."

"I'm not an expert either," Claire said, "but the concepts come from superstring theory, which we talked about in Modane: the mathematical attempt to unify quantum mechanics with the peculiarities of gravity into the elusive theory of everything. It was something Einstein was hoping to find but never did. We think that we can explain the properties of subatomic particles by thinking about them as different vibrations on a string as though they were tiny rubber bands. The string vibrates one way, it's one particle. It vibrates another way, it's a different one."

Arthur nodded. "I saw a TV show. But your voice is nicer than Stephen Hawking's."

"Yes, well, he's more clever," Claire continued. "One of the features of the theory is that the strings can only vibrate in specific dimensions of space-time. Actually, only eleven dimensions. Any more, any less, the theory breaks down mathematically. Of course, in our universe we can only perceive four dimensions so the other seven must be, well, think of them as curled up and inaccessible to our reality, very hard to describe in words, easier to conceptualize in the formulae."

"So there are seven additional dimensions?" Arthur asked.

"Ah, there's more to the story," Claire said. "The equations which arise from an eleven-dimension superstring theory suggest something more amazing. It seems the universe may be a three-dimensional membrane floating in eleven-dimensional space-time and before you get hung up on this impossible concept here's the important payoff. It raises the very real possibility that our universe exists in a multiverse of other universes. Try to picture a vast collection of bubbles or membranes, each one a separate universe, floating around in an unimaginably massive sea of eleven-dimensional hyperspace."

"How many universes are we talking about?"

"A big number," Neti said.

"One estimate is that there could be a googol of them," Claire suggested. "That's a one followed by a hundred zeros: trillions and trillions and trillions and trillions of them. Other models suggest it's maybe bigger, maybe infinite."

"Okay, I get the concept," Arthur said, "but I was asking about dematerialization and resurrection."

"Do you want to say more, Neti?" Claire asked.

"No, you keep going," the professor answered. "It's good your boyfriend sees how clever you are."

Claire shook her head at the comment and continued. "Normally, communication between each universe is impossible because we're glued to our own three-dimensional membrane by the physical forces of quantum mechanics like a fly is glued to flypaper. Only gravity, which is responsible for the warping of space-time, can make the jump into other universes."

"How far away are they?"

"Maybe closer than you think. A lot closer than you think. One set of calculations concerning gravity says that other universes can be as close as a millimeter away from us."

"You're kidding!"

"No, I'm absolutely serious. The math is very rigorous even if the idea is shocking. We may be only the thinnest curtain away from entire parallel universes. But the curtain can't be penetrated by us, only by gravity. Unless …"

"Unless what?"

"Unless dark matter is a bridge."

"She was on strong footing until now," Neti piped up.

"Go on, please," Arthur said.

"There's a controversial theory," Claire said, "that proposes that dark matter, which we know is invisible in our universe, is ordinary matter from another universe. There's also a theory that our Big Bang resulted from a collision between two parallel universes and that this was only one in perhaps an infinite number of Big Bangs to occur in the multiverse. So maybe the two theories are compatible. Maybe dark matter, like the dark matter in the Grail, came to us from another bubble."

"You said it was a bridge," Arthur said.

Claire shrugged. "Well, I don't know, but maybe it came across the curtain and maybe it can also take you back through the curtain."

Arthur nodded in vague comprehension. "The Resurrection Stone."

"Well, it's just a crazy theory," Claire admitted.

Neti smiled. "Now *that* I agree with!"

Arthur felt the need to stand. "Let's say Jesus drank from the Grail. He's imbued with exotic particles from the stone. He dies, he's wrapped in a shroud that gets acted on by escaping neutrinos to make the shroud image, and the dark matter somehow dematerializes his body and bridges him to a parallel universe? You're saying this is a physical explanation for resurrection?"

"I'm not saying anything," Claire said. "It's late. I'm tired."

Neti looked at her watch. "Yes, it's very late and we've got nothing here. I think we can rule out the Garden Tomb as being of interest. Let's pack our things and leave. Tomorrow—actually, it *is* tomorrow already—I've gotten us permission to spend the night at the Church of the Holy Sepulcher. When you go back to your hotel I hope you two young people will find something better to do than talk about string theory and the multiverse."

35

JERUSALEM, A.D. 33

Jesus was somber. He knew with blinding clarity what was going to transpire. He had acquired powerful enemies among the Sanhedrin elders even before he wreaked havoc in the Temple by challenging the moneylenders. Now his opponents were in a frenzy and the Romans would have to intervene—and when the Romans were drawn in men died.

Somehow the inevitability of it all was calming. He knew he would not run away, he knew he would not back down. Either course was anathema to him. So it was certain he would die. And it would not be a quick death, an easy death. It would be a hard death. He would suffer. But he prayed to God it would have meaning. Surely his life had meaning; surely his message of loving God and loving one's fellow man had meaning. Would he become just another martyr, ground down by the powerful and corrupt and forgotten when those who knew him themselves died, or would he have served a higher, more enduring purpose? If nothing was to be done to alter his fate, then surely his remaining task was to show his devotees that he was at peace and to teach them how a good and righteous man should die.

So sitting among his twelve closest disciples, men who had risked their own lives to follow him and his teachings, he smiled, determined to bask in a last warm camaraderie, a splendid Passover feast among friends.

They were in an upper room in a fine house on Mount Zion donated for the evening by a wealthy man who, as Thomas had told them, was the friend of their friend, Joseph of Arimathea. Joseph, while not a full-throated disciple of Jesus' preaching, had shown certain sympathies and made donations here and there to keep the cause afloat. The meal, spread before them on a low table, was simple but wholesome—meat, fish, bread, olives, and some wine.

They ate mainly in silence, for his followers also knew of the imminent danger, but any sense of despair that may have pervaded the proceedings was washed away by the utterly benign countenance of Jesus himself, who seemed to be enjoying the small pleasantries coming from friendship and a good meal.

But the room fell into shocked silence when Jesus suddenly stood and said, "One of you shall betray me."

The twelve men exchanged glances with one another and first Peter then others launched into denials and fervent expressions of their devotion.

Jesus nodded and smiled and put the talk to rest by taking a loaf of bread, blessing it, and breaking it into pieces. He said, "Take this bread and eat it for this is my body."

Astonished, the men did as he instructed and ate their pieces of bread.

Then Jesus took a pitcher of wine and said, "Take this and divide it among yourselves. This is my blood which is shed by many. After this night I will drink no more of the fruit of the vine until that day I drink it new in the kingdom of God."

The men passed the pitcher from one to another and when it made its way back to Jesus' hands Judas sprang up and stood over him, clutching a smooth black bowl.

"I bid you to take your wine from this chalice," he said to Jesus. "It is a hallowed vessel which comes from the ancient land of Moses."

Jesus took it, felt its warmth and marveled at its halo.

"How did you come by this treasure?" he asked.

"It is from a man who loved you."

Jesus poured wine into the vessel then beckoned Judas closer with a finger.

He whispered in his ear, "I know it is you who will betray me."

Then he took the bowl in his hands and drank the wine to the last drop.

Judas could do nothing to stop his shaking. He had run all the way from Gethsemane to the boarding house near the Temple where Nehor was staying. Nehor was waiting there with an Egyptian compatriot, an arrogant young man named Sacmis, which, as he liked to remind people, means "one who is powerful." While Jesus had acquired a following of earnest and high-minded men, Nehor had been attracting a following himself of altogether different sorts with baser objectives. Sacmis shared with his master an interest in the pursuit of alchemy, and though he was a tyro, he counted himself along with Nehor as a Qem, an ancient society that traced its lineage to Pharaonic times.

Nehor offered Judas wine to calm him but he refused it. He could not even sit to tell the tale of those horrible moments when he led the band of elders and priests and Praetorians to the peaceful olive grove where Jesus was sleeping, how the disciples had fled, and how Jesus had been roughly seized.

"Do you know what he did before they took him away?" Judas asked. "He kissed me. What have I done?"

"Did he drink from the bowl?" Nehor demanded.

"He did."

"Where is it?" Sacmis asked. He was muscular and hulking; next to him Judas looked like a boy.

Judas had it in a shoulder bag. "Here it is."

Sacmis took the bag, checked it, and passed it to Nehor.

"You did well," Nehor said.

"No, I am a traitor. He knows I am a traitor," Judas said mournfully. "I am cursed forever."

"Jesus is nothing if not smart," Nehor said. "Exceedingly smart. I am sure he suspects his martyrdom will advance his cause. He is a man of principles and so am I."

"And what are your principles, Nehor?" Judas spat. "You tried to strangle the prostitute, Anah. If Peter and Matthew had not happened by, you would have snuffed out her life. And for this, Jesus rightly cast you from his inner circle. I ask you now, why did you try to commit murder, Nehor?"

"Because I wanted to be sure, Judas. I wanted to test the powers of my fire stone. When I found it in the desert I knew it was a strange and powerful object. It had a halo. What stone has that? It was warm even when the nights were cold. What stone behaves thusly? I am an alchemist. I am trained in the manipulation of the natural world. So I knew it was special and I carried it with me from Egypt to Judaea where I came to make my fortune. And here I heard of Jesus of Nazareth, the greatest preacher the land has known, a man who is said to be so holy that he makes miracles. This was a man I needed to know. This was a man of possibilities."

"So you joined us to profit from him?"

"This is so, though at times I was almost drawn in myself by the power of his words. Has there ever been a man who could cast so fine a spell with words alone?"

"But you were never a true believer."

"I believe in myself, Judas. I find I am not such an able follower. I am more accomplished as a leader. And one night, not long ago, after an evening blessed with a great deal of good wine, I unwrapped my fire stone from the cloth in which I kept it and I said to it, 'What secrets do you hold? What can you do to make me rich? What can you do to make me powerful?' It had the rough shape of a bowl and as I am skilled in working metal and stone I ground it down to make it into an alchemical vessel where I might combine various substances and see if its properties led to promising outcomes. Perhaps, I thought, I might turn base metals into gold. Shaping the bowl was a wondrous thing since each flake of stone dislodged and each piece of dust thrown off had its own tiny halo. I worked through the night and as dawn approached I fell asleep in the dirt behind this very house. I awoke to a pelting rain, soaked to the skin, and when I stood I saw a dog drinking from the rainwater which had gathered in my bowl. A dog defiling my precious crafted bowl! So I kicked the animal and kicked it again and the second blow snapped its neck, causing it to die on the spot. I threw its carcass beside the rain barrel, retired to my bed for a proper slumber and thought no more of it until I awoke and decided to toss the beast farther along the alley so it would not fill my nostrils with the stench of its decay. But it was gone, Judas, gone."

"So?" Judas said. "Another animal surely dragged it away."

"That is what I thought, of course—until the next day when I set to work on the bowl again to finish shaping and polishing. I rose after a time to relieve myself against the wall and when I turned back to my work the dog was there! By the rain barrel!"

"How do you know it was the same dog?"

"It had the same white mark on its snout. It was the same dog, I tell you, risen; and it seemed to remember me because it looked me over and ran away as fast as a creature can run. I never saw it again."

"You cannot believe what you are telling me," Judas said. "Only a crazed man would believe this."

The remark angered Sacmis, who cursed at his insolence—but Nehor prevented him from striking Judas.

"I am of sound mind, Judas. I know what I saw. That dog drank from my bowl and returned from the realm of the dead. And I knew what I had to do. I had to test its powers on a man, or at least a woman. When Peter and Matthew thwarted me with the whore, Anah, my thoughts turned to Jesus. It was all too easy. I would not have to kill him myself and that was a good thing since I do like the man. The Romans will do the job for me tomorrow. I had only to offer him some Passover wine."

"My God, what have I done?" Judas wailed.

"Done? If I am proved right you have given him the gift of resurrection. And you will have given me the gift of immortality."

Jesus was crucified on a wooden cross on a Friday in the Roman execution ground outside the city walls in a place known as Golgotha. The Sabbath was approaching, a tomb had to be found for his bloodied and broken body, but none of his followers had the means to find him a resting place on short order. A solution emerged when the wealthy Sanhedrin priest, Joseph of Arimathea, came forward and persuaded the Roman governor of Judaea, Pontius Pilate, to let him take charge of the corpse. Jesus was carried to one of Joseph's unused tombs, near to the execution ground, which he had constructed for members of his extended family who lived in Jerusalem. After Jesus' body was hastily cleaned, anointed, and wrapped in a linen shroud by the tearful women in his life, the rock-cut tomb was sealed by a rolling stone and left for the Sabbath.

On Sunday morning, Nehor was nervously reading one of his Egyptian alchemical texts in his room when Sacmis bounded in, sweaty and out of breath.

"It has happened!" the large man panted.

"Tell me."

"The women, Mary Magdalene and the others, went to the tomb this morning to complete the burial rites. The tomb was empty! It has happened!"

Nehor calmly put down his text, rose and slipped on his sandals. His face was a picture of control.

"What are they saying?"

"Some, that his body was stolen by the Romans. Others say his disciples took it. But some are saying that he has risen."

Nehor slung his shoulder bag over his neck and felt the weight of the bowl against his side. He patted it with his right hand.

"Come," he said. "Let us test its true power."

A throng of men and women were gathered outside the empty tomb of Jesus talking excitedly and milling about, kicking up fine, white quarry dust. From a distance Nehor recognized most of the disciples, and as he drew nearer, Matthew, a long-haired youth with a sandy beard, pointed a finger with the same snarling look he had shown the day he pulled the Egyptian's hands from the throat of the whore.

"How dare you come, Nehor. You are not wanted here. Jesus cast you out."

Nehor responded with a bow of respect. "I never stopped loving him. Even though he cast me out from among his closest disciples he forgave me for my sins. He forgave all men for their sins and taught that we should forgive each other. Do you not adhere to his teachings?"

Matthew began to cry and said, "I will forgive you, Nehor. You have heard what happened here?"

"I have heard."

Nehor looked around and took stock of all of the disciples save Judas and cautiously asked if he was also here.

"He is dead. He hanged himself last night. He could not stand the pain of his deed. Someone gave him silver to betray Jesus."

"Do we know who?"

"The Temple elders, the priests, I do not know."

"Some are saying Jesus' body was stolen," Nehor said.

"Not by us!" Matthew exclaimed.

"What about the Romans?"

"Why would they? They would not wish to elevate his death by feigning a miracle. There is only one explanation, Nehor. He has been called to the side of God. He has been resurrected."

Peter was already walking from the tomb toward the city gate, clutching Jesus' burial shroud to his chest. Thomas was following, then James, Andrew, John, and the others.

"I must go," Matthew said. "We are meeting in a house on Mount Zion to discuss what has happened, to pray and give thanks. It is a stirring time. Jesus has risen!"

"What is Peter carrying?" Nehor asked.

"It is his shroud. The image of his body appears on it as if God Himself has painted it."

Nehor and Sacmis held back and waited for the throng to fully disperse. A few stragglers went in and out of the tomb and finally they were alone.

Entering, Nehor passed through the weeping room and stooped to enter the burial chamber. The day was already bright and hot but the limestone tomb was cool and dark. In the shaft of light from the tomb door Nehor could see that the stone burial bench was stained the color of rust with dried blood.

"Guard the door," Nehor told Sacmis. "I want no one entering."

When Sacmis was in place he removed the bowl from his bag and carefully placed it upon the bench.

He stood and stared.

He heard an argument. Sacmis and another man who said he was Joseph, owner of the tomb, coming to take possession of it.

Sacmis was denying him entrance but the man persisted and tried to push his way in.

Nehor looked back and saw a black-bearded, pudgy face pushing in far enough to see both him and the bowl.

Joseph shouted, "What is happening in here? This is my tomb! What are you doing with that bowl? Is this magic? Is it sorcery? I know who you are. Jesus cast you out!"

But the face disappeared as Sacmis manhandled Joseph away from the door. Nehor heard a volley of threats and counterthreats and the sound of rapidly retreating sandals when, he reckoned, Sacmis pulled a dagger.

Nehor stepped into the weeping room to speak to Sacmis when something happened behind him.

The burial chamber flashed bright, awash in light as if the tomb at once had been opened to the receive the rays of a midday sun.

He shouted at Sacmis to hold his ground at the door and painfully squinted into the light.

The light dissipated gradually and then he heard something.

Was it a voice?

He listened closely, hearing the words, "Dear Lord." It was the sound of praying.

With his heart in his mouth Nehor crept through the portal to the burial chamber and there he saw him bathed in a soft, fading glow.

He was naked. His hands and ankles bore the angry black holes of the spikes, his chest marked by scourging. But he was smiling warmly and he opened his arms in a welcoming gesture.

"Jesus," Nehor muttered numbly.

And Jesus said simply, "I have returned."

Nehor's head was swimming with things he wanted to know. Yet all he could manage to ask was, "Where were you?"

"In the realm of our Lord, our God."

Then Nehor blurted out, "What was it like?"

Jesus smiled more broadly. "It is for good and righteous men to know when it becomes their time. It is not for me to tell them. Where are my disciples?"

"On Mount Zion."

"I must go to them. Will you give me clothes?"

Nehor threw off his own robe, leaving himself clothed only in a loincloth.

Jesus donned the robe and saw the bowl on the bench, but it was no longer black. It was glowing white.

"This cup, this Grail, it is holy," he said. "Take care to protect it and keep it safe."

And Jesus lived among his startled and awestruck disciples for forty days, teaching them and praying with them. Fearful of the Romans, they endeavored to hide him away in safe houses but he himself showed no fear and boldly would go forth and appear in and around Jerusalem meeting with adoring followers who had heard of the miracle of his resurrection.

Though he would tell no one what he had experienced during his disappearance, he spoke in reverential tones of many things pertaining to the Kingdom of God. He talked of the path one must follow in life to attain God's grace and he commanded his disciples to disperse from Jerusalem that they might preach his gospel of salvation to all the people of the world.

On the fortieth day Nehor decided to act. He had been laying back, watching Jesus from a distance, shadowing his public sightings, accumulating evidence with his own eyes that the miracle of resurrection had transformed Jesus from a prophet to something much more resembling a deity.

On that morning he handed a papyrus scroll to Sacmis. "Take this to Peter and the other apostles. Today is the day I intend to send him back from whence he came."

"Tell me how, master?" Sacmis asked.

"The Grail is here and yet Jesus walks the earth. I have, as you know, cloaked myself and drawn close to him while carrying the Grail as he preached in public squares. Yet nothing happened. I have come to believe that the resurrection stone exerts its power only at the place where death occurs."

"But Jesus died on the cross."

"Did he? Perhaps he was beyond saving but barely alive when he was taken down. The Sabbath was coming. His body was laid out in great haste. Perhaps no one noticed the last movements of a dying heart. Perhaps his spirit left him within the tomb."

"That is what you believe?

"It is. And that is why I must get Jesus to return to the tomb. When that is done, if I am proved correct, I will convince the people that I am the chosen one to carry on his ministry on earth. We will found a new church, Sacmis, one that draws from Jesus' well but owes allegiance to the great Qem who came before us. We will be rich, we will be powerful and, above all, we will be immortal."

"How will you convince the people that you have been chosen?" Sacmis asked.

"I will die and like Jesus I will be resurrected."

"How will you die?"

Nehor smiled. "You will kill me."

In the evening, as the sun lowered in the sky and deepened in color, Nehor waited with Sacmis outside of Jesus' empty tomb. In the distance they saw a small procession, and soon, walking through the Golgotha quarry, past the site of his crucifixion, Jesus came forward with his eleven remaining disciples, Joseph of Arimathea and the women—Mary Magdalene, Salome, Joanna, and Susanna.

Jesus had Nehor's scroll in his hand. He approached and said, "I have come. What would you have me do?"

Nehor took the Grail from his bag and showed it to Jesus. After the resurrection it had returned to its natural black color. "Is this the bowl from which you drank wine on the Passover?"

"It is."

"Would you enter your holy tomb with me so I may show you yet another miracle?"

Jesus smiled at him and said, "I will come."

Then Jesus' followers cried out for him not to go, some saying that Nehor was evil, some, that it was a trick.

But Jesus said, "I have been among you nigh on forty days. I have delivered unto you my last earthly teachings. It is time I returned to sit at the side of God." Then he raised his hands in a blessing and said, "May eternal peace be upon you," and followed Nehor into the tomb.

A bright light flashed through the door of the tomb.

The disciples and the women shielded their eyes and fell to their knees in prayer. They strained to see.

In a short while a man came out of the tomb.

It was Nehor, clutching the Grail, white and glowing once again.

"He is gone!" he shouted to the people. "He has ascended."

The disciples rushed past Nehor and in twos and threes they entered and saw for themselves that the tomb indeed was empty save for the crumpled robe Jesus had been wearing.

Peter came forward and asked, "What did Jesus say inside?"

Nehor smiled and replied with the lie he had practiced. "He said that I would inherit his mantle as Son of Man. But he also said that I had to show you, his apostles, that I was worthy."

"And how must you do that?" Matthew asked skeptically.

"He said I must also drink sacramental wine and I must suffer and that I too will be resurrected. Then you will know I am to be the one to carry his message forward on this earth."

As Jesus' followers talked and argued among themselves, Sacmis poured some wine from a skin into the Grail and Nehor gulped it down.

They watched the Egyptian in fascination and heard him say to Sacmis, "Do it now. Make it slow, make it painful."

And before anyone could do or say anything, the large man pulled a short Roman sword from his belt and ran it through Nehor's gut, taking care to miss the most vital of the organs.

Nehor fell to his knees and let out a guttural yell of pure agony. He grabbed at the wound with his hands and they became wet and red.

"See?" he gasped, "I am dying."

The circle of men and women slowly tightened around Nehor as his lifeblood ebbed. All the while, Nehor's gaze was fixed hungrily on the Grail, which lay beside him.

Then Joseph of Arimathea raised his voice up and shouted, "There is one true Son of Man and one true Son of God and that is Jesus, our Christ and our Lord! I will not let this man, Nehor, use the holy chalice of Jesus' last supper to further his evil plans. He has never been and will never be Jesus' messenger. That duty belongs to you, his true apostles!"

Rushing forward, Joseph snatched the Grail from the dusty ground and took off with it down the slope of the quarry.

Nehor's eyes widened in terror and as he toppled from his knees onto his side he groaned to Sacmis with his last breath, "Bring it back."

Sacmis began running after Joseph, cursing and waving his sword, but when he got to the slope only paces behind the fleeing man he saw only a rubble-strewn hill and nothing else.

Joseph was gone.

Sacmis looked for him all evening and all through the night; and he would continue to look for him for the rest of his long life, recruiting others to his cause, other Qem, to whom he passed along the story of the Grail and the vast power that would accrue to them who found it.

Joseph hid that night like a rabbit down a hole in one of the many rock-cut tombs that honeycombed the quarry. Nehor's corpse was never found. Jesus' followers were of the opinion that Sacmis had taken his body and entombed it; because Nehor was despised, none but Sacmis were willing to entertain the possibility that he, like Jesus, had been resurrected. A few days passed and Joseph decided it was safe to come out from hiding and flee Judaea. He devoted his life to keeping the Grail and spreading the Gospel of Jesus.

Before he died, Joseph passed the Grail for safekeeping to a group of early Christians in the Roman province of Tarraconensis, who kept and venerated the relic but understood from his teachings that its power was best kept hidden lest evil men exploit it.

And generations later the Grail ascended, some would say closer to God, carried by monks to a high peak in Hispania to a mountain that would come to be called Montserrat.

36

"What time is it?" Arthur asked, blinking in the dark.

"Four."

"A.M. or P.M.?"

"P.M."

Claire was already awake, staring at the ceiling. She got up and parted the curtains, flooding the hotel room with light.

Arthur pulled the covers over his eyes and groaned for coffee.

There was a coffee machine in the room. She made him a cup and got into bed beside him.

"Some night," he said.

"Yes, some night."

"By the time we get ready and have some food it'll almost be time to do it again."

She drank from a bottle of orange juice without responding.

"You look tired," he said. "Did you sleep?"

"Not much."

"Any messages from your family? Is everything okay?"

"No messages, no."

"What then? You're off-kilter."

"I don't know that word."

"Off balance. Not yourself."

Her animation returned in a flourish of anger. "How can I be myself? Every day we stay here the danger only increases. We almost died at Modane!"

Arthur put his coffee down and said in exasperation, "Claire, it was you who suggested we come to Israel, remember? Complete the picture?"

"I know, I know," she admitted, shaking her head. "I thought it was a good idea; but all night I've been questioning myself. I think I was wrong. Let's go to Barcelona now, then somewhere nice, an island with a beach to get to know each other properly without the adventures. Just the two of us."

He held her and pulled her close, moving his hand tenderly up her thigh to her back. "You're having a delayed reaction to Modane. It's normal. We're here. We'll finish this. One more night. One more tomb. Tomorrow we'll go to Barcelona. We'll have our news conference with all the data we have. We'll deal with the authorities in Barcelona and Modane as quickly as we can. We'll go to Toulouse. Then I'll find us a tropical island with a nice sugar beach where we can make love all day and dance all night. How would that be?"

"It would be bliss," she said.

He kissed her. "Tomorrow."

The Church of the Holy Sepulcher is located within the Christian Quarter of the Old City adjacent to the maze of streets of the ancient Muristan district. Erected over the site many believed to be the true biblical Golgotha, the church in modern times is administered jointly by the Eastern Orthodox, Roman Catholic, and Armenian Apostolic Churches, and Neti had been able to secure nocturnal visitation rights for scientific study from the triumvirate.

They arrived at 11 P.M. and Neti parked on a side street close to the church courtyard. Lugging the same gear from the previous night, they entered the domed church, not through the great wooden doors at the main entrance but through a less-storied side door used by maintenance workers. Neti, acting as guide, took them through a series of storage rooms leading into the church where they emerged in the Chapel of Mary Magdalena and soon were standing in the rotunda.

A few incandescent fixtures had been left on for them, and though the light was dim, Arthur began to absorb the features that made the Church of the Holy Sepulcher different from any cathedral he had ever visited. For under the ornate dome of the rotunda, surrounded by massive marble columns, was a self-contained rectangular building, modest in proportions, with a fancy onion-domed cupola.

"The Edicule," Neti said, drawing their attention. "That's where the tomb is. That's where we're going."

They set the equipment and Grail box down on the marble floor.

Neti pointed across the central gallery, the Catholicon. "Down there and up the stairs is the shrine of Calvary: there's a stone with a hole where the cross was supposed to have been placed. It looks a little different from the Garden Tomb, no?"

Arthur nodded. "Night and day."

"You have to remember that this is all built on an area that in A.D. 33 would have looked not so different from where we were last night. It's impossible to even use your imagination it's so altered by two thousand years of successive shrines and churches. I think that's why ordinary people have a stronger connection to the Garden Tomb, while a majority of scholars favor the authenticity of this place."

The interior of the Edicule was dark. Neti entered first with one of her battery lamps and Arthur and Claire followed to get a sense of the layout before carrying in the monitoring devices. The first chamber, the Chapel of the Angel, was not much larger than a generous garden shed, its floor inlaid with panels of orange, white, and black marble. Dead center was a square marble altar, a pedestal with a flat glass top covering a slab of stone the size of a chessboard.

"That's supposed to be a piece of the rolling stone which an angel pushed away," Neti explained.

Arthur was looking past it to the portal that led to a second chamber. The arched passage, framed by creamy marble elaborately carved into a curtain motif, was low, preventing anyone from entering without bowing down.

Neti placed a second battery lamp inside and Arthur followed with his head low until he was through and could stand in the Tomb Chamber. This room was less than half the size of the other, and half its area was taken up by the stone burial couch. Directly ahead, partially obscured by Neti, he saw a painted icon of the Virgin Mary that overlaid a cupboard that, she told him, could be opened to reveal an older layer of the Edicule. To his right at knee height was a marble bench topped by Christ's supposed burial slab. Over the bench was a red marble shelf with the colorful iconography that represented the three controlling churches.

"Come on in, Claire," Neti beckoned. There's just enough room for three people, no more than that. I agreed I wouldn't put any instruments on the burial slab but we can use the floor."

"You think this is a good candidate for the actual tomb?" Arthur asked.

"Well, probably better than the Garden Tomb," Neti answered, "and certainly Catholics and Orthodox Christians think this is the right place. The history goes back to the fourth century when Helena, the mother of Emperor Constantine, the first Roman emperor to accept Christianity, came to Jerusalem looking for the tomb. So, this is a smart woman by all accounts and maybe she could be described as the first anthropologist because what does she do? She asks the people in the area where they think Jesus was buried. This was less than three hundred years after the crucifixion so it's not farfetched to think that people actually had a good idea. And they told her, 'there,' in the rubble of one of Hadrian's old temples, which had been erected on the site of Golgotha but had recently been demolished to build a new church for Constantine. That's where she was said to have found pieces of the True Cross, the Stone of Calvary and this tomb."

"But this is inside the city walls," Claire said.

"Now it is. Back in A.D. 33 this area was outside the Old City walls."

Arthur looked around. "I'm sorry, but this looks nothing like a rock-cut tomb."

"No it doesn't," Neti agreed. "Keep in mind this Edicule has been built and rebuilt four times over the centuries and the church around it has also undergone enormous periodic changes. This structure we're in is from the nineteenth century. Essentially the Edicule is like a Russian nesting doll, one building inside another inside another. The actual tomb is probably below us but it would take an earthquake literally to get the church authorities to agree to any kind of modern archaeological exploration. Okay, let's get on with it, shall we?"

Arthur and Claire went back and forth into the rotunda fetching the gear and setting it up in the tomb room and the anteroom. She was quiet, still not her usual self.

"Are you all right?" he asked.

"Just a little tired."

"Remember, tomorrow."

"I remember."

Neti was seated in the Chapel of the Angel in front of her laptop, checking the connections. She looked around.

"Where's the Grail?" she asked.

"In the rotunda," Arthur said. "Should I leave it there?"

"You can bring it in. It's okay."

He left and returned with the lead-lined box.

"Where should I put it?"

"You can put in on the rolling stone altar. They didn't say I couldn't put something on it. It's covered in glass anyway, which is probably not so clean since visitors kiss it all day."

Arthur gently placed the box on the altar and sat on the marble floor beside Claire. He looked up at the smoke vent and the fifteen hanging oil lamps. He wondered what the chapel would look like if they were all lit and the harsh battery lamps were shut off.

He would have liked to see how lovely Claire looked here in that enchanting glow.

Suddenly, the chapel got a few shades brighter. He thought it was his imagination but Claire and Neti noticed it too.

The three of them stood when the source of the extra light became clear.

It was the Grail.

Bright light was leaking through the seal of the box lid.

Neti's face changed. She seemed younger, more aggressive. "Open it!" she shouted. "Go ahead and open the box."

Arthur took a hesitant step forward and flipped the two latches. At that, the lid partly opened and the light was brighter still.

"All the way! Open the lid," Neti ordered.

Gulping, he lifted it until the box was fully open. The room became as bright as a sunlit day.

The Grail was shining like a beacon. It had changed color from jet black to snow white.

He felt Claire beside him and heard her say, "My God."

He was scared to touch it out of fear it was hot but when he realized that there was no intense heat he put his hand closer until his finger made contact. It was the same temperature as before.

Behind him he heard Neti say, "It's happening," and he assumed she was talking to them, but he was mistaken. She was speaking into the microphone of her laptop.

"What's happening?" he asked.

"You'll see."

Claire looked panicked. Her fear rubbed off on him. "Claire, do you know what's going on?"

"Arthur, I …"

She didn't finish the sentence.

A young black-haired man came barging through the Edicule entryway and into the chapel waving a gun.

Then a second man entered, more slowly, more confidently, also brandishing a pistol.

Arthur knew this man.

Jeremy Harp.

There hadn't been time to think, let alone act. Arthur was frozen in place and he felt Claire's body stiffen against his.

Harp feasted on the sight of the Grail.

"Give it to me, Malory," he said.

Arthur glowered at him.

Neti repeated the command. "He said, give it to him."

Arthur looked at Neti with contempt.

She's one of them.

"Come on then, Claire, *you* give it to me," Harp said, pointing his gun at Arthur's head. "Do you want me to kill him right here, right now?"

Arthur was woozy, disoriented.

"How does he know your name, Claire?"

"I mean it, Claire," Harp repeated.

Claire reached into the box and picked up the bowl. She handed it to Harp, who pocketed his gun to receive it in his small, soft hands.

Claire stepped back beside Arthur, the two of them on one side of the Altar of the Rolling Stone, Neti and the two men on the other.

"After all these years," Harp crowed.

"After all these centuries," Neti added.

"You know, Malory," Harp said, "one of the reasons for my success in business is a talent for picking the right people for the right job. After you joined the Loons and we learned you were a descendent of Thomas Malory, I had Martin Ash hire you. I was patient. I monitored your phone calls. I had my man do the burglary. I had you sacked to light a fire under you. I backed you to the hilt and you delivered."

Simone had his pistol trained on Arthur. "Claire did well too." He smiled at her. "I missed you."

She grimaced, refusing to reply.

"You're right, Simone," Harp said. "Claire did well, though she needed persuasion."

Arthur ignored everyone in the chamber but Claire. He turned to her and forced her to look at him.

"You're one of them too."

Her lips quivered and her eyes began to water. "I was curious, of course, and also honored to be asked to join. Neti was my mentor, Simone, my friend—okay, my lover—the men involved, some of the greatest living physicists. They told me things about the Grail that had been passed down over two thousand years, from alchemists to chemists to physicists. The Khem are rational and empirical people. We don't believe in magic, we don't believe in mystical things. We believe in science so we knew that the Grail had to have properties not from the earth but from the cosmos. Ever since dark matter was discovered we thought the Grail might be made of it."

"And now we know it is," Harp said.

"This is my subject, my passion," she went on, "but I ..."

"You what?" Arthur asked sadly.

"She got wobbly," Harp said. "She balked. We had to stiffen her spine."

"I decided to stop—after they killed Tony. It was madness. And I fell in love ..."

Simone's face reddened.

"Stop, Claire, don't," Arthur said.

"Okay ... but it's true. And then they threatened my family, Arthur. They have someone watching them outside their house. They said they'd kill them. I didn't know what to do."

"Your father's not sick."

"No."

"Another lie," he said. "Like the one about putting the Grail in this box. Lead doesn't block these particles, does it?"

"No."

"It didn't really make sense but if you said so, why would I doubt you? And these instruments—they don't do a damn thing, do they?"

Neti snorted. "Gamma ray detectors. Nothing to do with this exercise."

"And what is the exercise?" Arthur asked angrily.

Harp answered, his eyes fixed on the bowl glowing white in his hands. "Our oral history goes back to the time of Christ. A great alchemist named Nehor found the Grail stone, presumably a one-of-its-kind meteorite, and fashioned it into this bowl. He discovered it functioned as a portal. These days we talk about the multiverse. We shall see about that. Jesus drank from it, the dark matter entered his body and the rest is history. Did he go to heaven? A parallel universe? Are they one and the same? Do you see this melding of theology and science? Nehor, it is said, did the same as Jesus, drinking from the Grail, inside or near Jesus' tomb. It is also said he had one of his followers kill him but the Grail was stolen before he could, well, be resurrected. For two millennia the Khem have been looking for the Grail. Our aim was to bring it back to the exact spot where Nehor died."

"We don't know how extradimensionality works," Neti said, "but according to oral tradition, the place where you come back has to be the place where you died."

Harp nodded his jowly head. "Job one was finding the Grail. Job two was finding the right tomb. Look at the way the stone's behaving. We have the right place. Hopefully, we won't have long to wait for Nehor's return, the second great resurrection in history."

"And what happens if this Nehor materializes?" Arthur asked contemptuously.

"The dawn of a new era, *that's* what!" Harp cried. "Out with all the silliness and superstition, in with a rational culture based on science. The Khem will be both learners and teachers. We'll introduce Nehor to the world and let him tell his remarkable story. We trust he will be wise and articulate and inspirational. We will be the keepers of the Grail, we will be the leaders of a new scientocracy, we will be the ones to drink from it, and yes, attain a measure of immortality. I for one cannot wait to see what lies beyond this world."

Arthur shook his head. "What if Christ is the one who returns?"

Harp smiled. "We've discussed this. We're not unanimous but we've got a working plan. The rest of the Khem are standing by nearby to respond to any eventuality."

"Do you know how ridiculous you sound?" Arthur said. "A working plan? This isn't some project team discussion in a lab or a company. This is Christianity! You really are a pathetic little man. You're also a grubby, common murderer."

Harp's lips flattened then dipped into a frown. He held out the bowl. "Will you hold it for me, Neti?"

She took it from him.

Harp reached in his pocket then stretched out his arm, pointing his gun at Arthur.

"I've never killed a man with my own hands, Malory, but this is a very good place to start."

As Harp's pudgy finger curled around the trigger, Claire flung herself between Arthur and the altar.

There was an enormous boom and the bullet entered her chest.

She went down slowly, her knees turning to liquid.

Everything that happened next seemed in slow motion.

Harp stood there numb, dumbfounded that he'd shot her, his arm frozen outright.

Arthur lunged for the gun. It slid easily from Harp's sweaty fingers. As Claire continued to slump, Arthur grabbed her and fell to the floor.

The base of the altar must have offered some protection—while he heard another shot blast out, this from Simone's gun, the only effect was a boom and a shower of marble fragments.

Arthur turned the gun on his attackers. Down low, the only targets were legs. He fired at them at close range until Harp and Simone crumpled beside the altar, screaming in agony, offering him much larger targets.

Neti yelled in terror. Untouched by lead or marble, she dropped the Grail onto Harp's body and scrambled out of the Edicule in a panic.

Arthur's ears were ringing and he couldn't be sure if he was deaf or if everyone had gone silent.

He slithered across the floor to the bodies. The wounds were ghastly. They were no longer a threat.

He heard a moan.

Claire was alive.

He went to her and cradled her head. Her shirt was soaked through with blood.

"I've got to get help," he said desperately.

"No, don't leave me."

"I've got to get an ambulance."

"It's too late, Arthur. I'm dying. I can feel it."

He put his hand on her wound and pressed in a vain effort to do something, anything.

"I'm sorry, Arthur. I loved you."

"I can't lose you!"

He looked around and saw the Grail.

"Please hold on," he said, lowering her head gently onto the floor.

There was a water bottle in his backpack. He poured some of it into the Grail and took it to her.

"You've got to drink this. Can you?"

He lifted her head up and held the bowl with the other.

She gulped at it, coughed, and stopped.

"Please, more."

She finished it, looked at him one last time and stopped breathing.

He set the Grail down and put his arms around her, shifting her onto his lap. He wouldn't let her go. She was still warm, her skin still had a tinge of pink; she still looked beautiful.

He shut his eyes and felt the tears finding their way around his tight lids.

He prayed and rocked her in his arms.

His grief was overwhelming, like a bomb detonating inside his chest.

Suddenly a blinding flash penetrated his closed eyelids.

Claire was weightless.

He felt fabric in his hands and nothing else.

He opened his eyes and slowly stood, holding nothing but her bloody garments.

She was gone.

37

There was blood on the floor, rivulets forming along the seams of the stones.

A blue-gray haze of gunpowder lingered in the Chapel of the Angel.

Claire was gone.

Arthur fell to his knees at the spot where she had died, barely resisting an insane urge to plunge his hands into the pool of her blood, the way one might madly grope for a ring that had slipped off a finger into a muddy pond.

This was how it ended.

He had been a seeker—a quester.

He had succeeded where his ancestors had failed.

He had found the Holy Grail.

Was he more worthy than King Arthur? Thomas Malory? Was he purer of heart?

None of that mattered.

He had found something dearer than the Grail. He had found love and now he had lost it. Claire had streaked through his life like a comet—bright, shining; then gone.

She had risen.

He would have a lifetime to contemplate what had happened, to try to make sense of it. He stood up, angry and confused. His only thought was that the tomb had to be emptied. The bodies of Jeremy Harp and Simone were an abomination.

He dragged Simone from the Edicule by the ankles and returned to do the same with Harp, leaving them lying on their backs in the rotunda. He made two more trips, clearing out Neti's useless gear and the ridiculous lead-lined box. He dropped Simone and Harp's pistols into it after wiping them clean of fingerprints.

He had just shot two people.

Whatever life had in store for him, he didn't want to wind up like Thomas Malory, rotting in a jail cell.

There was only one thing left to do.

The air inside the Edicule was clearing. The Grail was where he had left it, atop the rolling stone pedestal, still white as a dove. The tomb felt altogether peaceful now, holy; but he could no longer stay. He would have to leave the church, hiding his face as best he could from the ubiquitous surveillance in the area. He thought about Barcelona, the planned news conference. That would have to wait. He simply couldn't go back there now, not without his Claire. He would return to England, take the Grail to the Bear, lay it beside Holmes' cane, tell his tale to the Loons, get good and drunk.

He took a last look around and reached for the Grail but then pulled back his hands to shield his eyes.

The portal to the chamber had exploded in white light.

Cautiously, he stepped forward and stooped low to see inside, drawn in, as powerless as a moth to flame. With one hand stretched before his face he stepped through the marble curtain and inched ahead until he was fully inside the Tomb Chamber.

A shaft of intense light had risen from the floor beside the rock-cut shelf, obscuring the icon of the Virgin, so bright it savaged his eyes like ice picks.

He clamped them tightly. He waited a second to look again, repeating the cycle of squinting and clenching until the shaft of light dimmed enough that he could see without pain.

And in the shaft of light a human figure began to emerge.

Arthur collapsed to his knees.

The figure was indistinct, opalescent.

Gradually, it materialized into something more substantial. He thought of his father's old Polaroid camera, the way it would ever so slowly form the image onto wet glossy paper.

He found his hands drawn together like iron to magnet, instinctively clasped in prayer.

Who was it?

Was it Christ?

Nehor?

Claire?

He kept his eyes fixed on the materialization.

In his heart he knew full well whom he wanted it to be, and he cried out over and over again, "Please God, please! Please God, please!" until the resurrection came to pass.

CPSIA information can be obtained at www.ICGtesting.com
Printed in the USA
LVOW11s0015270415

436195LV00001BA/100/P